REVELATIONS

MENELIK'SDAGGER

DAVIE FAIRBANKS

FOR CHLOÉ & JOSH

When no end was in sight and hope distanced itself from me,
I was picked up and carried by the love of those around me.
Glory be to God.

CONTENTS

CHAPTER 01

FATHER MICHAEL

Father Michael was feeling every second of his seventy eight years, finally reaching his room at the Vatican observatory in Castel Gandolfo. Dressed in a traditional cowl he wheeled a small suitcase across the threshold, sandals scraping wearily across the stone floor. He let the handle slip from his grasp, slapping harshly onto the floor. The sharp sound bounced around the sparsely furnished room. Continuing in a tired haze he finally rested on the corner of the bed, staring aimlessly into space.

Despite his years, it was often remarked upon how the priest possessed the energy of someone at least ten years his junior, and considered himself in God's grace to still be in such good health. It wasn't the journey from Cologne, Germany that consumed his every muscle with fatigue, but the reason for the journey in the first place: the anniversary memorial for his lifelong friend, Father Weiss.

It had now been almost eighteen months since Father Michael was first faced with the devastating news. However, due to complications surrounding the cause of death, it was several months before the authorities finally released the body for rights of burial.

It was never easy losing a friend, untimely or otherwise, but he had struggled to find solace for the act of murder. He knew his duty and wasn't conflicted in his faith, but in his grief, he discovered that his capacity for forgiveness had limitations.

Weiss' killer had never been caught and as long as he was out there, pain remained an open wound; the anniversary memorial only added ferocity to those feelings. A chaos of memories scrambling over one another, hoping to claw their way to the front of his mind, which most of the time he did his best to ignore, but a picture, a voice, a word would break through at random moments reminding him of a time he thought was past recollection.

Eventually willing himself to move, he collected the suitcase and lifted it onto the bed when he saw it; a letter laying perfectly on the centre of the pillow. His whole body went rigid.

He didn't receive very much mail and when he did it wasn't unusual for it to be left in such a manner. It was the handwriting that gave rise to his trepidation, the name and address on the envelope he recognised instantly as being penned by his late friend, Father Weiss; the man he buried a year ago.

Collecting the envelope he held it for a time, allowing his fingers to gently skate the surface. The elegant penmanship in a style of a time forgotten, complimented the coarse cream weighted texture that carried its worth. While knowing how his friend valued traditions of a simpler time, he was never shy in sending an email; knowing the act of merely receiving a handwritten letter was suggestion enough of its gravity.

His thumb stroked the Cologne stamp mark before turning it over, taking every care as he opened it. The folded paper inside was the same weight, colour and texture as the envelope, and carried a crested watermark.

_____

It read: *It has been too long old friend. I was just recalling our long walks along the Tiber.*   _____

No signature. Had the writing not been so familiar it could have been sent by anyone. Perhaps it was exhaustion, or the emotional trauma clouding his judgement, but upon first inspection it appeared a rather random, or even abstract sentence; either way it didn't seem to make any sense.

He stared at the letter, reading the words over and over again, hoping that something might fall into place. But the more he repeated it, the more his fatigue became apparent.

There were rumours before Weiss' passing that he may have been struggling with his memory; possibly showing signs of dementia. Father Michael never gave stock to rumblings of the ambitious, but as he looked at the writing, he couldn't help but wonder if his own unwavering loyalty had blinded him to the truth. *Had he really not noticed the deterioration of his closest friend?* he thought. The idea was upsetting and drained what very little energy he had left.

Returning the letter to its envelope he placed it on the desk, removed the suitcase from the bed and took its place, laying on top of the sheets. Weiss' words replayed over and over again like a mantra that made his eyelids heavy. His body felt like an uncomfortable dead weight with the rigidity of rigor mortis; its release more painful than its capture. But the discomfort was soon replaced with the reward of feeling himself sinking into the mattress; the promise of a deep sleep.

Suddenly his eyes sprung open bringing his descent to an abrupt halt. *Why has the letter only just arrived?* he thought, *And who put it there?* The questions released a surge of energy; now he was awake.

Returning to the desk, Father Michael opened the letter once more and stared at Weiss' words. Putting it down, he then examined the envelope, fingers once again tracing the ink as though it had captured an essence of his late friend. He turned it over and lifted the flap to inspect inside. There it was; the answer.

Below the gum line on the inside of the envelope was a symbol, drawn in the same pen as the letter; a spoked wheel.

It was an ancient symbol used by early Christians to communicate in secret. Hidden within the wheel were five letters. I,X,O,Y,E, the Greek word for fish. The letters were then used to created the acronym 'Jesus Christ God's Son, Saviour.' These were words that could not be spoken safely out loud. This in turn became the spoked wheel.

An uncomfortable tension returned to Father Michael's muscles. He hadn't seen the insignia used in this context for at least a decade. His initial worry was that the rumours may have been true. *Was Franz dangerously recalling past events as present?* But the mere fact that he held in his hand a letter from his late friend 18 months after his passing suggested something far more insidious was at play.

Father Michael read the words again...

It has been too long old friend.
I was just recalling our long walks along the Tiber.

Memories of their rebellious youth allowed him a brief smile as he searched for meaning. It was true they frequented the river that ran through Rome, but only at an early point in their seminary.

"That was probably 50 years ago!" he voiced, "When we found fellowship within…"

The Natsarim, he thought. A secret brotherhood embroiled in an endless holy war and its implications were dire.

It was nearly 10 minutes before Father Michael moved again, unable to escape the paralysing possibility that his friend, Father Weiss was somehow assassinated.

He blamed fatigue as the reason he'd been so slow to make the connection. The letter was an indication for the need to make contact, the wheel was its intention, to deliver information concerning the brotherhood; things he thought were in his past.

As a young disciple of the brotherhood, he recalled being introduced to agents sympathetic to the cause. Unassuming people who held connections to larger networks, such as independent or family run business. Father Michael's connection was a beautiful family that ran a small restaurant at the outskirts of the city. *The Busa's,* he recalled. It was a pleasant memory that offered a modicum of relief. But in truth it had been so many years he didn't know if they would even still be there. Tomorrow he would journey across the city to either validate his concerns, or finally let the memory of his friend rest in peace.

The next morning after a restless sleep, Father Michael rose early; dread still weighing heavily upon him. Despite an eagerness to uncover if the letter was more than it seemed or if it simply confirmed rumours of an ageing fragmented mind, he strolled the observatory grounds like a man without a care in the world.

Located at Lake Albano, several miles outside of Vatican City, it was far enough away that his presence would not be an affront to those in power, but close enough that movements and communication could easily be monitored.

It was still a functioning observatory, although it had lost its battle against the light pollution of a modern Rome; rendering the telescopes all but obsolete. However, many of the laboratories were still in operation, of which Father Michael made sure to potter in and out of every single one.

"What is it you're working on?" he would enquire.

Interrupting serious people doing serious work. Everybody was aware he would have just returned from his friends memorial and begrudgingly entertained the interruption. Father Michael pretended not to notice their growing frustration as he probed with mundane and sometimes stupid questions, before randomly saying…

"It was such a lovely service in Germany. I think Father Weiss would have liked it. Don't you?"

He could feel their utter relief as he left the room looking for his next unsuspecting victim. By around 2pm Father Michael had purposefully pottered in and out of every work lab in operation, interrupting almost everyone he came across. More importantly, he made sure that everybody had seen him; an old man lost in mourning dithering to occupy time. Now he was ready to leave Gandolfo.

As one last precaution he took a bus heading north-west towards Rome, before alighting several stops later, only to take a short taxi ride back into the neighbouring town of Albano Laziale.

With a constant and delicate smile, Father Michael stared out of the window with an almost child like fascination. The world around him seemed to have changed so much lately, and yet still felt so familiar.

The long narrow streets with cars parked half on the pavement, half on the road, clothing hung from makeshift washing lines on overhead balconies, dusty chalk roads and the terracotta roofs peering through the lush green on the hills.

The canvas was the same, but the paint was unfamiliar, more so now than he'd ever known before. Face after face passed him by and he searched each one.

It was clear the light of the world was fading, and you didn't need to be a person of faith to see it. The greater good, for the collective and community, had been replaced by tribalism, individualism, and God, had been all but removed from society. Priests were merely a novelty, a people unable to let go of archaic beliefs.

However, he didn't let that get in the way of enjoying a taxi ride through the heart of local communities, feeling the warmth of the sun and the breeze on his face. It was the first time since getting back from Germany that he felt himself start to relax, although the further out of the city he got, the less familiar everything looked. Something caught his eye as they passed a set of iron gates.

"Stop here," he said to the driver suddenly.

"Sei sicuro?" the driver replied. Are you sure?

"Si, si."

Father Michael alighted the taxi and stared up at the cheap colourful signage; The Trattoria Pizzeria. He didn't recognise any of it, but behind the iron gates were two discarded wheels; the type to have been used for old horse and carts, a modernised version of the wagon wheel he supposed. That was why he stopped.

He paid the driver and only once he was far enough away did he turn his attention to the restaurant. It wasn't at all as he'd remembered it. What was once a quaint family establishment with the charm of old Italy had been replaced by a semi-modern eatery that unfortunately sat very comfortably in its meagre surroundings. It was as if the entire area had been built up and run down all in his absence. As with many other lower affordable housing areas, it felt ignored.

Although now having absorbed the environment, Father Michael felt ominous eyes watching on from low rise buildings; *maybe I should have got the driver to wait,* he thought.

The main door to the restaurant opened and a young man stepped out, looking at Father Michael with greater recognition than he could offer himself. Not unlike the journey, the man looked familiar, but not the same.

The restaurant was still owned by the Busa family, although was now in the hands of the previous owners son, Paulo and his wife Stefania; whom was six months pregnant with her second child. The first was their four year old son, Francis, who played with his toy cars on the floor of the restaurant. Much in the same way his father did at that age, and hopefully his son after him.

Michael was relieved to see the interior had not changed much at all. The hideous, multi-coloured exterior signage was a poor representation of the authentic experience inside, but to locals he was sure it would be a hidden gem.

Father Michael was greeted with the familiar warmth of friends past and friends new, assuring the priest that they still honoured the old ways; pointing to the clever display of the wheels outside that appeared as discarded junk. He had to admit its intention had done just that.

Although, amidst the smiles and elation, there was a look that penetrated the facade with the sobering reality of why he was really there. He knew immediately there was indeed more to learn.

"We've been expecting you for some time now Father." Paulo said, the concern in his voice apparent. "We weren't sure if you were coming."

"I came as soon as I could."

"I'm… I'm so sorry, Father." Paulo said.

He was still a teenager the last time he'd seen Father Michael, but he was never without Father Weiss. Despite the calm reassuring demeanour, as he stood, the empty space next to him was palpable.

"And this beautiful woman at your side?" Father Michael asked, shifting the conversation to inject a more comfortable tone.

"Of course Father, sorry." Paulo said. "This is Stefania, my wife, my world."

"So nice to meet you," she said smiling warmly as she kissed both of Father Michael's cheeks. "Paulo has always talked fondly of you. Like an excited boy."

She laughed with Father Michael at her husband's embarrassment.

"And this little one," Paulo said pointing to his son, "this is Francis. Francis, come and say hello."

Francis looked up momentarily before continuing to drive his Sputafuoco cars across the tiled surface while making engine sounds with his mouth.

"You used to enjoy your cars too if I remember." Father Michael said.

"Don't get him started." Stefania quipped, "Some things never change."

"I think some of those cars are actually mine," Paulo admitted. "Hey Francis, we have a guest."

"And I don't think you ever left them to say hello either," Father Michael added.

Paulo laughed remembering.

"Yes, I think you're right. Why don't we have a seat?"

It was uncanny how much Paulo embodied his father. His gestures, expressions, almost as if time hadn't passed at all, and he was a younger man talking with his father as he had done so many years ago. But now he was an old man and the torch of burden was held by the next generation.

Over the next few hours they enjoyed lunch, a few glasses of wine and talked with affection as they filled in histories that passed like rapids towards the falls. These were the truly savoured moments, memories created, when one could exhale and look back to see how far they'd come before taking a deep breath to continue the journey.

There came a natural break in the conversation, when the silence reminded them of why they were together in this moment.

A shared look between Father Michael and Paulo saw Stefania politely excused herself from the table. The two men watched reverently as she scooped Francis into her arms, laughing with him as she carried him away, offering them the privacy they craved.

Paulo went to the main door of the restaurant and looked out beyond the fencing, making sure there wasn't anything out of the ordinary; there wasn't. He flicked the lock on the door and hung a sign in the window, 'Closed for 1 Hour'. Dimming the lights, he disappeared into the back of the restaurant, returning a few moments later carrying a newly lit candle for the table. In his other hand was an envelope, identical to the one Father Michael received.

"Please, take your time." Paulo said placing the envelope in front of him.

He left the candle on the table and joined Stefania, who was in the dining area after settling Francis. Not wanting to be a distraction, the two retreated to the kitchen and continued preparing food for the evening customers.

The envelope was simply marked, FAO Father Michael. Once again he admired the penmanship before using a knife from the table to slide under the fold and open the letter.

It read: *My dear friend. It is with a heavy heart that I write to you. In our conviction to preserve one truth we have blinded ourselves to another. It is only by the divine that I have stumbled upon a plot that surrounds a hidden prophesy, and where there is one there are two. I have acquired a parchment from those conspiring against the church. It is possible and likely that if discovered they would seek to silence me. How? I cannot be certain. The only importance is that they're thwarted from their plans which would ultimately destroy all that the Brethren have sought to protect for two millennia. An attempt to steal the Cathedrals' holy relics will set in motion events we have fought against our entire lives. I will endeavour to visit you in the coming weeks when I can be more forthcoming, until then I have*

placed our fate in the hands of Lucifer that he may bring light to the dark.
Let him guide you to the truth my friend, as only he can. _____

Father Michael's hands fell to the table and blood drained from his face as he attempted to absorb the stark truth. His friend, Father Franz Weiss, had been assassinated.

He realised at some point that he must have convinced himself that Weiss' death was, as the media reported, a horrible accident.

He was a man in mourning and despite his deep faith, reaching to find understanding. What better way than to have an overactive imagination create meaning out of a senseless act of violence; conspiracy without evidence. But in his hand was all the evidence he needed, confirmation that his friend had become another casualty in an ancient holy war.

Franz's death had been a buzz in the world media, lasting all of two days; how a priest became the tragic victim of a violent robbery. The report suggested he may have stumbled upon robbers as they made their bid to escape Cologne Cathedral with relics of the Holy Shrine, and was killed trying to protect it.

The feigned outrage surrounded the audacity to steel relics and desecrate a place of worship, rather than a priest being murdered in the middle of Cologne Cathedral.

Authorities pleaded with the public for anyone with information to come forward, which loosely translated meant they had nothing to go on.

The magnificent 12th century cathedral was famed for housing The Tomb of the Three Magi, also known as The Shrine of the Three Kings.

Inside what was once the largest structure in Northern Europe, lay a gilded triple-sarcophagus that contained the Magi's remains. They were discovered between the third and fourth century by Emperor Constantine's mother, Empress Helena, who had embarked on a Christian pilgrimage to Palestine, Syria and Jerusalem. As well as discovering the site of Christ's crucifixion and the True Cross, Helena bought and protected as many Christian relics as she could find. The Magi's bones were transported back to Rome and then moved to Germany in the twelfth century, where they would be displayed in a cathedral worth their status.

Throughout the middle ages Europe had become inundated with fake and forged relics, particularly those of the Christian persuasion. Today, several European countries each claim to have the skull of John the Baptist and several more the Spear of Destiny, others claim nails and sections of wood from the cross or pieces of Christ's tunic. With so many fakes in circulation, the shrine, like others, had been relegated to nothing more than a tourist attraction in a remarkable setting.

While coming to terms with the true nature behind his friend's death, Father Michael began reading the letter again, this time attempting to remove himself from it emotionally. He had so far not been able to absorb any of the important information from it, only what had affected him personally. The letter spoke plainly enough, although Franz's use of words had a wonderful way of containing very specific details at the same time as disguising their meaning.

If Franz's death, or the theft of the relics marked the beginning, then he was already playing catch up, or possibly already too late, he didn't know. But none of it would make any sense unless he could get his hands on the prophesy; and thanks to Franz he knew just where to find it.

Suddenly Father Michael didn't feel so silly about taking such elaborate precautions to cover his movements when leaving the observatory. He would now have to maintain the charade while attempting to uncover the truth, knowing once again that he would likely be watched from the shadows.

"Father Michael," Paulo's voice called out, pulling him from his thoughts, "are you okay?"

He didn't know how long he'd been sitting there lost in his thoughts, but the restaurant was slightly darker now as the evening drew closer. He smiled and nodded. Paulo turned the lights up in the restaurant, unlocked the door and removed the sign. He took a seat opposite the priest and stared with a solemn look of understanding, neither one speaking for almost a minute.

"May I pray with you, Father?" he asked, knowing there was nothing else left to say.

A soft smile brightened Father Michael's face with a humbling appreciation. The hands of the two men reached across the table finding each other in the middle, bowing their heads they silently prayed.

Before Father Michael left, Stefania gifted him a small box of pastries to take back to Gandolfo, hugging him with the warmth and affection of a beloved family member; it pleased him that they'd bonded so quickly. Burying his face into his mothers apron, Francis was tired and grouchy after his nap and refused to say goodbye, but he did wave goodbye along with his mother and father as the taxi drove away.

Returning to the bus stop at the edge of the city and as he had done earlier, Father Michael took the bus back towards the observatory grounds. Once again he found himself staring from the bus window, this time as he reflected on his unexpected afternoon, the gift that was Paulo and Stefania and of course Francis.

Had the news he discovered been delivered at another place or time, he wasn't sure if he would have had the strength to take it. Franz's passing had taken more of a toll on him than he would like to admit, but the husband and wife had shared more than just company with him, more than food and wine, they had given him strength.

Somehow he had felt the presence of God wrapping this family around him, like a protective blanket. Showing him the beauty in the continuation of life from father to son, and from father to son. A slight involuntary smile lifted Father Michael's expression for a moment, but as the bus came to rest at its destination, the lightness faded.

CHAPTER 02

ARCHIE

Charlotte Finbrook was about to embark upon a journey she could have never dreamed of. She'd arrived at the Pimlico address in London five minutes ago, but hadn't yet brought herself to alight the car. She was still staring up from the driver's seat of her city hatchback, in awe at the elegant three-storey terraced Regency building, home to her new boss, Archibald. T. Montgomery; and began to feel slightly overwhelmed.

The self-made woman from humble beginnings was now in a position to influence a nation to elect her new boss as the next Prime Minister of the United Kingdom.

Charlotte had a sharp mind and at times a sharper tongue that had a way of getting her into trouble. But straight talking was part of her charm and one of the reasons she had come highly recommended as the forerunner media strategist in a bid to run for Number 10, Downing Street; a position she had initially turned down.

When asked why she rejected the offer, she smiled sweetly, fluttering her eye lashes over her big brown eyes and replied, "Because I have a soul. And if you think I worked my arse off just so some pompous, soulless, ingrate can use my skill and data for their own self-serving agenda, then think again. Did you get all that?" she said facetiously.

The messenger smiled, seeming completely unperturbed by her comments.

"I believe I did," he replied.

Now she was one day away from launching that soulless ingrate onto the world stage. Of course he wasn't quite the man she was expecting.

Archibald. T. Montgomery, Archie to his friends, wasn't even a politician. A borderline genius, multifaceted polymath, a humanitarian, successful, charismatic, good looking, but not a politician. His family name was of old money, but other than his education Archie's success was entirely of his own making.

Determined to write his own passage into history, he served for a few short years in the military hoping to shed the privileged skin of his birthright. While he may have proved to himself he was cut from a different cloth, he soon realised the futile attempt at trying to escape the past, instead choosing to embrace the opportunities afforded him with the hope of enacting change.

His entry into the political arena was an accidental opportunity after a social media tirade with a high profile politician thrust him into the limelight. His arguments inspired the digital community to cry out for new politics, for new leaders, and they wanted Archibald. T. Montgomery to carry their torch.

The accidental opportunity arose from a culmination of events. The catastrophic handling of the H1N1 pandemic that killed over twenty million people across the planet, the global stock market responding in kind, crashing twice within six months, the middle classes being obliterated with illogical restrictions on trade, and now a tyrannical overreach of a globally forced utopian agenda they called, The Conscious Evolution.

Societal unrest was in free fall, citizens protested against their governments all over the world, but their desperate cries for help were only met with aggression from police and military bodies. It was quickly becoming evident that democracy had taken an opportunistic turn overnight towards tyranny, and the people needed a champion.

Although Archie wasn't one for the spotlight, his name had been thrown around like a rock star saviour as it was his company that developed a bio-tech smart-vaccine the media hailed as the 'miracle cure that saved the planet.' And better yet, he gave it away for _free_. The clear favourite to win this year's Nobel Peace Prize and now with the help of Charlotte he was preparing to throw his hat into the political arena.

For the past ten weeks Charlotte had been in what she called a data bubble. Spending every waking minute compiling and analysing statistical trends. Now, the night before they officially launch the campaign, the magnitude of the task was finally hitting her.

"Okay," she muttered to herself.

Taking one final deep breath, exhaling with a puff of her cheeks attempting to psych herself up. She collected her worn brown leather satchel bag and checked its various compartments; finally she stepped out of the car.

The square was dark and sparsely lit unlike the surrounding roads that buzzed with an electric neon haze, as if opulence was afforded the protection of discretion. Just behind her, at the centre of the square was a private garden for its residents, which was really a small park, and beyond that, the adjacent terraced twins completed St George's Square.

Charlotte felt so small, stood staring up at the building like something from a Dickens novel. A Victorian lamp hung over the black gloss door between two cream pillars, bleeding just enough light to fall upon the five small steps leading to its porch. An old iron shoe scraper sat just on the left, also glossed in black to match its surroundings. And she, a little orphan girl in Victorian London, attracted by the warm glow of light; longingly staring into the window of a world she could only dream of. *That was almost true,* she thought.

Suddenly she was finding it hard to catch her breath, her heart began pounding like she had just finished a thirty minute spin class, but not in a good way. She hurried to the roadside curb and quickly sat down fearing she might collapse.

Several seconds later, warm light poured onto the street, falling around her as the door behind her opened.

She hoped it was Johnny, Archie's personal assistant, but was unable to turn around to check, powerless to do anything but try and catch her breath, at this point just praying she wasn't having a heart attack. *Please don't be Archie,* she thought. *Please don't be Archie.*

"Charlotte, are you okay?"

Archie's voice said as his hand came to rest reassuringly on her shoulder.

His voice was deep with a warm soft gravel and projected with the clarity of a well-trained theatre actor, along with his touch it brought a much needed comfort she hadn't expected.

Charlotte turned to him and smiled, nodding as if to say *"I'll be fine, just give me a moment,"* hoping that she would be. But she wasn't, the hyperventilating was making her feel light-headed. She was confused, trying to intellectualise what was happening, as if somehow understanding it would make it go away. But she had never experienced anything like this before. And now on the eve of the most important day of her professional life, and in front of her new boss, she decides to have a melt down. *I'm so getting fired,* she thought, feeling herself just moments away from fainting.

Seeing her distress, Archie quickly stepped from the curb, ignoring the fact he was still wearing his very expensive suit trousers and sat on the road in front of Charlotte, crossing his legs. Taking both of her hands into his, making sure to keep eye contact, he smiled.

"Hey," he said softly. "You're okay."

She nodded along agreeably, her mouth smiled but the rest of her face didn't. However, now she was otherwise concerned that Archie would ruin his trousers.

"Stay with me," he continued. "Try and copy my actions."

Charlotte was still choking down little pockets of air as she watched him take long slow deep breaths, making sure his whole body accentuated the movement. She felt a bit silly, but followed, thinking passing out would probably be worse.

His hands were strong and warm, but soft. Hers felt small inside them. He had a cheesy grin, but it was a nice smile which was comforting. A strong jaw and light smile lines that were beginning to make him look more distinguished with age. And bright green eyes that looked incredible when he smiled, that she hadn't noticed until now, were really quite alluring.

Suddenly remembering where she was, Charlotte snapped out of her reverie, finding her breathing was coming under control. *Wow it's working,* she thought. Her heart no longer felt as if it was going to explode out of her chest.

"That's it, just breathe," Archie said.

Thirty to forty seconds felt like an age, staring uncomfortably into the eyes of her boss and holding his hands in the middle of the street, particularly at such a media sensitive time.

"I'm so sorry," she said, attempting to get to her feet. "I don't know what came over me."

But Archie continued to sit holding her hands, not allowing her to stand before she was ready.

"Just give yourself a moment. Has anything like this ever happened before?"

"Never," she insisted with objection.

She pulled her hands from his gentle clasp and looked around nervously.

"You need to get inside now," she said urgently with a hint of aggression.

Archie laughed as he got to his feet brushing down the back of his trousers.

"Feeling a little more like yourself now?" he said.

But it fell on deaf ears as she had immediately got to her feet and quickly climbed the porch steps leaving him standing in the road.

"What were you thinking?" She snapped at Johnny as she breezed past him into the house while he held the door for her.

Johnny looked at Archie slightly confused as to the role he played, but the two men shared a quiet look of amusement as Archie returned inside.

They were used to more reserved and restrained personalities in their company, formal to the death. It was strangely refreshing to have someone as spirited as Charlotte around.

Archie and Johnny were sat either end of an eight-seater oak dining table, with Charlotte's notes and papers strewn haphazardly across the surface. Almost four hours in and Johnny was suffering a rare moment of informality, his top button adrift and tie pulled low as he slouched back in his chair, slightly away from the table in an attempt to disengage. Archie on the other hand was slouched forward, hand holding the weight of his head as he tried his best to stay focused. But Charlotte wasn't showing any signs of her earlier fragility, standing between the two men like an animated conductor engaging both with rapid clarity and an impressive knowledge base, while simultaneously reading additional information from a slickly prepared presentation off the screen of her laptop.

A police siren wailed close enough to break her momentum along with the tired concentration of the room, as though the sound simultaneously triggered each of them into a hypnotic state. It was hard to ignore every single one, sometimes rooms fall silent reminding us that things were not okay. Before a year ago it was just another sound of the city, the police racing to a crime to keep us safe.

Now many people wouldn't even use the word police, they called them enforcers, nazis, fascists and a whole host of other names that suggested totalitarian control.

But tonight there wasn't fear in the silence, tonight the sirens were a call to arms, to fight the good fight. Of why the few people in this room were so desperately needed and why it was so important for the world to hear Archie's vision.

Charlotte was under no illusion. She knew Archie couldn't actually win the election, and as super-smart as he was, she wasn't entirely sure if that had even crossed his mind. But it didn't matter, that wasn't why she'd agreed to be a part of the team.

After initially turning down the offer to come and work for Archie, he contacted her personally to ask if she would be gracious enough to meet, at least to allow him the opportunity to present just what it was she would be turning down over a cup of coffee. She told him he was wasting his time, but out of professional courtesy agreed to meet.

She was nobody's fool, a city girl with street smarts and a highly tuned B.S. detector. It was going to take more than a quick cup of coffee to convince her that he wasn't like every other politician, part of the problem. But after just ten minutes she'd thrown caution to the wind and agreed to become part of the team.

She had never heard someone talk with such verve, to articulate a vision with a clarity as to inspire hope that even the sceptic would dare to dream. His ideas were transformative, revolutionary and, or, quite possibly mad. Or it might just become a blueprint in the next stage of human evolution. A historical epoch.

The world wasn't ready for such a seismic shift, that was why Charlotte knew he couldn't win and she didn't need the statistics to tell her. She was there because she believed when the world was ready, it would look back upon this moment and say, this was where it all started; here was its architect.

When the siren had faded far enough into the distance loosening its grip on Charlotte's attention, she was about to continue before becoming embarrassingly aware of her company's fatigue. Slightly relieved, she let out a sigh that contained whatever energy she had left and slumped onto a chair.

"Coffee?" Johnny offered.

"No, I'll never sleep."

He got up and went over to the coffee machine. It was big and shiny just like the ones from the coffee shops, with the full beans and milk steamer. Charlotte started to gather her papers together and organising them into a neat pile, Archie helped but seemed thoughtful; distant.

"Is everything okay?" she asked.

After a short pause he looked at her and said,

"I don't want to do this."

Charlotte stopped packing her things away and Johnny turned from the coffee machine, both concerned.

"I wanted to be an innovator, an inventor," he continued. "Someone that could impact the world with his mind not his politics."

"You are an innovator Archie, and you've already made an impact on the world. Your smart vaccine not only changed the course of the pandemic, but in the next few weeks will become a mandatory vaccination for all newborns. Do you know how many lives you've saved?"

Archie considered the question, despite its rhetorical nature.

"But there's so much more that could be done."

"You're right," she said. "But unless we put someone else at the helm, it's land we'll never find. Now, are you ready?"

"Let's just say, it's time," he replied.

And he was right, but it did little to settle her nerves. He had a way of responding with a truth that surrounded the question, which was a little infuriating, but not wrong.

"You're nervous?" Archie noticed, handing her his pile of papers.

"Yes. And no," she said, uncertain of either. "I don't know, I'm scared to death and excited at the same time. Kinda feels like the time my friend convinced me to bungee off a bridge in Australia."

Smiling as she remembered the moment. Charlotte packed everything back into her bag.

"Well you survived that ordeal."

"Yes, but I've heard your words. I've already taken the leap. Now we need everyone else to hear what you have to say. That's why we need to get this right."

"And we will," Archie replied.

"All I'm saying is that if they create a lot of noise it won't matter what you have to say, no one will hear it. So we don't need to get stuck in the conversation that you're just another rich white guy telling the world how to live. That's not the narrative. It might be the truth, but it's not the narrative."

Johnny couldn't hold back his chuckle and it brought a wide smile to Archie's face. The humour hadn't been missed by Charlotte, she just wasn't trying to be funny. She stood to leave.

"Get some rest. The car will be here for 9:30am to take us to the TV station, I'll meet you here. And don't give him anymore coffee," she said turning to Johnny.

Charlotte checked once more that she had everything before standing to leave.

"Let me see you to the car," Johnny said.

"My car's right outside."

"I know where it is!" he said with a tone suggesting this wasn't up for debate.

Her face softened revealing the woman behind the professional persona. She appreciated the gesture.

"Mr. Montgomery," she said turning back to Archie.

"Miss Finbrook," he responded in kind.

"So you're not coming tomorrow?" Charlotte said trying to make small talk as Johnny escorted her back to the car.

"I wouldn't know what to do with myself if I'm being honest."

"Shame, we could have done with the support."

Charlotte opened the door and slung her belongings onto the passenger seat.

"You care about him, huh?"

Johnny looked questioningly at her.

"I mean, this is more than just a job to you"

"Isn't it to you?" he said.

Charlotte laughed.

"You've definitely been hanging with him for too long."

Johnny laughed stiffly like an underused skill. It faded to a short silence.

"I suppose you're right."

"What is it?" she asked, feeling there was something unsaid.

He hesitated momentarily trying to formulate the right words.

"I fear not everyone is going to understand Mr. Montgomery. It's like you said, people tend to create a lot of noise and he could get lost in the commotion. There'll be times when you'll need to interpret the world for him. He trusts you."

This time it was Charlotte's turn to respond with a questioning look.

"The man's basically a genius. Other than statistics I'm not sure me interpreting anything for him would be good for anyone."

Johnny paused to rethink his approach.

"Have you ever had a conversation with someone when you know what you're saying couldn't be any clearer, but yet they just can't seem to grasp its essence?" he asked.

"I think I have an idea," she said wryly.

"And you can't seem to find the words to make it any easier to understand?" Johnny continued having completely missed Charlotte's humour. "Well, that's many conversations for Archie. He tried explaining it to me one day to help me understand the way he saw the world. He said the universe is efficient, not wasteful. Once energy has been used to create something, it had a lifecycle and the energy moves on, creates something new. So he trained his thoughts to follow the same pattern of efficiency. Once a solution presented itself he can disregard the preceding information and reuse the energy for further conclusion. So what may appear to some as naive is actually a superior mind unable to grasp the need for a simplistic conversation."

Johny anticipated a response, but Charlotte's unchanged expression suggested he'd probably lost her somewhere in the energy of the universe.

"If you asked someone for a light for a cigarette," he continued trying a new tact, "and they started to explain how to make fire by rubbing two sticks together, you might just look at them in the same way."

"Ahh." She said finally getting it, "Oh!" she blurted out, realising its implication. "I understand your worry, but the world doesn't need any more vacuous politicians Johnny. I'll do everything I can to keep the noise to a low hum, but once he has a platform and the people hear what he has to say, then he'll inspire their loyalty as he has ours. I truly believe that," she said touching his arm reinforcing her sincerity.

Johnny allowed himself a warm and unveiled smiled. If he had any reservations about Charlotte she had just laid them to rest.

"Drive safe, Miss Finbrook."

She gave a playful wink as she got into the car. Johnny returned to the porch steps and waited, watching until she was away before returning inside.

CHAPTER 03

COHEN

Amidst the deafening roar of the flames, the creaking structure cried out in warning of its imminent failure. But every direction Cohen turned, fire leapt to impede his escape; like a predator toying with its prey.

Oxygen thinned with every breath and the unnatural heat felt like it was cooking him from the inside. There was no escape, nothing to do but watch as fire swept across the ceiling like a rushing wave. Two dark spots began forming inside the ferocious flames and then an elongated third beneath, it was… a face? For a split second the unexpected image was a distraction from an impending doom; when he heard it.

"Cohen!"

Piercing through the deafening roar and creaking structure, something cried out his name, though it sounded like it came directly from the flames; causing further hesitation. It was just long enough for the flaming mouth to open and the gaping darkness to descend, suddenly engulfing him into an abyss.

Cohen gasped for air as he woke, pawing at his chest for something that wasn't there, as if the nightmare tried following him into the day; the smell of burning flesh lingering in his nostrils. While he was unable to recall specific details; he knew unequivocally the burning flesh was his own.

He was still wearing his filthy jeans and T-shirt, now soaked through with sweat; as were the Egyptian cotton sheets he was laying on.

It had become more commonplace in recent months to wake up in clothes from previous days with an alcoholic blackout of the last twelve to twenty four hours. However, he was surprised on this rare occasion to have made it to his own bed.

Snatching up a bottle of water from the bedside table, pain instantly coursed through his body causing him to knock over an empty bottle of Johnnie Walker Blue. It bounced harshly onto the floor, skipping across the wooden surface without smashing.

He gulped back the water, desperately trying to quench the dehydration that had become a daily pattern of abuse, and until just now successfully suppressed the plaguing nightmares that questioned his sanity. But now they were back.

It wasn't just the night terrors that had become the undoing of a once hardened and disciplined operator, it was the timing.

While on a contract in Europe, Cohen experienced an event that threw into question everything he had come to believe, the nightmares followed soon after.

He couldn't comprehend how a man with no fealty, no faith, who held no stock in fate, suddenly felt as though he was on a collision course with destiny. The nightmares; he believed were haunting glimpses into the future; premonitions. Now not even the alcohol could keep them at bay.

A part of him was still trying to convince himself he was simply losing his mind, but what he truly believed and what he'd never voiced, was that he had experienced God, and God had turned his back on him.

Cohen suddenly noticed his favourite trusty leather boots, curiously sat neatly on the other side of the room, socks balled up and stuffed into the openings. He was very much awake, but not entirely present. The spent water bottle slipped from his fingers and fell to the floor. There was a faint taste of blood in his mouth and his jaw pained with a stiffness and swelling, but it was the boots that continued to hold his attention; neatly side by side. *Not the actions of a blacked out drunk,* he thought.

Swinging his legs over the side of the bed he winced, the movement revealing further injury. Placing his hand on the right side of his rib cage he inhaled carefully, expanding his lungs until feeling a sharp pain; suggesting he'd either cracked or broken some. Following a spotted trail of blood from his jeans onto his dark t-shirt, spots increased to blots and patches, all probably his own and no memory to explain how they got there.

A noise from the shop below snapped him into the present; Nathan must have arrived and started setting up for the day. Looking at the old fashioned clock on his bedside table, the type you had to wind, it was nearly six thirty.

You could set your watch to Nathan's timekeeping and he didn't arrive at the shop until 6:55am sharp. A sudden shameful image flashed through his mind, of Nathan finding him passed out drunk and having to get him home. That would explain the boots and socks, and for him being at the shop so early.

He was sure Nathan could do without him getting under his feet; probably not having been the most pleasant person to be around in recent times, but he did own the shop and if the alcohol wasn't working, then keeping busy was the safest distraction. First he would have to get rid of the ripe smell of sweat and alcohol oozing from his pores.

After a hot shower, a pint of water and four strong painkillers, Cohen donned fresh jeans, a loose charcoal v-neck t-shirt that flowed softly against his skin; and of course his favourite trusty leather boots that he left to sag open with the laces untied. He scraped the long strands of damp hair from his face and tied them behind his head with an elastic band, he then headed downstairs to his shop; The Way of The Flower.

Situated opposite the old arches, south of the River Thames. Independent businesses were quite rare this close to the city, rent was expensive and now it seemed only franchises left their generic mark on the high streets. But Cohen managed to snap up the three storey buildings some years back as a repossessed freehold, and despite its high price tag, the value to Cohen wasn't at all financial.

Regardless of its odd location coupled with his reluctance for promotion, people ordered from all over the country and paid handsomely for one of his Ikebana displays. The art of flower arranging was a skill he had acquired from his time studying in Japan under Master Ueshiba. The displays had fortuitously become popular in some elite circles as the must have centrepiece.

An ignorance that bemused him; to culture the energy of harmony through a delicate balance of creation, only to be lost on its need for status. Although Nathan had done a good job of exploiting their exclusivity, commanding fees that varied from hundreds into the thousands, depending on the establishment or individual placing the order. He also told stories of the owner travelling to remote lands to discover and cultivate some of the rarest seeds, plants and flowers in the world; all adding to the shop's mystery and charm, but for the most part it did a good job of covering Cohen's constant absence.

He descended the stairs from his upstairs flat to a door that led into the rear of the shop's workspace. He was halfway down when the familiar smell of fresh coffee and freshly baked pastry pierced the sweet floral scented air, fused with a distinct undertone of incense.

Upon opening the door, he froze. Expecting to see Nathan sat at the work bench enjoying his breakfast and a newspaper, the way he did every morning before starting work, not an attractive blonde lady wearing one of his hooded sweat tops. Cohen's eyes darted back and forth around the room, still hoping Nathan would appear to give an explanation as to who this woman was and why she was sitting in his shop; wearing his top.

"Good morning," she said.

Her voice was soft and carried the warmth of familiarity, giving her an advantage over Cohen's lack of memory from the last several hours. He aired with caution, continuing to look around making sure they were alone.

The shop was long and narrow with a wider workspace and work-bench at the rear, where the woman was sat. Its location didn't allow much light to travel very far inside, leaving the workspace in a constant and steady gloom. Unless the overhead fluorescent lights were on it allowed anonymity, concealing you in silhouette. But from the bench you could see all who entered.

Cohen navigated around the multitude of vases that cluttered most of the movable space and peered out of the shop window, looking up and down the street for anything that might appear out of place; everything was quiet. Everything apart from the unanswered questions that were racing around his head.

"Well you certainly look better than you did a couple of hours ago!" she continued. "To be honest, I didn't think anybody could bounce back quite so quickly, even you."

Bounce back? he thought. While he knew he gave a relatively convincing appearance of functioning, the truth was he was still drunk and doing what he could to stave off a wicked hangover. Playing guess who wasn't exactly helping.

When entering the room he'd eyed a pastry bag and coffee invitingly laid out opposite the woman. She cradled her own drink and from the disregarded paper bag riddled with flakes, it suggested the other bag was probably for him. He placed his arms locked and rigid onto the work surface and bared down upon his guest as though she were about to be the subject of interrogation. For most it would have felt an intense and uncomfortable situation, but the attractive woman simply stared back with poise, her bright blue eyes never once breaking a gaze that held the warmth of her voice.

She noticed scars on the back of Cohen's hands, some that continued up his strong forearms and biceps; not the wounds of a florist. She sipped her coffee and smiled with unsettling ease.

Having failed to ruffle the feathers of his company, he petulantly took a seat opposite, tore open the pastry bag without invitation, ripping off almost half a croissant off with his teeth and poking the excess into his mouth with his fingers, never removing his eyes from her.

"How are you feeling?" she asked. "You took quite a beating."

Cohen just stared and chewed.

"So I guess that's the way you wanna go huh?" she continued. "Picking fights with people in the hope they might beat you to death? I suppose it *is* faster than alcohol. Do you even remember anything of last night?"

He ripped off another section of croissant, continuing to stare. He didn't care what had happened last night to him or to anyone else, only who she was and why she was here.

"I wanted to take you to the hospital," she continued, nervously filling the silence. "But you insisted on coming here. Of course I thought, a flower shop, where else."

She looked around at the array of vases and flowers that exploded out of them like a snapshot of a fireworks display, and then back at Cohen as if she was having trouble visualising the pairing.

"It's very beautiful," she said.

His blank and unwavering expression finally amused the woman to laughter.

"You don't remember me do you?"

She wasn't talking about last night and that's not what he was expecting. He quietly and frantically searched the recesses of his mind, desperately trying to place a situation or scenario where he might recognise her. There was a haze of familiarity but his fragile head couldn't tell him any more than that.

"I guess it has been a while. You really don't remember me? Jakaline Gotha…Leeny" she said, smiling broadly.

It wasn't her name, but her smile that had jolted his memory. Her eyes twinkled as her face lit up revealing the woman he'd met some years past, beautiful, untrustworthy, and last he knew, married to one of the most powerful and dangerous men in London. He pursed his lips and nodded an acknowledgement, that was about as close to a smile as he'd ever give.

"You never were one for talking," she said.

Cohen just watched, although now he was cautiously alert, scrutinising and analysing details. At first glance, Leeny was a confident woman with poise, but a tiny tremor below the corner of her mouth revealed itself when she smiled, and her fingers nervously played with the plastic lid on her drink unconsciously shredding its edges; she was more nervous than she was letting on.

"Why are you here, Leeny?"

She looked at him with the veil of reacquaintance lifted, hesitating before saying.

"I need your help."

He scoffed.

"Please just hear me out, it's not what you think."

"How did you even find me?"

"Oh you know," she said trying to inject a lighthearted tone, "dusted off some old phone numbers, called in a few favours. They said that I was probably wasting my time, but.."

"You are," he said, cutting her off. "I don't do that anymore."

His bluntness flustered her and she took a second to compose herself before continuing.

"You know I never did believe the rumours," she said, pausing to gauge his reaction, expecting at least a response of curiosity, but she got nothing but an ice cold stare.

"Until I saw you last night. I couldn't believe what I was seeing, I didn't want to believe."

"You should have listened," Cohen said with disregard, slurping his coffee and shoving the remainder of the croissant in his mouth, "Wasting everyones time."

"How the mighty have fallen. Problem is Cohen, I didn't find the man I was looking for. Instead all I found was a pathetic drunk begging for it to all be over."

Suddenly the English rose withered, now only thorns remained; but she had his attention.

"You know they said you'd lost it, a kill too far finally broke you. But that's not it at all, is it? No, the person I saw last night wasn't crazy. Lost maybe, desperate, but not crazy."

He didn't have the head for this and envisioned grabbing her by the arm, dragging her through the shop and slinging her out of the front door. But now she knew his location. He silently cursed himself for being so stupid. For years he'd managed to keep the shop a secret hidden in plain sight. Nathan Levinson was the name on the lease, even the title of the deeds were a subsidiary of Ikebana Holdings; a company formed out of Japan. And in one drunken night he'd given up his location to a woman who had connections to every major scumbag in London's underworld. While he loved the location, he always knew he'd have to sell up at some point and move on. Now was as good a time as any.

"I almost left you there," she continued, "and if it had been for any other reason, I would have. But it's my son,"

Her voice cracked slightly, but there was a steely resilience to her.

"He's missing."

Cohen's stare refused to soften, but he did now recognise the woman from his past, although she wasn't that woman; she was a mother now. He knew what was coming, despite her best efforts her theatre reeked of desperation, but more importantly, he just didn't care.

"He was in Prague on a school trip. It's the first time he's been away without me, he's only eleven. Josh is his name."

As if simply retelling a story of his first outing, like the truth was somehow disconnected from reality. But he understood the need for self preservation in the midst of a personal hell.

She took a picture from her bag and slid it across the counter until it rested in front of Cohen. He allowed his eyes to flit momentarily, but was more concerned in watching Leeny. Regardless of her plight and his fragile state, caution hadn't yet left him; as long as he was sober or close to it, it remained his default position.

"They said he told his friend he was just going to the shop," she continued. "Which was just two minutes from the hotel where they were staying, that was three days ago. Before you say anything, the first place I checked was my ex-husband. I mean the arsehole's never had anything to do with his son in ten years, but I thought, you know, that maybe someone could have taken Josh to get back at him. But he knew nothing about it and didn't even care. What sort of man doesn't care that their own flesh and blood is missing?"

Cohen knew Trenton was a cold-hearted bastard, but that was something even he didn't expect to hear.

"I've spoken to the school and the Prague police and Scotland Yard and... Everyone's doing what they can, so they tell me," she said, not believing the statement. "I can't just sit around and wait for these people... Look I can pay you, I have some savings and I can get more if you need it... You know I can."

"What is it you think I can do for you, Leeny?"

"Find my son!" she exasperated. "Why the hell do you think I sat here all night making sure you didn't choke on your own vomit? Because I give a shit about you? I'm here for him. I shut the door on this life a long time ago and swore I'd never return. But my son needs me, he needs you Cohen. The old you. The one that helped put his father where he is today."

Her words triggered fragments of memories that Cohen had been desperately hoping wouldn't surface so quickly; a tear falling as light faded from the eyes of an innocent man; sadness on the face of Christ looking down upon the moment from a cross that hung overhead. The backdrop of a magnificent stained glass window and crashing to his knees with a blood curdling scream that would peel a layer of skin from his throat. But there was something else, a detail he hadn't recalled or remembered; the smell of incense. The memory was so powerful it was almost as if he could smell it right there in the room. Leeny watched him as she had done all night, seeing only torment.

"I don't know what happened to you," she said, "if we're being honest; I really don't care, but something for nothing, you won't find redemption at the bottom of a bottle Cohen, that much I do know."

His stare snapped to her unnervingly as though she had read his thoughts.

"You think you're the only one who ever had an awakening?" she continued. "Unable to recognise the person staring back at you in the mirror? You should just be grateful you found your conscience."

A thought brought a softening expression as if she was staring into the face of her child.

"I suppose I was lucky. Josh was my conscience. When he was born it changed everything. In an instant the world became a different place, suddenly there was love in it. That was the moment I think I finally understood what unconditional truly meant. He was innocent and I wasn't going to allow him to become a part of our world; a place where hope goes to die. I couldn't have him turn out like his father, like you, like me. I wanted to give him a chance… and I never looked back."

She realised Cohen wasn't just listening, but studying her, and quickly adopted her previous hardened expression.

"How many times were you paid to end someones life? I'm only asking you to save one. You want redemption? Then use what you have to protect those that can't protect themselves."

Leeny could see her pleas had been unable to penetrate Cohen's un-wavering coldness. As hope faded, her steely reserve started to crack under the pressure.

"Please Cohen," she whimpered almost inaudibly as tears began fall-ing. "I'm begging you."

An interruption of keys jingling in the lock brought a pause to the conversation, but for Leeny it brought the urgency for an answer. It was 6:55am and this time Nathan *had* arrived.

The calm and quiet of the morning was suddenly at its end as he bumped and crashed awkwardly through the door, struggling to remove the key from the lock while holding two cups of takeaway coffee, one on top of the other. Wedged under his chin were two pastry bags, a folded newspaper under his arm and the strap of his shoulder bag slipping into the crux of his elbow that he had to raise to stop it dragging across the floor, eventually nudging the door closed with his bottom.

"Ahh damn it!" Nathan blurted as a few drops of beverage shot out of the lid and onto his shirt; unaware he had company.

Quickly wiping away any evidence of emotion with the palms of her hands, Leeny edged the photograph expectantly towards Cohen, her stare demanding an answer; one way or another.

There were few times in life when you were consciously aware that the decision laying in front of you wasn't just pivotal, but for better or worse would change everything. Cohen didn't know why, but this was that moment. Suddenly he felt extremely sober. Eventually a faint and reluctant nod of acceptance was met with a contained gasp. Unable to bring herself to speak, Leeny could only return the gesture with over-whelming appreciation; tears glistened in her eyes. He had given her a lifeline; hope if nothing else. She reached across and placed a grateful hand onto his; rough and scarred. Her's was delicate and warm. It had been a long time since he last felt the touch of a woman.

"Oh, good morning!" Nathan said, seeing the two silhouetted figures in the rear workspace, in what could only be described as a moment of intimacy.

"Good morning," Leeny replied, quickly retracting her hand.

"Sorry, I didn't realise we had company. Or that he was even alive." Nathan jested.

"He's alive," she replied playfully. "Well, breathing at least."

Cohen ignored their polite dance of introduction, just relieved there was someone else to do the talking. He picked up the picture and stared at the boy, committing as much information to memory as he could. There was a number on the reverse written with a black marker, which he assumed was Leeny's number in anticipation of him accepting the job.

"Sorry, would you like a coffee? Filter or flat white?" Nathan said; holding out the two takeaway cups on offer.

"No that's okay, thank you. I really must be going."

"Not on my account I hope?"

"No, no, I erm… really must be getting on." She said. "Sorry."

He put the coffees and pastry bag onto the work bench, wiped his moist hand onto his shirt and offered it in polite introduction.

"Nathan," he said.

As Leeny shook his hand, he couldn't help notice the familiar hooded sweat top she was wearing.

"Leeny," she replied. "Anyway I'm sure you boys have plenty to do before you open, so I'm gonna –"

She gave an awkward hitchhiking gesture with both thumbs towards the door. They both looked to Cohen for a reaction but his attention was still firmly on the picture of Josh. Nathan cleared his throat in the temporary silence to grab his attention. He looked up.

"Leeny's going," Nathan said like he was prompting a child to say goodbye.

"Okay."

"It was very nice to meet you," Nathan continued, almost as an apology for his friends behaviour as he unlocked the door for her.

"It was a pleasure. Good luck," she replied playfully before turning to leave. "Oh," she stopped at the door, "I'll wash this and get it back to you." referring to the hooded sweat top.

Cohen didn't bother to look up. She shared one last awkward smile with Nathan and was gone.

Nathan's smile lingered for several reasons as he watched Leeny walking away from the shop. Some were more on the playful and juvenile end of the spectrum, imagining how he would use the encounter to tease and joke at Cohen's expense; but mainly because it was good to see his friend up and about again.

For a time he wasn't sure if he'd be able to find his way back from whatever hell he had found himself in. And although he wasn't exactly his old self, there was a glimmer, and for now that was enough.

As Nathan went to lock the door he noticed a young priest on the opposite side of the road paying more than an enquiring look at the shop. When he realised Nathan had seen him, he turned and walked away without looking back. *Weird*, Nathan thought.

"Another black water?" he said, always finding new and unusual ways to describe coffee. Taking the space Leeny occupied, he passed over the filter coffee and pastry, curiously eyeing the photograph of the young boy and his friends attention of it.

Eventually putting the picture to one side, the two sat and enjoyed their breakfasts; Cohen taking a little more time on this one than the last. There was a comfortability in the quietude that spoke volumes of their bond, neither one desperate for conversation, both able to appreciate the fleeting opportunity that happened in-between the moments when life didn't.

After several minutes of silence Nathan finally asked,

"Who's the boy?"

"Leeny's son," Cohen said, returning his attention to the photograph. "He's missing."

"Oh I see. And I suppose she wants you to find him does she?"

Cohen nodded with a hesitation of uncertainty over his decision.

"And you told her no, right?"

He continued focusing on the picture.

"Cohen, please tell me you told the pretty lady no?"

Silence.

"Are you fucking kidding me? How many different ways of messed up do you want me to tell you this is?"

"Don't." Cohen gently warned.

"Don't? You're an assassin. You kill people, you don't find little boys for their mummies."

Cohen snatched up the picture and headed for the stairs back to the flat.

"And what happens when the thirst takes you over?" he continued. "What then? You can't even find your way home half the time, how do you expect to find some kid. You do know you've compromised us?" Nathan said.

Cohen stopped at the foot of the stairs unable to face his friend.

"I know."

Nathan stared at Cohen motionless at the foot of the stairs. Eventually expelling a deflating sigh, saying.

"Fine. I'll make some calls."

Stating the bloody obvious felt like a waste of breath. He knew if Cohen had said yes then it was as good as signing on the dotted line. Honour and discipline were once the bedrock of his way of life, and while the foundations may have cracked they hadn't altogether disappeared.

Cohen's barely faint nod conveyed more than appreciation, but right now it was all he could offer. He was about to leave when Nathan said,

"What about Leeny?"

Cohen looked at the shop. He loved this old place.

"See if you can scout a few locations," he said, "we'll look at it when I get back."

Nathan stood watching his friend slowly climb the stairs, every painstaking step until he was completely out of sight.

CHAPTER 04

BARRINGTON

Dr Barrington Ross couldn't escape the nervous excitement he was feeling. *What was it Helena was unable to tell me on the phone?* he thought. The driver swerved the jeep away from the main road and onto a path only distinguishable by tyre tracks; Dr Ross would have missed it had he been driving himself.

It had been several years since he had last seen Helena, but not until stopping to consider it did he realise just how long. *Seven, maybe eight years.* He was surprised how much time had passed, but like most friends and colleagues in academia, they believed there was a window of opportunity to make a name for yourself, and that required energy, focus and a bit of luck. Unfortunately the first casualties of this were always friends. You fit in what you can when you can, and never what you should. For Barrington it was lecture circuits and book tours. He always knew it was just a placeholder for something else, because at the last minute he'd blown off an opportunity to be the high-profile guest speaker at a prestigious event in London, something that could have taken his career to the next level. Instead he was happily racing through the Ethiopian desert, and didn't know why.

The jeep bounced so violently Dr Ross hit his head on the roof, he threw a wry look to his driver who held a slight grin, never removing his eyes from the road. He joined him in staring out at the terrain ahead. There wasn't really anything to see, just a vast plain of nothingness all the way to the horizon, allowing him the time to fill his head with romantic fantasies about the need for his presence. Of course he knew it was academic, but it never hurt to dream.

It had been a relatively easy journey, the flight had only taken an hour and a half from his home town in Addis Ababa, and he'd been on the road for just approaching an hour. All being well he would be with Helena in the next few.

He remembered having done the journey as a younger man, travelling eleven hundred kilometres by car. An eighteen hour non-stop ordeal and by the time he'd reached Aksum he could barely walk.

The evening was quickly drawing in, revealing a mesmerising canvas of the galaxy only few places in the world could offer. It didn't matter how many times he saw it, it was never lost on him.

The driver grunted at something pulling Dr Ross' attention to the road ahead. In the distance there was a set of headlights on the same path heading towards them. As they got ever closer, it appeared to be two vehicles in tandem, and judging by the dust trail being kicked up behind, they were approaching with speed.

The' driver decelerated to reduce any chance of miscalculation and steered the vehicle gently to the side of the trail. As the vehicles passed one another, Dr Ross pressed himself against the window, doing his best to see its occupants. But the dust being thrown around made it difficult. As the second jeep passed them, he caught a glimpse of Helena, who like him was pressed to the window staring back.

"Stop!" Dr Ross blurted urgently.

The driver brought the vehicle to a stop and Ross jumped out. The two other jeeps slowly came to a stop a little way up the trail and Helena emerged from the second vehicle. She removed her floppy wide rimmed hat and even in the low light he could already see her smiling.

She was a strong and shapely woman with shoulder length mousy blonde hair that had been pinned up by the hat. Not expecting to have seen him quite so soon, she bashfully tucked the loose strands behind her ears. She was wearing khaki shorts and a light shirt tied at the front over a t-shirt. He smiled both proud and amused, his old friend had become the clichéd embodiment of an archeologist.

Barrington on the other hand was slim with long limbs, giving him the appearance of being taller than his average height. At this particular moment he wished he was a little taller, whatever height Harrison Ford was seemed good. He'd opted for a casual look of cream trousers, a white shirt, brown shoes and his thick black rimmed glasses; which had become a sort of trademark in recent years. And although the climate made it less practical, he always carried a tie in his pocket; just in case.

They approached each other, both in silent excitement, and embraced as long and trusted friends; but there was more. Letting go, both stopped to look at each other, trying to take in all the lost years in one go.

"It's been too long," she said with a slight regret.

"You called, I came," Barrington replied warmly, "did you expect anything less?"

She looked at him and could see the boy she went to university with. The boy she always wished she'd told how she truly felt, but that was one marriage and many years ago.

"I hoped, I didn't know, but I'm so glad you came," she said. "It's so good to see you."

"And you. Is everything okay? You sounded…"

"Yeah… No everything's great," she said, like she'd almost forgotten why she called.

He found it a slightly puzzling response considering the urgency in which he'd been invited, but she didn't appear to be anxious or nervous, so assumed the news was good and could wait.

"It's not like you to be so cloak and dagger?"

She smiled with a subtle scoff, as if what he had said held significance. Barrington decided not to press the matter so quickly on arrival.

She looked back at the two jeeps waiting for her. A few of the workers had got out and their excited chatter was distracting her.

"Hold on a sec," she said jogging back to her jeep, "I'll be right back."

He watched as she began talking with the driver who appeared agitated, the excited chatter from the workers seemed to echo his contempt. Helena mirrored their intensity with ease and confidence, ordering them back into the vehicles before returning to Barrington as the two jeeps left.

"I told them I'd travel back with you," she said.

Linking arms they walked back towards Dr Ross' jeep, suddenly stopping with a discreet pull on his arm; far enough away from the driver's earshot.

"Look I know you're wondering what the hell is going on," she said in hushed tone. "As soon as we're back at the hotel away from…" She looked at Ross' driver to make sure his attention wasn't with them, "Soon okay?"

"Okay," he replied with a soft reassuring tone.

She smiled and rested her face against his arm, but suddenly let go.

"Oh wait!" she said.

"What is it?"

She slipped her hand into his trouser pocket and pulled out his tie; she giggled.

"Still the same Barrington."

Once again she linked his arm and rested her face against it, as they continued back to the jeep. "It really is good to see you," she said.

They'd formed a strong bond since their days studying at Oxford, and despite not having spoken in so many years, it was as though no time had passed at all. It was their fields of study that kept them away from each other, and yet it was often the field of study that brought them back together again.

Ross didn't really notice the bumpy ride back as much, apart from hitting his head on the roof a couple of times. He was too busy making the most of every minute, catching up on what they'd missed about each others lives; all while the question of what he was even doing here was burning inside him.

It was dark long before they got back to Helena's hotel in Aksum, a nice period four storey building that she swore was like a palace in comparison to other locations she had stayed in. Ross looked up at the building. It was clear from her description that he was expecting a little more.

"Trust me," she said grabbing his attention, "when you've spent ten hours in a hole in the middle of a desert, it's like coming home to five-star luxury."

"Well the flight was a little bumpy," he jested.

"Come on," she said leading the way inside, "the lecture circuit has made you soft."

Dr Ross looked up wearily at the building again before following her inside. She was right, he now lived a fairly moderate life and had become accustomed to a more catered existence.

Helena bounded through the reception with the confidence of someone that had been a part of the community for eighteen months. Stopping to greet every person she passed, the owners, their friends, the locals. It was an expected part of life in the community, had she not done so it would have been considered rude. All in all it had taken about twenty minutes just to get to the room, which was on the second floor. She warned Ross not to lean against the railings as the building was getting old. This time it was his turn to laugh. While he knew the archeological digs had made Helena more robust than him, he was still Ethiopian, he knew his country, and his countrymen.

He stiffly took a seat on the small chair by the window, knees together, back straight. Despite his friendship with Helena. he was quite conservative in his values, and all too aware of being alone with a woman in her hotel room.

There were moments in their youth when something almost happened, but never quite came to pass. Helena carefully placed her pack onto the bed, pulled off her over-shirt and threw it onto a growing pile in the corner; the dirty white t-shirt she wore underneath outlined her body perfectly. Barrington unexpectedly found himself staring.

"God, I need a shower," she said with desperation, stretching and rubbing her neck.

Reaching past him, she got almost purposefully and teasingly close, lifting her pillow to reveal a bottle of scotch. He didn't budge a muscle. Finding a couple of glasses, she poured them both a measure. There was the slightest hint of a sparkle in her eye as she handed Barrington a glass, his shyness was quite apparent and he got the impression she was enjoying it. He watched her like he was committing every moment to memory as she knocked back the drink in one go.

It had been quite dark since their initial meeting and he realised this was the first time he could really see her. Appreciating how long it had been and how much they both had aged. But Helena had blossomed and grown into herself, she had improved with age and her confidence was alluringly distracting. He could still see the girl from his youth, but now so could the rest of the world. He smiled and took a sip of his drink.

Without another word she entered the bathroom and he heard the shower start to run. He decided to distract himself and leaned on the window frame, watching as the local life passed by.

It was a vibrant part of the town and there were plenty of people milling around. A couple strolling arm in arm, three old men sat on chairs outside of a shop, laughing and joking with people as they passed by, and a couple of guys in a beautiful old faded blue Mustang, cruising slowly enough to attract admirers; giving him cause to smile. Cities were different all over the world, he thought, but people were fundamentally the same.

He turned back into the room, which could have easily been mistaken for a teenage boy's, clothes strewn on the floor, a crumpled up unmade bed and plates with the remanence of food from previous days, but he knew that was life on the road of an archeologist and not a reflection on Helena.

Barrington quickly picked up any extra clothes and put them on the pile in the corner, he then stacked the plates and straightened the cover on the bed. No sooner had he finished when the bathroom door opened and Helena emerged amongst the steam. She had a towel around her torso and another she was using to scrunch her hair dry. Ross did his best to avert his eyes, but caught a glimpse of the water glistening on her neck, one drop rushed to her collar bone and then slowed as it travelled beneath the towel towards her breasts.

"Pour me another one would you," she asked while rummaging in a large rucksack.

Barrington did as he was asked, poured a drink and sat stiffly holding the glass. Pulling out some khaki pants and t-shirt, she buried her nose in them and inhaled to see if they were fresh, they weren't, but they'd do. Returning to the bathroom she pulled the door over, but not shut, and continued to change.

"So I suppose you wanna know why I dragged you out here?" she called out from the bathroom.

"It had crossed my mind, but when I realised you were digging in the northern region of Aksum, I figured you'd found it."

"What?"

He didn't hear her. His attention was uncharacteristically fixed upon the gap in the door, just able to make out the curve of her bottom as she slipped into the khaki pants, and the dip of her waist as she pulled the t-shirt down. The door quickly swung open.

"What did you say?" she said seeming perturbed.

"What?"

Barrington was startled, embarrassed she'd caught him peeping. She did, but what he'd said was more concerning.

"You said you thought I'd found it?"

"Yes," he said as he quickly lowered his gaze.

But not before noticing she wasn't wearing a bra and her t-shirt sat tight against her frame.

"Menelik's palace," he continued. "That's why I'm here isn't it?"

She breathed a sigh of relief, which he thought an odd reaction.

"Is that mine" she asked.

Playfully taking the glass from his hand, he could only watch as she slowly tipped the glass and savoured the sip; her hair dampening the shoulders of her t-shirt.

It was clear she was teasing him, but he wasn't sure if the flirting was anything more than that.

"Well?" he pressed, hoping to distract himself.

"The palace? Oh we found it." She spoke in a way that suggested it wasn't big news.

A gasp, Barrington got more of a distraction than he could have imagined. She plonked herself on the bed beside him.

"I'm sorry, I shouldn't be so nonchalant about it, it's just that I've known the location of the palace for probably eighteen months now."

"What?" he exasperated.

Helena giggled. She felt a little guilty for doing so, but she had never really seen Barrington in a state of shock before, and it was both amusing and endearing.

"I was approached by a consortium a while back," she continued. "They said they'd read one of my papers, theorising its location."

"A consortium?"

"By the time they'd contacted me, they'd already used satellite imagery to confirm my thesis, and followed up by sending a team to conduct an extensive survey using ground penetrating radar," she explained. "Honestly I'm not even sure why they needed me, but I'm glad they called. Glad," she said again, thinking about the word. "Doesn't quite cut the mustard, does it?"

"Wait!" Barrington said as he attempted to assimilate. "So this consortium had access to satellite information? Funded a team to survey the area? *Then* contacted you, and funded the dig?"

Her answer was a quiet stare.

"And they managed to get clearance from the Ethiopian government?!"

"I guess so," she said matter-of-factly.

"Who *is* this consortium?"

"People who value anonymity above all things."

"Oh, come on."

"No, I mean I really don't know," she said. "They communicate through mediators, lawyers, private secretaries, things like that. From what I know they're of old money. Like, really old. I think I heard someone refer to them once as an 'Order', or 'The Order', but that's all I can tell you. Anyway, don't you want to know why I dragged you out here?"

But Barrington didn't hear anything past The Order. He thought perhaps she had been mistaken, or whoever was behind the funding was being flippant with their anonymity, because he'd heard of an organisation known as The Order before, but only once, and was told to never repeat what he'd heard to anyone. Not that anyone would believe him if he did.

It happened on what he used to call a down day. Not in regards to his emotions, but on the rare occasion that his studies and university classes didn't take precedence over everything, including food and hygiene, a down day simply meant to down tools, take the day off.

His friends had taken him to his first rugby match, a varsity game against Cambridge, but it was also an introduction for the excuse of consuming copious amounts of alcohol within the shortest time period possible. Much of the day remained a dreamlike memory that was broken into unrelated fragments, until the end of the night when he began to sober up, finding himself in a pub alongside his friends and a few faculty members that had also chosen to take a down day.

The groups numbers eventually dwindled and in the early hours he found himself in a drink-fuelled discussion with one of his professors, Veronica Lehman. Barrington was spouting quixotic notions of how archeologists were the authors of history and it was their duty to present findings unencumbered by personal bias or influence. She pointed out that while idealistic, it was the naive perspective of a student who had not yet met with real world consequences, political ramifications that could impact society as a whole, but more importantly, narrative always aligns with whomever funded the discovery. Scientific studies present themselves as independent, yet fortuitously their outcomes always seem to favour the profit margins of the ones who funded the study.

The professor warned him that interpretation was not authorship and his particular area of interest and expertise would undoubtedly lead him on a path that would reveal layers of the world he never knew existed, organisations and powers that wrote history the way they wanted it to be told, not the way it actually was.

Barrington was not a lover of conspiracies that couldn't be weighed against evidence, but

what the professor said was not nearly as sobering as the demeanour in how she'd said it, and it excited him.

Academia was fraught with people claiming elitist or cabalistic knowledge, but he'd only ever witnessed Lehman present herself as a lecturer whom refrained from exhibiting personal influence. Regardless of her extensive knowledge, she believed it robbed students of revelation and that in turn had the possibility of robbing humanity of the inspiration found in such rare moments. But not on this occasion. The knowledge she imparted, never to be repeated, surrounded a group known as The Order. An ancient bloodline that had woven itself into the fabric of the entire world.

In years to come, that very conversation would be the inspiration behind his book; Menelik's Dagger.

"Barrington?" Helena said again. "Don't you want to know why I dragged you out here?"

"Sorry," he said reengaging. "Of course."

Helena picked up her pack and gently laid it onto her lap. Her face was serious, but there was an elation behind her eyes. Barrington watched with an intense curiosity. If he wasn't there to hear about the palace, which he quietly considered to be a clever deduction, then he didn't know what he was doing there.

"You remember when we decided our majors?" she said, her playful tone gone. "We knew we wouldn't be able to see as much of each other."

"Yes, but we said we'd always make sure our fields crossed."

"And I hope they always do," she said, meaning so much more.

Pulling on some gloves, with both hands she reached into the pack and very carefully produced an object; securely wrapped in soft material and fastened with string. Placing it on the bed, she slowly and carefully unwrapped it, finally revealing an ancient dagger.

Barrington stood up and looked down at the object, then back at Helena and then back at the object, as if he wasn't sure what he was looking at. Adjusting his glasses, he bent over to give it careful consideration. It was still dirty with clumps of compacted earth clinging to the ridges, but truly remarkable; unlike anything he'd ever seen. As Helena sat watching him, she worried that the true excitement was being lost. Barrington proceeded to slip on a pair of gloves.

"May I?" he asked, gesturing for the artefact.

"Of course."

As Helena passed it to him, she didn't expect to feel quite as protective of it as she did, but she forced herself to part with it.

"It's magnificent" he said while inspecting it with great consideration, turning it in hand.

Helena watching him carefully, studied his face for clues.

"And you uncovered this at the dig?" he said.

She nodded. He stood to hold the dagger closer to the light, continuing to pour over its details.

"I've never seen anything quite like it" he continued, "From its design, I'd say…" He'd formed an idea but instead he said, "I don't know!"

Helena's heart was starting to sink, if anyone had known the dagger's origin, surely it was the man who literally wrote the book on it, or what she thought was it. The moment of doubt questioned her certainty, *perhaps I'm trying to force the dagger to fit history,* she thought.

"There's only one story that describes a knife like this," he said. "But it's a story I've only heard told in Ethiopia."

There was a soft warning in his words for Helena not to get her hopes up, but she knew this story, it was the one she was hoping for.

"It was said that the great and wise King Solomon had a harem of a thousand women."

There was always a slight performance when Barrington narrated, she remembered.

"Around seven hundred wives and 300 concubines," he continued, "but there was only ever one woman that truly captured his heart. If there was ever a story of star crossed lovers or serendipitous meetings, then it began with King Solomon and The Queen of Sheba."

Barrington sat next to Helena on the bed, his attention still fixated on the artefact, quashing whatever nerves had been previously present.

For a moment Helena had been transported back in time to the quad at Oxford. Sitting on the grass hanging on the every word of a young shy Barrington that sprang to life whenever he told his stories. The love and passion he had for his field was always shared in the tales; and Helena quickly realised what it was she'd fallen for all those years ago.

"It's one of the true great and tragic love stories of the bible," he continued. "When the queen returned to her homeland of Sheba, she did so having given birth to their child. King Solomon, so beside himself with grief, mourning the loss of his true love entered into a state of dramatic melancholia, and her story in the bible was suddenly at its end. But as we stand here today, in modern Ethiopia, we stand in Sheba, where in the writings of the Kebra Nagast her story continues."

There had been a true romantic under the straight suited surface of Barrington, and while it appeared, Helena couldn't have been more focused on a story she'd heard probably a hundred times. In truth, she wasn't listening to a word of it; not since the first sentence. Now she was just watching.

"The queen gave birth to a son and named him Menelik; son of the wise. He would grow up to become a great king and ruler of Abyssinia.

One day, he told his mother that he would journey to Israel to meet the father he'd never known, the great and wise King Solomon. The queen gave him a ring, gifted to her from Solomon, so that on his arrival the king would recognise Menelik as his son. For the son to recognise the father, he simply needed to seek his own reflection. Now as you know," Barrington said, skipping the narrative to get to the point, "some stories say that Menelik returned home with the Arc of the Covenant, others say it was the queen who had returned with the Arc. But where there is no conflict in the stories, was the gift he was supposed to have bestowed upon his son, Menelik; a dagger. An unearthly thing said to have been forged in the fires of hell," Barrington warned. "King Solomon invoked and enslaved seventy-two demon spirits with powers gifted to him from God."

"The seal of Solomon," Helena said, finding herself re-engaged.

"Exactly. It gave a son of Adam dominion over the forces of the underworld," Barrington replied. "An affront Satan could not bare."

The weight of the dagger suddenly felt heavier somehow, as though the story was bringing a mythical object to life in his hands.

Helena's brow suddenly creased, she had heard the story many times, but this part didn't sound so familiar. And although she believed she knew it, somehow the details had eroded.

"If the seal ever fell into the wrong hands," Barrington continued with a soft caution, "what enslaves can also emancipate, a chance to become of the flesh. Six daggers to form one were created, each dagger pierces the body of a sacrificed soul, enslaving them for all eternity in hell. The seventh dagger is formed from all of the six."

Barrington dramatically held up the dagger with both hands. At that moment, they both felt a cool air rush through the room. Very unusual timing that made them both chuckle nervously.

"This dagger pierces the body of the vessel Satan will use to walk the earth."

Barrington was back in the room with her, but quiet suddenly. This wasn't the dagger Helena was hoping for, the one from the story, and for that he was truly sorry. Although silently relieved, and for that he felt guilty.

It was clear the dagger had six points that joined at the tip as one, and the hilt starred in several directions, like the metal was crossing over or through each other, he couldn't be sure. *But it was just one dagger,* he thought. Barrington lowered his eyes as he handed the dagger back.

Whoever made the object, clearly wanted to believe in the stories as much as Barrington, the ones passed down through the generations of his countrymen, but as a renowned academic, he just couldn't bring himself to believe this was the dagger of Menelik.

Helena didn't seem quite so sad for some reason. He finished his drink and she poured another; topping up herself in turn.

There was still a playful energy to her that didn't quite make sense considering the information. *Perhaps she hadn't understood.* He eyed her curiously as she sat there with a subtle, yet visible smirk. There was something she wasn't telling him. She knelt by the bed and carefully placed the dagger in front of her with Barrington inspecting her every move. Without looking, her fingers searched the underside of the hilt, finding what they were looking for. Then, there was a light click and the one dagger fell apart in her hands, separating it into six individual sections.

Barrington jumped up from the bed and looked down at the pieces. Goosebumps pricked his body from head to toe, the hair on the back of his neck stood to attention and his eyes widened in disbelief.

"I was certain I knew what I had," she said smiling softly, her eyes almost watering with joy. "It was your stories. That's why you had to be the first to know."

Barrington hadn't yet been able to formulate any words or even acknowledge Helena was speaking to him. His heart raced with excitement. Without thinking he downed his drink, grabbed the bottle and topped up his own glass; downing it again. Helena laughed, finally the reaction she expected and wanted. It was several minutes before he could speak.

"This is…"

Barrington didn't know how to finish the sentence, but Helena jumped in, "One of the most significant finds in archaeology? Career changing? Funding for future projects for years to come?"

"Yes… Yes!" Barrington said, unable to stop himself smiling.

He joined her on the bed and filled both their glasses, although Helena's was already full and quickly started to overflow. Barrington raised his in a toast. He wasn't used to drinking to excess and the alcohol was taking a quick affect; stripping back the reserved conservatism.

"To you Helena, for making history!" he said, very slightly slurred.

He then went to clink glasses but stopped just short.

"And… for being one of the few that actually deserve it."

They clinked their glasses and took a sip, both unable to stop looking at the daggers.

"Do you know anyone that could independently verify?" she asked.

Thinking, he said, "There is a professor I could ask."

"How quickly do you think we could get it to him?"

"Her" he replied, "I could make a video call in the morning if you like. She'd obviously need to physically look at it, but I think she could probably make a good initial assessment on the call. It will give you a percentage at least."

Helena nodded with a smile, her excitement finally catching up and taking her breath. It was the same for both of them, words simply couldn't capture the magnitude. Barrington wouldn't have wanted to be anywhere else in the world right now, the find was a physical confirmation of his faith, and its historical importance couldn't have been overestimated, yet it was Helena that was his main focus. He had never seen her look more beautiful than in that moment. She was tired from spending a day digging in the scorching sun, her hair was damp and messy, and her clothes could have been army fatigues, but she was perfect. He cursed himself, wanting to be that man, the one that could sweep her into his arms and kiss her. *If there was ever a time it was now,* he thought. But he just couldn't bring himself to do it.

Their eyes had locked for far too long and she could see the want *and* hesitation in him.

It's not a day for regrets, she thought. Putting down her glass, she gently took his face into her hands, and softly kissed him.

He was completely taken aback, but for the second time in no time at all, he could feel the goosebumps return, this time with a wave of electricity that felt like it levitated him.

He stopped, their faces barely moving away from each other. Helena's heart began racing in panic. *Did I do something wrong,* she thought.

He stood up and carefully moved the daggers away from the bed, her watching his every move, thankful he wasn't picking up his bag and leaving. A shyness had come over her and a confidence over him. He returned and stood in between her legs, she looked up at him. Now it was her heart that was racing, and for the right reasons. He leaned in and started to kiss her, slowly laying her back onto the bed. For her, he found that man.

They made love and somewhere in the pillow talk, exhaustion took over and they fell asleep in each others arms. It was only a couple of hours before Helena awoke, as if pulled from her sleep. She looked at Barrington in a moment of tired confusion before remembering. She smiled tiredly and snuggled in close to him, he was still asleep, but his body reacted; his arm instinctively cradling her into him.

CHAPTER 05

FATHER MICHAEL

The sun was beginning to set as Father Michael headed back towards the observatory, slowly strolling the serene picturesque surroundings of Lake Albano, although his gaze never lifted from the smooth cemented pathways; weighed by thought.

He was just short of entering the building when something stopped him. Uncertain of why, he turned back to look at the sunset. It had set so many times in his life and he had stopped in awe at many of them, but none could compare to this; and he wasn't alone. It brought complete stillness to that part of the world, every person stopped and stared in silence, like it was something you didn't have the power to deny. There wasn't even a light breeze tickling leaves on a branch to distract you.

It was a scene from the original artist that every painter in history had attempted to copy, and paled in comparison. No oils or watercolours could truly capture the sheer magnificence of what was unfolding.

A beautiful deep golden sun encircled by a double spectrum halo, rich colours streaking across the sky in every direction that seemed to have no end. The few clouds that sporadically scattered the heavens wore a lining so bright it was as if they'd caught fire, against a sky that had turned from a rich blue to a pale lilac. When the last third of the sun sat looking over the horizon it burned vermilion, clothing the sky in blood red. When it finally disappeared from sight there followed a strange ethereal drone that seemed to come from every direction all at once, as though a trumpet from the heavens.

Everyone felt that moment, not just Father Michael. After the beauty, it had brought with it an eerie sense of dread. For most people it would be a passing feeling, but for Michael it was an affirmation. He needed to do as Father Weiss had instructed and seek out Lucifer.

Upon baring witness to a sunset scored into the heavens by the hand of the divine, Father Michael knew he had to follow the trail left by his late friend. To uncover the truth behind his murder and unveil the hidden prophesy.

He considered the folly nature of his actions, pursuing such a vague supposition eighteen months since events unfolded; after all he was never meant to make the journey himself. Weiss stated that he would explain everything when he saw him, a meeting that never transpired. However the letter also made reference to a location, somewhere Michael would immediately recognise, and though he may already be too late; not pursuing it had never crossed his mind.

To reach the prophesy he needed to purchase a flight to Arizona, but after only having just returned from Germany, such unusual behaviour would surely arouse suspicion; after all he wasn't exactly the jet-setting age. While tussling with the idea of just how he was going to make the journey, he found himself standing outside the office for the director of the observatory, Brother Mackie Bonsu; the one man in charge of all official Vatican travel.

Michael thought him somewhat of an unconventional man, and from their rare interactions, he got the impression Brother Bonsu would have rather avoided him. Admittedly, he felt the same, but couldn't be specific as to why.

No sooner had he knocked on the door that he realised it was in haste, he hadn't yet thought of an excuse of why he would need to travel.

"Come in," Brother Bonsu said.

Tentatively, Michael entered the room.

"Ahh, Father Michael," Brother Bonsu delighted. "What a lovely surprise. Please come in.

Thrown by Bonsu's enthusiastic welcome, whom was sat behind a large desk overwhelmed with stacks of papers. He peered over the top of his spectacles as he laid his pen onto the pile in front of him, interlocking his fingers to present his undivided attention; and intrigue for the visit.

"It seems you have beaten me to the punch," he continued.

"I'm sorry?" Father Michael said, slightly taken back.

"I had been intending to come and see you."

"You were?"

Brother Bonsu's unanticipated welcoming stunned Michael into appearing as the lost dithering soul he'd played all morning, only this time it was less of an act. It wasn't so much the welcome that threw him, but the apparent sincerity.

"I was hoping you might share the memorial with me," Brother Bonsu continued. "I was due to attend, but unfortunately my services were otherwise detained," he said gesturing disappointingly to his desk. "Please, sit with me."

He rose to remove a stack of books from a seat in front of the desk, then proceeded to close the door. Michael noticed him discretely peering out to see if anyone was loitering, or within earshot, before returning to take his seat.

"I hope you don't feel me inconsiderate," Brother Bonsu said.

"I'm not sure I follow," Father Michael replied.

"You and Franz were close. I don't want my enquiry to impose upon you, to risk inflicting unnecessary distress simply for my own gratification."

Removing the expressionless stunned veil, Michael's face softened to a faint smile that reciprocated the sincerity.

"On the contrary," he said. "It would be my pleasure."

Though cautious of revealing his own truth, it appeared as though Brother Bonsu was attempting to communicate, not least having used Franz's name rather than his formal title, a point he would expect to be challenged upon. *I'll bite,* he thought.

"You knew Franz?" Father Michael continued.

Brother Bonsu's gaze fell to a pile of papers in front of him, though it was the past he saw with fondness.

"I arrived here not long before Franz relocated to Germany," he said. "The first time we spoke was by letter, to liaise my assistance in his transition. At the time, I got the impression it was a job no one else wanted, which I'm sure you're already aware of."

Michael nodded along agreeably.

"But I was eager to make a good impression and so thought I would jot a short note to introduce myself."

There was a twinkle in Father Michael's eye suggesting he knew exactly where this story was heading, despite never having heard it before.

"His response was swift as it was sharp." Brother Bonsu continued. "Before even opening his letter, I was filled with an overwhelming sense of inadequacy. On the front was my name, as one would expect. But if he had written nothing else, the message still couldn't have been clearer. It was crafted with the most elegant penmanship I'd ever seen, I was instantly embarrassed about the scribble I'd left him. But just in case there was any doubt, Franz made certain to drive the point home."

"As only he could," Father Michael chimed.

"I can still remember his words verbatim. You would do well," Mackie said trying to adopt his best Franz impression, "You would do well to find a means of communication more suited to reflect the span of one's attention."

Father Michael chuckled nostalgically.

"I was in awe, which I'm not sure was the intended outcome. Though it seems there would be an irony to my penance."

Brother Bonsu gestured to the stacks of papers covering his desk.

"Every year I am now faced with applications for our summer camp. All written by the hands of a generation that see writing as an archaic means of communication… Franz would be laughing his ass off."

The two men shared a humoured truth that faded to reflective nostalgia.

"It was so elegant," be said, his tone suddenly direct and flat. "Distinctive. Something I would recognise even today, long after his passing. As undoubtedly I'm sure would you."

Brother Bonsu held a penetrating gaze, wanting to be sure his message was being delivered.

Father Michael wasn't as quick on the uptake as he would have liked, but suddenly realised that Brother Bonsu was suggesting either he was the one who left the letter, or at the very least knew of it. Scanning the room, books and papers, it wasn't only the desk that overflowed chaotically, but almost every surface of the office; as if inside the workspace of an eccentric scientist. Brother Bonsu looked on, waiting, as though confident of the outcome, willing Father Michael to see what couldn't be voiced.

Then he saw it, a symbol, the wheel. Of course being such an obvious form, he couldn't assume every single one held significance. But it began to repeat itself in several locations: the subtle background of a painting, the spine of a book, or most notably, at the side of the desk holding down a stack of papers as an improvised paperweight; a miniaturised replica of a ships nautical wheel.

"Keen mariner?" Father Michael queried.

"Not particularly," Brother Bonsu responded with a subtle yet mischievous grin.

Suddenly his distant behaviour was not so hard to understand, or Franz's silence on the matter. Depending on their position, brethren were concealed for protection.

"It was a very beautiful service," Father Michael said eventually, unguarded. "Of course Franz would have hated every minute of it."

He continued regaling the memorial service while Brother Bonsu immersed himself in its telling, closing his eyes at one point allowing Michael's voice to walk him through the day as though experiencing it first hand.

The following hour slipped by unnoticed as the two men traded without effort, their individual histories connected by loss had been their own histories waiting to be discovered, creating a bond and friendship as though it had always been. But the sweetness had a bitter aftertaste, when not just the palpable absence of their connection became painfully apparent, but the insidious means that brought them to this moment.

"There are so many questions I have" Brother Bonsu said, "that at this time, I am unable to ask. But I assume whatever Franz left you, led you here?"

"In a manner of speaking, yes… But not…"

"Before you say anything else, please, only tell me what you must, nothing more."

Father Michael appreciated the words of caution, realising Brother Bonsu must have sensed a slight lowering of his guard. He considered just how much he should reveal. *That Franz discovered a hidden prophesy? Which is most likely the motivation behind his death? That he placed the prophecy beyond the reach of those trying to silence him?* In the end, he simply said, "I need a flight to Arizona."

Brother Bonsu stared at him for several seconds, a blank unchanging, unreadable expression. Being unable to gauge his response caused a tightness in Michael's stomach. Finally Brother Bonsu let out a scoff of laughter that did little to settle him.

"Have I said something wrong?" Michael asked, concerned.

"On the contrary." he said in a manor reflecting Michael's earlier words.

He went on to explain that he had missed Father Weiss' funeral due to a problem surrounding the Vatican Summer Camp. Every year twelve potential candidates are invited to their facilities, in the hope of attracting some of the brightest young minds to further their pursuits in the academic sciences. However, one of the chaperones became seriously ill. With no one to take his place, the entire trip was going to be cancelled. A recommendation was passed down by Cardinal Oorloff to use an associate from outside of the Vatican. It wasn't his place to interfere, but as someone whom held the confidence of the holy father, it also couldn't be ignored. Not an ideal situation, but it did mean not having to cancel the trip altogether.

In the kerfuffle of re-submitting paperwork on behalf of the new priest, one applicant was overlooked. Now they needed someone to chaperone the candidate to connect him with the group, in Arizona.

"It's a funny thing faith. "So fragile. A whisper competing against the noise of desire."

Fixing his gaze upon Father Michael he then said,

"I saw the sunset tonight."

The words grabbed Michaels' attention almost the way the sunset had.

"In all the years I've spent looking into the heavens, it was like…"

Brother Bonsu couldn't find the words to finish the sentence, but looked up slightly as though he could still see it.

"Stillness, as far as I could see. Everyone stopping to just… be, to experience a moment."

It was almost as if Father Michael could see the sun on Brother Bonsu's face.

"And then I saw you," he said.

"I'm afraid I might be a little lost," Michael said with some sincerity, unsure of the reasoning behind the tangent.

"More so than you think. While everyone marvels at God's wonders, it's the prophet that holds the burden of its message. When you walked into my room I knew I was right."

Michael was shocked. He'd hit the nail on the head. Brother Bonsu laughed out loud, he looked like he'd spooked the old man.

"Rest assured, you're not alone," he said, picking up the application of a Phillipé Garcia and dropping it in front of Michael. "And I'm not talking just spiritually. The war has already begun my friend, the mouth of the serpent will soon vomit its spawn. Our enemy will have a face. Signs and wonders dear friend. Signs and wonders."

CHAPTER 06

COHEN

ohen stared vacantly into the expanse, where clouds met the sky on a wispy horizon. It was that endless ethereal vision that gifted him a moments respite, a peace that was uncomfortable in its unfamiliarity, but it was if nothing else, a distraction from an unseen battle against anxiety doing its best to consume him.

He tried focusing on the rolling clouds that were passing beneath the plane, head pressed firmly against the window, trying to hide the rigid tension beneath the surface; although anybody taking the time to look would see the obvious.

He had underestimated the symptoms his body would go through from such sustained alcohol abuse, but then he'd also underestimated just how long the abuse had been.

That morning, Nathan had looked at him in a way that he couldn't quite put his finger on. It was the air of an expression not experienced before, a tightness surrounding his eyes, a negligible squint, a look of quiet concentration.

It was hardly surprising having spent the last several months at the bottom of a bottle, so Cohen assumed the obvious, that Nathan's surprise at seeing him up and about semi-functioning, and with the unexplained presence of a woman, perhaps justified the look.

It was only when booking the flight did he realise *why* he was the subject of study. As he clicked on the website's calendar to select his departure date, the month was July, which he expected, give or take a month, but the year was 2014? *Clearly a glitch,* he thought, and a costly one if people couldn't book their flights until a year in advance. Just to be sure he clicked the time at the top right of his screen, a box appeared with the date, 'Monday 14th July 2014'. *That can't be right!?*

Scrambling to open the web browser in a quietly panicked hope that his computer was the problem, he typed 'Today's news' into the search engine. Randomly selecting one of the links, the website opened with a headline he wasn't concerned with. It was only the date that held any significance, but there it was again, 'Monday 14th July 2014'.

His perception of the several months of comatose self-destruction, was in reality closer to eighteen months.

All morning he tried desperately recalling memories that would fill in the chasms of darkness, but all Cohen got was flashes, nonsensical moments that he couldn't differentiate between nightmares and reality; and then nothing. Just the excruciating twisting and turning of his intestines as if they had begun to decay while he was still alive. A reminder of what he was failing to remember.

He had never experienced this kind of weakness before, enslaving oneself to a vice. The curse of a lesser men, believing he had somehow reached beyond the fragility of the human condition by pure determination of will and a religious execution of discipline. Now he was the embodiment of shame, unable to gaze upon his own reflection and recognise the man staring back, now he looked like everybody else, a target, a victim.

But Nathan's expression was also that of a friend, one who'd endured, shared the pain and continued to do so. The burden of responsibility for another human being was an unfamiliar concept to Cohen. He knew Nathan deserved better, to know the truth of what sent him into a spiral of self-destruction, he just didn't know how or where to start.

Maybe now was the time to unburden himself, share his madness, maybe it would do him some good. Perhaps when he returned from Prague it would be time.

Cohen pressed his head with greater force into the window, trying to stop the pain clawing its way up his throat. Anything that came close to a groan was dispersed by a slow release of breath from his nostrils, sounding more like a death rattle.

"Anything from the trolley?" a friendly female voice said.

He turned from the window to see a hard-worn, but professional smile of a young female flight attendant. The two men to his left who hadn't known each other at the beginning of the flight, now chatting like old acquaintances were quick to place their order.

"I've got this," the one in the aisle seat said, pulling out his wallet. "Well, hello," he continued with jovial confidence to the attendant, "I'll take two bottles of whisky, and my friend here will have the same."

"One moment please sir," she said. Smiling, and looked passed them towards Cohen. "Excuse me sir, would you like anything from the trolley?"

Cohen thought for a moment, wondering how much longer he could hold out. But looking at the two beside him, particularly the one in the aisle seat whose belly overshot his belt by several inches, and the grip on his wallet suggested a growing impatience, he knew once they'd opened their bottles and the smell of alcohol hit him, it would be difficult to resist. He envisioned ripping one of their arms out of their sockets and beating them just for a sip.

Instead he joined them in ordering two bottles of the same. For a man in his condition it was like ordering a paracetamol for a gun shot wound, but it would have to do.

The flight attendant placed the two single serving bottles of whisky and a plastic tumbler with ice on each of their trays before moving on. He turned back to the window, arms folded and hands clenched beneath his pits to quell any signs of the trauma he was desperately trying to hide; while the two men fuelled their bonding.

The seal cracked as the top twisted away from the bottle, a distinctive splash and pour into the plastic cup. A second later, the smell flaring his nostrils followed, then a tingling in his mouth as it tried but failed to salivate. Unable to hold out any longer he picked up the bottle in front of him and raised it in a friendly gesture towards the two men. Both responded by raising their plastic glasses. Cohen emptied the contents of both bottles into the container and with two gentle swallows it was gone. The background chatter of the two men suddenly fell silent as they watched Cohen's drink disappear with ease. He didn't mind being the subject of their fascination, he was just glad it had knocked the exuberance from their volume.

Shifting comfortably back into his seat, Cohen once again turned his stare towards the misty blue sky. The warmth in his belly quietened the screaming of his insides to a moan that he could tolerate, although now the taste had sparked a greed that would be another silent battle for at least the rest of the flight. He could see Nathan's face staring at him again. It was the same expression but beyond the stare laid grave concern. For the first time, Nathan could see what Cohen was only just beginning to realise, he was in no fit state for what lay ahead, but at least now they both knew.

Nathan had arranged a car that was waiting for Cohen at the airport's multi-storey car park, on the third floor in the north-east corner. A children's toy in the shape of a pink furry owl sat inside the rear window as an extra identifier. It was a small white town car with local plates and no outstanding violations, the keys were on the tyre of the driver's side at the front. It was clearly more of a women's car or teenagers, Cohen thought while having to adjust the seat back several positions. Struggling to fit his large frame comfortably into such a cramped space; he had to admit he'd probably put on a few pounds as well.

Putting the sports bag on the passenger seat, he opened the glove compartment. There was a portable GPS, a map, a revolver with one spare mag and a small bottle of Johnnie Walker Blue, everything he'd requested. Immediately unscrewing the cap on the Johnnie Blue and swigging down a few gulps, his thirst challenged him to drink it dry. But he replaced the cap, wiped his mouth with the back of his hand and put the bottle back inside the glove compartment, slamming it shut with a disappointed force.

Suddenly it was quiet. The muffled hum of a jet engine thrusted an aeroplane to lift off somewhere in the background, but inside the car, silence. A precious thing Cohen once craved and cherished now only promised torment. Memories he drank to forget became louder in the silence, sobriety gave him nowhere to hide. Although his thoughts were hazy and he was still coming to terms with just *how* much time had passed, something felt off. Without being able to think straight, he didn't know if it was him or the job.

He glanced again at the glove compartment, thinking about the bottle just sitting there, unfinished, tormenting him. He reached over to spring the latch again but caught a glimpse of himself in the rear-view mirror. He looked, not admiringly or superficially, but as someone trying to see beyond a reflection. His eyes were usually a bright hazel-green with an alluring glint that appeared to change in colour, depending on the weather or the colour of the top he was wearing, sometimes even his mood. He knew they didn't actually change colour, it was just a lucky reflective quality of the iris. But today, there was no glint in the ones staring back, no vibrant colour, just tired and bloodshot with lines he was only now seeing for the first time. A dark and dirty pigment of the surrounding skin made them appear sunken. His phone suddenly beeped with a text alert.

NATHAN: "A few unseasonal bees around the flowers this year."

The job was already proving to be more trouble than its worth, but he knew the shop was in good hands. He rubbed his face vigorously as if washing with air, trying to bring his focus into the here and now. Unzipping the sports bag, he took out the picture of Josh, looking at it as he had done in London. Eventually dropping it onto the passenger seat, he started the car and exited the airport.

Cohen made his way east on motorway six, towards Old Town, where a former associate and one time friend ran a bar; Viktor's. Prague wasn't exactly known for its criminal endeavours, but information had a way of passing through the city on its way east or west. And information was his trade. Viktor served a few terms in the military and a few more as a hired mercenary, this was now the safest way to stay close enough to the action without putting his family in harms way. Of course not doing anything at all would be the safest option, but he used to say, *"Once you had lifted the veil on death and seen yourself staring back, you could never truly walk away."*

At this stage, Cohen had nothing at all to go on. No one had claimed responsibility for the kid's abduction and there was no ransom. He wasn't surprised the police hadn't come up with anything, they never do. If they ever recovered a missing child it was generally pure luck, and most of the time it was just a body.

It wasn't their fault, their hands were tied, boxes needed to be ticked and protocols followed. Normally you'd have to wait for at least twenty four hours before anyone would even lift a finger. The problem is, the first twenty four hours in a child's abduction are the most critical, and Cohen was now close to five days after the event. He made the consideration even before accepting the job, that he may only be there to recover a body and not the boy. But still, for reasons he couldn't explain or justify, he had the overwhelming sense the boy was still alive.

The beautiful warm summer's evening offered a cathartic journey against the scenic landscape. It was around fifteen minutes into the drive when the fuzz and dullness that had pained Cohen's head since waking up started to fade, with it came the incessant voice screaming for satisfaction. The voice hadn't gone, it was just a little quieter for now. It was his own voice that was trying to break through, the one that normally made

REVELATIONS

all of the decisions. Right now it seemed to be waking up in a strange city and asking, *"What the hell are we doing here?"*

Without looking he reached across to the passenger seat and picked up the photo of Josh, pinning it against the wheel as he drove, eyes flitting between the picture and the road. The kid was the reason Cohen found himself in Prague, but he knew it wasn't why he came. He had come for one reason and one reason alone. To save himself; for redemption. Until Leeny had used that fateful word, her conversation was nothing more than background noise to him. She could have begged, pleaded and said anything else and it wouldn't have made a difference. *But that word: redemption.*

Not being a religious man, Cohen didn't quite know how it worked, opting for science over superstition, pragmatism over faith. The closest thing he'd had to religious thought was being in agreement with the Buddha, 'All life is suffering'. *That was an understatement.* But if there was a way to absolve himself from his past, to free his mind from replaying the torment of his own actions over and over, then he had to find it.

Again his eyes flitted from the road to the photograph, this time his attention stayed longer than it should, drawn by a hypnotic angelic innocence of the boy's smile. He thought he was seeing things as Josh's face began to change, a blackness burned out his eye sockets that cascaded down his face, melting it away like the wax of a candle. The smile was the same smile, but it now appeared more demonic than angelic, as if it had always been that way, but only now was he seeing its truth.

Suddenly, the photograph combusted into flames. Cohen jerked back in his seat instinctively propelling it away from him, but the picture fell towards his feet as it continued to burn. It all happened in a split second, but the reaction caused the car to swerve violently, narrowly missing several vehicles as he tried stamping out the flames, desperately fighting to regain control of the car. Horns wailed angrily as they passed swerving to avoid him. He managed to safely navigate the car to the side of the road, the last of the angry horns fading into the distance.

He took a breath before looking confused at his feet in the driver's well, expecting to see the smouldering remains of the photograph, but there was nothing. No smoke, no signs of burning, no blacked out eyes deforming the face, just the photograph of Josh as it had always been, smiling. But now it didn't seem so innocent. Cohen didn't pick it up straight away, instead leaving it under the tread of his boot as he tried processing what had happened, looking around to see if anyone was watching. They weren't. He instinctively flicked the latch on the glove compartment, grabbed the bottle and spun the top off at speed. He then stopped just as the bottle reached his lips.

It was happening again, just as it had eighteen months ago. The nightmares, the visions. It was as if hell was knocking at his door, toying with him until the very end. Whatever it was, felt closer, either in time or physical space, he wasn't sure. But there was something else, something just beyond his grasp, or perhaps beyond his understanding.

He had been trained to fight and to kill and made his name as one of the best, yet the only weapon he had against this unseen madness was the bottle in his hand. Suddenly, the idea of climbing back inside was an attractive proposition, maybe this time he wouldn't climb back out.

Cohen raised the bottle to his lips, the fumes tantalising his taste buds in celebration, but again he stopped. Somewhere in the deepest darkest depths of an internal abyss, a tiny light had come into being. Its voice so faint that a whisper could drown it out, yet there it was. At first he thought his once sharpened instincts might be returning, but this wasn't his voice, it was just *a* voice, and it was saying "*find the boy.*"

He looked down at the picture again peering at him from beneath his feet and collected it. Not being one for superstition, Cohen found it no accident that at this particular moment he was holding in his hands two choices. The picture in his left and the bottle in his right, one was a way forward the other a way back.

He put the picture back on the passenger seat and the top back on the bottle, placing it inside the glove compartment which he then closed; gently.

With the sports bag slung over his shoulder and map in hand, Cohen merged with the swarms of sightseers as he made the last part of his journey on foot. The concentration of tourism particularly in the Prague 1 district, created a palpable energy. Every cobbled street and archway danced with exuberance and excitement.

Unlike the other visitors to the city, Cohen's attention didn't loiter or elevate towards the preserved gothic spires and beautiful baroque buildings of Renaissance. It was focused with forward momentum, determined to move through and beyond without distraction.

The city's beauty wasn't lost on him. He had once upon a time breathed in the sights and seen miles of mosaic pavements pass under foot, standing as others do now, captivated by the black stone buildings and the 14th century Charles Bridge. The city had a way of grabbing your attention and stealing your breath all in the same moment. As cities go, Prague was one of his favourites, one of the few that hadn't succumb to the modern world. No cold glass and steel structures slammed ignorantly against the warmth and complexity of 19th century architecture. Franchises existed like any other city in the world, but they hadn't managed to steal its heart, not yet. There was still humility in her charm with so much cause to boast.

Viktor's bar was just north of Old Town Square on Jakubska, one of the few streets close to the city centre that was spared the tourist onslaught, welcome though it was. Upon first glance, the road appeared to offer nothing more than a connection to another road, but further investigation would lead to two bars. The Irish Bar and The Buddha Bar. But there was a third, Viktor's.

The entrance was a simple set of discreet wooden doors inside a cream painted building, no signage to promote its presence. Beyond that, a stairway that descended to a basement level bar; a place you had to know existed to be able to find it.

CHAPTER 07

ARCHIE

Archie had been contemplative since leaving the house this morning, staring out of the window as the car slowly made its way through the centre of London. Charlotte wanted to go over any final talking points before they arrived at the studio, desperate to break the silence. She was a talker and the quiet only exasperated the need for conversation, like a nervous tick, but she managed to contain herself; for now.

As the car passed by the Houses of Parliament and around Parliament Square, she joined him in looking out, once more feeling like a small child seeing the world for the first time, with awe and wonder.

The yellow stoned gothic architecture was megalithic, magnificent and humbling in its shadow. She had probably seen it a thousand times before and never once gave it the consideration it deserved. But now it was a destination, and in her own small way she had a chance to make an impact on what the building represented, what it stood for, to become a beacon to the world, now it was the Palace of Westminster.

She turned like an excited child to share the moment with the one person that gave it meaning, but Archie's thoughts laid elsewhere as he continued quietly staring from the window.

"Could you take us via the Strand please?" Archie suddenly said to the driver.

"The studio's just five minutes over the bridge sir?" the driver replied.

"We can take Blackfriars Bridge, there's plenty of time."

"Is everything okay?" Charlotte asked, concerned.

"Yes, of course."

"But people will be gathering for the march sir." The driver tentatively objected.

His eyes flitted briefly between Archibald and Charlotte in the rearview mirror, while navigating the road ahead. Archie raised his eyes to the mirror with a stare that lacked compromise. It sent a shiver down the driver's spine and without further debate, he turned away from the bridge and headed along the Embankment.

London was just one of dozens cities across the globe where people were gathering in peaceful protest against their government. For the first time in human history the people of the world had finally come together in solidarity. Against their overlords, against a tyrannical overreach of government. The equality people had been falling over themselves for in recent decades had finally come to pass. But it came in the form of oppression and the deconstruction of human rights. Simply put: we were all equally screwed.

The car passed crowds of demonstrators slowly making their way towards the march's starting point, almost a march in itself. Carrying placards and banners that read a variation of slogans highlighting inalienable freedoms and the right to exist. Many had attached black tape to cover their mouths as a visual display of silence and peaceful protest. Until now their voices hadn't been heard, in their desperation they hoped their silence would be.

Charlotte found it painful to look at their faces, but she couldn't turn away. The long awaited excitement and anticipation of the day was quickly being replaced with a sombre reality. Archie's silence was no longer in need of explanation. It was easy to forget what was being asked of him, that it was his shoulders that would bear the weight.

"Slow down," Archie said to the driver, unable to remove his eyes from the gathering crowds.

The driver nervously looked in the rear view towards Charlotte, hoping she would push back against the suggestion. She reluctantly and discreetly nodded to the driver that he should do as Archie requested despite her own reservations.

Peace was dependant on perceived provocation, and the driver believed a billionaire sitting in the back seat gawping at them like he was spectating a human zoo might just be provocation enough, but with no choice but to override his better judgement, he decelerated.

As suspected, the mere action of slowing the car attracted unwanted attention from various parts of the crowd, seemingly agitated with their audience. Feeling the growing tension, the hostile curiosity began to spread quickly.

The driver's foot nervously controlled the accelerator, ready to sink it into the floor at any second. He continued at a steady pace, which was only moderately faster than the moving mass, but not faster than the unrest that had rippled through them unseen. They began gesturing signs of profanity, cursing and becoming more animated towards the unknown figure looking on from the back seat of the limo.

The driver carefully scrutinised the mob, hands closing a tight grip on the steering wheel ready to take off at any second. And just as he'd suspected, the crowd started edging with intent closer towards the vehicle, the unrest threatening to escalate. A plastic water bottle burst onto the windscreen causing Charlotte to jump with a gasp.

The driver slammed his foot hard onto the accelerator, then with equal force and urgency, straight onto the break causing the car to violently come to a halt, almost throwing Archibald and Charlotte from their seats.

So focused on the crowd saddling up to the side of the car, he was distracted from the groups drifting into the road in front of them, successfully blocking its path.

Intimidatingly they quickly engulfed the vehicle, banging their fists on the roof. The sound was deafening and frightening, as bodies squeezed up against the vehicle, blocking out much of the daylight.

Archie could feel the fear inside the car, but still he continued to watch on solemnly, at the angry faces that had now morphed into a mob. One of its instigating members scowling at Archie, suddenly looked with familiarity… he recognised him.

"WAIT!" he screamed at the crowd.

But his plea was drowned by the chaos. They started to rock and shake the car from side to side, leaving its occupants hanging on to stop themselves from being thrown around.

"Hey… HEYYYYY! STOP, FUCKING STOP! STOP! STOP!" The man tried several more times, eventually having to physically push people away from the car.

Only when he'd upset enough of the crowd did the pounding abate, but only to hear his reasoning.

Inside, the car suddenly fell silent and still.

"You know who this is?" he shouted to the crowd.

"One of them!" a voice rose from the mob.

Again the pounding and shaking continued.

"No. Stop!" he pleaded again, forcing people back from the car with the growing risk of being turned upon.

"That's Archie! Archibald Montgomery."

The mob quickly fell silent, apart from the whispers of his name that started to spread among the masses. Light soon began filling the car as masses slowly moved away. The crowd blocking the vehicle opened to clear a pathway.

Confused, the driver cautiously accelerated to a slow and steady pace, still wary. The crowd started to clap, growing to an applause, erupting to elation as Archie passed them. He continued staring solemnly at the faces in the crowd, appreciating their support, but not once was he able to bring himself to smile.

It was quiet again as the the car made its way over Blackfriars Bridge, a different quiet than before. Charlotte no longer felt the urge to talk, wrestling with one dominating thought: *This was too much for one man.*

The young female sound engineer gave Archie final checks before escorting him on to the set. He took his seat on the couch as the live broadcast was going out, clearly out of his comfort zone as his head swivelled around at the lights, the cameras and the hustle that busied behind the scenes, everything it took to achieve the smooth running of a live show.

Charlotte was more worried than ever as she watched on, helpless to intervene. Her only last minute suggestion was for him to remove his tie. For some reason she remembered that detail from their first meeting. He seemed more relaxed, less stuffy than she expected and thought that should be the way he should be reintroduced to the world.

It was clear from the moment he'd arrived at the studio that Archie was nothing more than a fluff piece. A guest filling out non-news segments, which that morning included 'How to grow better greens in your garden' and 'Making your own mosaic quilt.'

His introduction had consisted of skating over his glaring achievements of a *'that was then this is now,'* attitude and painted a picture of an eccentric billionaire in need of a project, before the nations favourite morning TV presenters Susan Barrowman and Randal Morgan finally welcomed him to the show.

"So your miracle smart vaccine finally got approval from the British Medical Association," Randall said. "Which will see its mandatory roll out in the next couple of weeks. Perhaps you could remind our viewers of just what it is that made your vaccine the game changer."

"Well we weren't actually trying to develop a vaccine for a specific disease or virus," Archie said. "But the next evolution in bio-tech engineering."

"And that's the H3R0-Delta? or HRD as we've now come to know it?" Susan confirmed, pleased she'd managed to interact unprompted.

"That's right. When you consider the projection of current medicine, if we continue along the same trajectory in our fight against infection, we will inevitably lose, probably sooner rather than later. Viruses mutate, infections grow beyond the capability to contain them and our failure to act has put humanity teetering on a precipice. The HRD identifies areas of the body that lack a strong enough immune response to foreign material and is able to enhance the systems defence in that specific area."

Both presenters smiled with feigned interest, clearly not fully understanding the interview they were having.

"So, how does it feel to suddenly be thrust back into the limelight?" Susan Barrowman said, flashing a well-worn smile and considering her appearance more than her mundane question.

Charlotte was distracted by the amusement on the faces of the show's producers and production staff. Her heart sank with a fury. She wanted nothing more than to give them a large piece of her unfiltered mind, but that would just give them more ammunition. She was pained to watch as things unfolded, feeling as though she had led Archie like a lamb to the slaughter.

A producer for the show started to frantically wave his hands around attempting to draw the hosts' attention, no longer amused and desperately needing that to be relayed to the set. His upset quickly spread through the crew and production staff causing an uncomfortable tension. The hosts just continued smiling as instructions were being screamed into their ears. Charlotte watched on fascinated and curious as to the inner workings of a live production, but couldn't quite understand what had suddenly gone so wrong, everywhere she looked people were still doing their jobs, focused on the live broadcast. She looked back at Archie who was still contemplating the question. *It was dead air,* she thought.

Archie still hadn't responded. The producer was desperate for anyone to talk, silence was death to live TV and the interview was quickly becoming a car crash; the amusement was now her own.

The shot switched from Archie back to Susan Barrowman, whose professional smile was beginning to strain as it wavered under the pressure of the instructions rapidly delivered into her earpiece, "*Bloody hell, Say anything!*" But the complete lack of response saw the shot quickly switch back to Archie.

It began to move in on a close up of his face trying to capture or at least create drama. If the station was going to get egg on its face then this was the face they were going to pin it on. But they got more than they bargained for as Archie continued to contemplate the question, his beautiful brooding face soaking up the screen. He looked up at Susan, the camera capturing the moment perfectly.

Something happened. Charlotte felt goosebumps, but it wasn't just her. She noticed people all around the studio had stopped what they were doing to pay attention, panicking abated.

The same thing was happening all over the country. At first people laughed, calling friends and loved ones to witness the sensational car crash television interview, revelling in the discomfort of their favourite hosts. But in a nation of noise, it was the silence they heard and it was deafening. The laughter stopped.

Archie's eyes were a bright hazel green with a glint Hollywood stars would kill for, but bursting with a profound sadness they could only imitate. People weren't just watching they were feeling, and finally he spoke.

"Uncomfortable," he said.

It was as if everybody breathed in upon hearing the word, capturing the ears of a nation unable to move for fear of missing a second. Apart from two cameras that were being urgently directed to focus on just Susan and Archibald, framing Randal Morgan out of the picture. Realising what was happening, Barrowman seized the moment in upstaging her co-host and positioned herself for a one-on-one interview.

"What is it that's made you feel uncomfortable?" Susan responded.

This was her interview now.

"The cry for help."

A slightly stunned expression suggested she was expecting to hear something else; a typical polished speech perhaps, one that acted as a springboard to launch his political campaign, where soundbites could be played over and over, where she wouldn't have to work so god damn hard to drag out information that should be served up on a platter, anything else but that. It was honest, uncomfortable and that was because it was true. Every morning she wore a thinly veiled smile delivering puff pieces and human interest stories that were designed to distract. She laughed with her co-host while the thought of anything truly joyful in this world was becoming a vague memory, one so distant it was hard to know if it was real or just a dream. There were only two questions running through her mind, *Who the hell was this guy?* and *Is he really the genuine article?*

Her mind had gone blank but she covered professionally under the guise of considering the question, while having absolutely nothing come to mind she simply repeated his statement.

"The cry for help?"

"A final plea before an act of desperation."

"That sounds rather ominous."

"It should. It's what happens when governments put themselves before people."

"Well that sounds like the statement of a man running for office," she said professionally pulling the interview back into her lane.

"I'm sorry," Susan interjected before Archie could say another word, "we're going to have to interrupt this morning's broadcast with some breaking news."

"Shit!" Charlotte said under her breath.

Television screens around the country were turning to a split screen with a breaking news banner scrolling across the bottom; Susan Barrowman on one side and live images of violence breaking out across London on the other.

Upon seeing the images on a studio monitor, Archie was drawn towards the screen, consumed and saddened by what he saw unfolding. It was hard for people around the studio not to notice how genuinely affected he was, to the point of even momentarily distracting Susan.

"Erm… In a statement released by the Police Commissionaire," Susan Barrowman continued, "Metropolitan Police are advising people to avoid central London, particularly the West End, Trafalgar Square and Soho areas. They are calling for calm after violent clashes erupted at today's demonstrations. In the past hour, several organised groups have clashed with police, setting fires, causing damage to local businesses. There are as yet unconfirmed reports that an elderly male protester died at the scene after suffering a massive coronary failure. This may have been a catalyst behind the devolution of today's march. As I've said, these details have not yet been confirmed, but we will endeavour to bring you more news as it comes in."

The breaking news banner disappeared, swiftly returning the screens to regular viewing format. But Archie wasn't on the couch ready to continue the interview, instead they filmed him staring at the monitors, cutting between him and Susan as she once again flashed her well-worn smile.

"Well, as we've just seen," she continued, "there is indeed a great deal of turmoil on the political horizon. However, one could almost suggest the unrest has created an ideal opportunity for an eccentric billionaire to further his own legacy. Will you be running as an independent?"

She delivered the question with a sarcastic snap, knowing the combination of violent images and Archie's unconventional behaviour had led him on an unrecoverable path. This was now no longer dead air, it was filming the death of a political career.

"Would you care to comment?" she said, delivering a lethal and final blow.

This was the noise Charlotte had feared. Her heart was sinking like a stone as she watched from the sidelines. It was as if the entire studio had cornered him; the stifled smirks and sniggers making her blood boil. This time the producers let the shot linger on him, so the world could witness the free-fall. Archie all alone staring at the studio monitor still providing the live feed; oblivious to the picture they were painting; a man who fell at the first hurdle.

"It's a vapid existence that could witness the subjugation of humanity, yet lack the humanity to feel it," Archie said unable to take his eyes away from the monitor.

He spoke softly and quietly as though in intimate conversation, but the microphones clearly picked up everything he was saying.

"Men, women and children are on their knees and you talk of opportunity to further oneself, not better oneself."

Agitated, he turned from the monitor and stood in the middle of the set, making both Susan and Randall visually uncomfortable.

"You stare at these inanimate lenses pretending to convey emotions you don't truly feel. What *do* you feel?"

The presenters weren't sure if they should answer or not, looking like children being told off live on air.

"So you're nothing more than mouthpieces, whores at your master's bidding?" he added.

Charlotte had to cover her mouth to stop herself laughing.

"When did we agree that we are here to serve the government?" Archie continued "Allowing the parasitic consumption of people as though they are disposable objects, recycling them through generations."

Archie looked around the studio with disdain. All eyes were on him, stunned and silent; he scoffed.

"I'm clearly talking to the wrong people."

He then aggressively moved the monitor onto the set, placing it directly in front of Susan and Randal.

"This is my audience!" he said as he pulled off his microphone. "They deserve better."

He walked off the set passing in front of Susan's shot and stunned expression, leaving the viewing public relishing in their embarrassment.

The shot quickly cut to Randal Morgan.

"Have you ever thought about making your own mosaic quilt? We'll be showing you how right after this short break."

CHAPTER 08

BARRINGTON

Barrington woke earlier than Helena. Seeing her next to him, he almost wanted to pinch himself to make sure he wasn't dreaming. He looked across the room at her pack and saw the dagger resting on top; again he wanted to pinch himself.

He smiled, amused. Because just a few feet away was one of the most significant archeological discoveries of the last several hundred years, that would not only propel Helena's career, but as the foremost authority on the dagger he wouldn't be able to get out of the way of this even if he tried.

The reason he was smiling was that despite knowing all of that, he didn't care. And he didn't care that he didn't care. The only thing in this room of any value, or in the world right now was laying asleep next to him. He'd been wanting this moment and more of them ever since Oxford, and hoped last night was more than just a one off moment of celebration. As heartbreaking as that would be, it was also an outcome he was prepared for.

He got up, being careful not to wake Helena and helped himself to a shower. When he came back into the room, she hadn't moved a muscle, understandably exhausted from the last twenty four hours and he wanted her to rest. If her find was to be confirmed, which he thought it would be, then her excitement was only in its infancy.

He got dressed and searched the chaos of what he assumed was the kitchen, judging by the sink and a small portable stove top; like a free standing cooker that had lost the free standing unit. Finding a jar of instant coffee he paused, staring at the freeze dried granules in their glass container assessing just how desperate he really was for a coffee. He kept looking around for another minute or so, knowing it would probably be in vain, but looked anyway. Finally having to settle for the instant.

Turning on his laptop, the wifi signal reached one bar for a few seconds before dropping out. He picked up the computer and moved around the room, standing on chairs and crouching on the floor trying to find a strong enough signal, but it was no use. Taking out his smartphone, he used his data to search the internet for nearby hotels; only those that boasted excellent wifi service. Finding what he was looking for, he disregarded the phone and slipped on a fresh pair of gloves.

Sitting crossed legged on the floor, Barrington carefully laid the daggers neatly on top of their wrapping, one by one he very slowly scrutinised every detail. Taking a sip of his drink, his face instantly contorted in revulsion; having quickly forgotten the coffee was instant. He braved another sip and continued.

He held each blade only inches from his face as he admired them, turning them slowly in hand. He noticed some markings on the rear of the blade, that weren't visible while connected to the other pieces. It appeared to be a writing, but not one he was familiar with. The daggers hadn't yet gone through the cleaning process and were still heavily impacted with soil. Checking the other blades for the markings, the same was true for all of them, each one varying from the next.

The blades were slim, nearly eight inches in length and the sides were not at all sharp, but their points were needle like. Whoever designed such a thing had been clear it wasn't a tool for slashing or cutting, it had but one purpose. A thought that gave him a chill, reminding him of exactly what he was holding.

Starting to feel uncomfortable and the need to stretch his limbs, he checked his watch. He'd been sat in the same position for nearly an hour and a half and it hadn't felt like more than 20 minutes.

Helena began to stir, quickly realising Barrington wasn't beside her. She turned over to find him sitting on the floor. He was looking at her with a welcoming smile, but nervous, wondering how she would see him in the morning light.

"Hey." she said with a tired smile, her hand reaching out toward him.

He removed his gloves and sat on the bed beside her, brushing her hair lightly away from her face. She saw the daggers on the floor and smiled.

"You been up long?" she asked.

"No, just a few hours. I grabbed a shower, made a coffee…"

"Oh no!" she said covering her face, remembering how much he'd always hated instant coffee. "I'm so sorry."

She giggled, pulling him towards her and kissed him. He rolled over her onto the bed, both giggling like teenagers, intermittently interrupted with kisses.

"Let me get up and get you a proper coffee."

"You're going to stay here and I'm going to get breakfast," he said without compromise.

"No, no, no, let me get dressed."

"No!" he insisted, getting up from the bed. "I've already got it all worked out."

She sat up and leaned back against the pillow with her arms folded and raised eyebrows with an, 'okay impress me' attitude.

"If you can stand to be away from your palace for one night, I'm booking us into the four star up the road. You can have a hot bath, drink a cold glass of champagne and whatever other comforts you require. Feel the cool soft sheets on a kingsize mattress, oh and of course there's air conditioning."

She laughed. She loved his dry humour and the way he made her smile effortlessly.

"They of course have wifi, where as your palace does not," he continued, "So I will be able to make the video call to Professor Lehman."

"Oh my god, Lehman, of course!" she said with excitement, "is she even still alive?"

"Very much so," he chuckled. "So we have a couple of options. I can go and book in to the hotel, make the video call and come back with a lavish breakfast…"

He didn't want to say about the knifes authentication incase he jinxed it.

"Or, I can grab breakfast, *we* can go and check into the hotel later and make the call to Lehman together?"

Just thinking about the knife filled her with an energy and excitement that was hard to contain, it was almost palpable.

"You go," she said softly, her voice swallowing the excitement and filled with an unflinching trust. "Make the call."

He looked at her for a moment completely surprised at her decision. "Really?"

"Yeah," she insisted. "I mean, it's just a percentage right?" Professor Lehman flashed through her mind from her days at Oxford. "She was such a bitch to me, I couldn't stand her. But she really knows her shit. Yeah," she confirmed, "make the call."

"Okay," Barrington replied realising the trust she was giving him.

"There was one thing though," she then said with a wondering frown. "Everything you said sounded wonderful. And I'm not complaining, well sort of. But, I notice you didn't mention any repeat of… last night's activities…"

A smile beamed across his face. He looked at his watch. "Well," he said unbuttoning his shirt, "why don't we start as we mean to go on?"

She lifted the covers and he joined her in the bed.

"Please be careful!" Professor Lehman warned.

The video call disconnected and Barrington closed the laptop. He liked Professor Lehman, she was unapologetically British and wore it well. Her perfect posture, high cheek bones and pursed lips gave her the air of an old-fashioned school mistress, albeit a strikingly beautiful one. Maybe he was only noticing now because for the last ten minutes her face had filled the screen of his laptop, but then everything looked a little more beautiful today, he thought.

He sat pondering Lehman's advice while savouring the four-star air conditioned room. The call was more than he could have hoped for, but it left him feeling conflicted. He could already see Helena's face when delivering news that would change her career and life forever. But Lehman also reminded him what he was forgetting, about what *he* above all people knew; the reason why the daggers exists.

Like him, she had enquired with concern about who was funding the dig, the consortium, but Barrington chose to omit any knowledge of The Order. As Helena was unable to confirm or deny what she may or may not have overheard, there was no use in speculating. He did wonder if professor Lehman ever remembered that night in the pub so many years ago.

Lehman seemed perturbed, but Barrington wasn't sure if it was uncertainty surrounding the consortium's identity, or it was just Lehman being Lehman.

"What is it?" Barrington asked.

"You always were a little dumb struck when it came to Miss Braithwaite," she said, using Helena's maiden title.

"What's that supposed to mean?"

"She never was interested in the palace, Barrington. Whoever she's working for, wants that dagger. Have you asked yourself why?"

She was right, he thought. That was why he was initially relieved when he thought the dagger was just a replica. But every time he imagined seeing Helena's face as he delivered the news, of what the find would do for her, for her career, even for him; it blurred the lines. So much so, that he put aside the one thing he was there to provide: knowledge.

The mere fact he was holding in his hands an object that until now had been considered a myth. With absolute seriousness he had to consider the stories it told were also real. If one found Excalibur, you would attempt to pull it from the stone, Mjölnir, you would try to lift it. Menelik's Dagger, you would release Satan. But he wasn't holding King Arthur's sword or Thor's hammer.

"No man sleeps more soundly, than the one of character," Barrington's mother used to say to him.

One day, when he was all grown up and well on his way to an academic career, he challenged her.

"What about the one who lacks conscience?"

"What you avoid when you wake, you cannot avoid when you sleep," she replied.

It was the day he learned intelligence had nothing to do with wisdom. After that, he never challenged her again.

Still his mother's son, he knew exactly what to do. Leaving his things in the room, along with a chilled bottle of champagne on ice, he headed into town to source an array of ingredients for a lavish breakfast.

It wasn't long before Lehman's warnings faded and once again he was smiling without cause, strolling with an extra bounce in his step. While he and Lehman both erred on the side of caution, he knew once news of the artefact leaked, there would be a wave of international interest, museums all competing to be the first to display it. And then there would undoubtedly be pressure for a global tour, so all got the chance to witness the marvel. By then Helena's rise would be secure, and whatever plans the consortium have would have to wait. Sometimes, when objects with such historical significance are found, they never find their way back to the private owners. All Barrington had to do now was cause a leak.

He wanted to make sure everything was just right for Helena and had to go to several different places to get a selection of foods, mostly local traditional dishes. Wanting to show off a little, he threw in a few of his favourites from Arabian roots. He also found a nice coffee press and some freshly ground beans brought up from the south of the country. He thought Helena might appreciate it, although probably not quite as much as him.

Over the course of the morning he kept finding himself grinning at random moments, which Professor Lehman had found irritating on the video call and told him as such; he could feel himself doing it again. So caught up in thoughts of Helena, he hadn't noticed the crowd gathering a short distance ahead.

Eventually the bustle caught his eye, instinctively slowing his pace as he watched, trying to see what was happening.

A siren from an approaching ambulance made him jump, forcing him to step out of the road as it passed; kicking up dust and sand in his face. Barrington held his arms up to shield his eyes, squinting a stare that followed the vehicle's path. It stopped just before the crowd, about hundred and fifty yards ahead; right outside of Helena's hotel.

Suddenly picking up the pace, he didn't know why, but felt a growing concern. The crowd had formed a natural barrier as they jostled shoulder to shoulder all vying to see, in turn stopping Barrington. As he got closer the melee of voices increased in volume with onlookers voicing and narrating what had unfolded; or at least what they thought. A few were staring up, pointing at the building. A section of the railing had broken away and stuck out crudely from the second floor balcony.

A cold fear came over Barrington that he tried dismissing. He didn't want to entertain the possibility that any of this involved Helena, and yet he found himself running towards the scene, urgently pushing past the crowd to get a glimpse of what they were hiding.

He froze. What he saw paralysed him. No thoughts, no feelings; his body shut down. Her eyes were open and staring straight at him. She was naked as she lay twisted and contorted in the street. Someone at least had the decency to cover her with a coat.

She just seemed so different somehow, and for just a second he almost convinced himself that it wasn't even her; but Helena was dead.

He was just about to leave the anonymity of the crowd, to go to her, needing to feel her in his arms, and if he did then somehow he would realise this was all just a bad dream. But something stopped him. He looked at the faces of the people crowding around, a feeling of claustro-phobia rising, a tightness in his chest that was stopping him from taking a deep breath, no matter how much he wanted to.

Barrington knew Helena hadn't fallen, and began to search the faces in the crowd. If he knew the truth, then so did someone here. The only people he recognised were ones Helena spoke to when they arrived. But there were two others that looked familiar, the driver and passenger of the faded blue Mustang. Gripped with a fear he'd never known before, he slowly stepped backwards into the crowd, allowing the people behind him to merge in front to cover his withdrawal. Turning left at the hotel, again covering his retreat, Barrington dropped the bags of food he'd spent all morning collecting and ran.

CHAPTER 09

COHEN

Daylight faded with every descending step, with it the warmth of the summer air. The muffled beat of a harsh type of metal music pounded against the doors like a contained beast, growing with intensity as Cohen inched closer, finally hitting him like a wave as the doors opened.

Inside there was a long single archway of exposed brick, adding to the natural rough and rustic texture. The atmosphere still had the cool chill of a stone cellar, but every extra body helped raise the temperature until the end of the night when the walls would drip with a claustrophobic condensation. It reminded him of being home at the South London Arches, that and the subtle hostile atmosphere that emanated to any outsider; unless accompanied by a local, and even then.

The bar had a purposeful sallow glow of cheap lighting offering enough to see but not define. Accompanied by the flicker of randomly placed candles that caused shadows to stutter in eerie and unearthly ways, it was almost as if demons were tormenting and toying with Cohen as they danced across the walls. A feeling that only intensified as several patrons lifted their gaze with interest, a few with knowing intent others that aired with curiosity, but all felt the unease Cohen's presence brought.

He didn't look left or right only to watch stares avert, but continued a slow and purposeful walk, eyes fixed on an empty table at the rear. Taking a seat with his back to the majority of the bar, he closed his eyes and waited; listening.

His presence triggered stares that communicated silently around the room connecting those that seemed otherwise disconnected, fuelling an unseen tension.

Cohen was doing his best to focus his hearing beyond the harsh thump of music, beyond the reach and ability of the average person. It took a while longer than it normally would have, but after a short spell the music began fading into the background with the clatter of bottles and glasses becoming clearer and then also fading to reveal several groups of indistinct chatter. It gave Cohen a rough audible picture that he could pair with the mental image of the bar's layout that he assessed during his slow, purposeful walk.

Two men were sat by the entrance, one heavily set, three more towards the centre, a slight man at the bar talking with a female bartender, a second bartender, two more customers in front and a lively group of five overflowing from an alcoved table.

The group of five were nothing to worry about, no change in their speaking pattern or volume and the slight man offered no attention. But other silences and interrupted breaks in conversation gave rise to suggest several people were communicating with looks and glances. No cause for immediate concern but worthy of attention, which was soon grabbed by the sound of a chair's hurried scrape on the floor.

Unable to contain whatever insult his presence offered, the younger heavily built man near the entrance stood with aggressive determination, sending his chair scraping backwards, his seething attention fixed firmly on his victim's back. A micro-smile curled the edge of Cohen's mouth, pleased he was still able to sense the flow of energy between the passive and those with intent. The smile left as the energy in the room suddenly shifted. Cohen sensed he was no longer the focus, it was now with someone that wasn't visible to him when arriving.

A giant of a man appeared behind the bar, polishing a glass with the towel draped over his shoulder, he surveyed the room absorbing its current tension. At 6ft 6 and a width that could disrupt gravity, he towered over everyone in the bar including Cohen. His long reddish hair that was tied in a low ponytail hung to the middle of his back, while an equally long beard platted in the style of a viking gave him a look of a Norse warrior in a flannel shirt.

His eyes found the stranger with his back to the bar, his long dark hair concealing his identification, and then to the well-built man by the door, standing with aggressive intent ready to act upon his compulsion.

A calm but knowing look from the Viking giant was enough to see the man reluctantly take his seat in servitude, aggrieved to bear the affront.

The Viking man slowly poured a drink into his glass and began making his way towards the stranger. He took the seat opposite him, taking up nearly one whole side of the table and placed the drink in front of the man.

"Viktor," Cohen said before finally opening his eyes.

"Cohen," Viktor echoed in the same dull tone.

The battle hardened men studied each other in an uncomfortable silence, trying to gage a perceived truth. If their shared history had left them an ally or if friendship been circumvented for other reasons. Their eyes, like others that expose themselves to man-made horrors, shared a darkness that was less of a colouring and more of a light that had been extinguished.

Cohen's stare flitted for just a second to the drink and back to Viktor. In that moment the penetrating gaze that could send a coldness into your bones was gone. Viktor's face softened, replaced with a profound concern and then he saw it… defeat.

There were few men in the world that Viktor respected and even less that he feared, Cohen sat at the top of that very short list. But he could barely recognise the man sitting in front of him. This was a bad joke, an imposter. A soft, weightier imitation of someone he once knew, but his stare was all too familiar, something he saw in his line of work everyday. Every bar expects its regular scattering of alcoholics, he was just having a hard time believing it of Cohen; his once definition of discipline.

"What are you doing here?" he voiced without concern.

He had a strong Polish accent that he fused with localisms to try and diffuse the tone.

"I need information."

"You don't wanna start with, 'Hey, I'm alive, how you doing? How's Dida?' It's just the information you want?"

Just by looking at him, Viktor found it hard to believe that Cohen was in any shape for work. Eventually smiling with an amused scoff and disappointed shake of the head. Cohen wasn't baited to query, he just watched, waiting; knowing silence was the question people filled with answers.

"I'd figured you for dead," Viktor said.

"Not yet."

"You sure about that?" he sniped.

Cohen didn't quite smile but it was enough to break the tension.

"You look like shit, I mean it's good to see you, but…"

He was attempting to pick up where they might have left off, but the more Viktor looked at his old friend the less he recognised him, feeling pity more than anything else.

"You shouldn't be here Cohen," he warned.

"Am I not welcome?"

"No, You're welcome alright. Probably more than you'd want to be."

Cohen's silence demanded elaboration.

"I didn't even know you were still alive till yesterday," he continued, watching carefully for a reaction.

Being just as versed in interrogation as Cohen, Viktor knew what micro-movements to look for, a skill that saw him red flagged at every major casino.

"That's right!" he said. "Some guy was in here throwing your name around like fish bait, twenty four hours later, here you are. Now I could say that's a coincidence, but that will just get you killed."

"Anything to do with my admirer by the door?"

Viktor smiled, pleased that Cohen's instincts weren't as disheveled as his appearance.

"No," he said. "At least there's still part of you in there somewhere, but enough to stop you being dead? I don't think so. No, the admirer by the door is your past catching up with you. It's what happens when you slow down."

The humour fell flat.

"A friend of his broke a decree. Your decree," he added.

Cohen's expression remained unchanged, but again Viktor saw it register.

"What? You thought I didn't know?" he continued. "You gotta love the arrogance. You come to me for information and expect me to not know who you really are? How good would I be if I didn't know I was dealing with an Angel of Death? Or should I say former?"

There was glee in his eyes, finally able to release information he'd held for so long. But he got nothing in return, not so much as a micro-movement.

"And the guy throwing my name around?" Cohen asked.

"Not someone I'm dealing with," Viktor snapped sharply.

Cohen was under his skin.

"Listen, you don't just walk in here after however long and start demanding answers. I don't owe you anything. If it's just information you want then you can do like everyone else and let your money ask the questions. But the Cohen I knew would have already heard what I have to say, instead he'd start by asking the right fucking questions."

Viktor hoped his outburst might be the metaphorical slap in the face his old friend needed, which he wasn't exactly emboldened to do himself, but the stare looking back remained vacant.

"I just told you the guy by the door knows who you are, that I know who you were, and you sit there and act like I just gave you a weather report! I don't even know how you're still alive, you're a walking target now, a trophy for some up and coming kids résumé. The question you should be asking is 'who knew you were alive?'"

It was a good question and one Cohen appeared to take great consideration over. But this was what he was waiting for, silence being filled.

"It shouldn't take you long to work out who wants you dead. Clearly someone knew you were coming here before you did."

Victor slid the glass of whisky towards Cohen.

"It's on the house. I suggest you leave Prague while you still can. If you still can. It was good to see you."

Viktor stood to return to his work. Cohen knocked back the whisky and slammed the glass hard onto the table, its sound reverberated a stillness into the bar and Viktor.

"Sit down," he ordered under a growled whisper.

The Viking giant hesitated, but reluctantly slid back into his seat. Cohen played with the empty glass focussing his attention on it. He raised it to eye level to study, the way a jeweller might appraise a precious stone.

He realised Viktor had been compromised, to what extent he wasn't sure, but suggesting he leave Prague was trying to present himself as kin. He knew Cohen would never leave. He was right, but who knew he was alive? If Viktor knew twenty four hours ago, by his own admission, it placed himself in the firing line. But he was just a tool for someone to use.

The only thing Cohen could really trust in was his desperation to find redemption, he'd allowed himself to walk straight into a trap. He took a strange comfort in the notion they still needed him alive; whoever they were. He was here because they needed him to do something, otherwise he'd have already been dead. He figured that there was either more than one faction gunning for him, or there was more than one player at the table. The first left his chance of survival highly unlikely, the second only slightly better. Although it did present the opportunity for confusion. Now all Cohen had to do was find out who the players were.

"The information," Cohen continued, "a young boy went missing in your city six days ago."

"So you're doing Samaritan work now?" Viktor said trying to bolster confidence.

Cohen continued appraising the glass.

"Josh. He's ten years old."

"Six days?" Viktor said in an almost mocking tone, "I don't know what to tell you, but you might want to start preparing the parents for bad news. Now, I've got to get back to work."

Again Viktor edged to leave but didn't want to provoke an insult while Cohen continued to talk.

"You gotta love the arrogance," Cohen said softly. Gently placing the glass down, he turned his gaze on Viktor. "I come here for information and you expect me not to know who I'm dealing with?"

Viktor's nervous mocking tone was suddenly gone, replaced with the element of danger he'd been desperately trying to ignore.

"I'm trying to do you a favour," Viktor pleaded. "I told you, you shouldn't be here."

Cohen spun the glass on the table like a spinning top, Viktor watched on uncomfortably.

"No one's seen or heard from you in over a year, word was you hadn't taken any contracts. I thought you were dead, I mean, no one just walks away from this life, right?"

"You did."

"I was a merc," Viktor replied, "and as you can see, I didn't actually walk that far."

His attention was being annoyingly distracted by the spinning glass. He lowered his voice further.

"And I wasn't an Angel of Death."

Cohen continued to force the glass into further rotation. The silence coupled with the glass rattling against the wooden table was becoming torturous. Viktor's hand suddenly brought the spinning object to an abrupt halt, in turn their gaze went eye to eye.

"The boy," Cohen said.

For just a split second a veil lifted from Viktor's eyes.

"You know you're in over your head?"

Cohen's stare remained resolute as he played his part. He detested the theatre of it all. They clearly want him to have the information, but needed him to feel that he'd coerced it. Cohen placed a map on the table. Eventually Viktor gave a defeated sigh.

"I don't know if it's your kid," he said. "But there's one location you might want to check out."

He pointed to a spot on the map.

"Give my best to Dida."

Cohen got up to leave.

"Cohen," Viktor said, stopping his old friend.

He wasn't sure what he was going to say, although Cohen faintly nodded, as though he heard what hadn't been said, and continued out of the bar.

CHAPTER 10

NATHAN

Nathan sat in the gloom of the workshop staring at a picture on his phone, his face illuminated by the glare. Unaware that on the other side of the street, the young priest from that morning watched on with great interest.

The image holding Nathan's attention was the only connection he had to his former life.

It was an Ikebana display. An enchanting weathered log holding the stem of an azure, wild coffee chicory plant, a black rose lay on its side protruding from a split in the wood. Simple, elegant, poignant.

He remembered when ordering the Ikebana display from the south London florist, that he hadn't appreciated the art of Japanese flower arranging beyond its aesthetics. In truth, Nathan didn't even appreciate that. To him it was nothing more than a few ridiculously over-priced twigs and flowers, but still, he had to have it. So along with gracing his social media feed, it would hold conversation at dinner parties of how a Kado master created the display to bring balance and harmony into his life. That wasn't how it worked, but that was the story he'd tell.

As a not-so-young stockbroker, trying to remain relevant meant everything was status. Suits, shirts, shoes, socks, ties, a selection of watches, cufflinks, sports clubs, restaurants, exclusive night clubs and cars. He didn't know much about cars so he leased a Porsche, because, well, because it was a Porsche. Then there were the high-class hookers, champagne and small bags of white powder being consumed at increasing volumes, and of course a must have Ikebana centrepiece.

One morning, instead of sugar on his cornflakes, he found himself reaching for the cocaine, a hit in the toilets at lunch to make it through the afternoon, then it was party time.

When he could no longer keep up with the payments on the Porsche, they repossessed it. When he could no longer keep up with the payments for drugs, they broke things; normally body parts. After that, they were either satisfied or you were dead.

The best worst cheque he ever wrote was £3000 to a small south London Florist. Usually independent businesses harassed you for payment with letters and emails, threatening small claims court or collection agencies, but eventually they just went away. The last thing Nathan ever expected was the florist to come knocking.

Cohen found Nathan in his luxury riverside apartment laying half dead in a puddle of his own urine and excrement, and that was just the warning. Cohen never did tell him why he decided to take pity on him that day, it wasn't as if it was even an original story, a stockbroker who burned out living beyond his means; but he did.

What Nathan eventually learned, was the display Cohen crafted for him symbolised the Nathan himelf. Ikebana's were comprised of three levels: heaven, earth, and humans. The weathered log represented earth, its surface rough and unsteady: easy to fall between the cracks. The azure flower of a wild coffee chicory plant raised on its stem: the sky or the heavens. In between the two was the black rose laying on its side, this was the human element, more specifically, Nathan, half in, half out, consumed by the earth.

The display in itself was a breathtakingly accurate snapshot of his life at that time, and every once in a while Nathan would find himself looking at it, needing to remember who he was, then and now; although this time his thoughts rested with Cohen. The display had come full circle, now it depicted its creator.

He knew Cohen was no angel, though it was hard not to see him that way. After all, how else was he supposed to look upon the person that saved him, gave him a second chance. Nathan worried about Cohen and had done every gut wrenching day for at least the last eighteen months, pained not to be able to offer the same relief he had been gifted.

Every day he'd been arriving at the shop wondering if today was the day he'd receive news his friend had been found dead, beaten to death behind some back-alley bar. This was more subtle and at the same time more powerful, almost as if evil surrounded events, filling the air, always present. He couldn't explain it, but there was no denying he could feel it.

As a stockbroker, Nathan's talents were numbers, being able to see patterns and trends that accumulated to impact the markets. Cohen showed him how to harness his talent into other areas, to translate information from a range of sources that would paint a larger picture. Black market contracts were the invisible webs linking everything together, it was as good as insider trading if you knew what you were looking at. But not just on the stock exchange.

The morning laboured by one painful second after the next. Nathan had been busying himself preparing to transfer the business to a temporary online operation, at the same time as sourcing new locations for the shop.

Orders, invoices, inventory, everything was up to date, it generally was, but in this instance, such tasks served as a welcome distraction; checking and then double-checking. But he wasn't so distracted that he wouldn't notice a few out of place faces paying curious attention to the shop. And he saw the priest again which was starting to give him the willies. He text Cohen.

"A few unseasonal bees around the flowers this year."

It seemed word had spread on Cohen's emergence quicker than anticipated, only validating the urgency to relocate. Everything was in place just as he'd been shown, to appear as though nothing was out of place, and then he got to work.

Nathan was surprised at the lack of media coverage on the missing kid in Prague, especially with the local rags; human interest stories were their lifeline. After running a search on social media platforms, filtering IP addresses to the local area, he got a hit. Staceee33984 posted a video from her smart phone; police cars outside her building. There was nothing to see but flashing blue lights, but the post read:

OMG!!! Some kid got snatched. :0o

That was the only evidence he could find that the kidnapping had even happened. Nathan couldn't make sense of it. It would have taken more than money to create such a media blackout, but luckily Staceee33984 had slipped through the net; literally. Anything people tried to flush down the sewers found its way to the dark web, If you knew where to look. It wasn't long before Nathan found chatter on a contract around the time of the abduction; but he also found several others. It seemed Prague was having its fair share of children going missing and no one was talking about it.

By using the locations of the abductions, he triangulated a position that would put Cohen smack bang in the middle of kidnap central. All he had to do now was wait for him to do his thing.

CHAPTER 11

COHEN

Despite the beautiful summer's day, the room was dark, dank and had a mothy odour. Cohen dropped his sports bag onto the shallow mattress sending an explosion of dust particles dancing into the sun shard that split the room in two. He counted steps while crossing the room to pull the cord to open the corse weighted curtains. The mechanism jammed. A slightly stronger frustrated tug saw the cord brake, which he then used to tie them back to allow some much needed sunlight and warmth to engulf the room.

Comfort clearly wasn't high on the agenda when Nathan sourced the apartment. No names, entry logs or cameras, just a cash payment and a little extra for the service of discretion. A sum that would have afforded a nice suite in a luxury hotel he considered, looking at the metal twin framed bed with springs more likely to impale than support him.

A mixture of decorative decades reaching back to the 60s, cheap old wallpaper with sun bleached patches, sections peeling away from the surface, a dresser with broken drawers housing a dirty mirror and cheap lino on the floor, designed to look like wooden slats. But as Cohen pulled back the net curtains from the french doors, revealing a balustrade that overhung bohemian streets, he knew exactly why Nathan chose it and would have easily paid double for the location.

It was the second floor of a three storey apartment building, one balcony above and one below. The street ran east to west where the road sharply declined allowing a scenic view of the neighbouring rooftops. As usual, Nathan was right on the money.

The romantic evening sun covered the streets in fiery orange, adding a touch of quaintness to the milieu. A city village feel that was more popular with senior citizens, able to enjoy the area without the pageant of tourism.

Elderly couples sat in small cafes, milling from shop to shop, crossing back and forth the narrow streets to browse windows of small local businesses, bric-a-brac stores, bespoke clothing and bakeries. Traffic was minimal, save for a few locals toing and froing and a single motorbike courier heading west to the neighbouring village. Cohen checked his watch and returned inside.

Moving his bag, he took the risk of laying back on the bed to recall the old couple strolling on the street beneath him. The man's gate was just shy of 2ft and it had taken him twelve steps to cross the road, another four and a half from curb to building, averaging the width of the road at approximately 30ft. Paired with the approximate width of the building and rooftops running off to the west. The place of interest was no more than a mile away. Unfortunately the squeaking springs beneath Cohen were harsh and constant, which the room amplified to coordinate an attack on his senses. In an attempt to settle, he placed his arms behind his head, playing a quick mental game. He would lay perfectly still until the squeaking stopped, one squeak and he'd lose a point, more than five and he'd lay on the floor.

Squeak…   Squeak…   …

Cohen stared at the ceiling, mould gathering in the corners and paint that flaked and peeled back like an open sardine can, a room like any other he'd seen over the years, but today it was the only thing that felt vaguely familiar. Not so much the room as much as the situation. This was the part he used to like, the calm before the storm, when he would feel at his greatest peace.

Squeak…

He began to surmise that possibly one of the reasons for his former formidable status was due to his acceptance of death. Not of the life he would take, but the one he was willing to give; his own. To accept it as if there was no other possible outcome. Somewhere within, meditation had gifted him a clarity that reached beyond the senses. As if true peace laid within the acceptance of one's mortality. But now those senses dulled, pickling in alcohol. Wanting death wasn't the same as accepting it, and being willing to give what could so easily be taken wasn't quite the meditation he was hoping for.

Squeak, squeak, squeak, squeak…

Sitting up in frustration with the bed springs screaming at every motion, he finally stood. Feeling the need for air, Cohen quickly opened the french doors and leaned against the balustrade breathing deeply, playing down its urgency. After subtly inhaling and exhaling several times, he began feeling a little better but still sensed a negative undertone fighting to surface. He was uncertain if it was physical or emotional. At first he assumed it was just more withdrawal symptoms, dismissing the distraction with the most obvious explanation. But there was something else, something he was avoiding. The answer wasn't far from his mind and came quickly. It simply needed him to turn his attention towards it, something he'd avoided doing since waking up this morning.

The strange feeling was there when he accepted the job from Leeny and again when Nathan looked at him after telling him he'd taken it. It was there when Viktor questioned him about the contract and it was with him now. Fear.

A cold shiver ran down his spine. Looking around suspiciously, he moved in from the balcony with a sense of vulnerability, feeling as though he couldn't just be seen but was being watched. And he knew by whom.

Cohen opened the bag, snatched up the bottle of drink Viktor left and rummaged desperately around the bottom for the supply of diazepam he'd been given to help with the withdrawal symptoms. Finding it, he quickly flicked off the lid and knocked back a couple of pills like it was a shot, chasing it with a few gulps of Blue Label. The whisky had an immediate calming affect that helped to slow his breathing.

He sat back down on the bed, this time not even aware of the squeaking springs. Cohen's fist clenched comfortably around the neck of the bottle like a smoker nonchalantly holding a cigarette. He took another swig. Noticing the bag, he pulled it towards him and began distracting himself by taking out items. A leather jacket rolled like a towel, the city map, he swigged, the Glock and a couple of gun clips, zip-ties, GPS and a black leather belt, he swigged again. Next, he unrolled the jacket. It was a replica of the one he wore as an Angel of Death, only this one didn't have the titanium weave woven into its lining that could save his life, it just looked good. Another swig as he looked down at the items laid out on the bed, and then another and another, almost unaware of his actions.

It was dark when Cohen slowly woke. At first he was confused and bleary from the alcohol, before sitting straight up, feeling panicked and disorientated by the gloomy surroundings. It took him another moment to get his bearings, remembering where he was and why. Sitting on the side of the bed, he dropped his face into his hands, the squeaking now having returned with a vengeance. He used one hand to look for the bottle of drink, hoping there would still be something left, finding it just behind him; empty.

Eventually he stood and had to focus on his balance as something fell to the floor grabbing his attention. A single 9mm parabellum round rolled before stopping at his feet. He looked back at the bed where several more rounds nestled in the depression where he'd been laying, along with the Glock 17 sidearm.

Cohen picked up the round from the floor and dropped it with the others while tentatively collecting the gun. As he did so, the grouping of bullets quickly calculated in his head at fourteen. Setting the gun's safety to on, he ejected the clip; empty. Slowly, he slid back the barrel revealing the chamber and the missing fifteenth bullet. After removing the round, he inspected the casing. It was perfect, apart from a small scuffed dimple on the primer that suggested an impact from the firing pin. The gun had been fired.

The implications took the weight from his legs, sitting him down with squeaking he couldn't hear, staring with dismay at the small object in his hand. He swallowed, desperately wanting, trying to remember. But just like the several previous months of his life, there was only a void of darkness. The idea of not remembering trying to take his own life fuelled his fear and the fact he wasn't successful seemed to be pure luck, a misfire.

As he continued to carefully examine the bullet, he realised that it wasn't death that he feared, it was what was waiting for him afterwards.

Suddenly truth was an epiphany slamming him hard in the gut. There was never any reason to make preparations to save the boy, not when every decision he'd made since waking up this morning, or lack thereof, was a subtle death note, a subconscious suicide plan. Until now, he realised he had no intention of returning from Prague.

As Cohen descended further and further into his thoughts, his hand sought a round of ammunition. One by one he thumbed each projectile back into the clip until fourteen had been replaced, sat the clip on the bed beside him along with the gun.; never once looking at the weapon.

Before eighteen months ago he would have thought considerably less of anyone for even hinting at the hand of fate, or divine intervention.

But ever since that night in Cologne, Germany, how could he continue to deny?

He looked again at the scuffed primer on the fifteenth bullet. *Fate hasn't finished with me after all,* he thought, unable to believe he was using the word fate as an acceptable addition to his vocabulary.

Suddenly remembering Josh, Cohen had to concede that until now his actions hadn't even given the boy a fighting chance. What was worse, was that he'd been willing to sacrifice him, simply as an excuse to cover his own demise. After all the lives he'd taken, Josh would be just one more on a long list.

He may not have taken the kid or be the one to end his life, but by accepting a contract to save him, only to leave him to die, was as good as pulling the trigger himself. *Technically I would be breaking my own decree,* he thought.

As broken as he was, and as much as he knew he was in no shape to do what needed to be done, he believed he would at least now try. Although having only just caught up to his state of mind, he realised he'd placed himself in the lions den and armed himself with a fork. He got the overwhelming sense he was being used, manipulated. Not by Leeny or the people designing his downfall, which he was about to knowingly walk into head on, but by something else.

A powerful smell of incense suddenly overwhelmed Cohen's senses. So strong it was as if it was burning inside the room, or right outside. He grabbed the Glock sliding in the clip, remembering it was one round short. Very quietly he chambered a round and slid the safety off as he swiftly saddled up to the door frame.

Moonlight streamed through the window behind him outlining the room in silver edging, a light breeze from the open balcony stroked the net curtains into a gentle sway. He closed his eyes and focused his hearing outside the door, but heard nothing. *I know that smell,* he thought readying the weapon. He then opened the door at speed to a narrow slit, still nothing. Opening it a little further he peered out, it was quiet. Returning inside, he could still smell the incense, although it wasn't as strong, only now he wasn't sure if it was just a trick of the mind, a memory from another time.

But then he did remember, it was the same incense they used in Catholic Church's, like the one in Germany. He couldn't say why, but the thought immediately put him back on alert, looking around the room like he was expecting not to be alone. Shouldering up to the window frame concealing himself, he surveyed the road below. It was as everything should be for this part of town, this late at night; quiet. Swapping sides, he looked towards the road west, down the long decline. Nothing was out of place.

Cohen relaxed, flicking the safety on the gun while noticing a slight tremor in his hand, but disregarded it with a dismissive shake and flex. As he moved from the window, a flash of light caught his eye. He could have sworn whatever it was came from the west in the direction of the neighbouring town rooftops. It was just a fraction of a second, but if he had to guess it would be a green light, like that of a laser pointer kids use to try and blind the pilots of commercial airliners… or that of a weapon mounted laser. He stood at the window waiting to see if whatever it was revealed itself again, but nothing did. Curiously unsatisfied, he collected the NV-monocular sight. Returning to his position at the window he waited, scanning the rooftops. Still nothing.

He scoffed. *What was I expecting?* Cohen was beginning to realise the idea of trusting his own mind may possibly be his greatest liability. Alcohol hadn't only affected his recent past, but had made history uncertain. Suddenly the idea of discerning fact from fiction wasn't so easy.

"I'm in Prague," he said, attempting to anchor himself in reality. "A woman, Leeny, came to see me. Nathan saw her too. She asked me to find her son, Josh. He's been missing for five days. For six days."

Just a missing boy, he thought. The only conspiracy he could see was the one he brought to the table and was just about to convince himself of such when he caught a movement between two slim chimney stacks. A bird nesting perhaps? But this time, something did look out of place. Enhancing the zoom on a strange pipe, he realised it wasn't a pipe but a suppressor mounted on the barrel of a sniper rifle. He checked his watch.

CHAPTER 12

7147 GINA

The first thing you killed as an assassin was your conscience…

Gina was conflicted about the contract, but steadfast in her duty. She considered her conflict and the will to so easily override an emotion that if properly investigated, may offer caution. But there was always the possibility that it would birth a conscience, a mirror no assassin looked into by choice.

It was getting late and there was still no sign of the mark, but time was on her side as she scoped… waiting… watching.

The tier-one assassin had concealed herself in an almost perfect vantage point amongst a grouping of chimney stacks, but she wasn't alone. The adjacent building on the opposite side of the compound saw her counterpart Yuri, covering in a crossfire configuration with clear sight lines on anyone that came within fifty yards, although he had opted against her advice on his final position. Together they created a 360 degree kill box around the complex. She'd had a confirmed combat kill at just under fifteen hundred meters, so at this range it would be like shooting fish in a barrel with a blunderbuss.

She didn't play well with others so teaming up on a contract made her nervous. There were a lot of moving parts and no way to prepare for the mistakes of others… *But if he accidentally turns on his tac-laser again, I swear I'll shoot him myself,* she mused.

The building being watched was one of three identical villa style mansions that sat in a row at odds with the traditional architecture of the area, as if to make a statement. What that statement was couldn't be certain, affluence, arrogance or just bad taste?

At the end of a dark cul-de-sac was an uninspired three storey Mediterranean style villa with open floor planning, floor to ceiling windows, interiors in the style of a modern art-deco in seventies brown and boasting an underground swimming pool and sauna. It was a cold slab of rigid lines surrounded by the warmth of a city famed for its baroque, Art Nouveau. *A bullet for the architect might just be considered justice.* Floorpans for the other two identical properties provided them a complete schematic layout, bedrooms, bathrooms, WCs, even linen closets all committed to memory.

The multi-agency brief laid out a proposed tactical execution plan so things didn't end up a shit show turning Prague into the wild west. While its detail and precision was impressive to a point, Gina wasn't about to put her life in the hands of third-party intel.

Like any other contract, she arrived in Prague a week earlier to acclimatise and make preparations. Less impressive had been the attitude towards the target. Considering his previous status she thought it was complacent to the point of negligent, and that worried her.

Yes the man was a drunk, but decommissioned or not, he had once been called an Angel of Death. An underestimation could lead to miscalculation, the cost of which was your life, a price she wasn't willing to pay.

If you want to kill a giant, do it while he's sleeping. You don't wake him up and slap him in the face. But where, when and how the employer wanted the target killed was up to them, that's what they are paying for after all.

Her code 7147, or 7, 14, 7 was a childishly simple cipher representing the corresponding letters of the alphabet G.N.G. The acronym for her call sign, 'Good Night Girl.' There was a darkness in the irony the name implied which amused her. She had once considered The Long Kiss Goodnight, in reference to a film from the 90s about a female assassin, but 2012117 TLKG sounded more like a radio station, 7147 was just catchier. She did however assume the pseudonym Gina which was in playful reference to the actress Geena Davis who played the kick ass assassin in the film.

7147 had been making a name for herself in the last few years and the pull of bagging a tier-one A trophy was just too good an opportunity to pass up. It would elevate her status for consideration to the council and was definitely easier than toppling a regime.

The scope moved from the quiet residential streets to the property's periphery as it did approximately every thirty seconds. If the boy was inside there had been no sign of him. There were no deliveries suggesting they were holding a minor, no TVs playing cartoons or colourful children's programmes, toys or anything of a placatory nature that could be used to manipulate him in someway, or to just simply keep him quiet. Which meant he was confined, subdued or both.

Movement inside seemed to rotate around the second floor marking that as the boys probable location. She'd observed at least six armed operatives with automatic and semi-automatic weapons. They had been mindful to cover most of the large windows, although it had done little to obstruct the view from her vantage point.

"You think he'll show?" Yuri's voice crackled into the radio.

"He'll show," she said.

Based on what she knew of the mark's recent past she wasn't entirely convinced he would, but had no intention of letting down her guard. She kept a determined focus on the complex.

The only thing of interest in the last hour had been an extremely drunk older lady hanging from a man considerably and suspiciously younger, groping and exploring his chest under his shirt while failing miserably to maintain consistent balance in heels. They had taken an age to pass by, at one point stopping to embrace with a slightly stomach churning display. Yuri trained his crosshair on the rear of the woman's head.

"I could just put her out of her misery," he crackled into the radio.

"If it was a mercy kill, I'd shoot the guy," she replied. "Keep the channel clear."

It was quiet again for a while, every movement seeming to cause a rush of adrenalin in anticipation, but there was no sign of the mark. A stray dog became the next few minutes entertainment, watching as it moved from lamppost to lamppost peeing on every one of them. The radio crackled.

"What do you know, another bitch marking her territory," Yuri joked.

That was actually pretty funny, she thought, without responding.

"Movement, north-west corner," Yuri said, his tone alert.

7147's scope panned smoothly. Concealed by the shadows, there was a large man staggering close to one of the buildings, his shoulder scraping along the wall and bounced off as he countered his equilibrium. Drunken ramblings occasionally hit a volume that sent them rising into the night before dying to a low inaudible grumble.

"Just a drunk," Yuri crackled.

The crosshair of the scope hovered over the man in the shadows, unwilling to dismiss anything without scrutiny, though she didn't quite have an angle to make a proper assessment. Something felt off. She slid her finger from resting flush on the side of the rifle until she felt the trigger brush the surface of her skin. The man screamed out, argumentative with the night, throwing his bottle into the air at an invisible foe. Instinctively the scope tracked the projectile before steadily returning to the target.

"Is he talking with someone?" 7147 asked. "Do you have a visual?"

"Negative, he's alone."

"Then who's he talking to?"

"Hold on, scanning frequencies."

She didn't like it. The pressure under her finger slightly increased against the trigger. He was too far in the shadows to clearly make out his head, but from this distance she could still drop him with a single shot.

"I'm getting no frequencies, no one's communicating with him," Yuri said. "Check your PDA."

Yuri uploaded an image from his scope and transferred it to 7147's smart device. The image was a grainy replication using his night vision optic. He had the better angle and it clearly showed the drunk man alone, but from the quality of the image there was no way to tell if it was the mark, but she couldn't rule it out.

"If it is him, stick to the plan," Yuri continued. "Let him do his thing. He gets the kid, we get him on the way out."

"Roger that," 7147 said.

She released the pressure on the trigger. *Shit! What's wrong with me?* she thought exhaling, feeling relieved. In defiance of her extensive experience, she seemed to be contending with the nerves of a rookie, not felt since her first few targets.

When Gina accepted the contract she had purposely omitted her knowledge of the mark's past, hoping to receive a greater portion of their intel, surprised to learn that her information had exceeded their own, and she wasn't the sharing type. But what she knew combined with the sheer magnitude of the target's former reputation had managed to get under her skin. The same knowledge she privately chastised others for not having.

Angel's of Death were nameless, faceless people, afforded the authority to pass down decrees to the fraternity of assassins. A dormant rule that hadn't been exercised in nearly fifty years, until Cohen.

The mark passed a 'Non-Combatant' decree, meaning family, friends and loved ones could not be considered collateral damage, and or used as leverage in any way. It didn't stop separate contracts being taken out on individuals or family members, it simply meant you had to pay for the right of a higher body count. It was a way of separating blunt force tools from surgical instruments.

Decrees weren't strictly law and you could choose to reject them, but that inevitably ran the risk of consequence. What that was, nobody knew. But there was a second decree. 'The innocent'. This was in many ways like the first. Subjects could not be harmed or used in any way, but this was solely for children. The difference being, children could not become the target of a contract for any reason.

If adhered to, both laws had the potential to cost millions in lost revenue, squeezing the less skilled and inept contingent out of the game. But more importantly, protecting those that weren't able to protect themselves from would be murderers posing as assassins.

It was expected that there would be resistance, but most were just waiting to find out what the consequences of that looked like, and they didn't have long to wait.

Luiz Alves, a small time assassin from the favelas of Brazil had welcomed a contract in defiance of the decree. It was on behalf of the head of a powerful cartel, Marcos Rocha and brokered out of the U.S.

The contract was to eliminate Patricia Machado, a public official whose stand against crippling union policies were beginning to impact a moderate source of their control and revenue, putting money and power back into the hands of the people.

They wanted to send a clear message to her and anyone else considering taking up the mantle in her stead, so the contract also included her husband and three children. An eight-year-old boy, six-year-old girl and second boy of only two months.

With disturbing speed and ruthless will, Alves successfully executed the contract; apart from the little girl who had somehow managed to escape during the horrific ordeal. Alves was denied payment until he had fully honoured the contract, forcing him to hunt down and kill the little girl, Izabel.

The following morning, high up on the outskirts of the Rio favela, a place where you could witness the settlement in its entirety and where it could witness you. Alves' body hung from a post, blistering in the morning sun. The letters 'AD' had been calved deeply into his chest, signifying he had been delivered by an Angel of Death. He never completed the contract.

The broker Geoff Steiner, a wealthy talent agent out of the U.S. was found hanging from the 27th floor of his apartment building in downtown San Diego. It was an affluent area so inevitably news coverage was vast with helicopters littering the skies all vying to shoot the most dramatic footage for their nightly news editions, as only they could. It aired with heavy speculation of possible cult connections due to the carvings on his chest and the crotch of his trousers stained in blood.

He was found only several hours after Alves' body was discovered in Rio. Investigation into the death revealed ties to several brokered assassinations and links to an elite paedophile ring. Rumours were quick to circulate, implicating some of the most elite and high-profile Hollywood names one could imagine. No arrests were forthcoming, but when news of over a hundred children being emancipated from a child sex trafficking gang, along with some smaller inconsequential arrests, the rumour mill suggested deals had been made under the table.

It later transpired that the blood stained crotch on Steiner's trousers was due to the castration of his genitals, which the post-mortem discovered inside the lining of his stomach, somehow he'd managed to swallow it whole.

Upon hearing news of the deaths, the head of the cartel, Marcos Rocha, fled Brazil for the sanctuary of the High Atlas mountains in Morocco, to a beautiful remote retreat known as the Kasbah Du Toubkal.

At an altitude of 1800 meters amongst North Africa's highest peaks, it was a place that could only be reached by foot. Using a small militia, Rocha secured the location at gunpoint as they awaited his arrival throwing paid guests into the streets, forcing the local Berbers to stay and serve or face swift execution.

The mountain lodge was a picturesque hilltop refuge for travellers seeking an immersive experience of nature without having to sacrifice comfort. But the hidden paradise was abruptly transformed into a hellish fortress, scattering militia across the mountainside and in the lower village of Imlil where they would be able to blend in, spotting strangers from a distance. Inside the kasbah was his most loyal and trusted bodyguards.

Instead of running into a yoga enthusiast on the morning deck as they absorbed the panoramic vistas, it was now an armed militia carrying an AK-47 assault rifle.

Rocha knew his decision to come here was inspired. At this elevation they would be able to see anyone coming for miles, even an Angel of Death wouldn't be able to contend with the security nature offered.

In the coming days as fear and paranoia began to dissipate, he was able to truly appreciate the affect the kasbah was having on his senses. Not for years had he thought with such clarity or slept with such peace. There was an energy that couldn't be quantified, a history and culture that was absorbed without thought. He considered the lodge as a living breathing part of the mountain, shaped through history just waiting for him to discover it.

The arabesque motifs and Islamic architecture, the immersive and rich Persian textile, rugs, throws and cushions that accumulated to the feel of an Arabian palace. Even the dry heat and cool mountain air were more agreeable to him.

Closing his eyes, he breathed it in allowing it to fill his lungs, invigorating him to approach the day with a new found enthusiasm for everything Rocha.

On the face of the mountain, something caught his attention. It was a mound of some sort, possibly a pile of clothing. It was difficult to make out but it looked out of place amongst the mixed vegetation. He continued staring trying to define the object, squinting as he adjusted his vision. Suddenly a quiet realisation came over him and with it a wave of fear.

The mound he was looking at wasn't a pile of clothes, it was the body of a militia that had been guarding the retreat. *He may have lost his footing in the night,* Rocha thought, *falling to his death.* Still, his head swivelled urgently looking around, suddenly realising it was too quiet. Guards that should have been patrolling at an unobtrusive distance were not being intrusive enough.

He turned back to the mountain desperately scanning its face in search of other militia that would still be patrolling. But one by one mounds revealed themselves scattered across the mountainside, now not so hard to see, they were all dead.

Rocha took a step back from the terrace and found that he was standing in trails of drying blood coating the deck. Pools of it were swimming in the grooves, it was everywhere; a silent massacre.

When they found Rocha's body, it wasn't clear how he had died. Like the other two bodies that benefited from the contract, the letters AD had been calved deeply into his chest, but the wounds were not significant enough for loss of life. His face however, was frozen in a petrified state. What was certain is that Marcos Rocha died in extreme fear, the same fear he had spent his life inflicting on others.

Rumours amongst the local Berber population talked of a stranger that had descended upon the refuge from over the mountain, disappearing the same way after he'd freed them.

In five days on three continents, bodies spoke of the consequences that ignoring the Angels decree would bring. After that, even if you wanted to raise a contract that suggested collateral damage or hinted at the innocent, you would have a hard time finding anyone to execute it. That was until eighteen months ago.

"Incoming vehicle," Yuri's voice crackled into the radio.

Yuri was tracking a motorcycle approaching from the north, one of several they'd witnessed either collecting or delivering to the compound. Each one housed a large top box and a rider wearing a black helmet with tinted visor and a hi-vis vest.

7147 was reluctant to take her attention off the man in the shadows who had just turned towards a narrow opening between two buildings like something had grabbed his attention. It was as if his movement seemed to be purposefully concealing his face, like he knew he was being watched. *But how could he?* Neither sniper positions were particularly visible to the naked eye, almost impossible unless he stood and stared up into the night allowing his vision to adjust to the different shades of darkness. He hadn't even looked in that direction.

"Gina? You copy?"

"Copy," she said sharply.

Directing her scope north towards the vehicle tracking the rider all the way to the compound. She thought the hi-vis vest was clever. Motorcyclists wearing apparel that highlighted their presence were almost never stopped unless overtly flouting the law. Whatever they were delivering was almost guaranteed to arrive and did so at regular intervals throughout the evening.

The rider parked outside the property and removed a silver case from the top box, the type that would be packed with a thick sponge to house expensive or delicate equipment. After being checked at the door by a man not trying very hard to conceal the automatic weapon under his jacket, he entered the property only to emerge again a minute later, placing the silver case back into the top box and leaving the same way he came, towards the north. Every delivery was the same.

She looked again for the man in the shadows, *Shit, he's gone!*

"Do you have a visual on the drunk?" Gina said into the communicator.

"Negative. Probably gone home to sleep it off."

She didn't like it and began scoping any shadows that moved, crisp packets blowing in the wind, unassuming doorways and windows, as though danger was everywhere but nowhere to be found. It was quiet again.

Returning her attention to the property around the thirty second mark, she considered the increasing possibility of plan B. If the mark didn't show she was in position to take out at least four operatives before they could even consider returning fire. If properly trained, which they appeared to be, the remaining would concede the tactical disadvantage to the high ground sniper fire, needing to create a distraction to cover their retreat. It was more than likely they would dig in the hope that reinforcements would reach them in time. Of course by then Yuri would have blocked frequencies and they would make the extraction before help arrived, leaving no one alive.

Interference crackled into 7147's earpiece.

"Repeat your last," she said waiting for a response. "Yuri… do you copy?"

The radio crackled again with no response. 7147 raised her scope on Yuri's position. No sooner had it arrived when a painfully blinding flash of light from Yuri's tac-laser penetrated the lens of her scope followed instantly by a bullet exploding out of it. Then three more in quick succession, the second hit with a thud, the third hissed into the night air and the fourth pinged as it ricocheted off of the chimney; then silence.

CHAPTER 13

DR SARAH CARDEN

As Father Michael was arriving at the De Vinci airport in Rome, to meet with the young student whose misfortune had bought him passage to Arizona, the Vatican summer camp were already touching down at their destination; base camp for the Mount Graham International Observatory.

The group were understandably exhausted after having travelled for nearly twenty hours straight, their only interest now was to find their rooms and sleep, which most of them happily did fully clothed.

Despite the arduous journey, Father Trentini, a younger, slightly trendier priest then the holy city were accustomed to, insisted on introducing himself to their host Dr Sarah Carden, director of the observatory; currently on-site at the MGIO. It would take a further two and a half hour round trip up and down the mountain, but, "etiquette dictated it," he said.

The petite, full of energy Texan with a beaming smile wasn't exactly the respected astrobiologist Father Trentini had expected, but then Dr Carden hadn't seen many young brooding, hair gelled priests alight the Vatican either.

"Father Trentini, it's so nice to meet you," she said, "but you didn't need to come all the way up here just to say hi. You must be exhausted."

"It's very nice to meet you," he replied. "But after all the uncertainty and drama, I thought it prudent to personally express my gratitude for keeping the camp alive this year."

"Us? Please, without you stepping in we wouldn't even be having this conversation. The team are lucky to have you on board."

"Honestly, I was just glad I could help. Although it was a shame to hear in the confusion that one of the students was overlooked," Father Trentini said.

"Actually we got some good news about young Phillipé. They managed to find him his very own chaperone. They're en route as we speak."

"Oh that *is* good news."

"Father Michael … Do you know him?" she asked.

He paused briefly, before saying,

"No. I don't believe so. My knowledge of Vatican priests is rather limited, being from a small congregation myself. Though I've always thought it must be quite an ordeal overseeing the logistics of a place like Vatican City, or an international observatory."

Dr Carden watched as he absorbed the environment as though every detail held significance, wondering if his small congregation had been a sheltered experience. They were after all standing in a canteen and the building itself was constructed for function, not aesthetics. They couldn't be mentioned in the same breath as to the history and architecture of Rome. However, the equipment it housed was a culmination and continual evolution of humanities finest achievements, but the building was just a building. *Such was a simple life of a priest*, she thought.

"Now you're here, is there anything you'd like to see?" Dr Carden asked.

"No, that's quite alright, I wouldn't want to impose. I'm sure I'll see everything over the next few days."

For such a short conversation, that was the second time she hadn't believed him. The first was asking about Father Michael. He may not have lied about knowing him, but she got the impression he knew exactly who she was talking about, though it wasn't a concerning thought.

"Shoot, it's no imposition," she said. "Ask away."

He hesitated again, this time out of feigned politeness, before like an excitable child, he said,

"Is it true you have a telescope named Lucifer?"

Dr Carden's smile implied this was a question she'd been asked more times than she cared to remember.

"The Large Binocular telescope," she said, "or the LBT. Actually its full title is The Large binocular telescope, near infrared Utility, with Camera and Integral Field unit, for Extragalactic Research. But yes, it did adopt the acronym of Lucifer. Would you like to see it?

"If it's not.."

Sarah raised her eyebrows and dramatically placed her hands on her hips, as if to say "don't finish that sentence."

"Yes," he said instead, "I'd like that very much."

The main floor of the Large Binocular Telescope was a plain and raw setting. While it was a simple large metal warehouse with exposed structural beams, its centre piece was a sight to behold.

"It's an international project that sees cooperation between state and private contributors, such as The University of Arizona, the Vatican, and The Montgomery Institute to name a few," Dr Carden explained as they entered

Father Trentini felt like a perplexed ant staring up at the enormity of this inexplicable machine.

"You're in luck," she then added. "We're about to go into a rotation for a maintenance check."

"Rotation?"

"You'll see."

As if on cue, a voice boomed.

"All clear for maintenance checks!"

Father Trentini didn't know where the voice came from, or the several voices that followed it, repeating the phrase that echoed around the facility. A worker appeared from a platform halfway up the telescope, descended the steps and cleared the base perimeter.

"She's all clear," the worker said into his radio. "Rotate in 5… 4… 3… 2… Okay, Let's see her dance."

The worker then left the main floor as the deep clang of heavy cogs groaned into a melodic hum. There was a light vibration that increased until it could be felt in your bones, and then with a slight jolt, the entire structure around them began to slowly rotate. It was almost like a simulation of an earthquake.

Dr Carden was right! It was nothing like Father Trentini could have imagined. No oversized cylindrical tube with a scientist face pressed up against an eyepiece. Instead, it was a machine. Cutting edge technology from an array of scientific fields from all over the planet had come together to create the largest binocular telescope in the world. But if she'd told him it was an engine for a super cruise liner or it would transform into a giant alien robot, he would be none the wiser. He may not have understood it, but he certainly respected it.

"Not what you expected huh?" Dr Carden shouted rhetorically over the machines to be heard.

"Lucifer or Luci, as she's known round here," she continued, pointing to two large units attached to the structure, twenty feet overhead. "Part one and two are mounted at the focus point of the telescope and cooled to minus 213 degrees Celsius, which allows us to observe the near infrared wavelength range, seeing deeper into space than ever before."

When the structure finally came to a stop, Father Trentini stared at the two units Dr Carden had pointed out, with a strange longing; almost reverent. His expression then lightened to the point of a faint smile.

"213," he said under his breath as though thinking out loud. "Fascinating."

"Oh? Is the number significant?" She asked, no longer needing to shout.

"No. I just mean all of it, it's just all so fascinating," he replied, injecting enthusiasm into his voice.

But something about his behaviour suddenly made Dr Carden feel very aware of just how alone they currently were. Most bodies on-site were now performing maintenance in the sub-level machine room, meaning the only way they would hear anything was by radio. Without looking, her hand found the channel selector on the radio attached to her belt. She was on Channel 5, turning the dial two clicks anti-clockwise she would be on the maintenance channel; just in case.

Dr Carden had lost count of the tours she'd shown around the facility and never had the cause to feel unsafe, and she was sure there was no reason now, he was a priest after all; but somehow she did. It was something about the way he said '213' that unnerved her. She thought she saw something, as if a mask slipped, and for a split second revealed a facade.

"Quite something isn't it?" she said, subtly moving towards the exit. "An entire structure, approximately 2000 tons rotating."

"It's quite an experience," he replied, glaring at her as she moved away, but didn't move with her.

She turned to catch his menacing, ice-like gaze. It was as if he knew she'd seen something. Fear began twisting her stomach, but she managed to muster a believable smile. The moment had just stretched beyond uncomfortable when Sarah's radio crackled.

"Dr Carden," the voice said.

"Go for Sarah," she spoke quickly into the radio, maintaining eye contact with the priest. '*Sorry,*' she mouthed to him courteously.

"It's Heinrich," the voice crackled. "I've been trying to reach you, but your radio is on the maintenance channel."

"I know Heinrich, we're in maintenance checks. What's up?"

"I need you to John Hancock these parts if you want them on the next shipment."

"Okay, I'm on my way," she said.

Quickly re-engaging the button on the radio, she added, "I'm just on the LBT floor with Father Trentini, I'll be a couple of minutes."

She clipped the radio back on to her belt.

"I'm afraid I have to cut our tour short Father Trentini," she said while gesturing him toward the exit.

This time he obliged without hesitation. She was thankful to be on the move again, but didn't feel completely relieved until passing a couple of co-workers that acknowledged them as she passed. Everyone had jobs to do and rarely stopped for idle chit-chat, but with only fifty staff, no one was anonymous.

Reaching the canteen, Dr Carden stopped to shake Father Trentini's hand, firmly; Texan firmly.

"It was so lovely meeting you," she said. "I'm sure we'll catch up over the next couple of days."

"I look forward to that," he replied earnestly. "Please don't let me keep you."

She smiled and turned to leave. Though as she was walking away, she couldn't help wonder what it was that got her so spooked. His slick hair, dark eyes, piercing stare, a gentle tone of voice? It was the culmination that gave the priest an unfortunate, yet sinister air. However, now in the harsh fluorescent lighting of the canteen she was feeling somewhat guilty, allowing her imagination to have run wild, projecting unwarranted fears onto her guest. *And after everything he's done,* she thought, *stepping in for the group at the very last minute.* She stopped suddenly.

"If you wait here," she said, "I'll get Heinrich to drive you back to base before it gets too late."

"Too late?"

"We restrict travel on the mountain, particularly after dusk. The slightest miscalculation is the best way of taking route one to the bottom."

"So you stay on-site?"

"Pods."

Dr Carden pointed to the level above where they were standing, which could be seen through grated walkways, but judging by the expression on Father Trentini's face, he wasn't accustomed to observatory jargon.

"They're like small rooms," she said, "although to be honest I've seen bigger cupboards. But it's quiet, and a good place to get some shut eye."

"Thank you so much for your time Dr Carden," Father Trentini said, "it's been much appreciated, please, don't let me keep you."

"It's been a pleasure. You have yourself a nice evening now you hear," she said with a little extra Texan twang.

And she was gone.

Father Trentini continued to absorb the foreign environment and began exploring. Walking slowly around the two columns of three aluminium tables and fixed benches, draping his hand across the surfaces. Looking at the mundane posters on the walls and doors that gave cartoon reminders on personal hygiene, what to do in case of an emergency, or directions to another part of the facility; but his interest constantly reverted to the overhead walkways, toward the pods.

He observed an employee entering one, needing the use of a keycard to gain entry. Eyeing a doorway that directed its reader to the upper landing, he started towards it. But then, just as he was about to enter, a voice stopped him in his tracks.

"Father Trentini."

"You must be Heinrich," he said, turning with a broad smile.

"Yes father, I'm here to take you to base camp."

"How wonderful. I thought I might use the men's room before we leave," he said while prompting for direction.

"Good idea," Heinrich replied. "It'll take us just over an hour to get there, so probably not a good idea to stop on the mountain. Not really a place you want to get caught with your pants down, not with so many wild cats, if you know what I mean."

"Quite," Father Trentini responded to the strange and inappropriate statement, still waiting for directions.

"Sorry, second door on the left."

He then turned and headed for the bathroom, discreetly eying the pods on the upper platform.

Needing most of his concentration to navigate the 4x4 as he descended the mountain, Heinrich was only able to engage the priest with polite, albeit, broken conversation; constantly interrupting himself as he communicated with the observatory at specific turning points. He thought it was refreshing that someone such as the priest would show an interest in the logistics and running of the MGIO, and not just in the telescope. People never fully appreciated just how much work went into keeping an international science project running like clockwork.

Heinrich was the head of a seven person team that dealt with telescope maintenance, heavy equipment operations, plumbing, telecommunications systems; and even road maintenance. On top of that, there was a 24 hour, on-call duty system to manage.

"I wonder how far you'd see into space without my team?" he would jibe, but never seriously.

Along with the scientists, there were several small teams that dealt with operations, but on the mountain, they would say it was just one team, and everyone respected that; but it was still a welcome change to field the enquiry.

As they approached base camp and Heinrich no longer needed to split his attention, he became more chatty, enjoying the company of the young priest.

"I'm not quite sure on the etiquette," he said. "But if you're not too jet-lagged, did you want to join me for a beer father? Sorry if that's not appropriate," he added as an afterthought.

Eyeing the identification lanyard that hung around Heinrich's neck, along with his access card, Father Trentini smiled.

"Not at all," he said. "That sounds most appealing."

CHAPTER 14

FATHER MICHAEL

Father Michael had not been looking forward to traveling again so soon after arriving back from Germany, but he was dreading it far less than chaperoning an enthusiastic adolescent on a fourteen hour flight; followed by a three hour car journey.

The last twenty four hours had been a whirlwind of emotion, chaotic and confusing, yet he would only stop to ponder the reason for his travel once. What he couldn't have envisaged was just how much of a welcome distraction the young man would prove to be.

His young candidate, Phillipé Garcia, had been easy to spot. Innocent and doe-eyed, scanning every face that passed him in the hope of one revealing themselves as his guide. He was tall and slim with the soft features of youth, unkept curls, a shirt buttoned to the collar and trousers that were at least two inches past their sell-by date; judging by the way they sat above his ankles.

His eyes widened with reverential fear upon seeing Father Michael, whom was easier to spot in a traditional hooded cowl; which tended to effortlessly attract attention.

Mackie had described the boy as an exceptional talent; quiet and reserved. What Father Michael met was a bundle of pent-up excitement still coming to terms with the trip.

"Being flown to the Vatican observatory, by the Vatican. Whoa!" he said, making a gesture of his mind being blown while talking at an excitedly fast pace, barely stopping to catch his breath as though he'd consumed several high energy caffeine drinks. Under the circumstances,

Michael thought the boys reaction was quite endearing and understandable, but hoped the quiet side wasn't too far away.

He convinced Phillipé to browse the shops for any last minute items, and found a quiet spot in the departure lounge to gather himself; hopefully mustering a spirit to match his travel companion.

He thought he should feel more fatigued than he did, but not since he was a young man was there such a sense of fidelity driving him. Though he wasn't naive enough to believe his ageing body possessed the agility of his mind, years had robbed what youth took for granted. What remained was a sense of duty, a willingness to make the necessary sacrifices; sacrifices a younger mind may be more reluctant to face.

He'd been so busy following Franz's trail that he hadn't stopped to wonder if he was even the right man for the job. *After all, strength of courage wasn't the strength of confrontation, and wars weren't won by philosophers,* he thought. Malevolent powers had already taken one life that he knew of, and at his age he could offer no opposition the next time they tried, wondering if perhaps the mantle wouldn't be safer in younger hands.

As the thought crossed his mind, he saw Phillipé, a hundred yards away making enquiries in an electrical store, leaning over the counter, hands clasped behind his back, only removing one to point at the device before returning to its position, as if an old soul trapped in a young body. The thought made Father Michael chuckle internally, quickly remembering their introduction, when he simulated his mind exploding, saying,

"Whoa!"

But in that moment, with overwhelming certainty, he knew that he was supposed to meet someone. Perhaps not Phillipé, but someone that would have to make a greater sacrifice than himself. *Was that the prophesy?* he thought, *was God sending someone?* But without the necessary information, he dismissed the idea as quickly as it came.

So caught up in his head, he hadn't seen Phillipé approaching.

"Is everything okay, Father?" he asked.

Jolted from his thoughts, surprised to see the young man stood right in front of him.

"Phillipé!" he exclaimed. "Sorry, I was in my own world. Did you manage to pick anything up for the journey?" he enquired, noticing a fresh bag in his hand and directing the conversation away from himself.

"Oh yes Father, I did."

He took the seat next to the priest and excitedly opened the bag to reveal the purchase; a digital camera. By the time they'd boarded the

REVELATIONS

plane, Michael was astonished that the boy had already learned its every function. It had a viewing screen that could be rotated 180 degrees, so the very first picture he took was a selfie with Father Michael, both smiling with his arm around the priest's shoulder.

With his face pressed to the window, young Phillipé watched as over four hundred tons of metal separated from the tarmac to take flight, and the world shrank to the size of a model village. He then turned his gaze skywards as they inched ever closer to the clouds. When the plane eventually emerged through the suspended layers, his gaze continued looking towards the heavens, a sense of possibility and wonder lighting his face. About ten minutes in, the pilot's voice came over the intercom.

"We're approaching a cruising altitude of 31000ft and the weather ahead is calm and sunny."

The announcement broke Phillipé's focus and he turned from the window, finally settling into a more subdued excitement. Somehow the youthful exuberance wasn't quite as annoying as first imagined. Listening to him talk about his passion for science, fuelled by his faith. About the recent discovery of the 'Higgs boson', the pursuit in understanding dark matter, and string theory, which he believed was a misunderstood construct of the universe and should be thought of in terms of DNA; a blueprint.

Most, if not all of it went over Father Michael's head, but he found himself engrossed and inspired by the young man, wondering how the Rabbi's must have felt when a twelve-year-old boy named Jesus, held an audience in a synagog debating scripture.

But one thing Phillipé said stood out above everything else, that he was hoping to reach the observatory in time to see the blood moon. So preoccupied with current events, Father Michael had completely forgotten that tonight would be the first of a tetrad. He didn't see how it could be just a coincidence, not after witnessing such an inspired sunset. *Signs and Wonders*, Mackie said to him. *Signs and Wonders.*

The journey finally caught up with Father Michael sometime during the third in-flight movie, when he fell asleep and remained so until Phillipé woke him for the descent.

Halfway into the three hour car journey toward the International Observatory, a sort of nausea began to take hold. He thought that maybe the barely edible in-flight meal was starting to churn his stomach. He knew it couldn't possibly be the car as he never suffered with travel sickness. Then it dawned on him. For a short time he had managed to forget his mission. He was used to being versed in scripture, not clandestine operations, and had to remind himself that he wasn't really a chaperone, but part of a brotherhood; seeking information that had got his best friend killed. The nausea was his body doing its best to remind him of that, the closer they got to their destination.

CHAPTER 15

ARCHIE

The studio was in a silent state of shock and confusion as Archie left the set. What he had said affected everyone in some way, but he looked almost sad as he handed his microphone pack to the young sound engineer, as though the burden of the world was his to bare alone. He smiled and thanked her before leaving.

With so much in his head, he didn't see Charlotte as he walked passed her and out of the studio.

The brief interaction with the sound engineer hadn't gone unnoticed by Charlotte. The young woman was smiling reverently at Archie, looking at him in a way she hadn't only ten minutes earlier. It was curious, Charlotte thought; before following him out of the studio, keeping at a distance that allowed him some space.

Charlotte didn't know how it was possible, but the return journey felt even more silent than the ride there. The driver that collected Archie had been allocated to him all morning and now drove quietly back to the pick up address. He kept his eyes on the road but every time he looked into the rear view, it wasn't at the road behind but was snatching a glance at Archie. He'd driven any number of movie stars, celebrities and politicians and was always content to do his job quietly and professionally, but on this occasion he found himself primed to speak.

"Is it straight home, sir?" he eventually said as an ice breaker.

Archie had felt the conversation coming but didn't feel the need to encourage it.

"Do you have time for a scenic route?"

"Of course sir," he responded with energetic enthusiasm. "My next pick up isn't until four p.m. is there anywhere that you'd like to go?"

"Not particularly. Just around."

"Right you are sir," the driver said in his snappy cockney accent.

"I'm sorry," Charlotte said, finally breaking her silence.

Archie looked at her quizzically.

"I should have seen this coming," she continued.

Archie smiled warmly the way he always did when he wanted to make people around him feel comfortable, except this time his smile only made Charlotte feel worse. Seeing her discomfort he gave a slight chuckle.

"If you'd have seen this coming, I would have given you a raise."

"I don't understand."

Archie continued the same docile expression as he stared from the window at the passing scenery. Charlotte's mind raced over the situation in her mind wondering what it was that she missed.

"I mean, sure they were being dicks about the whole thing, but you turned it around, you had them right where you wanted them. Wait…"

The answer came to Charlotte before she could finish her question.

"You planned it?" she asked.

"No," Archie replied, "but I saw an opportunity."

Charlotte was blown away trying to wrap her head around the information. Archie was aware their conversation wasn't exactly private.

"I'm sorry I didn't catch your name," he said to the driver.

"Dave, sir."

"It's nice to meet you Dave, I'm Archie and this here is Charlotte. Do you mind if I ask, how long have you worked for the station, Dave?"

"About to go into my tenth year now, sir."

"And do you enjoy your job?"

"Oh yeah. You know, you get to meet a lot of interesting people but mainly I just like to drive. It's uncomplicated and ninety five percent of the time it's stress free."

"And the other five percent?"

"Let's just say precarious situations, sir."

"Ahh," Archie voiced with regret. "This morning, I'm sorry about that."

"Well, we live to fight another day sir."

"How would you like to live to fight another day being an exclusive driver, with a ten thousand pay bump, pension and health benefits covering you and your family?"

"I'd say you've made an excellent transition from politics to comedy sir, good for you."

"I like this guy," Archie said to Charlotte who watched the interaction with fascination.

Dave continued to try and gage Archie's response in the rear-view mirror, but his expression was unwavering as he waited patiently for the driver's answer.

"You're serious?" he asked.

"I have a question," Charlotte intervened with a sudden protective quality. "Did you happen to see the interview, Dave?"

"I did ma'am, yes."

"And what did you think?"

"Honestly?"

"Of course."

"I think I was just offered a job by the next Prime Minister of the United Kingdom, ma'am."

Charlotte sank back into her seat with the breath stripped from her speech. She looked at Archie with a puzzling incredulity. *What was it about this man that achieved loyalty with seemingly little effort?* Unaware of his impact, Dave continued the journey through the city using his extensive knowledge of its back roads to circumvent the closures. The car eventually slowed to a halt as it approached a temporary police cordon. In the distance the chanting voices of protestors rang into the air and inaudible bull horns crackled orders from police in unsuccessful attempts to disperse the crowds.

"The road's temporarily closed," the police officer said addressing Dave. "You're going to have to turn around."

"What's going on?" the driver asked.

"Some of the protestors broke away from the designated march route so we've had to shut down parts of the city. You'll have to go back towards Hyde Park Corner and head north to get around, south across the river if you're heading east."

Looking east along Piccadilly, Archie saw a large group of protestors making a stand with police keeping a safe distance due to lack of numbers. Charlotte and Dave both jumped as Archie's door opened.

"What are you doing?" Charlotte said with complete disbelief.

"Finishing the interview," Archie replied.

Smiling he turned and looked the length of Piccadilly.

The police stood by and watched as Archie began the long walk down Piccadilly towards the circus of chaos, flanked either side by buildings of history as though each step took him further and further into the past. The Ritz, 1906, The Royal Academy of the Arts, 1768, Fortnum and Masons, 1707 and Burlington House, 1664.

But to Charlotte, it was the future that was striding forward with a determination that relegated history to a backdrop. Archie was larger than life, but as she watched him continue in the direction of the smoke on the horizon, slowly moving from sight, it was as though he was being consumed by the city, the buildings and the violence.

She hadn't put up much of a protest of his insane notion to address a hostile crowd in the throws of expressing their frustrations with an alarming display of violence and destruction, because she'd assumed his tomfoolery would be halted by any one of the hundreds of police that lined the streets in high-vis attire. She was wrong.

The brightly coloured enforcers were nothing more than yellow wallflowers lining the length of the street like a runway directing Archie towards certain disaster.

Panic began building inside of her to the point of an outburst.

"They're not stopping him!" she said.

Dave watched the faces of the police as Archie passed them by. Smiling, exchanging underhanded comments and sniggering in anticipation of what they hoped his reception would be. Their unison gave the impression of not acting by self governance, but by orders.

"Dave!" she pleaded.

He could see genuine fear gripping her in a vice, something he couldn't imagine feeling for an employer, but strangely understood.

"Those fuckers want him to get hurt," he said, thinking out loud.

Charlotte snapped a look at him.

"Sorry, I didn't mean…"

"ARCHIE!" she screamed out.

But the cacophony ahead was a wall of sound her voice couldn't climb.

"Get in the car!" Dave barked with a sudden urgency.

"What?"

"Just get in!"

Charlotte jumped in the back and fastened her seat belt, uncertain. As Dave manoeuvred the car in the direction of Archie, several police moved to block his path, a couple of them armed with semi-automatic weapons they made sure were on display.

"Sorry sir," one of them said approaching the driver's window, "can't let you pass."

"Fuck this," Charlotte gritted.

Tugging at the seat belt several times to release it, eventually getting herself free, she alighted the car to make the journey on foot. Once again her path was blocked as police began surrounding her.

"What are you doing?" she asked the policeman nervously.

"I'm sorry ma'am. For your own safety, I can't let you through."

"What are you talking about? He's just walked passed you," she said gesturing up the road towards Archie.

"If someone managed to slip passed the police cordon, they've done so at their own risk. But I still can't let you through."

Bravely she mustered the courage to push past them, but was forcefully and aggressively pushed back. She was shocked and frightened at how confident and blatant they were being, only fuelling her fear for Archie.

"If you persist," he continued, stepping into her personal space, where his towering, heavily protected frame would deliver the greatest impact.

"I'll have no choice but to arrest you."

"Come on," Dave said.

Taking Charlotte's arm, he coaxed her away.

"Fucking nazis!" she shouted, seething.

But the officer who had been standing in front of her could only laugh, as if almost proud of the suggestion, with his colleagues joining him in the belittlement.

Dave approached the car when a single raindrop fell upon the windscreen with a tap, pulling his attention skywards. The bright sky had taken on an unusual motion, as if accelerating. Dark rainclouds pushed in from the east passing over their heads, plunging the day into an ominous gloom.

As it continued along Piccadilly overtaking Archie, Charlotte's attention snapped to her side attracted by movement in her periphery. But it was just a shadow. Which was a relief, because what she thought she saw didn't make any sense. A humanoid shaped shadow scuttling over the police car with an animal like quality, a beast. But *just a shadow,* she thought.

As caliginous clouds continued to steal the light, a deep roll of thunder cleared its throat, and with a tumultuous boom its power was felt in the ground beneath their feet. Lightning streaked across the sky like fiery serpents, before punching through the heavens and descending towards Piccadilly.

A bolt collided with The Daughters of Helios, an art installation on the top of a building beyond the statue of Anteros; three female golden idols depicted in mid-dive as if having leapt from the building. Sparks and debris rained down as people stood agasp, watching as one of the daughters fixings gave way and started to fall. Her perfect form plummeting to the earth like a golden angel from the heavens before crashing into the installations counterpart; The Horses of Helios. At the foot of the building, four stallions galloping side by side were reduced to three in the blink of an eye.

The heavenly display brought the rioters to a standstill. Gasping as lightning struck the building, they cheered as the golden statue began to fall, and continued to celebrate as it destroyed one of the four horses. All were compelled to watch. All but two.

Charlotte flinched as thunder roared and lightning struck, but so concerned for Archie's safety that she'd continued to maintain a concerned eye on him. His movements on the other hand hadn't faltered at all, which had been an instinctive reaction to anyone else present. The growing threat in the sky was reflected on the ground, and yet somehow, above and below, a calm surrounded him, not as if he was in the eye of a storm, so much as its cause.

She glanced around, to Dave, the police, press, bystanders, wondering if anyone else was witnessing this. But everybody just stared upwards at an unpromising sky as though from a less evolved time. *This man, this very moment,* she thought, *was being ordained.* She could feel the electricity in the air, coursing through her body like excitement waiting to burst. *He was sent to change the world.*

Almost as a response to her thought, lightning cracked so loud it was as though it split the sky, with it a torrential downpour reduced visibility. Archie was suddenly gone from sight. But another sudden flash revealed his dark unflinching silhouette through the pouring rain.

As Archie reached Piccadilly Circus, the weather had done little to dampen spirits and quell any rebellion; rioters continued jubilating in the city's destruction. Although it had extinguished some of the burning cars, high-end flagship stores at the foot of Regent Street blazed victoriously.

Some of the dissidents started to notice Archie approaching, the billionaire wannabe politician, suddenly with no protection. Faces turned towards him, knowing their anger would soon follow, his heart began to race. It was just like the car earlier that day, although now there was nothing between him and the crowd. No Dave ready to slam his foot on the accelerator to get him out of trouble, or Johnny willing to break someone's arm if they posed a threat. Any idea of a peaceful march was now just a distant memory.

Airborne cameras picked up the unfolding situation and images were broadcast live to online news stations. Only this time it wasn't just a nation watching, but a world.

At first, what seemed to be a courageous act was now the moronic actions of a dead man walking. No one said it, but that was the only reason people were really watching. They didn't necessarily wan't to see someone beaten to death as an outpouring of rage against the machine, but still, they couldn't turn away.

A quixotic Archie was suddenly surrounded. As he cautiously tried moving away, his back came into contact with a burnt-out car; there was nowhere to go. The crowd encircled him so tight it was like a human boa constrictor. He wouldn't have been visible had the camera view not been aerial. People across the globe watched on, breath bated, but one particular group studied their screens with more than just a passing curiosity; The Order.

Any second now Archie would disappear under the weight of bodies only to be discovered upon the crowds dispersal.

All they were waiting for now was the one person to instigate an initial action, after that the conclusion was inevitable; as would be the headlines.

It was clear the mob were expecting a spineless, pathetic, whimpering charlatan that would fall to his knees at the slightest hint of ferity, to expose him for what he truly was. As did the onlooking press, the police and the viewing public.

Archie's head slowly began to rise above the mob, and then his shoulders, almost as though he'd begun to levitate. People watched on with disbelief at what was unfolding, but soon realised the mob were raising

Archie up. Lifting him above their heads, they set him down on the roof of a burnt-out car.

He looked out at the crowd standing in the pouring rain, the desperate, tired faces of the men and women that had reached breaking point. News helicopters captured unfolding events, as did a few camera operators that braved the crowds to get as close as they could. Everyone watched and everyone waited, until finally he spoke.

CHAPTER 16

COHEN

The green tac-laser flickered once more shooting a beam of light into the sky before dying. Cohen ripped off the malfunctioning device from underneath the barrel with a sense of disgust, continuing to hold aim on the opposite sniper position.

There was insult felt at the inexperience of the people sent to kill him, but at the same time he was strangely thankful. Had the two operatives been of any worth then he no longer would be. The mistake the second sniper made was to track the bottle after he threw it, the movement giving away their position. Old senses were still working hard to revive themselves, but he wasn't close to being what he needed to be, not yet.

Cohen watched the opposite chimney stacks for the next few minutes ready to fire at the slightest movement, but the night remained still, a literal dead calm. Retrieving the ceramic blade still protruding from the back of the first sniper's neck, he wiped the residual blood on the corpse before sheathing it above his right ankle. He checked his watch.

Then, searching the corpse, he took and equipped an earpiece and radio, followed by two magazines from the sniper's kit bag, which he laid side by side and a small tablet display velcro'd to a pouch on the operative's chest.

After turning it on, the screen meandered to life revealing a dull but high-resolution display, perfect for night viewing without attracting unwanted attention. *Unlike the tac-laser,* Cohen mused. He guessed his way around the tablet pressing various icons and discovered the schematic layout of the property. After studying it momentarily, he disregarded the device and returned to the weapon, continuing to scope the rooftops.

Using light from a lamppost as a marker, approximately four hundred meters from his position, Cohen fired the rifle. The oversized suppressor kept the weapon to a whisper, but he missed, high and left. Recalibrating the weapon the first dial two clicks, the second dial one click allowing for temperature pressure and wind value, he fired again, missed. One more click gave him a direct hit, shattering the streetlight. Adjusting his aim, he shot again and again taking out lights like they were metal ducks at a fairground attraction, plunging the area surrounding the villa into darkness. He continued until both spare clips were spent but for two rounds, every shot more confident than the last.

Checking his watch again, Cohen noticed the tremor in his hand. He then took a couple more of the pills Viktor had given him. Laying the rifle across his lap he placed his back against the chimney and waited.

There was a dull heavy feeling in his head as it sobered, something he never really got used to and one of the reasons why drunks prefer to stay drunk. *That wasn't an option tonight.* His mind however was beginning to feel as if it was being woken from a prolonged coma, racing with a profusion of thoughts like a flip book of maddening imagery.

But it was strangely peaceful on the roof sitting beneath the stars, even with the dead body of a sniper laying at his feet. The cold metal of the weapon resting under his hand didn't just feel familiar, it felt right. He was a natural born killer and once upon a time had made his peace with that. The truth he was looking for now, however, was more elusive.

Cohen closed his eyes and felt the cool breeze wash gently over his skin, taking a deep breath as if in unison with nature. Opening his eyes he looked out over the rooftops into the calm of the night. *Stop running,* the voice in his head said.

He had to finally concede something profound was happening to him as opposed to the idea he was simply losing his mind. On the face of it, it was a notion that may have been irrational, but the more he resisted the more it brought him to the edge of insanity. The only madness now would be trying to deny there were other forces at work; a truth he wrestled with.

What part he had to play in all of this wasn't clear, only that he was being used somehow to do… something. What, he didn't know. Only that after what he had done, redemption was a notion he wouldn't revisit in a hurry, not sober; there could be no reprieve. This was his penance, to atone without hope of forgiveness. That was mercy.

Approximately thirty minutes passed when he saw a light approaching from the North. He checked his watch; *right on time.*

Taking up the rifle he aimed on a transformer box to the side of the villa complex and fired the two remaining shots. Sparks discharged from the box before it failed, plunging the villa into darkness. Wiping down the rifle he placed it next to the corpse and left.

The motorcycle driver confidently navigated the long descent towards the villa, maintaining a good speed despite the blacked out roads, its single light on high beam giving maximum illumination. Pastel colours from the buildings came to life, fleetingly leaping out of the night as the beam washed over them.

Suddenly, out of nowhere, a man wandered into the road directly into the vehicles path, seemingly unaware of the imminent danger. With no time the rider reacted skilfully, using all of his experience to swiftly apply deft pressure to the breaks. With the back tyre sliding from side to side almost losing traction, it managed to gain control bringing the bike to a halt just before colliding with the stranger.

"You stupid…"

Before the rider could finish his sentence, Cohen raised his silenced Glock-17 and fired. The shot propelled the rider backwards off the bike. Cohen grabbed the handlebar stopping it from falling and quickly flicked down the kick-stand. He then dragged the rider's lifeless body off the road and laid him in a sidings between two houses.

The unexpected blackout ignited tension inside the villa, putting everyone on high alert.

"Check your corners," a voice of calm said, piercing the gloom. "Cover your man."

There was enough moonlight to easily navigate the space and see the others, but not enough to define an expression or see objects in darkened corners, particularly with everyone dressed in black. One by one small powerful flashlights began illuminating small sections of the villa, looking for anything out of the ordinary.

"Might be a problem with the grid," one of the operatives said as she cautiously peered from an upstairs window. "Looks like it's affecting the area."

"Stay alert," the calm voice replied.

After around twenty minutes of continued darkness the nervous tension subsided back into routine. Twenty minutes more and the darkness had become a part of that routine. That was until a wave of light from an approaching vehicle danced across the ceiling immediately placing everyone into a state of readiness.

"It's just the driver," the female voice said.

The temporary illumination of the reception quickly plunged back into a moonlight gloom as the engine from the motorcycle was cut.

"Right on time," the operative in the reception said.

He waited for the inevitable knock at the door before making his way over. He carefully opened it just half a yard to conceal the gun he held out of view, estimating his aim at head height. He then looked the motorcycle courier up and down as he waited, helmet on, visor low and the metal case at his side.

"You're late," the operative said.

"No, I'm not," replied the courier.

"Naaaahhh," he blurted musically, "I'm just fucking with you. Come in, but take the helmet off.

The operative turned back into the room at shouted nonspecifically, "Yo, pick up."

Cohen noticed the gun in his hand. He removed the motorcycle helmet and watched the operative carefully, knowing he would only have a split second to react if he realised who he was. He'd concealed a knife in his right hand with the rear of the blade flush against his forearm. Gambling on the drivers anonymity, he entered the villa.

"You know where to go," the operative said, turning back to him.

"What's with the lights?" Cohen asked buying some time, relieved not to have been forced into action.

"Grid probably, who knows."

"Before I grab the stuff, you think I could use the little boys' room. I've been busting a gut with that tank pushed up against my bladder for the last hour. I'm about two minutes from pissing my pants."

He matched tones and speaking styles as it tended to relax people to the point of letting down their guard.

"Use the one down here," the operative said with a smile, flashing his light towards a door.

"Thanks."

As Cohen took a couple of steps he accidentally knocked into a small table, almost losing his balance.

"Careful… fuck's sake."

"Sorry, I didn't see it," Cohen said bending to rub his knee.

After an exasperated sigh, the operative led the way by torchlight to the bathroom, giving Cohen time to assess the room. There were three operatives downstairs and two that he could see on the raised platform above. He assumed there would be at least one or two more on the floor guarding the boy.

His chaperone shined the torch inside the bathroom so he could at least see the layout before closing the door and concealing him in complete darkness. Before the operative had a chance to turn around and leave, a powerful hand covered his mouth and nose yanking his head backwards while simultaneously sliding the knife into the soft of his neck, instantly severing his vocal cords. There was a moment of struggle that quickly subsided as his body went limp.

After gently laying him on the bathroom floor he picked up the torch and placed the gun in his belt. Taking a small remote from his pocket, he readied himself to exit.

"I forgive you," the operative said.

Cohen spun around wide eyed in horror, knife at the ready. But the body he'd laid down remained at rest, staring endlessly into nothing. His eyes had captured that final moment of fear, when he realised with unequivocal certainty that death was upon him.

He wasn't sure why, but Cohen followed the empty stare skywards. No longer was he standing in darkness, but confused to be dwarfed and humbled by the magnificence of a cathedral. A view to conquer egos. He was a mere spec in the nave where walls ascended and arched nearly 150 feet above him. *Surely a feat only divinity could inspire,* as he lowered his gaze, to his surprise a man of passing years stood right in front of him staring back. Not just at him, but into him, exposing him from depths he would not dare to tread. But there was something else, pain, suffering… sadness. Lowering his gaze again, descending further into disbelief at seeing a knife in his hand, impaling the old man's chest. Blood was seeping from the wound and staining his hand.

"I forgive you," the old man said as he reached out gently touching Cohen's cheek, leaving behind a bloodstained finger print.

Reeling from the touch he found himself in sudden darkness once again, but for the beam of light coming from the small torch in his hand.

Breathing heavily he desperately searched his pockets for the bottle of pills. Finding them, he tore off the lid with equal desperation and knocked back the bottle. It was empty. He clenched his hand to stop it from shaking and closed his eyes tightly to focus on calming his breathing.

He knew he didn't have long before they noticed the operative was out of position. *Breathe in for four, out for four.* Sliding the remote back into his pocket, Cohen removed the high-vis vest, collected the helmet, readying himself at the door, as ready as he could be. He shined the torch beam across his face, not looking directly into the light, but enough to adjust his eyes to it.

Before he could open the door, a flurry of bullets began bursting through, splintering holes, showering him in debris. Cohen dropped to the floor behind the dead operative and pulled his body onto its side, using it as a shield. He could feel the thud of the corpse absorbing the projectiles. After the short flurry the shooting abated, it was quiet.

He could hear muffled voices communicating, preparing to move in. Cohen stood, picking up the dead operative… and then dropped him.

Hearing the sound of a body slumping to the floor, one of the operatives outside made an approach, carefully turning the handle he slowly opened the door. Cohen pressed the remote in his pocket, activating the personal alarm he'd positioned on the small table outside when pretending to bang his knee into a table.

The open space of the villa filled with a deafening and constant high pitched alarm, bright pulses of intermittent light rapidly strobed, blinding and disorientating the operatives. Cohen yanked the door, the agent's hand on the other side was pulled forward along with him. He slammed the motorcycle helmet down onto the operatives head nestling it inside and spun it 180 degrees, snapping his neck before pushing him back the way he came. The body fell into the third operative, only obscuring his aim for a split second. There was just enough time for Cohen to move in. He sliced the assailant's wrist as he raised to take aim and drive the blade under his chin, he was dead before he could feel the pain of either.

A shot rang out, Cohen's shoulder lurched forward and down. He instinctively rotated throwing the blade up and back to follow the trajectory of the force that hit him. The blade ricocheted off from the balustrade causing the shooter to flinch. Fighting against the disorientation the shooter reacquired her target and took aim, But Cohen was quick to follow the throw with a shot from his silenced pistol, he didn't miss.

A second shooter appeared on the upper level from the stairwell behind her, letting off several wild shots, one smashing the strobing light.

It was chaotic cover fire more than anything, but stray bullets were as deadly as aimed ones. However, it gave him the time he needed to pull his teammate to relative safety and reassess his situation.

Cohen took cover beneath the walkway, keeping his back to the wall he followed its protection the length of the room, painting a trail of blood behind him.

It was still once more, moonlight outlining bodies that decorated the cold affluence. He closed his eyes, listening. On the walkway above the sound of the female operative's breath, a slowing wheeze, clinging to life that was seconds away from beyond her grasp, then silence. Her partner slid a fresh clip into the gun. Beyond that the faint muffles of feet shuffled on the floor above, there were two sets.

It was a tapping sound, like that of a water droplet that saw him open his eyes and look to the floor beside him. Blood dripped steadily from his fingers from the wound to his shoulder. Reaching under the jacket he felt the wound, the bullet was still in there.

He scanned the room for something to try and make good of his situation, unable to take a shot without compromising his position, however a reflection in the window gave him the position of the shooter above him.

Using the wall for partial cover, the operative tactically positioned himself so that anyone entering from the stairwell had no chance. Back up was probably already on the way, all he had to do was wait. Suddenly there was a sharp sting, almost like a small electric shock as he felt a cold blade draw across his neck. Cohen had climbed to the upper level, appearing like a wraith from the shadows behind him before slitting his neck.

CHAPTER 17

FATHER MICHAEL

The harsh glare of fluorescent lights in the canteen rippled rhythmically across the surface of the coffee hypnotising Phillipé into a tired haze. It was his first time experiencing jet lag and his brilliant brain was even too spent to comprehend despite travelling for twenty hours, it wasn't yet tomorrow but still the day before.

Too exhausted to move a muscle, his gaze found Father Michael sitting on the adjacent bench; also staring idly at a coffee. He too was in a paralysed exhaustive state and caught Phillipé's gaze. Finding their deflated images perfectly mirroring one another amusing, they began to chuckle. Its contagion escalated, each fuelling the next into a persistent giggle, finally erupting into fits of laughter.

Unaware they were no longer alone, Dr Sarah Carden, director of the observatory, entered the canteen only moments earlier. It was quite a sight seeing the ageing priest and young candidate in uncontrollable laughter, revealing a connection that transcended their age.

"Well, isn't this a sight to behold," she said.

Her strong, sweet Texan accent, alerting them to her presence cut the laughter dead.

"Dr Carden," Father Michael said, stifling his laughter and respectfully standing.

His smile was part greeting, part hangover from the impromptu humour.

Phillipé was quick to follow suit and stood to greet Dr Carden, although his smile had vanished and shyness was suddenly very apparent.

"And you must be Phillipé?" she asked, giving a hardy Texan hand-shake. "Howdy,"

he nodded and pursed his lips with an awkward smile. *Now he's quiet,* Father Michael thought.

Dr Carden was a petite woman, which looked exaggerated against Phillipé's height. Straight blonde hair that hung to her lower back and almond eyes that tilted when she smiled, Phillipé was quite taken. He thought she looked just like a real life manga fairy from one of his comics, minus the wings.

"It's so nice to finally meet you," she continued. "We'll make sure you have the best stay with us. And don't you worry, summer camp might be a day ahead, but I'll see to it that you don't miss a thing. I'm even inclined to say you might see a little more, bit of a VIP package."

She winked. Phillipé continued to smile and nod, while his cheeks flushed with red.

"Sorry," Father Michael said.

Allowing Phillipé some much wanted relief from the attention.

"That was probably not the greeting you were expecting."

"Oh shoot, we're used to it up here. We like to say you got a bit of the mountain madness."

Michael and Phillipé passed an inquisitive look to one another. Their adorable double act timing was as if they'd known each other for years.

"A combination of jet lag and low oxygen," she continued. "It's a little like being drunk. Most of the time people just get a fit of the giggles, but people have been known to hallucinate."

Michael's eyes widened with interest, Phillipé's frowned with concern.

"Anyhoo, first things first," Dr Carden continued. "I wanted to apologise for bringing you all the way up here and not dropping you off at base camp, but I needed Father Michael to sign off on some urgent paperwork, just to make it all official. However, I did take the liberty of setting you both up in your very own pods. So for tonight, you'll be staying with me and the crew on-site."

Excited by the prospect, Phillipé smiled youthfully at Father Michael. Dr Carden then gestured for them to follow her.

"Let's get you boys settled in."

As they ascended the stairs to the upper platform, Dr Carden noticed that Michael looked a little pale.

"How are you adjusting to the altitude?" she asked with genuine concern. "We're at an elevation of over ten-thousand feet here, so it can be a little tricky if you haven't had a chance to acclimatise."

"I'm okay," Father Michael said.

But by the time they reached the upper platform, his breathing was becoming increasingly heavy.

"There's a small cylinder of oxygen in your pod. You don't have to take it," she said not wanting to insult him, "but, I'd highly recommend you do. You can thank me in the morning."

Father Michael humbly nodded his appreciation. The altitude *was* a lot tougher than he had expected.

After showing Phillipé to his pod, Dr Carden showed Micheal to his quarters, which was situated on the adjacent platform. He was a little taken aback upon seeing the interior. It was how he imagined solitary confinement might look in a prison, and certainly not one for the claustrophobic. A narrow 2x3 room with a slither of a bed and a miniature basin and mirror, there was barely enough room for one. And yet, Dr Carden closed the pod door behind her when they entered.

Once hidden from the eyes of the world, she threw her arms around him and squeezed him tightly.

"It's so good to see you," she said.

Affectionately resting her head on his chest, as one would imagine a loving daughter to a father. She pulled away suddenly, having inadvertently heard his wheezing chest and the need to expand his lungs to their full capacity. Sitting him on the suspended canvas bed, she pulled out a small canister of oxygen from underneath. She then placed the mask over Father Michael's face and he breathed deeply, its affect and relief were immediate.

"Thank you," he said, looking at her with an affection he wasn't able to do until now. "You haven't changed a bit."

"A little older maybe, a little more jaded," she replied, unable to stop smiling, but there was truth in the statement.

She took a seat on the bed next to him.

"Sorry, I know it's not much," she said, looking around the pod. "But I thought it was best you were close."

"It's fine," he insisted.

Michael didn't care about the pod, he was just happy to see her.

"Mom said she saw you at the memorial."

"Yes. She looked well. Don't worry, she's a strong woman."

"She's doing better now, but losing uncle Frankie was hard on her. Of course it was hard on all of us, but, well, you know…"

"Uncle Frankie," Michael chuckled, "it always sounds so strange when I hear that."

"He hated it," she said.

"No, actually, He loved it. And you. There wasn't anyone else in the world he trusted more. Why else would I be here?"

"About that…"

Sarah's expression suddenly became grave.

"What is it?"

"The priest the Vatican sent, Father Trentini. What do you know about him?"

"Nothing. He was a recommendation from Cardinal Oorloff. Why do you ask?"

"I don't know, I just don't get a good feeling about him. Well I didn't, then I did, but now I definitely don't."

Even though Father Michael knew he was tired, he wasn't sure anybody would have been able to follow that thought process.

"Heinrich, one of the workers is missing," she continued. "Last I saw, he was driving Father Trentini back to base. He was supposed to bring the camp up this morning, but never showed. His truck is still there, but no sign of Heinrich. And he's not the walkabout type."

"But why would you think…"

"There's more," she interrupted. "Earlier, after the summer camp left the site, I was going through entry logs. Heinrich's card was used to gain access to several of the pods. I went to look and they'd been turned over. Whoever it was, was looking for something."

"Did they find it?"

"No, it's safe," she replied. "But are we?"

"I need to find out what the prophesy says."

Father Michael's response didn't do anything to placate Sarah's feelings, but she understood why. Jumping with a fright as the pod slowly began to open, she only let out a sigh of relief upon seeing Phillipé's face appear at the door.

"Oh my, Phillipé, you gave me such a fright!"

Not used to keeping such obscure secrets, her behaviour seemed glaringly guilty. Phillipé remained silent, which wasn't unusual to Sarah, but Father Michael could tell something was wrong. He wasn't just quiet, he was scared. The door opened further, revealing a knife pressed to the boy's throat, and further still to show the hand that wielded it; Father Trentini. He was pressing the point of the blade under Phillipé's as yet undefined jaw, with a force that was causing blood to trickle down his collar.

Trentini threw the boy inside the narrow, over-occupied space, and he fell to the floor. Instinctively reacting to help him, Michael received a hard stamp to the leg, causing him to reel back in pain.

"Hey!" Sarah shouted as she stood to confront their assailant.

But no sooner was she on her feet when the back of Trentini's hand struck her with a force that sent her slamming into the wall, hitting her head with a thud. Phillipé looked up from the floor with a scared, but venomous stare.

"You want to be a hero?" Trentini said to the boy. "Don't worry, you'll get your chance."

No longer donning the dark robes of a priest, but of a covert military operative, he sheathed his knife in a vertical chest harness before taking out his sidearm, pointing it nonchalantly inches from Sarah's face.

"I'm afraid we haven't had the pleasure," he said to Father Michael. "It is thee infamous Father Michael isn't it? The man who once raised his hand against the Holy Father."

The shocking revelation saw Dr Carden and Phillipé look at Michael with disbelief.

"He's not my Holy Father," Michael said nursing his leg. "Luciferian!"

Forcing a manic laugh, Trentini got intimidatingly close to Michael's face.

"Oh, but he is," he said.

When Michael didn't flinch, he eventually pulled back.

"Look at you," he said, his face contorting with disgust. "Blinded by your righteousness."

"You won't get away with this!" Sarah said.

"Oh really? I wonder what gives you such confidence? Your dead colleague? The gun in your face? This is an international observatory, Dr Carden. A weapons free zone at the top of a mountain. I could shoot you and every single person in this facility, and still be out of state before anyone even knows you're dead. How's the face? Feeling confident?"

Sarah submitted her gaze to the floor.

"Now, if you're done with your Nancy Drew bullshit. Where is it?"

Sarah remained defiantly quiet. Trentini shook his head in disappointment, as if in response to a child causing a minor offence.

"I blame the media. Film, television, shit like that. People have become so overexposed to violence, they're numb to its affect. I see it more and more nowadays. Immune to accept reality, like you're waiting for someone to burst through the doors at the last minute and save you."

Pulling the knife once more from its sheath, Trentini admired the blade.

"You might be the doctor, but I've always found a shock to the system is the most efficient way of instilling a much needed sense of reality. Do you concur?" he said.

Gesturing the knife towards Phillipé, he watched Dr Carden as she squirmed. He then moved the knife back towards Father Michael. When a subtle nuance of tension revealed itself, he quickly pressed the length of the blade across the priest's throat.

"No!" Sarah blurted instinctively.

Trentini smiled. *This was too easy.*

"I can show you where it is," she said. "Please, don't."

But Trentini just continued to watch his knife as it pushed into the soft, loosened skin on Father Michael's neck. It was as if in his fascination he pretended not to hear her, or that stopping wouldn't give him the satisfaction he was looking for. The sharp bite of the skin breaking was like an electrical current causing a sharp inhale, but he didn't dare move any more than that.

"Please!" she begged.

Finally he stopped.

"You see, we can all play to the drama Dr Carden. But in the real world, that just gets you killed. Now I'm going to ask you one more time. But before you answer, understand this. I swear to *your* god, I will kill every person in this building if you fucking lie to me. Now, where is it?"

There was a darkness in Trentini's eyes that sent a shiver into Sarah's soul. She was still trying to come to terms with the idea that her friend and colleague, Heinrich, was dead, and this was all really happening.

It was in this exact moment she realised that she had never truly believed her uncle was killed as part of some wider conspiracy, that he was assassinated by an organisation from inside the church. As devastated as she was, she wasn't about to disrespect his memory and her own mourning by filling her head with fantastical ideas.

She believed that her Uncle Frankie did stumble upon a secret. Given the number of stories that had emerged from the church in recent years, that part wasn't really a surprise. But if the narrative surrounding his death was true, then whatever he sent had implications beyond anything she could comprehend. What she did know, or at least believed, was that if she did nothing, the cold killer stood in front of her would hold to his word, and more people would die.

"I can take you to it," she said.

"Tell me where it is, then we'll go together," Trentini replied.

"The main floor of the LBT. On the upper platform there's a a lock-box, combination 9297. Inside there's a laptop case."

"You," he said to Phillipé, "on your feet."

"I told you where it is," Sarah pleaded. "Please, I'll take you, just let them stay here."

Grabbing Phillipé by the scruff Trentini dragged him to his feet.

"Don't worry, we're all going. Now, show me your hands," he said to Phillipé.

The boy held out his hands palms down. Trentini then flipped over the left hand and gently ran the edge of the blade across his wrist. Phillipé winced as a vein nicked and a thin fountain of blood shot out hitting the ceiling. He quickly grabbed his wrist with the other hand and applied pressure.

"What the hell are you doing?" Michael demanded.

"He's got that look," Trentini said. "Like he wants to do something stupid, you know, be a hero."

Phillipé avoided his stare, but Trentini noticed a fleeting glance toward Dr Carden.

"I think it might be because he's got a little thing for our Dr Carden here."

Phillipé's cheeks flushed red. Trentini laughed.

"Yeah, that's it. He likes the doc. Well Romeo, now you've got something to do with your hands. Look at me the wrong way again and it'll take more than a bit of pressure to stop the bleeding."

He turned to Dr Carden and smiled.

"Well, what are you waiting for?"

Sarah wasn't sure what he meant by this.

"Lead the way!" Trentini demanded.

Dr Carden began to slowly guide the group through the facility, being sure to take a route least used at such a late hour. There weren't as many personnel at this time and the building became almost silent, but for the eerie creaking of contracting metal as the cool night set in.

But somewhere in the silence was a hive of activity, scientists collaborating, collecting and compiling, because these were also the functioning hours of the LBT, of Lucifer.

Despite Phillipé's hand becoming increasingly wet with blood and the barrel of a gun being sporadically thrust into the base of his spine, when they eventually arrived at the main floor, for just a few moments, he managed to forget the ordeal.

Looking up, mouth adrift, he was in awe. *It was beautiful!* he thought. Although not entirely having a frame of reference, he felt as though this was his Everest.

He couldn't remember a time when he wasn't looking at the stars. Staying up until the early hours in the back yard with his Dad, wrapped in blankets. His mum would sometimes bring them a warm drink and sit with them, although she never looked at the stars, instead, her wonder was him.

Phillipé was just four when his parents bought him his first telescope, and nine by the time he'd constructed his own. Dreaming that one day he would be looking through the most powerful telescopes in the world. Only ten years later he couldn't have imagined the bizarre circumstances that would culminate to bringing it to fruition, but here he finally was.

An excruciating sound overpowered Phillipé's hearing, replacing it with a disorientating ringing that bordered being painful. He was shoved forward. Everything was moving in slow motion, and while Dr Carden was screaming at him, he couldn't make out what she was saying. He could only think that she reminded him of Kanade Tachibana, a character from his manga comics, the way she would scream out as she was about to attack. *Was that what was happening?* he thought. *Is she going to attack me?* As she got closer, he had the sensation of falling.

It was like a dream, where he would wake just before hitting the ground; but it felt like he'd been falling for a long time now. Finally, when he hit the floor, his hearing returned with a thump and the world around him began moving again at a normal speed. He wasn't sure how he'd fallen or why Dr Carden had jumped on him, or why she was bleeding all over him.

"Get help!" she screamed with tears in her eyes.

"You're hurt," he said, "You're bleeding!"

Finally, he had spoken to her.

"You're going to be okay, Phillipé!"

Father Michael knelt and held onto the boy's hand. As Phillipé looked back at him, he caught a glimpse of someone else on the floor. It was Trentini. He was lying face down with his eyes open, gun still in hand, and a small trickle of blood dripping from the corner of his mouth. He was dead. Phillipé's eyes continued beyond the false priest and rose up beyond the scope he'd been waiting his life to see, all the way to the opening in the observatory roof where the Large Binocular Telescope could explore the furthest reaches of space. And there in perfect formation was a moon cloaked in blood.

He looked back at Dr Carden, her eyes blazing a teary blue.

"Kanade Tachibana," he said, "Angel."

And closed his eyes.

CHAPTER 18

7147 GINA

On the roof outside, 7147 was regaining consciousness aided by the sound of gunshots piercing the night. Still disorientated, she could feel the rifle in her hand and instinctively manoeuvred to press her eye to the scope. However, the shattered lens quickly brought her into the here and now, and with it, a searing pain covered the left side of her face. *He must have thought I was dead,* she thought.

Looking at the rifle she knew she was lucky not to be, realising the faulty tac-laser Uri mounted onto the weapon must have not only given away their position and got him killed, but inadvertently saved her life.

The laser penetrated the scope causing a natural recoil from the pain as it came into contact with her eye, a split second before the scope exploded. The perfectly fired bulled exploded out of the lens slicing a wound across her cheek and removing the upper section of her left ear. The laser also caused its own damage, leaving her with 20% vision in her left eye. The damage was just superficial and her sight would return in the next day or two, or so she hoped.

A flurry of shots pulled her attention to the compound which was now somehow in complete darkness, save for a strobing light emanating from inside. The shooting stopped and the strobing light soon disappeared.

She needed to get herself back in the game, but her weapon was next to useless with no scope, and it was too dark to take the shot raw using her weaker eye. The thought of going close quarters entered her mind, but not long enough to be a serious consideration. If she was going to kill the Tier-1A assassin then distance would be her only friend. *Uri,* she thought. His weapon would still be on the roof. With his scope she could still make the shot. Leaving her rifle she grabbed the kit bag and quickly made her way down to the street.

Quick and painless was what she thought as she studied the wound on the back of Uri's neck.

"I don't want to be that person Uri, but, I did tell you to choose a different spot," She said while taking up a prone position and saddling right next to his corpse. "Still, saved me a job."

Picking up the rifle she scoped with her good eye. The trigger sat uncomfortably under her right index finger and she could feel the lower left half of her face awash with the blood still seeping from her wounds. She wiped the excess blood on the back of her hand and focused.

"Nice Scope," she said as she surveyed the property.

A muzzle flash from a single shot lit up a window on the third floor. Her crosshair swiftly moved towards it, but there was nothing to see. A few minutes went by before another shot was heard. She had no way of knowing, but thought that whatever was happening was drawing to a close.

Gunfights were often like the antithesis of a classical movement, with the crescendo always being at the beginning. Although there is sometimes a spectacular finale, it's often a frenzied solo going out in a blaze of glory.

Anticipating the target's exit, she adjusted her scope towards the main entrance when the most disturbing guttural scream she'd ever heard rose into the night. It triggered a memory that transported her back to a time she thought was long forgotten, words imparted by her uncle; her honorary uncle.

"The first thing you must kill as an assassin is your conscience. Either you kill it, or the day will come when it will kill you." Lessons for an eight-year-old girl.

Not so much a mantra but a reminder that a moment's hesitation caused by a conflict of conscience was sometimes all that stood between life and death.

She didn't understand at the time, but it was a lesson in checks and balances, not of government but of the mind. It was about the lines we were willing to cross and the reasons we crossed them.

The family that helped raise her, presented her with a gift. The most beautiful, precious and tiny rabbit she'd ever seen. She was still fairly small herself for an eight-year-old, but was able to hold the rabbit easily in two hands. It had fluffy wispy brown and white hair, ears that drooped either side of its cute face, framing it as it looked up at her with those large brown eyes. They said it was called a mini lop, but she didn't care, she just thought he looked like a real-life Disney cartoon, and he was all hers.

In time, she would come to learn that the family never did anything without attaching a life lesson to it. This was about learning to be responsible for something more than just herself. So every morning she rose with the dawn and cleaned out the hutch, laid fresh food and bedding and all before breakfast. If she didn't, then no one else would and the rabbit, which was entirely her responsibility, would die.

A week or so passed and another gift was presented, she had never known generosity like it. This one was a small box wrapped with a bow. Inside she found a four inch locking blade with a matt-black handle and two pearlescent spots. It was received with almost the same enthusiasm as the rabbit; unbound gratitude. It wasn't an unusual gift for a family that had not forgotten how to live from the land, foraging, tracking, surviving. Its presentation suggested acceptance, as well as exciting lessons to come, but for the first one… Kill the rabbit. *A lesson in cruelty,* she thought. But this was about attachment, weakness, vulnerability, things used to bend your will. Remarkably, even at her young age, she had understood that and the value in what was being taught.

It was with a heavy heart she extended the blade for the first time. It had that new stiffness to it, but she managed to lock it into place without cutting herself. It was clear that great care had been taken in selecting the knife, it sat perfectly in her small hand allowing authority over the object.

The family gathered to watch as if proudly witnessing a right of passage. Without hesitation she opened the door to the hutch. Having created a strong bond in a short amount of time, the rabbit enthusiastically bound towards her. She lifted it, cradling him in one arm while holding the extended blade in the other and turned to face her brothers, sisters, aunts and uncles, all honorary.

"This is Angel," she said. "She's family now." Raising the blade she gestured towards all who watched. "Anyone who tries to hurt my family… I'll kill them."

Uncle smiled as he watched the little girl put Angel back into the hutch. The lesson had been less for her and more about who she was, and more importantly about who she would become.

The guttural scream 7147 heard that night sent a chill down her spine, which was not an easy thing to do. Her conscience was still very much alive. The compound sat in a still darkness with no sign of movement for several minutes.

She trained her gun on the main entrance and waited. Any second now… Another minute went by before she began to get restless. *If he was still alive he should have left by now.* The faint sound of sirens took her away from her scope momentarily as she listened, trying to estimate how long she had. Just then, something in the dark caught her eye, moving slowly away from the compound. She adjusted the scope accordingly.

"It's him!"

A rush of adrenalin triggered a wave of goosebumps as she focused with her weaker side. The boy he was carrying didn't appear to be conscious, a dead weight draped between his arms.

This was it, a slow moving target in an open field of view. She exhaled, pressing her eye against the scope, her finger sliding from the side of the rifle to the trigger. The cross-hair from the scope pinpointed the upper centre of the targets back, aiming for his heart. The bullet would almost certainly take out the kid at the same time, she was counting on it. The pressure under her finger built as the trigger began to retreat, suddenly pausing to reverse her actions.

"What the hell!" she said removing her eye from the scope.

Someone had shone a light onto the target, but she was unable to see where the source was originating from. Returning to the scope to confirm what she was seeing, there it was, a definite light.

"Where's it coming from?" she agitated.

It was a pointless task to aimlessly scope when there was nowhere to check. The area was in darkness, the source would have been obvious. 7147 wanted to believe that Uri's rifle might have been fitted with some sort of new thermal imaging scope, or that the laser had not only damaged the left eye, but somehow affected the vision in both. Because what she was seeing she couldn't bring herself to believe.

It was too faint to see with the naked eye at that range, but through the high powered sight, a faint glow surrounded the target, appearing as wisps of white smoke. The only reason she could reconcile what was unfolding was the boy who remained shrouded in darkness.

Whatever it was wouldn't be there for much longer, she thought. 7147 slowed her breath and re-took aim. Once more she felt the trigger give as she began applying pressure. The target stopped, she wasn't going to get a better opportunity than this. Just as she was about to apply the final squeeze, he turned around.

With the boy's dead weight draped across his arms he stared up into the night sky, staring at... *Me?*, she realised.

"But that's impossible. What the hell is he looking at?"

All she had to do was pull the trigger and the Tier-1A trophy was in the bag. Again she caressed the trigger, but without conviction, watching him watch her, the unexplainable light, the boy, her mission, the contract, her cover... she finally let go of the rifle.

As if somehow connected to her choice the target turned around and disappeared into the night.

CHAPTER 19

COHEN

Josh didn't look much like the innocent, bright happy boy in his picture. He was more like a fallen soldier on the field of battle, the type that are left to die slowly, bleeding out from their wounds. Cohen didn't know how much blood was left inside his frail body, but he knew he didn't have long.

Cohen felt the burn of lactic acid in his thighs as he ascended the road's incline. The strength and fitness he once had was now purely muscle memory, and that had been all but exhausted at the compound.

As he looked at the emaciated boy, his pulse barely registering, his own heart was pounding with a relentless force. It wasn't giving up on him, but driving him, as if beating for the both of them.

He wondered how he was still alive, knowing he shouldn't have been. *Why didn't they take the shot?* he thought. It didn't make any sense. While he couldn't see the operative, he knew they were there. It was as if he could feel the target on him. *Why didn't they shoot?* he perplexed again when something in the dark caught his eye, distracting him as he walked.

What he saw were only shadows on the building, but there was something ominous about them, like a living thing, watching him, following him, or perhaps it was just the boy.

Josh's eyes started to roll back in his head, in a desperate moment of panic Cohen shook the boy with a force that lacked experience of youth. Thankfully a groan offered relief, the boy was still with him.

Cohen widened his gait with concerned effort pulling Josh close to his chest.

"Stay with me kid, " he said to the soldier.

Was this what redemption looked like? he thought as fear and desperation built inside of him, a helplessness he was unfit to understand, because for the first time in as long as he could remember, his thoughts weren't for him.

"Joshua," he said, softening the harshness of his tone. "Open your eyes."

The boy's eyes twitched as if they were blinking while still shut and then slowly opened.

"Hey," Cohen said, smiling.

At least he hoped it was a smile and not a weird grimace, it had been that long he couldn't be sure. He only knew that it didn't feel altogether comfortable.

"I'm going to take you home now, okay?"

Josh looked up at him unaware of what was going on. Only that the man holding him was bleeding from his shoulder smelling of burnt gunpowder and whisky. The boy closed his eyes again.

"I need you to keep your eyes open Josh, okay?"

He looked up again.

"Just for a little while. Can you do that?"

Josh nodded sluggishly, bringing a second consecutive smile that suddenly vanished from his face at the sound of a car engine.

Headlights appeared out of the dark from the road to his left approaching at speed. Cohen dropped to one knee taking Josh's weight onto his leg as he cradled him with one arm. Cohen's right hand reached inside his jacket and rested upon the holstered weapon. The vehicle narrowed its distance without showing any signs of slowing down. Cohen's fingers curled a soft grip around the handle. With the kid in his arms he knew there was no point in running; the car would be on them in a matter of seconds. Just as he was about to pull the weapon, he locked eyes with the driver. It was Viktor.

Skidding to a stop only yards in front of Cohen, Viktor leapt out of the car. For a big guy he moved with an agility and speed that was revealing. Opening the rear passenger door he carefully helped lay Josh across the back seat, noticing the bullet hole in Cohen's shoulder.

"Jesus! What have they done to him?" Viktor said looking at the boy.

"He hasn't got long," Cohen replied. "Did you manage to find a doctor?"

"He's waiting for us."

Before the car pulled away, Cohen made sure Josh was secure and as comfortable as he could be under the circumstances. He stared silently from the window, eyeing the shadows on the building with an ominous curiosity. Considering the symptoms of his withdrawal he wondered if his eyes were deceiving, but just as the car sped up he caught sight of a shadow that wasn't. Something was staring back at him.

"What is it?" Viktor said looking in the rear-view mirror to see it they were being followed.

"Nothing," Cohen lied. "We need to hurry!"

"You're hit," Viktor said keeping his eyes on the road, "how bad?"

Cohen looked at his shoulder, forgetting for a moment he'd been shot, remembering only helped register the pain.

"It's not deep."

"Good, the doc can take it out after he sees to the boy. How's he holding up back there?"

Cohen turned in his seat to check, only now noticing his hands were coated in blood. He pulled short from touching the boy with them, apart from his fingers to check for a pulse.

He watched him for a short while, the way a father might reflect over their child as they sleep. Viktor stole a pondering glance at Cohen while his attention was on the boy.

The two men had witnessed enough death to last several lifetimes, numbed to its affect on the human condition. Overexposed to a side of the world that ripped and tore at your soul at every opportunity it got until there was nothing left… or so you thought. But the death of a child brought an accumulation of suffering, from all that had passed before, from everything you thought you'd escaped. It was as if humanity clung to you, like something greater than your life depended upon it, something unseen. Cohen's accumulation was a count not worth thinking about, only that if the boy died, Viktor wasn't sure it would be a rage he would ever be able to escape.

As Viktor skilfully navigated the streets, Cohen scowled a thousand-yard stare out of the windscreen, unable to see anything but his most recent memories, breathing with a heavy venomous contempt as if still there.

After dispatching the operative on the upper walkway, Cohen made his ascent to the second floor, instinct causing him to pause before reaching the end of the first flight. He closed his eyes and listened trying to gauge a picture of what couldn't be seen.

A subtle and constant low hum, the type generated by electrical equipment or a motor, caused subtle vibrations in the wall. Movement from an individual, not at all stealth like, and something else, much closer. Raising his silenced pistol to the partitioned wall between the first and second flight, Cohen fired three times, clack, clack, clack. The sixth operative who laid in wait on the opposite side of the partition fell lifeless to the floor, landing at his feet. Clack, clack. A double tap to the head to be certain. The quickening breath whistling through the man's nasal passage had given his position away.

Cohen turned the corner sharply, his gun in perfect unison and climbed the final few steps. In front of him was a short corridor, a set of double doors leading to the bedroom and a chair with a glossy magazine on its seat, but nowhere for anyone to conceal themselves.

He made a cautious approach to the side of the bedroom door, keeping his body away from the centre, whoever was inside was anticipating him. Leaning over he clicked the handle and, expecting another showering of bullets, let the door swing ajar while taking cover against the wall. But there were no bullets, just an unfiltered buzz and hum of electrical equipment.

Raising his gun he entered at speed, his sight swiftly acquiring a target in a white medical coat with his back to Cohen.

"You're wasting your time," the man said.

Cohen's gun held on the target, locked in place while his eyes scanned the room. A series of medical equipment had transformed the space into a temporary hospital. The doctor, unconcerned with Cohen's presence didn't flinch from his duties, continuing to shine a torch into the boy's unresponsive eyes.

"You're quite fortunate," the doctor said, turning to face Cohen for the first time. "If the equipment hadn't had its own battery reserve, your antics in cutting the power could have killed the boy."

Cohen had to concede this was not what he expected. Blocking out whatever the doctor was saying, he quickly tried reassessing the situation. The low hum he could feel had been coming from the medical equipment that he could only assume was monitoring the boy's vitals, alongside an interconnection of tubes, drips, blood bags and a refrigeration unit. At its centre was an emaciated, small, skinny boy almost unrecognisable from his picture.

Cohen's aim remained locked in place as he tried to make sense of everything. The refrigeration unit housed blood bags, one almost full attached to the tubes carrying it to or from the child. Judging by its appearance, it looked to Cohen like a transfusion, having seen and even helped to administer similar procedures in a field hospital.

"If you attempt to move him he'll die," the doctor said smugly as if reading Cohen's thoughts. He showed no signs of fear at his presence, or the fact he was aiming a weapon at his face.

"Which sort of defeats the object of you saving him I would imagine."

The doctor's self assured arrogance was difficult for Cohen to bear, but not reason enough to shoot him, satisfying though it may be.

The doctor continued attending to the boy as if the intruder wasn't there. Cohen watched carefully as he collected a new bag from the cabinet and proceeded to take down the full one, his gun stalking every movement. He marked the label and hung the bag inside the refrigeration unit alongside others.

The boy's body twitched several times distracting Cohen's attention. As the doctor refrigerated the blood bag, Cohen didn't notice him remove another. The contents of which had a darker tone compared to the usual claret of blood, as if it had been tainted. He then poured a small amount into a beaker

Cohen's eyes continued tracing the tubes running from the boy's arm to the bag, and the slow drip of blood that began collecting in it. His entire body began to surge with a rage as his eyes desperately searched for the tube that was supposed to carry the blood back into his body... but it wasn't there. The rage was a preemptive instinct of what his eyes were only waiting to confirm, the boy's blood was being drained.

The doctor was probably right, if he tried to move the boy he could die, but if he didn't, he definitely would. A faint sound of sirens in the distance meant a decision had to be made. Cohen's only dilemma now was that he didn't want to shoot the doctor. What he wanted was more time, he wanted this man to die slowly, painfully, but the closing sirens were stealing that opportunity. As Cohen turned his attention to the doctor he caught sight of him consuming the last contents of whatever was in the beaker.

The doctor closed his eyes allowing a euphoric shudder to run the length of his body, before opening them, looking directly back at Cohen. His eyes had suddenly become sinister and dark, an unnatural black. Without warning he flew at Cohen like a rabid animal, gnarling with a bloodstained mouth and scream to match.

With his gun being locked into place ever since entering the room, Cohen calmly pulled the trigger. The bullet clearly struck the doctor centre chest, but did nothing to thwart the attack. He didn't have time to get off a second round before the doctor slammed into him with the force of a truck, sweeping him off his feet and sending him hurtling backwards until finally slamming into the wall. Landing in a heap on the floor, the gun fell beyond Cohen's reach.

The doctor growled, baring and gnashing his teeth as he leapt into the air landing on top of Cohen who could only jam his forearm into his neck to stop him from biting into his flesh. Cohen didn't have time to consider the man's impossible strength or the fact it was taking all of his to stop him restructuring his face.

He managed to pull his knife from his boot and with a satisfying force plunged it into the doctor's side. He expected weakness to start taking hold but the only fatigue was his own arm giving way as the gnashing teeth inched ever closer with no less force.

Removing the knife he slammed it in again and again and again, it was having an affect, but not quickly enough. In a last ditch attempt, Cohen dropped the blade and slammed his fist inside the hole he'd created, grabbing a fist full of intestines, he yanked. The guttural scream that came out of the doctor didn't sound possible for a human to make.

Suddenly, the doors to the bar flew open as Viktor burst through, swiping a table out of his path to clear a route. Cohen was close behind with Joshua cradled in his arms.

"In the back!" Viktor urged.

The large space under a sallow glow of lighting was mainly used for storage; bottle crates, beer kegs, chairs and tables all piled and stacked. A small area had been cleared and a few tables pushed together to form a make-shift workspace.

The doctor, Honza, was waiting for them along with Dida, Viktor's wife, a small, rotund powerful looking woman. There was no white coat to identify the doctor, just a collarless powder blue shirt, beige khaki's and Viktor's word.

As soon as Dida saw the state of the child, she flew past her husband and took Joshua from Cohen's arms, never giving him a second glance. His part was done for now, but he felt less than helpless as she walked away with the child, wondering if he'd failed him. Dida laid Josh across the tables that waited his arrival and Honza sprang into action. He checked the boy's vitals while going through the bloodstained medical notes Cohen retrieved from the compound. Removing a syringe and several vials from a small medical pouch, the doctor selected one and gave the boy a shot.

"Where's the blood?" he snapped with impatient urgency.

Cohen slid a canvas bag from his shoulder and handed it to Dida. The doctor removed several blood bags, noting the various labels marked with different blood types.

"What's this?" he said. "These are all different! What are you trying to do? Kill him?"

For the sake of the boy Cohen gritted his teeth. Viktor stood back observing the situation, particularly his old friend, quietly growing with concern. Honza soon found what he was looking for and laid one of the bags to the side.

"Imbecile," he muttered under his breath.

Viktor's frame slightly gave as if expecting an inevitable reaction. But to his surprise Cohen's attention stayed with Joshua, small and vulnerable. His skin was turning a sickly yellow, which was only being enhanced by the storage lights. His face so sunken and withdrawn it was beginning to reveal the skeletal structure beneath.

In no time at all, Honza and Dida began a feed that would slowly return blood back to Josh's body. Unable to watch any further, Cohen turned away and quietly left the room. This was not what Viktor had been expecting.

He gave it a minute before checking on Cohen, finding him sat at a table in the middle of the bar staring endlessly into space.

"You've got that look," Viktor said trying to inject a lighter tone. "What does it all mean?"

Cohen didn't stir, refusing to look away from whatever thoughts held him. As long as he was around the boy he knew he wouldn't be able to see beyond the suffering, beyond his rage, and he needed to.

Viktor grabbed a couple of glasses and a bottle of Black Label from behind the bar and joined him. Pouring, he slid a glass in front of Cohen. The smell stirred his senses and broke the trance. While it was a more spicy scent than the smokey chocolate he was used to, he still collected the glass and stared at the contents looking for answers, the same way he'd blankly stared into space.

"You're trying to work it all out huh?" Viktor asked, studying his old friend.

Eventually Cohen abandoned his thoughts.

"You ever seen anything like this?"

"I don't even know what this is," Viktor replied. "Honestly, I'm not sure I want to."

"Is that how they managed to operate in your city?" Cohen sniped.

Viktor smiled at the confrontational insult.

"That was an easy target," he replied. "So the saint of all sinners has returned. And where were you for the last few years? The bottom of a bottle? Running away from what you'd become? What you are?"

Cohen immediately regretted his challenge, but didn't give the satisfaction of revealing it.

"And you still haven't faced it have you?" Viktor continued. "No wonder you're such a fucking mess. I could see it the second I laid eyes on you. This was never about the boy, it was a suicide mission. You came here to die."

Cohen's face remained like stone, but Viktor's words had resonated.

"Problem is," he continued, "you're just discovering what everybody else already knows, you're not that easy to kill."

Viktor cradled his whisky and sat forward as if readying to impart knowledge.

"The guys in the unit used to tell stories about you," he continued. "About things they'd seen, but couldn't quite explain. I never wanted to stop them, it seemed to give them something they needed. An idea that they were going into battle with someone touched by the divine. Thing is, when you're on the battlefield, you don't want to be the one standing next to the guy that death passes over. I mean they didn't just believe you cheated death, but were somehow protected from it."

Normally Cohen wouldn't have taken much stock in stories from history he had no way of impacting, but under the circumstances it concerned him greatly.

"And you?" Cohen questioned with uncertainty.

Viktor smiled again, for a moment seeing the young Cohen he met so many years ago.

"I just like the stories," he replied. "But that's all they are right, stories?"

Viktor sat back in his chair studying his old friend as he pained over his thoughts. He savoured a sip of his whisky, as though having earned the right for imparting prevailing wisdom.

"So, you worked it out yet?" he asked.

Cohen's furrowed brow posed the question, *worked out what?*

"There's no mystery surrounding the boy," Viktor continued, "it's just the same shit we've dealt with our entire lives. There are bad people in the world and there are…"

"Worse," Cohen said finishing the sentence.

"Right!" Viktor continued hoping his friend was finally hearing him. "It was never about the boy. That's just how they got you here. Hotel California."

Cohen was finally hearing what his friend had to say.

"Check out any time you want, but you'll never leave," Viktor added.

"We have a problem," Honza interrupted.

In the back, Honza had laid out the blood bags with the labels clearly showing the varied types. Six bags marked as O+(Positive), five AB+(Positive), one O-(Negative), and two separated from the rest that had a distinctly darker colouring, marked with Josh's name alongside B-(Negative).

"I've started the first bag," Honza said, "we can administer the O negative next, but with his levels already so dangerously low even that could be a risk."

There was a brief silence as they waited to hear more.

"We need more blood," Honza added, realising he wasn't speaking with his normal colleagues.

Cohen eyed the B negative label marked with Josh's name.

"What's wrong with these ones?" he said pointing at the separated bags.

"You see the colour?" Honza queried. "That blood isn't pure. It's been mixed with something."

Victor eyed the bag with interest.

"Mixed?" he said. "With what?"

The doctor was hesitant to answer.

"Honza, what's it mixed with?" he pressed

"I don't know, I don't have any way to test it. You said you just needed help with a transfusion, not all of this."

"But you have a theory?" Cohen asked.

"I found a puncture wound on the back of the boy's neck," Honza continued reluctantly. "It suggests a procedure was done on more than one occasion. But unless I can test the blood…"

"What procedure?" Cohen asked.

"I could be struck off for even suggesting…"

"And you were thinking this would lead to a promotion?"

It was a fair point, Honza conceded.

"It's an idea relegated or manipulated in the realms of pure conspiracy. But the colouring of blood, the entry wound on the neck would suggest 'Adrenochrome.'

Viktor and Cohen passed a quiet look between one another.

"I take it from your silence you know what I'm talking about? Honza said. "Well that's disturbing. But it doesn't alter the fact that we need more blood. Which leads me to the next problem."

"I can get more blood," Viktor said. "I have a contact at the hospital."

"I wish it was that simple. The boy has an extremely rare blood type. We were fortunate to have an O negative, his body could assimilate the antigens, but like I said, with his levels so low, even that's a risk."

"How rare?" Viktor asked.

"1%," Cohen replied.

Honza and Viktor looked at Cohen taken aback by his knowledge.

"Yes," Honza said, "but how…"

"He can have my blood," Cohen interjected.

"I don't think you fully understand," Honza said. "Anything other than an exact match at this point will kill him."

Dida had been listening to them squabble incoherently while she attended to Josh. Dabbing his brow and letting him feel the affection and comfort of his hand being held. She hadn't wanted to add confusion to the conversation by giving another opinion. There was more than enough what with her husband's blunt force, the doctor's supreme arrogance and Cohen's aloof ambiguity, she thought the boy would probably die before they reached consensus.

It was obvious to her as it should have been the doctor, that once Cohen had expressed knowledge of the rare blood type, he wouldn't have then suggested giving his own had it not been a match.

She prepared a space adjacent to the boy and moved the apparatus to start a transfusion.

"You're bleeding," Dida said taking Cohen's arm and leading him to the table.

"Wait, what are you doing?" Honza asked. His objection falling on deaf ears.

Her actions silenced the room to spectate as she began cleaning the wound to Cohen's shoulder. Without another word Honza donned his glasses and began inspecting the injury alongside her.

"I will have to remove the bullet before we start," he said, falling in line. "If we are to do the transfusion you understand I won't be able to give you anything for the pain?"

Cohen's attention was on the boy and stayed there, but a gentle nod acknowledged he'd heard the doctor.

Viktor had the next best thing and quickly retrieved a bottle of Blue Label from behind the bar. There couldn't have been a greater gift than the inviting amber-nectar Cohen had craved all day, now within his grasp. As he went to reach for the bottle he realised he held no desire for it, not even for the benefit of numbing the pain, and rejected the vice that only hours earlier had been a necessary function.

Viktor watched on as Cohen removed his belt, folded it over and bit down hard. Reflecting on his conversation in the bar only moments earlier, he realised that Cohen also hadn't taken a drink their either.

The surgical tool penetrated the surface of his skin causing a searing pain that electrified every nerve ending in his body, while Honza did his best to extract the bullet.

"This is barbarism," he said stopping suddenly with frustration

He had never used such basic tools for a difficult surgical procedure.

"What's the problem?" Cohen asked, his teeth clamped onto the belt.

"You should be in a hospital," the doctor exasperated, dropping the surgical tweezers onto the medical tray, "where there are actually instruments and machines designed for this. I'm flying blind here, I could cause tissue damage, nerve damage and without an X-ray…"

"Doc," Cohen said softly.

Once he held the doctor's attention, he turned towards Josh laid out on the table while Honza followed his gaze. Without need for further proof, the doctor could see plainly what he was looking at. The man sat in front of him had clearly already sacrificed so much to rescue the boy, and still he had more to give. And judging from previous scars, this unfortunately wasn't the worst he'd ever endured, maybe not even tonight.

Allaying his fears he picked up the instrument.

Pain was just an attention seeker, Cohen thought as it took hold of him once more. He focused his mind, meditating it away from the suffering to a place he'd created for such occasions. An ethereal forest untouched by the human world, where he could be alone. Where every step sang with the crisp crunch of twigs and leaves under foot, rays of sun that pierced its canopy producing shards of light that played like children of the forest, radiating beauty and colour to everything they touched.

REVELATIONS

Amongst the sounds of insects and birds there was a backdrop of water that trickled from hidden brooks, pooling to a crystal clearing. By the edge of the water a small boulder became his throne in this unspoilt oasis, where he allowed peace to find him, even if only for the briefest of encounters.

As he approached the clearing he could see a small boy sitting on a rock, staring out at the water. It was Josh. Not the sickly boy he'd been charged to rescue, but the bright, happy version he imagined from the picture. The boy looked up at Cohen and smiled before returning his gaze upon the water. Cohen smiled and joined him in looking out, both seeking a temporary sanctuary.

Until now, Cohen couldn't understand why he'd been the one chosen to save the boy. Not by his family, but by something pushing him in a direction. Thoughts that had questioned his sanity now justified an impossible conclusion, they shared the same rare blood. If he couldn't save the boy then no one could.

Honza, with Dida's assistance, removed the bullet from Cohen's shoulder and started feeds for the transfusion. Dida had to coax her stubborn and groggy patient to lay across the tables, even finding him a cushion to lay his head upon. Now all they could do was wait.

CHAPTER 20

FATHER MICHAEL

When words failed, silence filled the air, and it was deafening. Only broken by gentle heartbreaking sobs that slowly and excruciatingly overpowered the quiet.

Allowing observatory personnel to take over, Father Michael delicately coaxed Dr Carden away from Phillipé's body, who was in an inconsolable state of shock, convinced it had all been her fault.

When Trentini struck Dr Carden in the pod, she fell into the wall, inadvertently pressing down the communication button on the radio. Realising what she'd done, she maintained her position to continue holding the button; aiming to relay her situation to the maintenance team.

While she was aware the facility was a weapons free zone, as Trentini confidently pointed out, Texan's weren't. Several of her colleagues, herself included, held carry permits for their vehicles. All she could hope was that they were hearing the unfolding situation over the radio and reacting accordingly.

The maintenance bay had direct access to the car park for the easy transfer of heavy machinery, meaning they'd be able to get to their cars and back with time to spare.

They would be aware there was no lockbox on the LBT platform, and she hoped they'd realise she was playing for time. Even the code was just the passcode to her phone, she just hoped the details made her sound more convincing. All she had to do now was direct Trentini towards the main floor as he basked in certain glory. While being frogmarched on a route of her choosing, she asked,

"What could you possibly expect to achieve from all of this?"

REVELATIONS

Trentini smiled, it wasn't sinister but a genuine response to her question, as if enjoying the naive inquiry of a child.

"Something amusing you?" she said.

He grabbed the back of her jumper and with a yank slammed her into a wall; pushing the barrel of the gun under her chin. Father Michael and Phillipé could only watch on in helpless horror.

"For we wrestle not against flesh and blood," he said inches from her face, "but against principalities, against powers, against the rulers of the darkness of this world, against spiritual wickedness in high places. Did I get that right father?" he said without taking his eyes off Dr Carden.

"I know my scriptures," she said defiantly.

Trentini took the barrel of the gun and pressed it into her cheek, just below the bone causing a searing pain, she cried out.

"You don't believe your scriptures," he said with venom through gritted teeth. "They're just stories to you people. Why else do you think you work in a monument built for his glory? A shrine to the Morning Star? Erected by the Vatican no less. Because you believe? I mean they named it Lucifer for Christ's sake. At what point will you people see a red flag? And you," he said turning to Father Michael. "The pilgrim, a man whose own best friend sent him here to die for a hidden prophesy."

He became giddy.

"I have to admit, I've been kind of anticipating this moment for a while. To see the look on your face when you realise the prophesy isn't even yours… it's ours."

Trentini watched as hope faded in Father Michael's eyes and laughed.

"There it is. Priceless."

Grabbing Dr Carden by the hair, he threw her forward to continue leading the group towards Lucifer.

"I'm curious," she said.

"Jesus, don't you ever shut up?" Trentini said, exasperated.

"When you first saw the telescope," she continued, knowing she was treading a fine line, "what was so interesting about its cooling system?"

"For someone with such a lack of faith doctor, it may be a little difficult for you to understand. It wasn't the cooling, it was the temperature."

"Minus 213 degrees?"

"You see, even in its construction, he uses your scriptures to mock you."

Dr Carden didn't know what he meant by this, but it didn't matter. She'd delayed him more than enough and hoped that had given the cavalry time to mount a defence, if they'd heard the communication. But when they entered the main floor, Trentini spotted one of the workers trying to move into a better position and didn't hesitate in letting off a shot. Father Michael and Sarah instinctively hit the floor as bullets started to fly, but Phillipé just stood there, looking up at the telescope. Trentini's initial shot had gone off close to his ear, causing disorientation. Unable to get a clear shot on the workers, he turned his gun on Dr Carden but Phillipé wandered blindly into his path as he pulled the trigger. Dr Carden lurched for him, but it was too late. In the same moment, Trentini's body began to jolt and twist as he was hit with a flurry of bullets, killing him before his body hit the floor.

A little later in the canteen, while Sarah was still coming to terms with the night's events, Father Michael was opening and closing cupboard doors looking for facilities to make a sweet tea; something to help calm the nerves. Finding what he was looking for, he placed the hot drink in front of her, and took a seat several yards away, literally giving her space.

She cradled the cup, staring at it in reflective silence, although it wasn't as Father Michael thought: shock and gathering the shattered pieces of grief. Instead it was something else. She wasn't entirely sure what. A tranquil rage perhaps. But she'd added herself into the firing line with self-deprecating thoughts due to her lack of belief in the narrative. And even now, as she contended with understanding, Father Micheal was the one who'd spent the last twenty four hours with Phillipé, who'd formed a bond. Still he had the strength of character to allow *her* space, to see to *her* needs. She looked over at him, unaware he was being watched, staring into the empty space that Phillipé had occupied only hours earlier. It was a heartbreaking picture if you knew. An ageing priest, a man searching for the truth behind the death of his oldest and dearest friend, and now this innocent boy.

It was a sight to quell any residual hangovers of life threatening experiences, feelings of self-absorbed guilt that were forcing her into action. She put down the cup and left the priest for a short time before returning carrying a case in one hand and a small object in the other.

Father Michael was slightly taken aback as a laptop case was placed in front of him not having realised Sarah had even left the room, but he knew exactly what this was. He looked around to make sure they were alone, including eyeing the overhead walkway. They were.

"Here?" he asked.

"No."

The energy in her voice suggested a renewed purpose. And though she hadn't intimated, her body language suggested he should get up and follow her, right now!

"I'll need my bag," he said.

In the aftermath of the tragedy, any personnel that weren't present at the incident were sent back to base camp. Dr Carden, Father Michael and the maintenance team all had to wait on-site for the Graham County Sheriff's department, leaving the main office completely empty.

There were several workstations consisting of large pine wood desks that housed up to four monitors; a little more computing power than a laptop. Sitting Michael at her desk, she placed the case in front of him and laid the small object she was holding on top, it was Phillipé's camera.

"It was with his things," she said. "The only thing that wasn't still packed. I don't know if there's anything on it. I figured, if there was…"

She didn't need to finish that sentence. Taking from his lead, Sarah placed herself at another workstation several feet away, allowing Father Michael the space he so desperately needed, even if this gentle, stoic man didn't know it himself.

Picking up the camera, he looked at it with slight trepidation. Not because of sentiment but because it was modern technology, which he found most intimidating.

Locating the power button he pressed it instantly, lighting the display screen with the last image taken. It was a selfie of Phillipé inside of his pod, smiling and making a peace sign with his fingers. It brought a smile to Michael's face that quickly filled with pain. At the side of the screen was a small circular button with arrows pointing up and down, left and right.

He tried the left arrow, changing the image on the screen that caused a scoff of laughter. It was blurry and out of focus, taken from the moving car; the journey to the observatory he presumed. His laughter was remembering how quickly Phillipé had learned the functions of the camera, which clearly hadn't transpired into good photography. He continued flicking past the images of random moments with each raising a smile as though seeing an abstract version of their journey in reverse, until he got to the final image. Phillipé and himself on the plane. Phillipé's arm around his shoulder, both of them smiling.

Finally, a tear fell from Father Michael's cheek, landing on the laptop case. He watched as it was absorbed by the canvas, suddenly forcing him to remember why he was there.

He placed the camera to one side and pulled the case towards him, once again tentative in his action, although this time it was due to the weight of responsibility and moving another step closer to finding out why Franz was murdered.

Unzipping the case he took out a laptop. *More technology*, he thought. He raised the screen, pressed the power button and waited. His hesitancy must have been obvious because Sarah asked if he was okay.

"It's a laptop," he said.

"Yes," Sarah replied, as if to say '*What did you expect to find inside of a laptop case?*'

But his eyes pleaded quietly for help.

"Let me take a look," she said.

Without getting up, she used her feet to roll the chair across the floor and slid up beside him.

It was a cheap over-the-counter home edition laptop in beaten up plastic casing. Sarah pressed the power button and Father Michael looked at her with raised eyebrows.

"What? I was just checking," she said. "It needs power. I'll see if I have an adaptor."

But as she slid the computer towards herself, it felt unusually light. She began to look over it and noticed a USB slot on the bezel that had no internal connection. She pushed her finger into the hole.

"There's something in here," she said.

After applying a little more force, the casing on the bottom started to come loose. She ran her finger around the gap until the bottom completely fell away and with it a slim flat box dropped to the table. It was only a little smaller than a standard A4 piece of paper. Michael and Sarah just stared at it, neither one wanting to be the first to move. Eventually, Sarah picked it up and respectfully presented it to Father Michael.

Taking a deep breath he slowly lifted the lid. Inside was a single piece of parchment laid perfectly flat and sealed in a plastic wallet: The Prophesy.

"Can you translate it?" Sarah asked.

"Yes, I think so," Father Michael replied, concentrating on the document.

Holding it up to the light he said,

"It's Greek. Possibly a translation… it could be the original, without an author it's hard to say. Or if it's even authentic," he warned. "Get a pen."

Sarah quickly sourced a biro and pad from another workstation and sat poised and ready. Michael began to recite.

"In the past God overlooked such ignorance, but now…"

Sarah immediately stopped writing. *I know this,* she thought.

"He commands all people everywhere to repent," Michael continued. "For he has set a day…"

Sarah interrupted,

"When he will judge the world with justice by the man he has appointed."

"Quite," Father Michael replied.

"Why do I know that?" she asked.

"Good Bible studies?" Michael jested. "It's Acts 17, 30 to 31. When he will judge the world with justice by the man he has appointed. He has given proof of this to everyone by raising him from the dead," he said finishing the transcription.

"So it's fake?" Sarah sniped. "Uncle Frankie was killed for this? Aren't you going to say anything? Aren't you…?" she said with increasing anger.

Michael was still looking carefully at the parchment, unperturbed by Sarah's reaction. He put down the prophesy.

"My bag," he demanded.

Thrown by his response, Sarah passed Father Michael his bag and watched as he rummaged through before finally pulling out a small torch.

"Get the light," he said.

But she just stood there, trying to work out what he was doing.

"The light."

Realising her idleness, she rushed across the office to turn them off, leaving them in the dim glow of the security lights. Michael clicked his torch and the beam illuminated the parchment in a purple glow, it was a fluorescent torch. He held it close to the parchment and almost equally as close to his face.

"What does that do?" she asked.

"Parchment was not always readily available or affordable in most cases. So it was at times washed and re-used," Michael said as his eyes strained to focus. "This helps you see it."

"And you carry that stuff around just in case, huh?" Sarah said in an attempt to be amusing.

"Well you never quite know when you'll come across an ancient manuscript just lying around," he quipped.

"So what does it mean if it has been re-used?"

"In later times, they realised that under certain lights, the washed writing could still be read. So it became a useful way of keeping pieces of information hidden or to pass around secrets."

"Is there anything there?"

"Oh yes," Michael responded.

"Well, what does it say?" Sarah said slightly too loud. "Sorry."

Again Father Michael began to read. There was just enough light coming off of the torch for Sarah to take notes.

"The Prince of lies believed he could deceive God as he deceived man and walk upon the earth before the breaking of the first seal. The moon will wear a cloak of blood before it weighs the sins of the sun. I will then break a new seal and send forth a messenger, baptised in Holy fire before his resurrection, and bring forth the wrath of my judgement."

Sarah rushed to turn on the lights and read the transcription back to Michael.

"Is that everything?" she said.

"Yes. There may have been more, but it appears this is the part of interest."

"So that's it? You deciphered it?" She asked, uncertain of what that meant.

"I've translated it," Michael corrected. "But the prophesy is not cryptic, it speaks plainly.

It's broken into three pieces. The first is why Satan has tried to deceive God and found a way to physically walk on earth, before the first seal is broken."

"Wait, what?" Sarah said, hoping she'd misheard.

"What?"

"Satan walking on earth. I mean, that's metaphorical… right?

Michael exhaled softly, his body sinking ever so slightly with a veil of sadness as he considered his response. But the implication of the subtle reaction brought Dr Carden crashing into a new reality; where science was no longer the bedrock. Suddenly, Trentini, the religious zealot, didn't seem quite so mad after all. *In fact, he was right, she thought.* She didn't believe the scriptures. Not the way he did, not in a literal translation, but in parable, allegory and metaphor. However, knowing her scientific mind, that was not a light she could just switch off and it wasn't a time for lessons in theology. Instead she sided her broken skepticism and lead with what she knew.

"I thought the seal could only be broken by Christ? The first of the seven seals, the book of revelation, right?"

"Exactly," Michael confirmed.

"How would you even begin to do something like that?"

"I don't know. But I'm guessing that's what our killer meant when he said the prophesy is… theirs," he said while sinking back into his seat.

Weighed down by the stark revelation, suddenly everything was clear, everything made sense to him.

"What is it?" Sarah asked nervously.

"What's the second piece?" she said quickly.

"The moon will wear a cloak of blood, before it ways the sins of the sun."

They looked at each other, all too aware of what tonight was.

"Let's not get ahead of ourselves," Michael said. "Tonight is the beginning of a tetrad, four blood moons over the next two years. It could be any one of them. Or none," he warned.

Sarah switched on one of the computer monitors and began running a piece of solar mapping software.

"What are you doing?" Michael asked.

"You tell me," she said waiting for instruction. "What am I looking for?"

He looked at the parchment before asking,

"Is there a way to bring up constellations?"

Sarah pressed a single button and the screen immediately displayed constellations, cross referenced against a map of the solar system. Pressing another button turned them into their pictorial representations and started accelerating the trajectory to see alignments in the near future.

After around ten minutes of staring at the screen like it was showing a national news event, a few desks away the office phone started to ring.

"Hello?" Sarah said after picking it up.

She was expecting the Graham County Sheriff's department, but her frown suggested it was otherwise as she looked to Father Michael with slight puzzlement.

"Do you know a Veronica?" she asked, covering the mouthpiece.

Veronica? Michael thought.

But his exhausted mind was so busy with everything else, he couldn't think of anybody with that name.

"Says she's a professor?"

"Oh, Professor Lehman?" he voiced.

"Yeah, I think that's her," Sarah said while holding the phone towards him continuing to cover the receiver.

Father Michael's delight in remembering her was quickly overshadowed with why he knew her. Professor Lehman was affiliated with the Natsarim. Before even picking up the phone he knew events had gone beyond containment. *She must have been in communication with Brother Bonsu to find our whereabouts,* he thought. *But why?*

"You carry on," he said to Sarah.

She returned to the desk to continue watching the mapping software when her phone vibrated; No Caller ID. She looked at Father Michael who was engaged with his own call, before answering.

"Hello? Mr Mont...? But how did you... No, I'm fine," she said still clearly shaken. "That's very kind of you... A young student, Phillipé Garcia. No, I'm okay, everyone else is fine, a little shaken maybe, but... Yes, of course. No, I'd like that. Thank you for reaching out."

Sarah was slightly thrown from receiving a heartfelt call from one of the contributors to the observatory, but was soon distracted by an image on the screen.

"I think I've found something," Sarah said, grabbing Michael's attention.

Father Michael quickly jotted something onto a pad, tore the paper and placed it in the sleeve of his cowl before cutting the conversation short and joining Sarah at the computer.

"What is it?" he asked.

She was curious about what information Michael wasn't sharing, but didn't think it would be able to trump what she had.

"I wasn't sure what I was looking for at first," Sarah said, "but it was like you said, the prophesy isn't cryptic."

She then pointed to the screen to show the alignment of the sun and the moon.

"What is it I'm looking at?" he asked.

"Oh," she blurted, realising she hadn't put up the contrasting visuals.

After moving the cursor to click on a few on-screen buttons, it revealed the moon positioned above the constellation of Libra and the sun under the right hand scale.

"Its sins are being weighed," he said, staring at the screen; stunned.

"That's it right? That's what we were looking for?" Sarah said excitedly.

Suddenly Michael became slightly unsteady on his feet, needing a moment to sit down.

"Are you okay?" she asked, quickly jumping up and helping him into the chair.

"Yes. I think I'm just still trying to adjust a little to the altitude."

In truth, it was the overwhelming sense of reality that was buckling Michael's knees. It was a rare thing to recognise a moment as it happened, but in a fleeting thought, he saw it all.

God inspiring a man with a vision of the far-off future. For him to set it down upon parchment that would survive for a millennia. While new stars are born and old ones die moving through the cosmos, waiting to reach an alignment that was foreseen over a thousand years ago; waiting for him.

"Can I get you something?"

"No, I'm okay," he insisted. Wanting and needing to push on. "When is the alignment due?"

"In the next seven days."

Through Uncle Frankie, Sarah had known Father Michael for most of her life. When her uncle died she never imagined him having to endure pain like that ever again. But seeing him now, she wanted to cry. His stare fell distantly to the floor, lost, defeated and alone.

"I don't know what I'm supposed to do," he admitted.

A quiet followed. Helplessness was contagious as Sarah could find no words of comfort, unable to provide solace. She could only picture the smug smile of that killer Trentini, which infuriated her. Desperate to break the silence, eventually she said,

"What did he mean?"

The question pulled Michael from sliding into an abyss. He looked at her.

"He said, 'He uses your scriptures to mock you?" she continued. "What did he mean?"

Michael quietly considered the question for a few moments, distracting him from his melancholy.

"I thought about that. Minus 213 degrees, perhaps it was in reference to scripture. M 213. The only one that really makes sense is Matthew 2.13," he said. "And when they were departed. Behold, the angel of the Lord appeareth to Joseph in a dream, saying, arise and take the young child and his mother, and flee into Egypt…"

"What is it?"

He looked directly at her.

"And be thou there until I bring thee word: **For Herod will seek the young child to destroy him…**"

It was clear from her expression that she was expecting something plainly spoken.

"An ancient relic was discovered in days gone by that not only invoked the power of Satan, but allowed the wielder to embody him, make him of the flesh. Their success is ensured by our prophesy."

"I don't understand," Sarah said honestly.

"God would not need to send anyone to stop them unless he knew they were to succeed."

Needing to take a moment to grasp the reality of what she was hearing, anger became her overriding emotion.

"Herod was alerted to the birth of a child, a prophesied saviour, King of the Jews. When the Magi arrived in Judea having followed the alignment, Herod then ordered the massacre of the innocence, killing the first born male of every house in an attempt to destroy the child of God. They are aware of the alignment, and where Herod failed, they seek triumph. To kill a child of God."

"So more people will die?" Sarah asked, clearly desponded by what she had heard.

But it went unnoticed as Father Michael was inspired with a new sense of urgency, almost speaking over her.

"Is there any way to see if the alignment points to a geographical location?"

Flustered and upset she took few a seconds to regain her focus.

"Erm… a location?" she said, "well, okay, yeah, just gimme a sec."

Taking data from three different screens and jotting references onto her pad, after a few minutes she turned the screen towards Father Michael.

"London," she announced.

Sarah watched Father Michael with growing concern as he silently considered the information. Eventually he took a piece of paper from the sleeve of his cowl, the same one he'd placed after speaking with Professor Lehman.

"I need to make a call," he said.

CHAPTER 21

BARRINGTON

With tears streaming down his face, Barrington ran as fast as his legs would carry him, making sporadic turns where he could, just incase anybody decided to follow. But the streets were long and wide and spotting him would have been easy had anybody tried.

On pure adrenalin alone he made it all the way to the main road leading out of town before having to stop and throw up. A passing couple looked on with concern, giving him a wide berth.

He didn't care. Now wasn't the time to worry about social acceptance or conservative values, he thought while wiping the remenance of vomit from his mouth and looking back down the road to see if he was being followed. *I don't even know what I'd be looking for,* he thought, scanning faces to see if anyone was paying attention to him.

They were. Anyone who'd noticed the out-of-towner running for his life through the streets until throwing up was definitely looking in his direction, and with good cause.

His head swivelled back and forth trying to find a landmark, or anything that might stand out as he attempted to get his bearings. He'd been to the city quite a few times, only now realising what little local knowledge he actually had.

Ezana Park was on the other side of the road, suddenly jumping out from its surroundings. The lush green of the trees and shrubs seemed like the only things not bleached by the sun, beckoning him like an oasis. *Just for a few minutes,* he thought.

The park was wedged between two roads in and out of the city, and a third linking them together, forming a triangle island. It was a small space but there was still enough foliage to block out the surroundings, making it feel more isolated than it actually was.

Finding a large set of boulders under a leafy canvas, a kind of organic installation, he assumed, Barrington sat down and looked out at the park in front of him, or more for anyone who's attention might loiter on him for too long.

It was a good position as he could see anyone coming from enough distance, meaning he could make a run for it if needed. Although if he had to he didn't much like his chances, after all, he was definitely no Indiana Jones.

It was more than just a passing self-deprecating thought, but one that broke his heart and bore the weight of responsibility for Helena's death. He could still see her eyes staring at him and started to shudder, slowly at first then almost violently. His face fell into his hands and he sobbed with his entire body, bombarded by an array of emotions, confusion, fear, cowardice, guilt and now anger. It was all too much to get his head around. *Why would anyone want to hurt such a sweet…* but before he could finish the thought, he realised he was still wearing his backpack. *The knife!* Scrambling to drag the bag from his back, hoping the artefact hadn't been damaged, he pulled it from the bag. Thankfully it was intact, but now there was no joy to be had when staring at it, the only thing he felt was what he thought the only thing anybody should feel in its presence: utter dread.

Barrington began replaying the last twenty four hours in his head, searching for a reason, clues, something Helena may have said that would point him in the right direction. Picturing her face, he almost smiled.

She had looked so happy the night before. The two of them lying face to face, her head on the pillow, smiling as they talked, laughing into the early hours. For just a short while, he even let himself believe this might be the start of something more, much more, a pairing he'd wanted since Oxford.

Helena spoke of her divorce and regrets of marrying so young. How, like Barrington, she'd allowed work to get in the way of relationships, friends and family. The break up with her husband was an amicable affair and they'd managed to remain friends. She even went as far as to describe her life as being safe and boring.

He stopped tormenting himself, *The knife was the only explanation for any of this*, *but who knows?* He recalled the agitation of the workers when first arriving, and there was no way of knowing who they could have told, or who she'd contacted since the discovery. And that wasn't even taking into account who funded the dig. *Who were the consortium? The Order?*

Only now did he realise with sadness, at Helena's reaction when he said "Cloak and Dagger." Unfortunately not even she could see its implications.

Resting the artefact, Barrington took out his phone with the mind to call someone. The need to not be alone was becoming overwhelming. Unable to think straight, he began scrolling through an endless list of contacts, hoping one would jump out as the person he needed in this moment. As he continued scrolling through the names of people he called friends, he realised there wasn't a single one there. They were colleagues, people that could serve his career, but not genuine friends.

That's when he realised that he *was* alone. A fact that hadn't dawned on him until this very second. He felt more surprised than melancholy. *And for what?* Barrington thought. *Academia?* He never considered himself a selfish man, far from it. But as a reflection of his life flashed before him, brought about in no doubt by the stark perspective thrust upon him, he realised that's exactly what he was.

Somehow he'd missed it. So caught up in striving for excellence, for… but that wasn't it either. Even now, with no one to hear his thoughts, he still couldn't be honest with himself.

He wasn't really oblivious to his own narcissism. He'd been ruthless in pursuit of recognition, so the Helena's of the world would no longer pass him by, to hear the reverent applause at the mention of his name, lorded for his work while feigning humility.

He looked at the dagger sat on the backpack. It was a bill from God; the price he paid.

Looking through his phone, there were several missed calls from his friend, or more like his colleague, Roger Hammond. He guessed he could call him. After all, they had enjoyed some fairly heavy and sometimes quite personal conversations over the years. Although often generated by alcohol-fuelled post speaking events. However, with such close connections and considered loose-lipped, Roger didn't strike him as the most secure source. Plus he had only been subjected to details of the Hilton event he turned down. *If he hadn't, would Helena still be alive?* he wondered.

There was also a missed call from an international number, but not one he recognised. He thought for a moment it might have been Professor Lehman but the dial code wasn't from the United Kingdom, however, the timing of the missed call was odd, considering.

Something was telling him to return the call, his thumb hovering over the button, when a gentle wind caressed the leaves overhead, distracting him.

He looked up, almost having forgotten where he was, only a few blocks from Helena's body.

If this really was about the knife then she was being watched. Which meant they would have seen us together. It was just a matter of time before they realised he had the knife and the feeling in the pit of his stomach returned. He didn't know what to do or where to go, only that he couldn't stay here.

Suddenly remembering the four-star hotel he'd booked for Helena, he realised his passport and overnight bag were still in the room. A part of him wanted to go back to see Helena, not wanting to believe any of this was real, but it was. Instead, he returned to the hotel.

A short time after leaving Ezana Park, a faded blue Mustang cruised by.

As Barrington crossed the hotel foyer, his state of paranoia reminded him of a Jason Bourne movie he'd seen recently, where the character being followed panicked, getting himself killed in the process. Suddenly he got the feeling his brain would be the last thing he'd see.

He did his best to cross the foyer in the most casual way possible, making it all the way to the room without being shot.

Once inside, everything was calm, just as he left it. Not as he'd built up in his mind and ransacked by henchmen looking for the dagger, or finding one sitting there with a gun just waiting for him to return.

He paused when seeing the bottle of champagne still in its bucket with the ice now melted. Pulling himself from remaining idle, he collected his passport, overnight bag and left as quickly as possible.

He was about to exit the hotel when deciding to engage the receptionist, smiling enthusiastically as he booked an eight o'clock dinner reservation for two, knowing he'd never return.

Barrington didn't know where to go, only that he needed to get out of town. No, better yet, out of the country. Composing himself, he began walking the road east, expeditiously, but not so much that it would attract attention.

After around thirty minutes and several failed attempts, he managed to flag a ride on the back of a small wheat grain truck heading east, passing the airport, before travelling north towards Eritrea.

It was surprisingly easy to get comfortable between the large sacks, Helena would have been proud of him. He shifted a few heavy bags, giving the impression of hunkering down. In reality, he was actually just positioning himself not to be seen from outside of the vehicle.

He let out a sigh of sheer relief and his body responded in yearning for him to close his eyes, and for a moment he did. But no sooner were they closed when a vision of Helena lying dead in the street flashed into his mind, springing them back open. He was now scared to close them again.

The further away Barrington got from the city the more he was able to relax. If only for a short while, it gave him time to let the reality of what was happening sink in. But the more he thought about it, the more it felt surreal. It was like he was imagining the whole thing.

Taking the knife from his bag he stared at it as if somehow it would reveal the answers, but all it did was confirm a dire reality.

When they arrived at Aksum airport, Barrington thanked the driver, giving him 2500 Birr for his trouble and silence, equalling about fifty dollars U.S.

"You never saw me," Barrington said, surprising himself.

The driver was all too happy to comply if it appeared he was helping someone circumvent authority. He still had a delivery to make and wished Barrington well as the two parted ways.

The journey helped Barrington organise his thoughts a little. Fight or flight hadn't been a recurrent experience in his life and he found it frustrating being unable to formulate a simple thought process. But now at the airport, he had a plan.

He would take a flight to Europe and put the dagger in the hands of a governing body. Any one would do, and any one would be mad not to take it. An item like this would cause an international stir, and based upon his testimony, an investigation would be inevitable.

The dagger would be wrapped up in red tape for years. It wasn't justice, but it was a start, and might just be enough to keep him safe.

He purchased the first ticket available, which would see him fly back to Addis Ababa to take a flight to Madrid, Spain, stopping at Cairo for the connection. It meant travelling for maybe fifteen hours and that wouldn't even see him reach a final destination. It was an overpriced ticket, but he was paying for safety not travel and for that would be willing to pay more.

As he started across the airport concourse, a bottleneck of passengers began building in front of the departure lounge with people becoming animated.

The Ethiopian military had suddenly descended upon the small airport conducting extra security checks with a violation of force, snatching bags from passengers to search them.

Barrington stopped. He didn't need to be a clandestine operative to know whose bag they were looking for and slowly started backing away.

Before he could turn around, one of the military guards noticed his behaviour and started towards him. Barrington had never felt his heart beat so fast before as he turned around and began moving alongside a passing group, peeling off to another to confuse his pursuer until safely reaching the exit.

Outside, he could see the guard still looking for him in the terminal but he soon lost interest and retuned to his post.

Who are these people? he wondered. *Are the government involved? Or does someone have the ability to employ their services at a moments notice?* Either way, Barrington knew he wasn't flying. But if whoever was after the dagger had this kind of power then it was the kind that would be able to monitor his movements, but to what extent he had no idea. It seemed like now was a good time to let paranoia get the better of him, if it meant staying vigilant, it meant staying alive.

He looked around for any potential rides. If flying wasn't an option then going by road was the only alternative. Even with the power of the military behind them, their were so many ways in and out of the country, making roadside checkpoints just a waste of resources.

A small military unit exited the terminal as they continued to conduct searches. Barrington had to move and fast. Stepping into the road, he waited for a gap in the traffic to cross before suddenly stopping. Approaching on the other side was a faded blue Mustang. The same he'd admired only the night before, and its occupants who'd been present at Helena's body this morning were scouring passengers as they passed, though it appeared not for collection.

The military were closing in, now just meters away and the driver of the Mustang's searching stare was about to fall upon him. *This is it!* Barrington thought. There was no where left for him to run.

A truck quickly pulled to a stop dangerously close in front of him.

"Get in!" the driver said.

On his way out of the airport, after making his delivery, the driver of the wheat grain truck had spotted Barrington. Noticing the military closing in behind him, he thought he looked like he could do with some help. Fortuitously, stopping when he did obstructed the view of the Mustang driver.

This driver let Barrington ride in the cab, although he said he wouldn't be offended if he found it more comfortable amongst the wheat. In truth it was, but Barrington didn't want to be disrespectful, especially after being saved from whatever he had found himself running from.

They remained quiet in the truck until far enough away from the airport. Finally, Barrington found himself no longer looking over his shoulder or in the wing mirror every ten seconds.

"I'm Solomon," the driver said, breaking the silence.

"Of course you are," Barrington responded ironically.

He was starting to get the sense that meeting Solomon was no accident, a thought that offered him a modicum of reassurance.

"Barrington, Barrington Ross."

It was the first time he could remember introducing himself without his illustrious title of doctor.

Solomon spoke with an infectious energy and humour that helped distract Barrington from his situation. He never pressed him on why someone that looked and spoke as Barrington did would be hitching a ride on a wheat grain truck and avoiding the military, but Barrington got the impression that some of Solomon's deliveries might have been more than just grain.

An hour or so into the journey, Barrington was losing the battle to keep his eyes open, when his phone rang on vibrate, jolting him almost clean from his seat and his heart into acceleration.

Taking it from his pocket he looked at the screen. It was the same international number from the previous missed call. He wasn't sure what to do.

"The only way to know, is to answer," Solomon said.

He's right, Barrington thought. Just as he plucked up the courage to answer, it rang off. A few seconds later it rang again. Still hesitant, he answered...

"Hello?"

"Is this Dr Barrington Ross?" a man's voice said with a softly aged gravel.

"Who's this?" Barrington said quietly.

"My name is Father Michael, a friend of Professor Lehman. I hope you don't mind, but she gave me your number."

"I'm sorry, but this really isn't the best time," Barrington said and disconnected the call.

It wasn't in his nature to be so short, but he didn't have it in him to find the courtesy.

He figured Professor Lehman had told a friend about the find and now they wanted to get a jump on its reveal; probably to control the narrative on how it might impact the church. With so much going on, he couldn't remember if he'd told Lehman not to mention it to anyone. Or maybe he just assumed as an experienced Oxford Professor she would have had more scruples. Either way it annoyed him.

The phone rang again. Feeling his frustration building he answered.

"Please don't hang up," Father Michael said immediately. "I fear your friends life could be in danger."

The words stunned Barrington to the point of finding it hard to catch his breath. Solomon looked at him.

"Are you okay?" he asked.

While Barrington was unable to respond, he was listening intently.

"Hello. Are you still there?" Father Michael continued.

"Yes," he said, finally swallowing, desperately holding back tears.

"I'm sorry to sound so dramatic," Father Michael said. "But I assure you, I couldn't be more serious."

"I know," Barrington replied.

He wasn't sure that was the right thing to say, but needed to let go of some piece of information.

"Has something happened?" Michael asked.

"Tell me what you know," Barrington replied without compromise, not wanting to reveal more than he had to.

Without him noticing, Solomon threw a look as if impressed. He didn't know what his new travel companion had got himself into, but this was the first time he thought he might just have the backbone to get through it.

"Professor Lehman tells me you were once a student of hers," Father Michael said. "You and your architect friend…"

"Helena," Barrington snapped.

"Indeed. She said not only were you extremely talented, but that you're one of the few people in the world that actually know what this artefact is."

"That's what I know. I asked what you know?"

He was starting to lose his patience.

"Dr Ross, you know what this knife is. It has but one purpose," Father Michael said. "What I know is that there's a very ancient and very powerful bloodline who will stop at nothing, and I mean nothing, to get their hands on it. They believe they will be fulfilling Luciferian prophesy. You need to…"

"She's dead," Barrington said with a calm fury that dispelled his tears.

Silence followed.

CHAPTER 22

ARCHIE

The events of that day reverberated across the globe as Archie's impromptu speech went viral with over a billion views recorded in 24 hours. Social media, broadcasters, newspapers, magazines, even inside the walls of parliament, the name Archibald T Montgomery fell from their lips, he was an instant phenomenon.

Images circulated of Archie standing on top of a burnt-out car in the middle of Piccadilly delivering an impassioned address to the masses. Rain fell and faces turned towards him as shops raged with fire and electronic billboards blazed, branding the historical moment with logos. It was an image for the age.

In the coming weeks, Archie was invited to guest on every major late-night chat show around the world. It was the type of coverage usually reserved for generic Hollywood blockbusters where every host would ask the exact same scripted questions so the guests could deliver the exact same scripted answers. If you'd seen one, you'd seen them all.

But Archie used each and every opportunity to expand on his vision, his manifesto. So if you saw one, you were only scratching the surface.

Suddenly the subject of much debate, not just on breakfast television, mid-morning chat shows and lunchtime cookery programmes, but by academics, financial experts and philosophers, by presidents, prime ministers and politicians the world over. Many painted Archie as a messianic figure, others a delusional dreamer. But while debates raged and intellectuals did their best to discredit his ideas, they simply couldn't. And the more people listened the more restless they became, disillusioned with their governments and untenable living standard.

Protests were becoming violent opposition as riots began echoing across the globe, demanding the implementation of a new epoch, a Montgomerian era.

For Archie, it wasn't long before the frenzy of demands outweighed the physical ability of being in two places at once, but like everything else, he'd planned for that, amassing a team that when called upon would be ready to implement his ideas. But Charlotte was the only one who would be able to articulate it as if he were there himself.

As expected, she mounted a strong defence of exactly why she shouldn't and wouldn't be taking a public-facing role. Being a media strategist, she'd already gone above and beyond the remits of her job description, and this was just a step too far.

Her objections fell upon the deaf ears of the mature stylist who smiled back politely to acknowledge that she was listening, but she wasn't. She was too busy picking at a blue, off-the-shoulder piece from the Alexander McQueen spring collection until satisfied with the drape, while Charlotte's new assistant Teresa watched on in protective silence.

Charlotte stood self-consciously clasping her hands in front of her, trying to hide what she could with her toned slender arms. The stylist finally stepped back to assess her creation.

"Stand up straight dear," she said, smacking at Charlotte's hands.

The behaviour agitated Teresa, but she held her tongue. Feeling a little like a child being dressed, Charlotte unclasped letting her hands fall to their natural position. Though her pouty expression didn't help, the stylist still wasn't happy about something.

"Let's lose the necklace," she said.

Clearly uncomfortable with the suggestion, Charlotte instinctively placed her hand to her chest covering the small gold cross that hung delicately from a slither of a chain.

"It'll just be for the interview," she added, proceeding to unclip the necklace. "Nothing should take away from this beautiful neckline darling, you're like a swan princess."

It was so small and delicate, weighing nearly nothing at all, but Charlotte could feel it missing from her neck, as if more than the cross was being taken from her.

The stylist beamed a smile.

"You are simply breathtaking my dear. Don't you think darling?" she said addressing Teresa with her everyone pay attention to me voice.

Charlotte was indeed beautiful but Teresa could only muster a smile that showed her utter contempt for the display of self-ingratiating importance. It was the only time that evening Charlotte found a smile, though she did her best to hide it.

Charlotte never considered herself aesthetically and so presented herself accordingly.

"We're ready for her," the stage runner said, poking his head around the door after knocking and not waiting for a response.

Charlotte gave one last worried looked to Teresa before being swept up in following him along a brightly lit narrow hallway where pictures of previous guests lined the walls, each more famous than the next. He continued narrating his movements into the headset with the stylist on Charlotte's heels picking at the dress until the very last second.

"Guest 2, in position in 20 seconds," he said.

20 seconds, she thought, feeling panic rising.

Charlotte suddenly felt as though her life was spinning out of control, not in her comfort zone where she could be the snappy, quick-witted charmer, pulling strings from a safe distance. Instead, this was front and centre. *Not the place for a bellflower,* she thought. It was a private reference to herself from when she was a small child. Because the bellflower usually sat at the border of a garden, on the periphery. It went unnoticed and thrived in the shade. Not only useful, but a very pretty flower if you took the time to look.

Her chest started to feel tight and breath shallow as the narrow hallway started to close in. She couldn't feel her legs walking but assumed she must have been because the end of the hallway was approaching with a smooth nauseating momentum. And then everything went dark.

She could hear her name. It wasn't being called, but presented. Out of the dark a blinding light found her before being thrust onto the L.A. Stage. Live TV and a doe in headlights, she was warmly greeted by the show's host, Craig Ferguson. She instinctively put her hand to her chest, but her cross was no longer there to offer comfort.

The entire evening had been so overwhelming, it went by in a blur and she couldn't recall details with any certainty. It was like waking from a vivid dream, but when trying to remember, it vanished.

The second she left the stage, Charlotte bolted past the coordinator and stylist and straight into the bathroom where she proceeded to throw up violently. Teresa rushed to her aid and stood waiting outside the cu-

REVELATIONS

bicle. Finally the latch on the door clicked and Charlotte tentatively emerged.

"Just tell me straight," she said, reverting to a South London defence, bracing herself for the impact. "In terms of a car crash, did I scuff a bumper or was that a fifty car pileup with fatalities?"

"I erm, it was…" Teresa said, uncertain of how to formulate a response. "I'm sorry, I don't have the appropriate car crash analogy, but…"

"But what?"

Charlotte's mind raced with what she already knew was coming, she just hoped that she hadn't irreparably damaged Archie's reputation. She would of course hand in her resignation. It was the right thing to do and would at least salvage something from the wreckage.

Teresa took Charlotte's hand and led her back to the dressing room, passing a few busy people that worked at the studio, all of whom had time to stop and stare at her. *This really is bad*, she thought.

There was a TV in the dressing room streaming the live broadcast. Ferguson had introduced the top billing guest, currently the highest paid actor that year promoting the next instalment of an unprecedented superhero franchise. However, he hadn't yet stopped discussing the previous guest; Charlotte.

"I don't know what's happened to politics, but I like it," Ferguson said, in his toned down Scottish accent.

"Sophisticated, intelligent, funny," the guest said, "British politics just got glamorous."

"British politics?" Ferguson exclaimed, "this is bigger than that. Have you ever heard a politician speak like that?"

"Until just now, I hadn't heard a politician say anything new for fifty years."

The audience applauded. Turning to address the camera and live audience directly, Ferguson said,

"Now I know we're just a late-night comedy show and anything we touch on politically tends to be done with a satirical edge. I enjoy comedy and the fact I have a job where for just a few minutes, five days a week, I get the chance to make someone laugh, someone smile, even for just a fleeting moment. But I think, and I'm sure you'll agree, that it's been getting harder and harder lately to ignore the bleak existence the world is hurtling towards at what seems like an accelerated pace. However, ladies and gentlemen, I can honestly say to you that after tonight's show, I believe we may have just discovered a light on the horizon."

The high profile guest stood up to clap Ferguson's speech, the audience applauded wildly.

Watching the show from London, Archie turned off the television and set down the remote onto the coffee table next to a spread of magazines. Vogue had just bumped this month's model, now it was Charlotte gracing the front cover.

She was wearing a white blouse, a power tie and ankle length pin-stripe skirt, under the title 'The Woman Behind The Man.' Archie allowed himself a faint smile, though the magazine beside it was no less impressive.

Time went with the image now being used as wallpaper and screen-savers on devices the world over, even as clickbait on social media and news reels. Archie, stood on top of the burnt-out car, drenched from the rain as he delivers an impassioned speech to a sea of mesmerised damp faces. High-end shops burnt in the background and iconic logos lit up the famous electronic billboards, though the image had been doctored to put the magazine headline onto one of the screens: 'Hope.' It had also been edited into black and white, leaving only the burning shops and logos in colour. Even Banksy had chosen to immortalise Archie with an image appearing on a wall in Piccadilly.

After pouring a small brandy, he stood at the first floor balcony window and stared into the night. His other hand draped at his side held a photograph he hadn't seen in many years, and despite holding it, he still hadn't brought himself to look. Instead he pondered his reflection, slowly turning his head and noticing the details. He raised his chin slightly to appear more powerful. *No, regal,* he thought.

A polite knock at the door saw Archie quickly slide the picture into his pocket, turning from the window just as Johnny entered the room, who immediately noticed that Archie was uncharacteristically having a brandy outside of the study.

"How do you think she did?" he asked, knowing the TV appearance was the last thing on his mind.

Archie turned his thoughts to Charlotte giving him a much needed moment of relief from his own turmoil, fleeting though it was.

"As expected," he replied with the faintest of smiles. "Her team is in place?"

"Of course."

A beam of headlights bounced off the surface of the vehicles parked below, pulling Archie's attention to the north end of the road and returning to his burden.

A black executive car with tinted windows flanked by two motorcycle police escorts had just turned into the square and continued uncertainly along the dimly lit street.

"They're here," he said.

Two innocent words that delivered tension and stillness into the room.

"If for any reason tonight doesn't…"

He stopped himself from finishing the sentence.

"Just make sure Charlotte's insulated," he said.

"Of course."

Johnny wanted to offer something more, some semblance of comfort, maybe a modicum of what Archie had given to the rest of the world, but the intimidation of being in the presence of genius had a way of suppressing vocabulary that it wouldn't extend to equal his emotion. Instead, noticing the wall safe was open, he filled the silence by crossing the room to close it, hoping the action would break the density.

Usually the safe contained only a few items, a skull, a neatly stacked pile of cash, thirty thousand or so, which was considered walk around money for Archie. A gun with a box of ammunition, and a book 'Menelik's Dagger', by Dr Barrington Ross. The only item missing was a photograph and it was the only thing that spoke to Archie's state of mind. He closed the safe and slid across the wooden panel concealing its location.

Feeling a fraction of Archie's world, it was with a heavy heart that he collected the suit jacket draped over the back of a chair, and like a matador with a cape shook it lightly allowing any creasing to fall.

The gesture prompted Archie into action. Tabling the brandy, he slipped his arms into the waiting sleeves but his vacant stare suggested that his thoughts were still elsewhere.

Johnny raised the jacket over his shoulders and brushed down the suit. Archie turned to face him as if for approval.

It was a good choice of attire. The finest charcoal three-piece courtesy of Saville Row, a grey shirt with a cutaway collar and matching silk tie in a Windsor knot, finished with a formal shoe from Christian Louboutin. The fit accentuating his form of a tight waist and broad chest, the colour complementing his dark groomed features and chiseled lines. He was the embodiment of power, yet his eyes held the gravity of a man facing destiny.

Johnny looked down at the newest addition to the wardrobe, a platinum band on the ring finger of Archie's right hand; something that hadn't been present earlier that day. Taking his hand and sliding the ring forward, it revealed an abrasion encircling the finger beneath.

After receiving a phone call earlier that day, no sooner had the line disconnected when with perfectly choreographed timing there was a knock at the door. Johnny answered to be met by a small stooping man that resembled a human mole, a feature only accentuated by the circular glasses perched on the end of his nose.

He carried with him a large wooden box, like that of a painter's supplies or an old typewriter carry case. Behind him at the foot of the stairs was his chaperone, a giant of a man whose presence needed no explanation. Without request the small man rudely shuffled inside.

"I'm here to deliver the invitation," he said in an annoyingly high register.

Placing the box on the floor he opened it to reveal a tattoo machine.

Johnny gently kissed the abrade area and carefully slid the ring back into position.

"The Order awaits," he said. "Everything is panning out exactly as you said it would."

Archie turned an unflattering gaze upon him.

"Not exactly," Archie scathed.

Johnny's frame quickly deflated, averting his eyes suddenly uncertain of himself. Archie returned his disapproving stare to the window, to the blackened heavens pierced with celestial lights.

"The Natsarim alignment is almost upon us and you managed to let the dagger slip through your fingers. If either side come into its possession, its humanity that will be left in the balance."

Archie's stare fell to the waiting car and police escorts.

"Now The Order are not the only ones in play. Not exactly as I planned."

"Do you think they suspect?" Johnny asked.

Archie made his way from the room.

"If I don't return you'll have your answer. Until then, find Dr Ross."

With great worry Johnny watched as Archie descended the stairs until gone from sight.

The waiting driver held the door for Archie, before taking his own seat behind the wheel. Opening the glove compartment he took out a semi-automatic pistol and placed it on the passenger seat beside him.

Archie was concealed from the driver by a frosted glass panel, although it became transparent at the touch of a button, and from the outside world by tinted windows. The driver's voice came over the intercom system.

"Do you have any electrical devices on your person sir?"

"No," Archie said as he sat back in his seat and waited.

After a small electrical hum, a green light on a panel in front of the driver illuminated, letting him know his passenger had been scanned. Archie was telling the truth.

The intercom sparked to life again.

"Please raise the armrest and place your invitation onto the scanner."

Swallowing his agitation he raised the padded rest beside him. Inside was a glass plate he eyed curiously. Unknown to Archie, his slight hesitation caused the driver to pick up the gun.

"Your invitation please, sir? We're on a schedule."

Looking at the glass panel, Archie removed the platinum band, exposing the abrade section of his finger and placed his palm against the plate before spreading his fingers. A dull light switched on revealing the invitation. At the base of the finger sat an invisible tattoo, only exposed using ultra-violet light; a serpent eating its tail. The driver returned his gun to the glove compartment.

"Thank you," the intercom sounded.

Archie then replaced his ring and lowered the armrest.

The car left 26 Grosvenor Square and headed south of the River Thames. It was a short ride before arriving at the London Heliport in Battersea, where Archie was transferred into a waiting executive helicopter.

The armed pilot checked her passenger was buckled into the soft tan leather seat and wearing the aviation headset before making a quick ascent, sharply following the river west of the city.

Once they hit cruising speed, the vibration and muffled drum from the rotors accompanied by the swirling pattern of street lights below were doing a good job of making Archie feel more relaxed. He consciously sank a little deeper into the chair, willing himself to keep calm, when he remembered the photograph. Carefully he took the picture from his pocket, reading the inscription on the reverse.

"Simon 8 years old - Trenton 2 years old"

He hesitated and finally turned it over. The boy staring up at him from the picture was his older brother Simon. Handsome, with soft blonde hair and a smile beaming with pride as he held his baby brother in his arms; a two year old Archibald.

It brought an all too fleeting moment of warmth, before being consumed with a bitter cold that stole the light from his eyes.

Memories of his youth fragmented and eroded over time. Things he'd blocked out for so long, now could no longer be recalled with any honesty. But what remained was a feeling, an essence, one he could still feel when holding the photograph. Although he didn't know for how much longer.

Simon passed away from cancer when he was just 10 years old. Archie, being only four at the time, remembered very little about his brother. Although he did recall a time where he felt an immense adoration. Now, however, he wasn't sure if even that ever really existed.

What he could remember, with an overwhelming clarity, was the feeling that love died with his brother. It was less of a scar he bore and more of a wound that would never heal.

In the years after his death, Archie's parents constant use of Simon as an unreachable benchmark forced him into a lifelong competition with the memory of a dead child, distorting what remained with loathing.

He was all too aware family traditions demanded rights of passage only be granted to the first born, for which they reminded him at every given opportunity. No matter what his achievements, he always knew it should have been Simon sitting there instead of him.

As a teenager, the incessant bombardment of family tradition, bloodlines and rituals had left him disillusioned with his lineage. They talk of unrivalled power while hiding in the shadows, congratulating one another on accomplishments, which as far as he was concerned amounted to nothing more than DNA. He could have chosen to do anything with his life and never fail. Their influence was endless and the risk factor to any endeavour was inconsequential; the dice were loaded.

As the helicopter continued to distance itself from the lights of London, a luminescent three quarter moon settled against the sleek crystal of a clear night. The landscape below darkened to a series of indistinguishable agricultural fields and forestry, but Archie estimated that they were probably somewhere over the region of the Chiltern Hills.

The pilot deftly descended to a height barely clearing the tree line and held course for almost a minute. Suddenly the forestry gave way to a large clearing and at its centre was an ominous building. Its plain but gothic architecture seemed misplaced.

The grey bricks made it impossible to make out any distinguishing features, other than how creepy it looked. A quality only exaggerated by the moon as its only source of illumination, reflecting off of a glass dome protruding from the backside of the roof; an odd feature considering the construction. That, along with the distinct lack of roads or access routes to the property. The only way to get there was to navigate by foot through a privately owned and patrolled forest, or to fly.

The face of a security agent burst out of the darkness as the pilot engaged the spotlight to land. After directing the helicopter's descent, the agent made a careful approach amidst the powerful thrust of rotors kicking up dirt and grass from the immaculate acres of lawn.

"Mr Montgomery?" the security guard shouted to be heard. "Follow me please sir."

Archie stepped from the helicopter, met with a strong hand on his back forcing him low to avoid any unnecessary mishaps. The security had been impossible to see in the dark, which he assumed was the point of the black attire, but now in the open air being marched across a moonlit lawn, he could make out several more silhouettes emerging from the darkness. All were positioned equidistance from each other forming a perimeter around the property.

A compact submachine gun hung from a strap under the agent's right shoulder, which Archie assumed was the theme reflected across all of the detail. The agent stopped fifty yards short of the building.

"Sir, if you follow this line directly to the front entrance," he said, "from there you're to continue down the hall."

As the agent gestured a direction, Archie noticed a small tattoo on the inside of his wrist, three circles inside a soft triangle. The agent was aware of the attention given to the ink, but silently backed away leaving Archie alone.

Surprised to be left alone and unable to see the line the agent was referring to, Archie stepped forward with uncertainty. Suddenly, a sack was forcefully yanked down over his head and powerful hands from what felt like every direction grabbed hold of him. The ground beneath disappeared as he felt himself hoisted from his feet and carried forward at pace. At first his sharp panicked breaths sucked the material against his face making it harder to breathe and his heart raced unsustainably. Johnny's words replayed loudly in his head,

"Do you think they suspect?"

Fear sent adrenalin coursing through his body. It was a rare emotion in Archie's life, having risen to not just meet every challenge he'd ever faced, but to emerge victorious. He assumed it was the point to all of this, to elicit fear and remind their guest of where the balance of power truly lay.

While he was willing to accept that which was beyond his control, he had no intention of allowing them anything that was. He inhaled deeply trying to savour the rare nuance of emotions, controlling his breathing and slowing his heart until his body relaxed; acquiescent to its inevitable destination.

The cool night air disappeared as he was taken inside, removing his socks and shoes before placing his feet on the ground. The hands made short work of removing every item of clothing until he was stood naked with only the bag upon his head.

In a degrading and vulnerable state, Archie waited obediently for what was next, intimidation, threats of violence or worse, but nothing came. Slowly and carefully he removed the bag from his head to find himself stood in an expansive room, 30ft high, 50ft long and every inch covered in black marble slate. Six flaming torches, three on either side provided just enough illumination to make out a shimmer across the surface of the floor in front of him. He edged forward, squinting in the low light trying to get a better look. It was water. *A cleansing pool,* he thought. A requirement of purification before stepping onto hallowed ground.

While certain he was alone, he was equally certain nothing was unseen and began his descent into the water. Immersed to his chest, he slowly waded through the warmth to its centre before completely submerging. Upon re-emergence he was surprised to be faced by a lone cloaked figure wearing a black mask with no holes for eyes offering a robe draped across outstretched arms.

Archie climbed the steps to accept the robe and the cloaked figure stepped away, somehow able to expertly navigate the pool's edge without the need for sight.

Light appeared from beyond a set doors, revealing them to their guest. Panelled with Tiffany stained glass, the light threw colours dancing onto the floor, bringing warmth to the otherwise cold empty space.

Donning his robe he approached the doors and slid them apart.

CHAPTER 23

THE ORDER

Seven figures sat motionless shrouded by cloaked robes. While unable to see their eyes, Archie could feel the judgmental stare of each of them upon him. There wasn't an individual on the planet he feared and that was even true now, but collectively their power shook him to his core.

"You may enter," one of the members granted.

Smooth marble gave way to cold coarse stone as Archie's bare feet crossed the threshold. A palpable energy instantly enveloped him and the temperature sank several degrees turning his breath white. Still wet and naked under his robe he should have been feeling the bite of the cold, but somehow the garment kept his body perfectly warm.

The Order were seated on high backed chairs of dark wood and claret cushioning, around a vast stone table positioned perfectly beneath a glass dome; the same he'd seen from the helicopter.

The chamber itself appeared to be a separate construction from the rest of the mansion. Large boulder stones that made up the walls and floor were more in keeping with ancient castles or monuments; the burning torches continuing the theme.

The table itself was a flattened boulder, creating a ceremonial centrepiece. The base continued below the floor and possibly beyond the foundations. It appeared the reason for the building's construction was to conceal its existence. Painfully intricate patterns, sigils and symbols were carved into its surface while lines divided it into eight equal segments with each differing from the next. Apart from the section facing Archie, where the surface had been left untouched.

At the centre was a small indented circle where seven platinum bands lay, the right hand of each member rested on the table with their ring fingers emanating a faint but luminous tattoo. Unlike the car there was no UV light to cause such a reaction, but still they glowed.

Removing his ring, Archie approached the table and placed it in the circle alongside the others, and like theirs his tattoo radiated.

Unlike the members, the chair waiting for him was just an ordinary chair, plain and uncomfortable. It was intended to remind its occupant of their status, not just in the room but in life. Kings, queens, presidents and prime ministers had all once stood where Archie was standing now, and sat in the very chair before him. Finally he took his place completing the circle.

"Why now?" a female voice asked sharply.

Archie panned the seven figures, eyes shrouded by the lip of their hoods, before raising his stare to the glass dome overhead and the sky beyond.

"A shadow looms," he replied.

"You don't believe in shadows," a male voice snapped, "isn't that why you requested to be released from your lineage?"

Archie hesitated before lowering his head in shame.

"Yes."

"You were warned on the consequences of leaving the protection of the family, were you not?"

"I was."

"And now your son, our blood, is in the hands of The Natsarim."

Archie could not bring himself to respond.

"Then why now?" another female vexed.

Archie returned his gaze to the seven, this time with more confidence.

"I was born not only to a bloodline but to a generation at war with the past, a past it is ill-equipped to conceive. Every spawning must forge a new, but never in history has the chasm between generations been so vast."

"You talk of their world, not of ours."

"I talk of a shared existence. Advancements in technology, access to information, things I was encouraged to pursue," Archie protested. "To align with a generation that arrogantly believes we know all there is, forgoing the experience of our elders. Only information yet to come is of value. So no matter how much I looked back, truth evaded me.

"And now?"

"Some time ago you tasked me with acquiring an ancient relic, a skull. At the time I didn't give it much consideration, only humbled by a request from The Order."

"Lack of consideration I can believe," a female voice said. "But humility? That's a little outside your repertoire Archibald. Spare us your fawning."

He gave a faint nod acknowledging their candour.

"It wasn't until I took possession of the skull," Archie continued. "I remembered what I tried so hard to forget. Lessons of our history, our bloodline… our rituals. Fortuitously, this led me to a prophesy of The Natsarim. Where an alignment will mark the arrival of one who will bring our destruction."

"What of it?"

"The alignment can only be brought about when the Seal of Solomon is revealed. We sit in the shadow of a convergence, which means you've found Menelik's dagger. You ask why now? Because that was your design. That I return not in faith, but in knowing."

A silence followed. Then in unison the seven members raised their hands to their hoods. Archie's heart started to race, this was the moment he'd been waiting for his entire life. Placing his hand on his upper thigh expecting to feel the photograph in his pocket, only now remembering that's where it still was. Without it he didn't quite feel prepared but watched as the seven members revealed their identities.

As he sat there trying to absorb the magnitude of what was unfolding before his eyes, a lifetime of wondering, speculating, he couldn't escape just how underwhelmed he actually felt.

There was nothing special about six of the ageing faces sat before him. As he looked from right to left, he either didn't know or could only muster a vague recollection from childhood memories. But it was the seventh that held his attention the most. Positioned on the far left was the youngest of The Order, his father; Jonathan Montgomery IV.

"Wilhelm Katz," Jonathan said taking to his feet and introducing the other members.

Starting on his left he continued around the table.

"Melcher Mayer, Sonja Gotha, Isabella Borbon, Jessop Steiner, Francis Magnusson."

Archie respectfully acknowledged each member as they were introduced.

"It's remarkable that after so many years you recall our teachings with such clarity," Sonja said.

She was positioned at the centre of the table directly opposite Archie and aired with a sense of seniority.

"Knowledge gained is but a cypher without experience," Archie Said.

"Then it's not you that pursues destiny, but destiny that pursues you?"

Duelling with equals was an unfamiliar territory for Archie and his clever anecdotal responses held no quarter, he needed to tread with more caution.

"Because from your recent performance in London," Wilhelm said, "it would seem you've made your ambitions quite clear."

"Reckless though it was," Jessop barked.

"What isn't clear is your allegiance," Wilhelm continued.

"You question my loyalty?"

"Your ambition," Isabella interjected. "For millennia empires have risen and fallen, but The Order is a constant. We survive because we do not succumb to the short-sighted ambitions of younger minds. True power is but a whisper Archie, a delicate manipulation of one's will. To wield this power takes more than understanding, it takes belief, in something greater than oneself."

"But surely it must start with belief *in* oneself," Archie responded.

"Ahhh, the arrogant conundrum," Sonja said softly, lowering the temperature of exchange. "Clearly we're not happy with the position you have put yourself in, and yet without it you know that you would not be sat where you are now."

"We had of course considered an alternative," Francis scoffed.

"However," his father Jonathan finally spoke. "In the past you have, as you said, proven yourself resourceful. We will grant your wish to return from exile."

"And you will be free to further your political ambitions," Isabella added.

"Under our benevolent guidance of course," Wilhelm butted in.

"Of course," Archie aligned.

"But first you must pay tribute."

To his surprise a masked figure stepped out of the darkness and placed a large knife and chalice in front of him on the table, before once again disappearing into the shadows. He had thought them to be alone, only now realising there was more to see than could be seen. He eyed the objects on the table.

REVELATIONS

"Well," Melcher said. "Are you prepared to make an offering?"

Again Archie's stare panned the seven faces before stopping at his father. Taking up the knife holding it aloft the chalice, he curled his fingers into a tight fist around the blade until blood began falling into the waiting vessel, never breaking eye contact with Jonathan, nor did Jonathan with him. With ravenous eyes the six other members could only watch as the blood fell.

"The shadow that looms is the one we will cast upon this world," Sonja said swallowing her salivation. "And yes, the seal of Solomon has indeed been revealed, though not yet in our possession."

Archie listened as blood continued draining into the cup.

"Preparations for the ceremony have already begun," Jonathan said. "Return the dagger to us and you will take your rightful place at the time of convergence."

"Fail and next months Time magazine will be a short eulogy on what could have been," Melcher added.

"You do understand, regardless of the political position you've placed yourself in, there can be no other priorities before this?" Isabella warned.

"What of my son?"

As the cup continued to fill, Archie could feel his blood pressure falling and lightheadedness begin to take over.

"Had the boy's mother not interfered, your son would have already been home and safe," Wilhelm said. "A problem that will be rectified within the hour I'm told. We have his location, a team has been sent to recover him."

"Once the seal is in our possession, our response for this heinous act will be felt a thousand fold," Isabella added.

"If the convergence marks the birth of their destroyer, then we will leave no stone unturned to see him destroyed at birth. Like Pharaoh, God has chosen his plague."

With the chalice three quarters full, Archie slumped forward onto the table barely holding onto consciousness.

Jonathan rose to collect the vessel. Unconcerned with his son, he drank from the blood before passing the chalice to Wilhelm, who then drank and passed it to Melcher, Sonja followed, then Isabella, Jessop and finally Francis. With all seven now on their feet, they raised their hoods once again concealing their faces.

Through a fading darkened vision, Archie could see the figures baring down upon him. A cold rush of air made every hair stand on end and not even his robe could defend the chill. The wind swirled around the chamber, pulling at the hoods of the seven and threatening to extinguish the torches. With what little strength he had Archie pushed himself up from the table to try and see, but a shadow blacker than night descended from the dome and his consciousness was no more.

CHAPTER 24

VIKTOR

Allowing Josh and Cohen some space and privacy, Viktor, Dida and Honza took seats in the bar. Dida affectionately sat on Viktor's lap, which was her default position whenever possible. There she would play with the platt of his beard like an unconscious comfort blanket, something he never tired of.

On the table she'd placed a champagne bucket containing ice and a bottle of Belvedere vodka. The tradition of conclusion, an earned gratuity to savour and reflect.

They all drank, but none quite as convincing as Dida, who smoothly knocked back her shot and then studied Honza each time he reached for his, as though masculinity was being judged... it was!

He tried appearing relaxed, but despite his best efforts the doctor's fears were evident.

As much as he wanted to know what the hell was going on, he also quietly just wanted all of this to be over so he could get back to the privileged lifestyle he'd worked so hard to acquire.

It was living beyond that lifestyle that found him here in the first place. Incurring a debt of desperation led him to a world he didn't belong in or even understand.

"They'll be okay, right?" Viktor asked expectantly.

"I think so, yes." Honza said, "That man... Cohen, he saved the boys life, in more than one way I'm guessing."

Dida smirked at Viktor who held a subtle smile watching Honza pry for information he shouldn't, but couldn't help himself. She poured another shot for the doctor, eyeing him carefully.

Honza could feel the atmosphere suddenly shift, *What had I said?* he thought. He nervously reached for his glass, but Dida shook her head causing him to freeze, now fearful of his own movements or what was happening.

Viktor whispered into Dida's ear and she immediately left the table, making Honza extremely nervous.

"I didn't mean to…" Honza began rambling with an apologetic tone.

Viktor raised his hand to quieten the doctor's whining, which did well to amplify his fears.

Dida returned from behind the bar holding a manila envelope and handed it to Viktor. Without checking the contents, he tossed it onto the table towards the doctor. The wad of cash inside spilled some of the notes onto the table, but Honza could only eye the payment like a dog staring at a bowl of food waiting for permission to eat.

Dida returned to Viktor's lap and nodded to the doctor, as if giving him permission to move. He picked up his glass, knocked back the contents and collected the envelope, shuffling the notes back inside before sliding it awkwardly into his pocket; submissively nodding in gratitude.

"You understand that's not for your services?" Viktor said.

"I… what do you mean?" he replied.

"Your silence," Dida said.

Her words were few, but coupled with her stare, she had just delivered a cold threat that scared the doctor more than anything else he'd faced that night.

"Of course," he said nervously, gesturing locking his mouth and throwing away the key.

It quickly dawned on him that he'd just crossed a one-way threshold. Having taken payment, he knew he was now bound to these people whenever they chose to call. And to a promise of retribution if he ever voiced his unspoken vow. However, once he'd accepted his fate and felt the fat weight of money in his pocket, he was emboldened to persist in understanding.

With stirring curiosity, or perhaps it was a bad mix of vodka and adrenalin, he started to ask questions. Viktor was happy to engage him with old war stories that without alcohol would have scared him to his core, but all he felt was a naive excitement.

A veil had been lifted on a world he had no idea existed and would never be able to see the same way again.

Dida had heard the stories on so many occasions she could have re-peated them verbatim, every now again playfully stealing the punchline of a story. Honza began to feel more at ease in their company, seeing a charming and unusual couple with stories that were just a little more magnificent than the norm.

"Is that how you met…?" Honza gestured to the back room.

He didn't want to say his name, sensing an unspoken reverence to-ward Cohen. Viktor shook his head, the quiet that followed only con-firmed his suspicion.

"You want to know about the man lying back there?" Viktor asked. "Okay, I'll tell a story. I was heading a private security detail in Co-lumbia, extracting a French diplomat for U.S. intelligence. What was supposed to be in and out, ended up a shit show. A militia attacked the embassy, killing on-site. It was a slaughter."

Viktor sat back, remembering. Seeing him lost in thought, Dida stopped playing with his beard.

"We had no right to make it out of there alive, but we had this guy, Trent, not your typical military type, but a genius tactician."

Viktor was in awe.

"And unflappable," he said. "He could devise a plan in the height of battle, when everyone else was just trying not to shit their pants, and he did. But a plan is only as good as the one executing it. Well we had Cohen."

It was the first time Honza saw a sign that this colossus of a man ac-tually feared something.

"I don't mind telling you," Viktor continued. "Its a scary thing, seeing the perfect plan in the hands of the perfect killer. Even when they're on your side."

It was a second or two before Viktor could talk again.

"We blew up the embassy, making the militia think we were buried in the rubble, giving us the time we needed to make it out on foot, devising a strategy that would see us pass through the Darién Gap; an 80km stretch of dense jungle between Columbia and Panama. The mi-litia lost our trail, but now we were exposed to the elements and rebels patrolling the Gap. So we've got this French prick."

Viktor searched for a word.

"The ambassador," he said. "He'd acquired some sensitive informa-tion that the U.S. Government deemed high priority, top secret shit.

Typical of the U.S. to turn a blind eye to atrocities, just as long as it gives them an edge. I mean look at operation paperclip for fucks sake."

Honza didn't have a clue what he was talking about, but the way Viktor spoke, he thought maybe he should.

"Anyway. For that reason we were also ordered to ignore his travel companion, an 'adopted son'."

Viktor said using air quotes.

"Couldn't have been any more than eight years old. It was a difficult order for the team to stomach, stand by and pretend the man's affection for the child was anything then what it really was, especially after everything we'd been through to get him out.

We stopped to make camp and Cohen took first watch. He always took first watch. He tried as best he could to block out the sounds, the stifled cries and whimpering, but in the end, he snapped.

When he entered the tent, the diplomat knew exactly why he was there and panicked. He grabbed the boy and put a knife to his throat, trying to remind Cohen of the mission, of his duty and how important it was that he was delivered to the U.S.

The boy had grown up in depravity and desperation. The only thing we could hope was that he was too young to really understand what was going on. But his experience was beyond anything we could imagine. He did understand. He could see the anger and frustration in Cohen's eyes. A rage of defeat that circumvented his will... our orders.

He knew as much as Cohen wanted, he was impotent to act. But the boy still found a way to smile, as if to thank him for even attempting to intervene, to tell him that it was okay. That fucking smile," Viktor said, remembering. "The boy pushed himself onto the knife."

There was admiration in Viktor's sadness.

"After that, it didn't matter what we'd all been through to get this guy out, that we'd just been through hell for nothing. Fuck the mission!" he said. "For Cohen, the second that boy smiled... well, it was one hell of a long night after that. He began to slowly extract the information, and he was good at it. He got anything that had made the ambassador remotely valuable, and then he really went to work on him, even found out stuff they didn't know he had and wasn't being asked for. It was a contradiction. An inhumane act of humanity."

Viktor needed to take a drink. Everyone needed to take a drink.

"The lust for his blood was insatiable," Viktor continued. "Not just to be his destruction, but to bathe in it. Only wishing he was alive to be killed over and over again, unable to quench his thirst."

Viktor got lost in his line of thought, trying to remember why he was telling the story in the first place. Even Dida listened intently, hearing details he hadn't shared before.

"Anyway," he continued, "what we didn't know at the time was that the diplomat was being extracted on behalf of an organisation, we knew them as The Room of Seven. A group more powerful than any government I've ever seen. What he knew... well, you'd have to ask Cohen. He vanished that night, disappeared into the jungle. He knew after killing the diplomat that he'd made enemies within a shadow arm of the U.S. Government, not to mention leaving his unit high and dry.

A few years passed and he showed back up on the radar. About the same time news began circulating of an assassin that passed a decree on the killing of innocent children. For the few people that knew about Columbia, they knew they'd found their man. A contract was created to try and flush him out. Something that would spit in the face of his decree.

As far as all the players involved were concerned, it was the genuine article; a kill order on a politician in Brazil, which included her husband and three children, all surplus to requirements. Along with the assassin, who was nothing more than shark bait, blood in the water to entice him into the open. They knew he would go for the real prize, the head of a drug cartel who'd allegedly initiated the contract. But he was flown out of Brazil to North Africa on a private military jet and surrounded by special forces posing as militia, not to mention the impenetrable compound where he was held up, somewhere high in the mountains that could only be reached by foot."

Honza poured a shot for himself and quickly downed it, gulping almost as much air as drink, hanging on every word that fell from Viktor's lips. He was all too aware of the penchant that men have for exaggeration and embellishment, but Viktor had clearly been understating specific details of the story, which only helped to secure the believability and fuel his imagination to fever point. He sat forward leaning on the table, drawn to hear the conclusion. Dida left the men to finish the story.

"So, what happened?" Honza pressed.

"Well he's here isn't he?" Viktor said, but didn't seem happy about it.

"But what did he do when he found out the contract was a set up?"

"He doesn't know."

"I don't understand?" Honza said.

Without warning, the strong forearms of Dida wrapped a wire around the doctor's throat, yanking him backwards off the chair.

"I organised the contract."

Viktor poured a drink as he watched Honza's legs kicking desperately to try and gain control. His face ballooned with the pressure of blood and his eyes looked like they would pop out of their sockets. But the kicking soon faded as the doctor's life slipped away. Dida let his body fall to the floor and Viktor handed her the drink. He picked up Honza's lifeless body and threw it over his shoulder. He looked towards the back room. Dida placed a reassuring hand on his forearm.

"They'll be here soon," she said.

CHAPTER 25

COHEN

The two patients perfectly mirrored one another, connected by more than just the medical apparatus between them. A tube extracted blood from Cohen on the left, carrying it to Josh on the right. The boy was still unconscious, but their heads were turned towards one another as they lay there, sharing the rarest blood on the planet.

Josh was starting to show signs of responding to the treatment, faint glimmers that gave Cohen a sense of relief. It was beyond anything he believed he was capable of, which surprised him.

Adjusting his head to the discomfort of the cushion he turned from the boy and stared up at the anaemic yellow glow of lights, as though looking through the building, through the bricks, the beams and pipes, staring straight into the heavens. Exhaustion sank into his bones taking the fight from him, it even hurt just laying on the hard table.

He hadn't fooled himself into believing one act of saving a little boy could suddenly wipe out a lifetime of atrocities, but he had to admit that it did feel good.

It was a warm evening, but Cohen was getting colder by the minute. He'd played down how much blood he'd lost, feeling the young doctor already looked overwhelmed enough, any more excitement and his head was likely to explode. It was just easier this way. Whatever was left, he knowingly and willingly gave to the boy.

I'm ready, he thought, wishing it was that easy. That God would suddenly grant him reprieve and his eyes would open on this world no more. Fatigue set in and his eyelids drooped; resistant.

As he continued staring up at the lights Cohen's vision began to morph into a kaleidoscope of colours, twisting and turning until eventually a beautiful stained glass window emerged.

The pictorial image on the window was a scene depicting Mary, looking down upon her son's torn, lifeless body as he lay across her lap following the crucifixion.

At first he thought the memory might have been triggered because of the way the boy's body was sprawled across the table next to him, almost lifeless, or perhaps because it symbolised the destruction of something pure, something innocent. But it was more than that. Memories that alcohol had helped keep at bay were now beginning to break through. What Cohen was running from had finally caught up with him.

In the shadows of the triforium, a pierced gallery sixty feet above the cathedral's nave, his frozen breath lingered upon the air as he watched, waiting. He'd been observing the target all week, but tonight would see the contract's completion.

When first arriving at Domplatte Plaza he'd been met with an unexpected intimidation. Not just another building or landmark, but a presence; Cologne Cathedral. The megalithic gothic monument baring the dark stains of a modern world stole his gaze skywards, ascending twinned spires that reached into the heavens.

It was the largest facade of any church in Europe and one of the largest in the world. Intimidation was in its imagining. At its heart lay the very reason for the cathedral's existence and one of two reasons he found himself in Germany that week, the 'Shrine of the Magi'. A reliquary containing the remains of the Three Wise Men, as told in the New Testament, and one of the most profoundly important relics of Christendom.

The contract was to take possession of a single skull. The second reason was to take the life of the priest charged with the relics keep; Father Weiss. His death only served to fuel the narrative of having tragically lost his life while stumbling upon a robbery in progress, a collateral damage clause.

However, his employers had been very specific about the date of the contract's execution: 11th February 2013. Without being privy to any further information, he was assured this day above all would offer a window of opportunity.

That night, attendance of the cathedral had in fact been a lot lighter than normal, as suggested it would be, but he didn't stop to ponder its reason.

After the doors closed to the general public returning the inner sanctum to a fragile silence, his target, Father Weiss, emerged from beyond the north end of the transept.

Slowly he moved in and out of view as he passed the archways, heading west towards the cathedral's entrance. The entrance was beneath the triforium, so for a short time remained out of view. But Cohen had witnessed the routine all week and it was always executed with the same precision, with an attention to detail he could only admire.

Without being able to see the ageing priest, he knew at this moment he would be placing his hand flush against the main doors, eyes closed in prayer; unconcerned whether the invocation was for the world beyond the doors or the one protected by them. Turning to face the glory of the cathedral, everyday seeming humbled in her presence, Father Weiss continued his journey the length of the nave.

It was several minutes before the priest came back into view and approximately six more before he reached the central altar, where once more he would reflect in prayer. Then continuing beyond the altar towards the Shrine of the Magi, concluding the liturgy in approximately twenty five minutes.

Only when Weiss had passed the central alter did Cohen finally begin to make his move. Mirroring each step with that of the priest, all be it fifty meters away, to avoid separating sounds that could journey to an ear with just one stride. He timed his movement to reach the stairs leading him to the transept at the same time Weiss would be arriving at the shrine. Once descending the gallery steps, continuing south, the target would be trapped at the head of the church with no way back without passing the assassin.

As calculated, by the time Cohen reached the central altar, the target was knelt before the shrine deep in prayer.

Until now he had only witnessed the ceremony at a distance; an observer analysing superficial elements. He was unaware and as such unaffected by its gravity, which he now felt in abundance. But there was something else, something he couldn't quite grasp… almost like a presence.

It had been an entirely different experience sharing the vastness in such a private setting, as apposed to being amongst a noisy melee of gawpers, as if the building revealed something in its silence.

For a week Cohen had explored the space operationally, tactically, unaffected by the foundation of belief the structure rested upon, and yet until now he'd been unable to see what was so glaringly obvious. The dizzying magnificence was simply a distraction from the truth, Heaven was in the details.

Stepping from the altar, his trusty leather boots began to silently traverse the mosaic tiles as he closed in on the target. Candles that lined him both left and right flickered, catching his attention. He eyed them as he took another step and again they flickered, this time he noticed the flame push in his direction.

He instantly recalled his tutelage under Master Yoshida in perceptions of fluctuating energies; that which flowed from and toward you with positive and negative affect.

His uncertainty was that the flame had not bent towards the priest as he would have expected, but towards himself, cautioning an unseen presence whose intention may be even greater than his own.

Cohen pressed forward, and yet somehow the presence seemed to follow. Not in the flames of the candles, but the building itself, which he knew didn't make sense. Suddenly everywhere he looked eyes seemed to be watching him, staring up from the mosaics tiles beneath his feet, the stained glass windows that encircled him in every direction, saints raised on pillars baring down upon him, angels and cherubims, and just in front of him, raised above the priest… Christ upon the cross. And although he had been depicted with his eyes closed, Cohen could swear he was staring directly at him.

He convinced himself that being immersed in the pageantry had somehow managed to get under his skin. The history, the building, the aromas, the elaborate garments all combined to elicit doubt, nothing more than a magic trick of the mind. It was after all one of the most powerful organisations in the world, that had seen empires rise and fall in its wake.

With an arrogant steely determination he pressed forward, overriding *their* power with his will.

But as he did, the beautiful calved oak choir stalls flanking him on either side framing him between panels of delicate frescos, began to feel claustrophobic, even inside this heavenly expanse. Every step felt as though it was wading through wet sand, sinking further and further as palpitations rose.

In each of the stalls, numbering fifty one, he could feel the nameless, faceless souls of the past watching his every move with condemnation, but there were two seats where the feeling was particularly powerful. On his left, at the east end of the aisle and its equivalent on the right. The one to his left was reserved for the Pope, on his right, the Emperor.

Ignoring the periphery of his vision, Cohen focused directly on the target who was now just yards away. The priest's head suddenly rose from his knelt position, but only to rest his eyes once more upon the shrine sat before him.

Ignoring any further hesitation, Cohen delicately removed a knife sheathed at his waist. The distinctive sound of the cold blade striping the leather delivered a stillness into the target, suspending what little animation there was. Father Weiss knew he was no longer alone. With a soft sigh and a groaned effort, the ageing priest rose to his feet and slowly he began to turn around.

Covering the last few yards with surprising swiftness, practically gliding across the tiles, Cohen was there to meet the priest just as he completed his turn. His left arm cradled around the priest's back, almost as an embrace, their eyes meeting for the first time, staring at each other like a reunion of long-lost brothers, filled with pain and sorrow.

The priest then felt a strange heat permeate from his abdomen and ripple like a wave across his body as weakness began to take hold. The stranger's arm was now the only thing keeping him from falling. Their eyes still locked in an impenetrable and confusing gaze as he gently lowered Weiss's body to the ground. The priest winced.

Cohen desperately wanted this to be over quickly, but he couldn't risk inflicting a wound associated with a professional killer, only prolonging the suffering for them both.

Weiss looked down at the knife protruding from his stomach. then back at his killer. There was no sign of anger. A pain that lived beyond the physical, but no anger. As he reached out, his fingers gently brushed the cheek of his deliverer with affection, leaving behind a small stain of blood.

"I forgive you," Weiss whispered.

Strength waned as the ageing priest's life slipped away, until the final limp weight fully rested in Cohen's arms. In that moment something inside the assassin broke. For the first time he regretted taking a life, unable to justify or reconcile the kill.

This priest he'd observed through the week, a man who had shown nothing but great character and nobility, whom had dedicated his life to an idea greater than himself, had just used his final breath to offer forgiveness.

His eyes glazed with a watery layer that would eventually form a tear, but deep controlled breaths suffocated whatever emotion was attempting to rise. He removed his arm and gently rested Weiss's head on the ground, before looking up at the shrine, as though seeing a dwindling hour glass.

Using a frequency generator to create an inaudible hi-frequency pitch, the casing of the shrine shattered with ease. A waft of stale air escaped as beads of sweat began to form over Cohen's temple, his heart racing, not in anticipation or excitement, but dread.

Again sensing he was not alone, his head swivelled back and forth surveying the surroundings. He listened carefully for what he couldn't see, at the same time scanning observation points that he himself might have chosen. Sections of the raised gallery or temporary scaffold platforms used for restoration, that would also assist him in making his escape. But there was no one to be found and he was running out of time.

Removing an oversized alter candle to acquire its even larger holder, he returned to the shrine. Raising it aloft, readying the cumbersome battering ram, he then paused.

There in front of him in all of its glory was the Shrine of the Magi. A triple gilded sarcophagus, with two laying side by side and the third on top to form a basilica. It was exceptional. Elaborately decorated with pearls, cameos and precious gemstones, it was surrounded with excruciatingly fine and intricate metal work. Its panels displaying golden images of historical significance. Prophets, apostles, Mary, Jesus, the baptism and crucifixion and of course, the resurrection. Its value couldn't be quantified and despite its obvious aesthetics, it was only the contents his employers were interested in. The skull of a Magi.

Cohen slammed the base of the holder into the relic with an unrelenting force that sent a sound wave reverberating through the cathedral and probably beyond. The shrine gaped a crude opening of irreparable damage, releasing a rancid odour built from a millennia of decay.

He frantically tore at the opening, breaking off golden ornaments and panels, before reaching inside, blindly navigating the human remains until he found what he was looking for.

He held the skull in his hand studying it, unable to conceive why people went to such extraordinary lengths to acquire such useless things, but it kept him in business, he thought.

REVELATIONS

Setting it down, he reached inside once more and removed a second skull. From inside his bag he removed a further skull and placed it inside the shrine, bagging the two he'd removed.

As if on cue, distant voices bled into the main area of the cathedral as people made their way to investigate the noise. Cohen returned to Father Weiss's body to retrieve his knife, looking up at the cross that hung overhead with a curious fascination.

He wondered how this mere man had amassed such loyalty. The men *he'd* studied were scholars of war, men of renown that had made their names great in the shadows they cast. And just like that, without effort his mind began to recite from one of its teachers, Napoleon Bonaparte.

"I know men, and I tell you that Jesus Christ is no mere man. Between him and every other person in the world there is no possible comparison. Alexander, Caesar, Charlemagne, and I have founded empires. But on what did we rest the creations of our genius? Upon force. Jesus Christ founded his empire upon love; and at this hour millions of men would die for him."

Uncertain of how he could recall a quote he couldn't even remember knowing only reignited his unease and the need to get as far away as quickly as possible. Removing the knife from the priest, he turned to exit before unexpectedly crashing to his knees.

He clutched his stomach as a searing pain began to spread throughout his body. Looking with confusion at the stains on his knife, then at his stomach, blood began cascading over and through his fingers. The wound was in exactly the same position as the one he'd inflicted on the priest. Cohen was certain he hadn't accidentally caused his own wound, but despite his trauma he knew he couldn't be found here.

He struggled back to his feet when a small group led by a young priest entered the cathedral, making their way from the north transept. Suddenly they fell silent. In the narrowing distance ahead of them, a killer stood over Father Weiss's lifeless body, a blooded knife still in hand.

Wondering if he would be able to make it to a safe house before passing out, Cohen looked down again at his wound, but there was nothing there, no wound, no blood cascading through his fingers. Disturbed, relieved, he ran. But before more than three steps passed, something took hold of him.

It was a void inside of him, an absence of life where his heart felt as though it was breaking a thousand times in a single beat, a darkness where love lacked the ability to exist; it was pain beyond any physical torture he'd ever endured. And then he felt it. Something physically penetrated his chest with a force that sent his arms stretching out as though he himself were being impaled on a cross. The knife in his hand pointed skywards and his shoulder bag hung clenched in the other.

He was a prisoner in his own body, unable to move or see the crude depiction of justice he was forming, but he could feel it, in every cell of his being. A scream so powerful it peeled a layer of skin from his throat, filling every inch of the cathedral and causing onlookers to flee in terror, all but one; a young priest.

And just like that as his body collapsed to the floor, it was gone. Whatever force had taken hold of him had gone. Though he knew it never really would be.

CHAPTER 26

JOSH

Joshua's eyes opened. Scared to move and wondering where he'd been moved to, his gaze trolled the raw cement ceiling, rusted pipes and tube lighting.

There was damp mixed with the stale smell of alcohol in the air and the surface he was laying on was hard, unlike the soft bed he'd been previously chained to. Not that it mattered, he didn't know where he'd been before, but if they'd moved him, *maybe it was because someone was looking for me*, he thought, *maybe they were getting close*. It gave him hope.

Sensing he was alone he carefully shifted his head to the side, unexpectedly bringing into view a large man sprawled out on the table next to him; he didn't look so good. But seeing him instantly caused his tummy to cramp, the same twisting feeling he had been suffering from every day for the past week.

His instincts were now to fear everything and everyone, and this man looked as scary as they come, although there was something strangely familiar about him.

He remembered a recent smell of burnt gunpowder and whisky, and looking up, seeing stars in the sky above a man carrying him, who said he was going to take him home. *It wasn't just a dream*. Silent elation began to unravel Josh's tummy with hope, but something still felt off. *Why is he hooked up to a machine as well?*

Sitting up, he looked around to make sure he really was alone. Everything was quiet. Pulling the tube from his arm he disregarded it, leaving blood to slowly drip to the floor as he got down from the table, being careful not to make any noise. Still slightly unsteady on his feet, Josh approached the unconscious man.

He was scruffy, pale, a bullet wound in his shoulder and hands that looked like they were covered in dried blood, but he still had that smell. It wasn't what you would consider inviting, but to Josh it was the scent of his protector. It was masculine, it was strength, comfort, it was larger than life.

Placing a sympathetic hand onto his forearm he instantly reeled, not expecting him to have been cold to the touch. He knew the feeling of blood draining from your body all too well, as though you'd never feel warmth again.

Mimicking procedures he'd experienced throughout the week, he placed two fingers onto the man's cold wrist, hoping to find a pulse. He didn't know if he was doing it right, but was sure he could feel something. It was very faint, but the man was still alive.

Josh's eyes followed the tube from the man's arm to the medical machine and then to the tube dripping a steadily increasing puddle of blood on the floor. *He must have been dying,* he thought.

A child's helpless panic began to rise inside of him, crippling him, his face contorting, preparing for the tears that would soon follow, wanting nothing more than to curl into a foetal ball; wanting his mother.

But I'm not a little boy anymore, he determined, wiping the barely formed tears on the back of his hands. He wanted to call out for help and almost did, but something stopped him. Instead he quietly began to check his surroundings, being careful not to alert anyone to his presence.

There were three half-sized windows high on the wall that appeared to be at street level, which he knew placed him in a basement. *A good escape route,* he thought. That was until he noticed a door with a dull green light above it, reading 'EXIT'.

He climbed on top of a barrel, tiptoeing on its edge to get a view of the road outside. There wasn't much to see, it was still dark. What he could see was a quiet narrow street and a single parked car a little way up on the opposite side. Suddenly a pair of feet crossed in front of the window, the surprise causing Josh to jerk backwards. The barrel rocked and threatened to topple over, but he managed to grab hold of the window sill just in time. Steadying his balance and bringing the barrel beneath him under control, he continued peering from the window, trying desperately to see who the feet belonged to, but the man was so big he couldn't get an angle to see his face. What he could see was another man draped over his shoulder like a rag doll.

Slowly, as if in sudden shock, Josh climbed down from the barrel with a slight trembling in his body. He needed to get out of this place and fast, but his only hope was lying unconscious on the table. *If he couldn't escape, maybe he could hide,* he thought.

Approaching the door at the far end of the room he peeked into the bar. It was quiet. All the chairs were stacked on top of the tables, but for one. In the middle were three used chairs, although one of them had been knocked on its side. On the table was a silver ice bucket, a clear bottle and three small glasses, but no sign of anyone.

He made his way through and crawled behind the bar. Not sure what he was really looking for, he found a manilla envelope stuffed with cash, lots of cash. Underneath was a revolver and a canvas coin bag. Stuffing the envelope and gun into the bag, he returned to the back room, his head swivelling frantically looking for somewhere to hide.

He eyed the exit door, again toying with the idea of running, but at ten years of age didn't quite fancy his chances. He looked at the shelving, the tables, crates and barrels, asking himself where he would go in the ultimate game of hide and seek. He concluded that the piled crates forming pillars against the wall could be manipulated, allowing him to stand amongst them without looking like he'd disturbed anything. Then when he got a chance, he would run, find help and eventually get home.

He started towards the crates when he noticed a table with several bags of blood laid across it, uncertain of why he hadn't seen them until now. He then looked back at the man who had saved his life. Putting down the canvas bag, he picked up a pouch of blood and approached the machine. The label on the blood read 'A positive'.

All week he'd been hearing people talk about rare and special blood, and that whatever was inside of him people were clearly willing to kill for. He returned to the table and picked up a bag marked 'Josh's blood', reasoning if it was so valuable then perhaps it could help, *and hopefully piss them off.*

Returning to the machine, needing a chair to reach its functions, Josh hung the new bag of blood, reversed the machines flow and removed the secondary feed that was still dripping on the floor.

All week he had done nothing but watch as doctors repeated the same functions for him, and was sure he had got the sequence right, but nothing happened. Checking the connections, he remembered something else. He then flicked the drip tube below the bag, and waited. Eventually a single drop, then another and another. A small accomplished smile lightly curled his mouth, it had only been a week, but it felt like forever since he'd done that. It made him remember his friends on the school trip, laughing with them in the hotel room and the teacher knocking on the door telling them to go to sleep. He hoped none of them had been taken because he knew there were more like him. Lots more.

Jumping down from the chair he attempted to move the crates. Most contained empty bottles, but the stacks were a lot heavier than he'd imagined and had difficulty moving them. Sitting on the floor like he was ready to row an oar, Josh pulled at the bottom crate with all his strength. The stack scraped on the floor as it started to move, the top swaying, threatening to topple, but it was just too heavy. He stopped.

The exertion was beginning to make him feel light-headed, but he knew he could do it, he was a strong boy and one of the fastest in his class. He pulled again with an even greater effort, when something strange came over him. Without enough blood in his system, his energy suddenly evaporated and the room began to spin out of control.

He slumped onto his back breathing more rapidly, trying to stay conscious as he stared helplessly at the window and how close he was to being free.

Lights from an approaching vehicle flashed across the wall, briefly illuminating the room before plunging it back into its yellow gloom. The vehicle stopped right outside and the engine cut. Muffled voices began conversing, but it was too blurry to make anything out. He could just about make out the person who'd passed by the window earlier moving in the opposite direction. *He's coming back*, Josh thought.

The doors of the vehicle began opening and closing, but it wasn't just one vehicle, he heard at least eight doors and what sounded like one sliding, like the type you'd find on the side of a transit van. What followed was a parade of dark trousers and boots marching past the window in the same direction. They were heading to the bar.

Rolling onto his tummy, Josh started to drag himself towards the crates, hoping he could somehow slide himself amongst them. As he inched closer, he could hear the rumbling of feet descending the stairs into the bar. He wasn't going to make it. Using his last ounce of energy to roll onto his back, so he could at least breathe, he listened to the melee of voices gathering in the next room, his vision was starting to fade. The last thing he remembered was the sensation of his body rising into the air, floating towards the dull green light.

CHAPTER 27

COHEN

With Josh in his arms and a bag of blood gripped between his teeth, Cohen quickly and quietly made his way from the exit to an exterior enclosure, where a steep metal staircase covered by a steel plate overhead led onto the back alley.

As he began to ascend a lightheadedness forced him to pause, cautioning him to his state. It quickly passed, but any exertion was gambling with his consciousness. Holding Josh, he pushed with his head against the metal plate to open it, again feeling a slight vertigo he exited into the alleyway.

Two men in dark tactical attire were enjoying a smoke in their downtime, waiting by the three vehicles parked outside. One was a heavyset military type and the second, a young wet-behind-the-ears rookie judging by his incessant chatter. Even in Cohen's current state, he was more than capable of stopping him. It would be a matter of seconds before Viktor discovered he'd taken the boy and be racing out of the exit behind him. He stepped into the alley and approached the empty lead vehicle, stopping at the passenger side.

"Get the fucking door!" he ordered.

The brazen action did as intended, instilling them with enough uncertainty to act. Without question, the younger man opened the door for Cohen who secured Josh into the passenger seat, while the heavier guy watched curiously and suspiciously.

Suddenly realising who he was, he scrambled for his gun which he'd left inside the vehicle. The young man was mid-sentence when Cohen turned from Josh, put the barrel under his chin and pulled the trigger.

A spray of blood washed his face as the excruciating sound of the blast bounced rapidly between the walls of the alley, causing a painful ringing in his ears, welcoming back the disorientation. It gave the heavyset operative the time he needed to reach his gun, he turned, aimed and pulled the trigger. A second shot rang out and the man collapsed lifeless to the floor with his finger over the safety.

Gritting his teeth to brace himself for what followed, Cohen emptied the rest of the clip into the second vehicle, incapacitating it and blocking the third from being able to follow. The ringing became so severe that along with his equilibrium, his vision blurred. Staggering back to the car he managed to get a new clip into the gun and himself into the driver's seat just as the metal plate over the back stairs flew open. Despite the impairment he knew the road ahead was straight for at least 150 yards before he'd need to turn. He took off at speed with the car bouncing and scrapping off of the walls. His vision clearing just in time to take the sharp corner.

Viktor, along with associates, started to pour into the alley, but only in time to see the vehicle kick up sparks as it scraped the wall before turning right at the end of the road. A stillness came over him, almost as if he'd just caught a glimpse of his future. He took a long slow deep breath, staring at the space where the car had just been, while the men around him panicked, fumbling frantically to move the bodies and an immobile van. A few ended up reversing the working car all the way to the other end of the alley to chase a ghost. Viktor knew the city and the target better than anyone and if you weren't right on his tail, you weren't anywhere.

He was embarrassed to see their disorganisation at work. They wouldn't have lasted an hour in some of the shit holes he and Cohen had seen. Leaving them to frolic around in the dark, he turned and calmly walked back to the bar.

"Oi, where the fuck are you going?" one of them said.

Viktor looked at the man as if to respond, but there was nothing to say. He knew that unless The Order caught up with Cohen and finished him for good, every person in that alley had just signed their own death warrant. He turned back and continued inside.

Getting out of Prague was easier than expected, although Cohen had to be a little creative to avoid the sudden increase in police presence; an order that was beyond Viktor's power.

With the city lights behind him and dark country lanes ahead, he peered over the steering wheel fixated on the road like a wide-eyed novice, lights on full beam and gripping the steering wheel so tight it was cutting the circulation from his fingers. He was all too aware of a fragile consciousness and doing everything he could to hold on to it.

Initially he headed south of the city, using main roads to make the direction of his journey more detectable. A trail that would lead anyone tracking to hopefully anticipate his escape towards Vienna, arranging to intercept him sometime before Austria. But once out of the city he took the road west towards Frankfurt, to someone that would be able to fly them out of the country under the radar.

Not until noticing the sun creeping over the horizon in the rear view did he realise how long he'd been driving for. There were no signs they were being followed, but every so often he would look up at the sky. It was habit more than anything else, but tracking was rarely done at ground level anymore.

Josh was still unconscious, but every so often Cohen felt his wrist for a pulse. When they started the journey it was beating at a pace he worried would induce a coronary failure; even at ten years old. But it had slowed to a steady rhythm, which alleviated some anxiety, though not to the extent a nice bottle of Blue Label would. He pulled into a clearing where the foliage concealed the car from the main road and sent Nathan a text.

"The sister of a Red Rose?"

For obvious reasons they used obscure floral references to communicate pre-arranged codes. It could be used to identify a whole host of situations, but on this occasion it was a pilot and location, Traeger Schäfer of Hanau; a town 25 kilometres east of Frankfurt.

The sister of Red Rose is Snow White, not the Snow White from the Disney adaptation, but from the tales of The Brother's Grimm; Snow White and Red Rose.

"You know the Brother's Grimm were born in my home town of Hanau," Traeger would mention without fail every time you flew with him.

After serving in the German military, he ran off book and was possibly one of the most audaciously insane pilots Cohen had ever come across, and the only one who could still make him nervous doing so. They called him The Baron. But he always enjoyed hearing him tell an unusual Grimm fairy tale right before dropping him off in some backwater hellhole. *The Juniper Tree, might have been the one he would have told before coming on this contract.* He thought.

Now Traeger flew commercially and from time to time the two had been known to break bread, although not since he helped Cohen escape Cologne. A detail that until this very moment had slipped his mind.

The thought agitated him enough to step out of the car and stretch his legs. Noticing some wild berries he tried distracting himself by foraging a few, wrapping them in a napkin and leaving them in the glove compartment for when Josh woke up. He paced a slow circle, staring at the phone waiting for a response, though his vision drifted beyond the phone to the grass he walked. As he completed the small circle he was stopped by the epiphany of being back where he started, where it all started.

Traeger was the only other person who really knew what happened to him that night, and had witnessed the fear of God in Cohen's eyes. That alone was reason enough to never want to see him again; ashamed in his own skin. And last night he'd only faced the memory of Cologne because he thought he would never open his eyes again, but it made it all feel like it was just yesterday.

A warm morning breeze washed over him. He turned to see if Josh was still in the car. He was. It was strange because he was sure he felt a presence, as if someone was standing right next to him. Suddenly Cohen could no longer feel the pain of his wound, the weakness of blood loss, the withdrawal of alcohol, but there was something else. Something far greater that he didn't know was there until it wasn't. Anger, rooted to the core of his soul.

He stood looking across the golden canola fields being kissed by the morning sun, trees scattered on the horizon stretching out their branches in praise, and felt peace. Not an appreciation for life in that moment, but actual, absolute and underserving peace. It was beyond anything he could have ever imagined.

The phone vibrated in his hand pulling him into the now, shattering the peace and returning his possessions; pain and anger. But its power lingered in his memory as a destination.

Looking at the phone, he'd received a response from Nathan. Traeger was in play.

As Cohen returned to the car, the moisture of a cold sweat started to break. Using his knife to slice into the backseat, ripping out the cushioning, he pulled out a wire from the frame. Wiping the steadily increasing stream from his forehead, he fashioned the wire to the handle over the driver's side door and attached the bag of what remained of Josh's blood. Connecting it back to his arm he reluctantly opened the tap.

The concoction of blood and adrenalin was unrelenting, but necessary. Burning as it swept through his veins and into his chest, there was a sharp stabbing in his brain. His body went rigid as he slammed his feet into the well of the car. Not wanting to wake the boy, he desperately ground his jaw to stifle the groans that leaked a soft whimper. After the mixture's initial impact passed, Cohen's body collapsed back into the chair. It was nothing short of torture, but the only thing he could do to stop himself from passing out, albeit carefully and incrementally.

As he looked at Josh sleeping peacefully, innocent despite all that had happened to him, he wanted to smile. It was an image to soften the hardest of hearts and yet he still couldn't allow himself. He realised now that when he was standing in the canola field, gifted with a serenity undeserving, he wasn't alone. But when the presence had gone, it left something behind. He couldn't smile because, whatever laid ahead, this was just the beginning. He put the car back on the road and headed for Hanau.

CHAPTER 28

BONSU

There was serenity to be found in the early hours of the observatory, which often saw Brother Bonsu still at his desk long after technicians had left for the evening. So he was taken aback when the faint sound of tapping caught his attention before instinctively covering what he was working on with other papers on his desk.

"Hello?" he gently tested.

The door handle slowly turned and Mackie could do nothing but hold his breath. After hearing of the cruelty in Arizona he feared the worst. The latch clicked and the door swung ajar, a tray emerged in its opening followed by its carrier.

"Cardinal Oorloff!" Mackie exclaimed.

"I apologise for calling on you at this late hour," he replied. "I was just sitting in my office when I recalled how much you always cherished this time."

He closed his eyes embracing the stillness, before opening them again to look directly at Mackie.

"Mmmm, so quiet," he said.

There was a breathy melodic resonance to his voice that sounded how one would imagine a snake might if it could talk, complimented by his slender skeletal features. Despite the polite dance it was clear the two men were not trusting of one another. The cardinal placed the tray onto the desk taking note of the paper resting beneath Mackie's hands. He then took a seat.

"You came all the way from the Vatican?" Mackie queried.

"Well in light of this business at our facility in Arizona, I thought perhaps it prudent to stay abreast."

"Of course," Mackie said.

But his candid nature had caught him off guard.

"Tea?" the cardinal asked.

"Yes, thank you."

Mackie took the natural movement as opportunity to shuffle the papers in front of him and slide them into the desk drawer, but it didn't go unnoticed by Cardinal Oorloff.

"Please don't stop on my account," he said continuing to pour.

"I'm sure if the cardinal hadn't meant interruption he would have called."

"I suppose he would."

He handed him the cup and saucer, accompanied by a small biscuit resting on its edge.

"Thank you," Mackie said placing it on the desk in front of him, acutely aware the cardinal was studying his every move.

"Has any new information come to light?" he enquired.

"Not as yet," the cardinal responded. "But it will. It must. But in doing so we also have the reputation of the church to consider."

"Why would the reputation of the church be in any danger? Surely we were the ones attacked."

The cardinal smiled as he sipped his tea. Mackie followed suit, but only after the cardinal had tasted his. Placing down the cup the cardinal collected his biscuit.

"Come now Brother Bonsu, you aren't naive enough not to have foreseen the optics. The priests recommendation came directly from me."

The biscuit snapped in two. The cardinal was unpleased his tension had revealed itself.

"I fear implications would put the Holy Father into the public firing line," he continued. "Hard though it may be to believe, I'm here because I need your help."

Realising the cardinal was there to protect himself helped Mackie breathe a little easier. He collected his biscuit, biting into it as he considered Cardinal Oorloff's dilemma, when he noticed him replace his own broken biscuit back onto the plate. Mackie raised his vision to find the cardinal's icy gaze staring back, a taste of almonds climbed his throat and into his nasal passage. He tried clearing his throat, but that only seemed to hasten the poison. He smiled to himself as he felt his throat tighten, staring at the uneaten broken biscuit on the cardinal's plate.

"Why did you take that letter from my study?" Oorloff said with disappointment. "It was a selfish act that has caused needless deaths. It seemed only fitting the deed should be repaid."

"I was simply the messenger," he said with a gleeful smile.

"You'll forgive me for not stating the obvious." Oorloff said wryly. "There was no malice in withholding Father Weiss's letter, quite the contrary, we did it to avoid exactly what we're now facing. The hopeless crusade of your brethren to stop that which cannot be stopped."

"So my death is a righteous one."

"Oh don't be soar. I did tell them this was all so much more complicated than it needed to be. Contractors, assassins or whatever they are, when sometimes a little flattery and a biscuit is all you really need."

"This changes nothing," Brother Bonsu said, sounding as though he was trying to speak with a hand gripped around his throat. "The brotherhood already know."

"Oh I'm not here to stop anything. By all means rally the troops, the more the merrier. No, your death merely serves a purpose Brother Bonsu. To offer up a narrative that won't be investigated. Your brethren will soon follow."

He noticed the miniature nautical wheel on the desk and flicked it into rotation.

"You Natsarim and your silly symbols," he amused.

Watching as Mackie fought a losing battle, a slither of air slowly wheezing from his final breaths, face bloating and eyes bulging as though any second they might burst from his skull, until finally he collapsed on the desk.

The sound caused Cardinal Oorloff's driver to rush into the room, but only to see the dead brother sprawled across his desk. Oorloff moved around the table to check the drawer Mackie hid the paper in; words of the prophesy.

"Is it important?" the driver asked.

"No," he said closing the drawer. "Collect the cups and tray would you, I'll meet you in the car."

The cardinal left the room.

As his chauffeured vehicle made its way back to the Vatican through the quiet roads of Rome, they passed a congregation of police vehicles surrounding a small church. The sirens were silent as the blue lights flashed ominously against its facade. One of the police personnel happened to notice the cardinal's car driving past. He removed his cap and bowed his head in reverence. The cardinal returned the gesture with a faint smile and nod of appreciation.

Inside the church they had discovered the body of a young priest, the real Father Trentini who'd been horrifically impaled upon a section of iron candle holders, his arms stretched out as though in mocked crucifixion.

Upon its sight one of the police fell to his knees and started to pray.

The cardinal dialled a number on his secure phone.

"It's done," he said.

He listened for a moment and then disconnected the call. Taking from his lapel pocket a small unmarked envelope no more than a few inches in size, he held it for a moment before removing a white card from inside. It was embossed with a golden serpent eating its tail. He stared from the window with thoughts lingering victoriously, before saying softly to himself, "If no one's around to hear the fall of man, does he make a sound?"

"Sorry sir?" the driver said.

But the cardinal just continued smiling, staring from the window.

CHAPTER 29

TRAEGER

When Cohen and Josh arrived at the hanger, Traeger was finishing the final checks on his pride and joy, a dark blue Cessna 172 light aircraft. There wasn't much that could pull his attention from her once he got working, but he did stop to take in Cohen as he alighted the car. He tried giving the appearance that everything was okay, but Traeger knew an injured man when he saw one. However, he was surprised at the dishevelment and somewhat amused at the extra weight his old friend was carrying. Smiling broadly he stretched out his arms in greeting.

Ignoring the pain that would follow, Cohen embraced Traeger with all his strength. Even before he'd stepped from the car he could tell his old friend was unwell. Thinner than the last time he saw him, to the point of gaunt; sallow skin and sunken ghost-like eyes.

The embrace of the men lasted a little longer than would have been normal, but then there was more to say, albeit unspoken. Eventually they broke away and Traeger held his friend at arm's length to take him in.

"To be honest, I was expecting worse," he said. "Nathan explained everything. How's the kid?"

Cohen looked back at the car, Josh was sleeping soundly. It was clear Traeger was blowing over the obvious. *How's the kid?* he thought, H*ow are you?* is what he wanted to say, but instead he said,

"He's strong. I could do with getting some fluids into him though."

"Is he awake?"

"No, but he's got a tap," Cohen said raising his hand to show the cannula still attached to his own.

"Matching jewellery. Nice."

"You think you can put something together?

"Shouldn't be a problem. What about you?"

"Yeah, I could do with some fluids," Cohen said, "if you've got a bottle of something lying around."

Traeger scoffed.

"Okay. Let me put something together. Make yourself at home," he said exiting to the back office.

Suddenly Cohen felt like a painted target stood in an open hanger with just the plane, the car and him on display. Seeing a crappy old kitchen table off to the side, probably salvaged knowing Traeger, he checked on Josh and then like everyone else that entered the hanger, gravitated towards it.

He perused a partially unfolded map of Europe that was laid across the surface. It seemed Traeger had already plotted a flight path for England, stopping at Le Touquet on the French coast, probably to refuel. His attention was suddenly distracted by a loud clattering entering the hanger, turning to see Traeger wheeling a gurney towards the car.

"Gimme a hand with the boy," he said.

"You just happened to have this lying around?" Cohen quipped as he joined Traeger to help.

"You'd be surprised at the amount of medical emergencies I see."

"Yeah? Like what?"

"Like now dick head. Get the door!"

Cohen chuckled to himself. First time he could remember doing that since… well, he couldn't remember the last time.

The two men carefully removed Josh from the car and laid him onto the gurney, though Cohen's attention was split between the two, unable to reconcile his friend's deterioration while watching him attend to the boy's needs selflessly.

Once Josh was resting comfortably and starting to take on fluids, Traeger brought a drink for Cohen, though not the one he was expecting. From the office he carried a small tray holding two cups and a metal tea pot, met with a blank expression of disappointment. Traeger laughed and poured.

"Green tea. I thought you loved this stuff?" he said handing Cohen a cup.

Cohen stared at the leaves swirling around the vortex of transparent liquid. Not because he was disappointed in the drink, but because looking at his friend was just too difficult. The Baron he knew was like a real-life comic book character that was just too big for the pages. An adventurer that could find your smile in the darkest of places. And when you're in hell, a smile can save your life. He may not have known it, but he had saved Cohen's life on more than one occasion.

"A brain tumour," Traeger said addressing the elephant in the room.

Cohen stared up from the drink wearing a weighted expression, but words suffocated in his throat.

"I started getting spells. You know, a little dizzy here and there, nothing serious, and then six months ago I blacked out. Angela insisted I saw a doctor. She knew I'd never go if I was left to my own devices, so we went together. They gave me four months."

"Six months ago?" Cohen confirmed.

"Now every night when I go to bed Angela kisses me, wondering if I'll still be there come morning."

Traeger's thoughts lingered on his wife.

"Traeger, I'm…"

He interrupted Cohen's sentiment dismissing it with a wave of his hand.

"Yeah, yeah. You're sorry, Angela's sorry, everyone's sorry," he said. "But like I explained to her and what I want you to understand now is this. I'm not being robbed of life Cohen, of time. I'm being gifted it. Every single minute of every single day."

The hanger fell silent momentarily.

"You want to hear something funny?" Traeger continued. "For years Angela had always been on at me to go to church with her."

Cohen listened intently.

"Then about a year ago," he continued, "I couldn't tell you why, but I had this strange yearning that I had to go, so I spoke to her about it. She said it was God calling me home. Can you believe that?"

His skin stretched with unnatural lines as he smiled. Cohen stiffly offered one in return, though his eyes betrayed him. Traeger had become used to veiled looks of sympathy.

"I always loved my wife," he continued. "Despite the fact she believed some ghost was running the world. But honestly, for all the shit I'd done in my life, I really wanted to believe her. Of course it's all just a bunch of stories right?"

"Right," Cohen offered unconvincingly.

And Traeger's knowing stare suggested he was unconvinced.

"But when I stood outside that church," he continued. "About to go in for the first time, I was probably more scared than I've ever been in my life, because I know what I've done. I said to myself, 'how can this all be just a lie, if the fear is so real?' I couldn't do it. Angela had to actually take me by the hand and lead me in."

The thought of that day brought a smile to him.

"And then I remembered you."

"You're right that is funny," Cohen said dryly.

Traeger scoffed a smile at his friend uncertain if he was being coy, naive or just dishonest.

"That night in Cologne. I saw it in your eyes and don't you try and fucking deny it."

Cohen could see his friend needed some semblance of peace so remained silent. Though he'd been denying it every day for the past eighteen months.

"I thought somehow my part in all of it had damned me," Traeger continued. "That this was my judgement."

"And now?" Cohen asked with more than passing interest.

"Now I know. It isn't judgement, it's forgiveness, it's mercy."

An anger ran through Cohen's body tightening his muscles and furrowing his brow.

"Forgiveness?" he sneered through gritted teeth. "You think some God giving you a brain tumour is forgiveness? I can understand your wife, civilians or people that haven't seen the true horrors of this world taking comfort in some force that runs their lives. But you?"

"You're still standing outside the church Cohen, you're just afraid to go in. I get it, I do. But you need to wake up. It was us, we were the horrors of the world. God was never absent, no matter how much we denied him."

Cohen couldn't believe what he was listening to. He wanted to scream at his friend but was conscious of waking Josh. He leaned forward.

"You think it was God that got you through Panama?"

Traeger mirrored Cohen's movement and leaned in.

"Yes. I do."

The response was powerful enough to retreat Cohen back into his chair. He wanted to say something, but he was stunned to look at Traeger with incredulity.

"You don't get it," he continued. "I've lived my life in a way that doesn't deserve for me to be here to take stock, to prepare, to be able to say goodbye to loved ones. And for the last two months I've lived every day as if it was my last, because in that moment it really was; it is. A mercy so beautiful, so un-fucking-deserving, I thought why me? Why do I get this gift? That's when you appeared in my mind. As clearer picture as I've ever seen. It was like, my memories, but I wasn't seeing them, I was being shown them."

Traeger watched as the blood drained from Cohen's face, fear overcame his eyes. He may not have noticed had he not experienced the same thing standing with his wife outside the church.

"So I knew I'd see you again. I know man, I know how this all sounds, like I'm losing my shit. But I knew there was still one thing left for me to do."

He looked over at Josh and smiled to himself.

"You know you're not as funny as you used to be," Cohen said.

Both men smiled at one another before quickly morphing into a painful and silent goodbye, which Traeger broke by saying,

"Why don't we think about putting this bird in the air and getting the little one back to his mother?"

A short while after refuelling at Le Touquet, somewhere over the English Channel, Josh awoke, taking a moment to get his bearings. He rubbed his eyes and stared curiously from the window, eventually realising he was in a plane. He looked to his right where a strange thin pale man was sat smiling at him as he piloted.

"There you are," Traeger said. "I was hoping you would wake before we landed."

Josh tried to speak but his throat and mouth were completely dry. Traeger reached behind him for a rucksack and dropped it in the boy's lap.

"Here, you must be starving."

Josh opened the bag to find a stack of drinks, sandwiches and sweets, it was like a mobile sweet shop. Traeger reached in and pulled out a bottle of water.

"You'd better start with that," he said.

Josh sipped the water and gingerly swallowed to limit the pain of his throat absorbing moisture.

"Where are you taking me?" he croaked.

"You're going home Josh. Back to your mother."

He sank back into the seat still waking up when it dawned on him. Quickly he started looking around the plane.

"That man? The scruffy one," he said.

Traeger chuckled.

"He wanted to be here, but he still had some things he had to do. Here," he said opening a pocket on the rucksack, "he left you something."

Traeger took out the napkin of berries and handed it to the boy. Josh put down the bag of goodies and took the napkin before opening it. Seeing the berries he then offered them to Traeger.

"They're just for you," he said.

Josh sat back, ate the berries and drank his water.

"Oh I nearly forgot," Traeger said. "The scruffy guy, Cohen. He told me to tell you thanks for saving his life."

CHAPTER 30

CHARLOTTE

In London, political negligence had now moved into the realm of sheer incompetence, after yet another embarrassing scandal surfaced surrounding the prime minister. The UK's already charged atmosphere was a tinderbox waiting to ignite, and if it did, it threatened to spark a fire that would spread around the world. The public wanted his blood, but accepted his resignation.

Anyone with eyes to see or ears to hear knew exactly what came next, but still they scrambled to fill the power vacuum with all the same faces, trying to placate the masses with all the same promises. *'We've heard you, and we will change,'* they said.

But gone were the standard cries of the political landscape, schools, taxes, inflation, immigration, all replaced with one single demand: *We want Archibald. T. Montgomery.*

It wasn't 24 hours before waking up to the familiar sight of an ominous hazed sun, shrouded by the smouldering ashes of cities that burned through the night. And with it the historical and unprecedented move to announce the name of their champion as a candidate on the ballot of a snap election. Archie gracefully accepted. Power was with the people.

That alone was enough to turn the tide of hope, not just for a nation, but a world watching.

After an extended, gruelling but successful by-proxy promotional tour, Charlotte was now only hours away from returning home. Along with her new 23-year-old, geopolitical post-graduate assistant Teresa, she was in the process of packing the last of her things and could hear her phone vibrating.

"Where the hell…? Tee can you see my phone?"

Teresa was in the middle of eating some room service toast that hung from her mouth as she began to look. The two searched around the room picking up and disregarding clothes and a plethora of shopping bags, but couldn't locate the source. Finally Teresa checked under the bed, there it was. Just as she reached it, the vibrating stopped.

17 Missed Calls: Archie.

"Oh shit!"

She handed the phone to Charlotte.

"Aren't you supposed to be keeping me organised?" Charlotte dryly amused.

Teresa looked around at the chaotic mess of the room, uncertain of how to give a polite answer, but her raised eyebrows conveyed just what a task that was. Charlotte was about to hit call return when Archie's picture appeared on the television behind the presenter of a local news station.

"Turn that up," she said.

Finding the control under a magazine, Teresa turned up the volume as an assertive knock arrived at the door.

"Noooo…" Charlotte said, instinctively and amusingly linking the events.

She knew when it came to Archie, anything was possible, but ignoring the door momentarily focused her attention on the television.

Presenter: "In a recent interview with his Holy Father the Pope, he was asked what he thought about the man in line to receive The Ordo De Christi and his meteoric rise on the world stage."

A video clip of the interview started to play. The Pope was sat forward on a high backed armchair with his careful attention on every word of the interviewer.

Off Screen Interviewer: "Do you think that in these turbulent times that it's possible that Archibald Montgomery is a man sent by God?"

The Pope reclined into his chair as he took time to consider a question of such magnitude.

The Pope: "One does not have to be sent from God for him to work through you. That being the case, I do believe that he has chosen this very extraordinary young man, so in essence, yes. Why not?"

He smiled warmly.

As the screen returned to the presenter the assertive knocking repeated itself in quick succession. Unable to focus on the broadcast Charlotte frustratingly looked at Teresa who proceeded to answer the door.

"Erm, Charlotte."

With a sigh she rose to join Teresa, taken aback to see four men and two women wearing semi-casual, but functional attire and a uniformed serious expression.

"Miss Finbrook," one of the women said in a regimented tone.

"Yes," she replied uncertainly.

"I'm Delia, head of your security detail."

"My security detail? I don't have…"

Delia thrust a smart device forward.

"Please place your thumb inside the window on the screen, everything will be explained momentarily."

"Archie!" she blurted.

Charlotte looked at the device and pressed her thumb against the small rectangle. The woman snatched away the device and waited for confirmation.

Charlotte Finbrook: Authentication.

When the text turned from red to green, a colleague handed Delia a smart-tablet which she passed directly to Miss Finbrook.

"Please close the door and hit play on the device," she continued. "We'll be here when you're done."

Being surprised at the interruption, Charlotte looked at her as though she was still trying to catch up. Delia leaned forward and slowly closed the door on behalf of Miss Finbrook.

Now staring at the inside of the hotel door, Charlotte turned her attention to the tablet, unaware that Teresa's attention was concerned on her. Taking a seat on the bed, on top of disregarded clothes, she hit play. The screen burst to life with a pre-recorded video of Archie.

"I thought by you having an assistant you'd be easier to reach," he started with his normal charming self. "I was really hoping to speak to you before news broke."

Both Charlotte and Teresa's attention was stolen and soon stunned by an announcement on the television, the resignation of the United Kingdom's Prime Minister.

The news triggered a not so unrelated memory of Charlotte's first meeting with Archie.

A small South London coffee shop. She'd purposefully chosen a part of the city where his comfort wasn't the first thing on the agenda. It was a petulant test, but carried worth. She had of course expected him to be agreeable to the demand, but only so his team could make last minute arrangements to change venues; an obvious power play.

The call came that morning as expected, but only to confirm her attendance; now she was a little nervous. But the crisp morning and a low winter sun filled her with confidence and energy that she could enter the coffee shop, look the handsome billionaire in the eye and say something to him he hadn't heard in his entire life: No.

She arrived thirty minutes early, as per every meeting she'd ever attended. Now sat idling over a coffee gone cold, rehearsing in her head the most graceful way to reject his offer.

The door opened pulling her attention, but sun reflecting from its window hit Charlotte directly in the eye, blinding her momentarily. Painfully squinting she tried to adjust her vision by shielding her eyes with her hand, when a shadow came between her and the sun. As it disappeared behind the silhouette standing in front of her, she could have sworn the receding rays looked as though wings were being concealed. And there standing in front of her was Archie, almost as if he'd appeared from the sun itself, smiling, edged in a golden corona.

A remarkably fortuitous entrance, she thought, but not enough to sway her decision. She'd expected the meeting to be a swift affair of no more than ten minutes, but two hours into the conversation and they hadn't barely begun talking of work. She took time to observe him, how people responded to him, how his energy infected everyone around him in a way she'd never seen before, let alone in a wannabe politician.

"Yes," she said without having to be asked the question.

"You don't know what it is you're saying yes to," Archie teased.

"Oh no I do," she said. "I just hope you do."

He laughed as if everything she said had been foreseen.

"Okay. Then I guess statistical analysis it is… For now."

She'd always wondered what he'd meant by that, but assumed it was that her role had a shelf life and the clock was ticking. Knowing Archie as she did now, she realised he had plans beyond a horizon she was ill-equipped to see. But that wasn't the reason for the memory, it was the interview on the TV. *A man of God*, she thought. As preposterous as it seemed, it wasn't the first time the thought had entered her mind.

She recalled the day now dubbed The Piccadilly Speech and the absolute fear she felt watching Archie approach the venting masses, one man against the world. That was when she felt it. Every hair standing on end as lighting streaked across the sky, bursting through the clouds. Now she wasn't so sure it had just been a trick of the light on their first meeting. Now she had to seriously consider if what she'd witnessed were actually wings of light, because there was something undeniably special about this man, even the Pope could see it.

The untimely reverie had distracted her from the important message and by the time she focused on the tablet, Archie was saying,

"See you in a couple of days."

The screen went blank.

"That's unbelievable," Teresa gasped. Unaware Charlotte had zoned out.

"Shit."

She tried getting the device to replay but it wouldn't respond. A fracas from the television stole her attention once again as Teresa continued to watch her.

A smiling Archie was doing his best to wrestle past reporters thrusting microphones and cameras into his face as he tried entering his North London home.

"Have you given any thought to how you would make your choice on cabinet ministers?" one said.

"We've been approached by MPs from both sides of the aisle," Archie responded, "but we're not interested in career politicians, only those who can affect change matter now."

"How about your number two?" another shouted. "Who's that gonna be?"

The melee suddenly became quiet as Archie turned to face them.

"The only person it could be of course. Miss Charlotte Finbrook."

Her breath taken, Charlotte placed a hand to her chest, the way she would when drama struck, only this time it wasn't just a gasp. Overwhelmed, she found herself needing to take a seat on the bed, unconcerned with the disregarded clothes and bags. *Oh no, it's happening again,* she thought as her breathing quickened. Unable to expand her lungs she tried remembering how Archie calmed her the last time, but thinking of him only seemed to exasperate it.

Feeling the warmth of Teresa's hand suddenly but gently taking hold of her own surprised Charlotte. The assistant sat beside her on the bed and said nothing, closing her eyes she bowed her head and prayed in silence. Charlotte was so taken by what she was seeing, uncertain of how to respond or process it that she hadn't immediately appreciated her anxiety completely evaporate.

When Teresa removed her hand she'd left something behind, the slither of a chain draped from Charlotte's clasp. She opened her hand and there in the palm lay her necklace. She was so unexpectedly grateful to see its return, bewildered and impressed beyond measure; speechless. Only able to quietly watch with new admiration as Teresa stood and began to address the packing situation.

"How did you…?"

But she avoided any questions by opening the door and calling Delia inside.

"Miss Finbrook will be ready to leave for the airport in the next thirty minutes," Teresa said. "Please see the cars are ready."

Delia nodded in the affirmative, turned on her heel and left the room. Looking at the delicate plain silver cross in hand, Charlotte's fingers touched it with longing affection, it held more value than she'd realised.

"I don't think I'm ready for this," she admitted.

It wasn't like Charlotte to expose weaknesses or offer up vulnerability, but with the world in such utter chaos, she didn't want to be just another part of the problem. Becoming distracted by a meteoric rise where ambition would cast aside purpose.

"He would never give you more than you can handle," Teresa said, continuing to gather discarded items. "There's a reason you're here. But, if he's going to send you out a sheep amidst the wolves, you might want to just keep that close," she said indicating the necklace with a playful wink.

"What if he's made a mistake?"

"He doesn't make mistakes," Teresa said confidently.

Charlotte was a little thrown by her sharp unwavering loyalty.

"So you really think Archie's made the right choice?" she tested.

"Who said anything about Archie?"

Stunned by the unexpected response, Charlotte's gaze returned to the cross in her hand.

CHAPTER 31

ARCHIE

Aided by a host of security detail, Archie's new and fiercely loyal driver, Dave, led his boss through an onslaught of reporters that continued to bombard him with questions, which were now merging to nothing more than a cacophonous blur. Once safely inside, Dave directed the security to move the crowds beyond the gates with a polite but firm hand. Most dispersed quickly enough, but there were always one or two paparazzi skulking in the shadows.

Archie gratefully closed the door on the wall of sound and rested his back against the door, his constant smile soon vanished. Closing his eyes, he breathed deeply trying to appreciate the sporadic and diminishing moments of solitude. Suddenly realising he wasn't alone, he opened them again. Leeny was stood at the top of the stairs watching him.

His head swivelled left and right with unfamiliarity as he regarded the home. A pristine display of modern lines and a cool palette that projected style and affluence, managing to sterilise any warmth.

Everything had its place, which is why Archie's attention was taken by a small white envelope out of place on a side table.

"It arrived today," Leeny said.

His stare lingered on the item for few seconds, though he already knew its contents. A small white card embossed with a golden serpent; an incontestable invitation from The Order for the ceremony.

Finally he returned his wife's gaze.

"Where is he?" he asked.

"Sleeping."

Leeny took note of the bandaging on Archie's right hand as he began ascending the stairs.

"Well?" she asked once he'd reached the top.

"He's safe."

"For how long?" she pressed with venom.

Archie caressed her cheek with affection and thoughts disconnected to the touch. She leaned into the warmth embracing the rare moment before it was suddenly taken away, and without word he continued on to his son's room. The sigh that followed expelled a silent pain, inhaling deeply provided the strength to endure, before following on.

As Archie looked down upon Josh sleeping soundly, safely, he let go of the theatre that had been keeping him functioning for so long. Its release slightly collapsed his posture and began dissipating anxiety from every cell in his body.

Josh's skin was starting to regain its youthful glow, apart from the dark circles still surrounding his eyes; a remanent of the ordeal. He looked a little older now, as if the experience had somehow prematurely aged him.

As a father the success of seeing him sleeping in his own bed could never outweigh the failure of losing him in the first place, the over-whelming sense of relief coursed his entire body, draining him weak. Subtly he leaned against the bedpost to disguise his weakness, lights dimmed and flickered momentarily as though in unison. Leeny noticed, but was unconcerned.

When the moment passed, Archie returned his full attention to Josh, lovingly adjusting the parting of his hair. After a short time he asked,

"How's he been?"

"Asking for you," Leeny said, watching from the doorway. "Wondering why you hadn't been to see him."

"You explained?"

"To a point," she replied.

Archie turned his stare on her.

"What am I supposed to say?" she defended quietly. "He now understands the value of our blood, but not its implications. I told him his father was doing all he could to protect him."

He was struck silent as her words triggered memories of his older brother Simon, and to his own father. Finally he said,

"I see so much of Simon in him."

A sadness came over him as he closed his eyes to remember, but the pairing only reminded him of pain and how powerless he was as a boy to save his brother, and now as a man to defend his son. The same power his family boasted of and yet had alluded him his entire life.

When he opened his eyes there was a darkness that had befallen them, one that was reflected in the surrounding shadows.

"You would have thought a war for the soul of this world would see more than one man standing between two ancient rivals," he said bitterly. "Scavengers pecking at the flesh of power."

Leeny joined Archie by the bed placing a reassuring hand on his back.

"Be thankful for their arrogance," she said. "It allows them to deny what's right in front of them, what the rest of the world already acknowledges. You are no mere man, Archie. Endure. Tomorrow it will not just be a son or a country that looks to you, but a world."

Archie held onto her words as he moved to the window, despite only yards, she could feel his thoughts pulling him further away.

"You know there was a time I tried to run?" he said, almost ashamed. "That was why I joined the military, to escape from what I knew was inevitably waiting for me, like light trying to escape a black hole. I soon realised there was literally nowhere on earth I could hide, so moved in a direction that gave the appearance of a conviction I couldn't feel. Simon could. He said he could feel it the day my mother brought me home from the hospital. But I never did."

"You never mention your brother," Leeny concerned.

"Do you have any idea what it's like to be told as a child that humanity will rest on your shoulders, without the conviction of belief to see it through? No one to turn to, to guide you. If not for Simon I wouldn't have ever known who I truly was, and yet without him there was no one to believe in me, so how could I believe in myself? The truth of my existence died when they took him from me."

"You said Simon died of cancer."

"Yes. And now I only wish that were true," he said. "Do you know what one must do to show their allegiance to The Order?"

Leeny didn't like where this was going.

"The Abraham sacrifice," she acknowledged with caution.

It was an act of mockery against God. When Abraham dutifully obeyed the Lord with the offering of his first born, only to have an angel intervene saving the child in the final hour. The Order's conviction was to take a life the Lord did not.

Suddenly she realised what Archie was telling her, Simon was a sacrifice.

"Your father's on the council," she exclaimed.

His unwavering bitter stare gave confirmation, but there was something else.

"Not just my line," he said. "Sonja Gotha."

"My grandmother?"

Leeny was stunned and perplexed. The unexpected and disturbing news hit her quickly, remembering stories she was told of her uncle's accidental death; he was just ten years old. She looked down at her son sleeping as a quiet painful agony took hold, reminding her of just how close she was to losing him.

When the initial shock began to subside she found herself needing to take a seat as wider implications began to set in.

Their arranged marriage, which was not just common place, but expected to maintain purity of the bloodline. But she knew The Order never did things by chance and plans are generations in the making. If both of their lines sat on the council, then their marriage was orchestrated long before their meeting, and Josh was nothing more to them than a calculation, a lamb raised for slaughter.

"I don't understand," she said in desperation. "If they're already on the council, why would they need Josh?"

"To harvest his blood for the coming ritual. If the scripture is fulfilled then power will reside with one, not seven. The Order would no longer be the seat of power in this world and they have no intention of abdicating."

"They're going to try and replace you?"

He nodded solemnly.

"If Lucifer can rise to challenge the seat of power, is it so inconceivable that they wouldn't rise to challenge him? And now with Josh's blood they have everything they need."

"Except the knife," Leeny said. "Where is it now?"

"The Natsarim secured its passage into the country," he replied. "It arrives tomorrow."

"Naive of me to think they were our greatest threat."

"Don't be mistaken, they're no less so. Although it seems neither side truly understand the scriptures or have read the signs."

He looked at Josh proudly.

"Their time is at an end."

There was a subtle shift of shadows around the room as if in response. Archie could feel its energy make its way under his skin, not as a separate force, but something that was completing him; making him whole. Finally Archie started to feel what Simon had always professed.

"The convergence is not in the stars of The Natsarim prophesy," he said. "It is here now, in the union of the unholy trinity. An Antichrist to take power over the world's faith, A False Prophet embraced by all with promises of peace and security."

Again he brushed the delicate golden hair on Josh's head.

"And the one who will rise up to sit upon the throne of this world."

Suddenly Leeny could also feel the energy of the room. There was a moments trepidation before allowing it to embrace her, filling her with affirmation, empowering and emboldening her with a righteous confidence. Knowing their journey was a path beyond sight, she rose with poise and approached Archie, fixing his tie.

"The Order has sent the invitations for the coming ritual," she said. "As the next prime minister of the country we must honour their preparations."

Both mother and father looked down upon Joshua sleeping.

"Remind them that the mortar in the foundations of every new empire is blood," Leeny said.

In that moment Archie was filled with adoration towards her, not with intimacy or affection, but as a loyal protector, a soldier of legacy. But there was something else…

"What is it?" he said.

"The florist?" Leeny concerned.

"A loose end."

"Loose ends unravel tapestries," she warned.

CHAPTER 32

BARRINGTON

Barrington watched people impatiently jostle for position by the baggage reclaim at Heathrow Airport, London. Families, couples, frequent flyers, backpackers, and the one small child that seemed to be present at every conveyor belt, trying to remove a suitcase twice their size and weight. He couldn't have been more than eleven, not small, but skinny, reminding Barrington of himself at that age.

The boy was with family, a younger brother, older sister and mother doing her best to keep a watchful eye on all of them. As would be their custom in the absence of a father, the boy was adopting the eldest male role as he saw it.

Despite obvious struggles to remove the case from the conveyor as it slowly pulled him several feet from where he started, eventually it toppled over the edge displacing frustrated passengers.

Untroubled by the commotion he was causing he turned to look for his younger brother, finding him being silly with his older sister. Feeling frustrated, he was about to call out.

"Would you like a trolley?" a voice said.

The boy turned back to see Barrington offering the empty trolley and without invitation he hoisted the heavy suitcase onto it.

"Thank you," he said.

"Do you have any more I can help with?" Barrington asked.

The boy stretched his neck to look back and forth along the conveyer, eventually seeing what he was looking for and pointed. Barrington returned to the belt apologetically trying to ease through reluctant passengers.

"Please," a young woman said standing aside to let Barrington pass.

Endeared his actions weren't for himself he thanked her, slightly taken by her beauty and removed two more suitcases, before shyly thanking her again. He tried not to stare, but despite her wide rimmed sunglasses, he could see bruising that could have only flowered from the eye. But the fresh scaring to her cheek and bandaged ear suggested a probable accident as opposed to anything more sinister.

"Skiing," she said with an alluring South American accent.

Barrington wasn't sure how to respond.

"Skiing, you know? Whoosh!" she shimmied a cute gesture.

"Yes," he said embarrassed, "Sorry, I didn't mean to. Anyway thank you. Again."

He shuffled away with the two heavy suitcases. The woman chuckled to herself.

Barrington returned to the trolley stacking them two and one while the boy directed him towards his mother.

"That's very kind of you," she said, smiling gratefully.

It's my pleasure, Barrington was about to say, but the mother continued.

"But he will have to learn to do this for himself one day. He cannot always rely on the kindness of strangers, however well intentioned."

Barrington looked at the boy who seemed defeated by the comment.

"I have a feeling he'll be okay. He has a strong guide."

"Hmmm," she scoffed with a smile of caution.

Noticing his own suitcase passing by, Barrington excused himself momentarily as he took it from the conveyor.

"Well this is me," Barrington offered as a stranger's goodbye.

"Goodbye," the boy said.

"Goodbye," his younger brother imitated.

The mother gracefully offered an appreciative nod and subtle smile. Taking her lead the daughter did the same. Barrington returned the gesture and merged with the moving crowd.

With all his effort the young boy leaned his weight into the trolley. It didn't move at first, but he wouldn't give up as the wheels slowly started to turn. Once gaining momentum it became easier to manoeuvre and he led the family towards the exit.

It took all his strength to keep the trolley under control, especially when a rude hipster in a pork-pie hat and overbearing neck tattoo unapologetically banged into him, as though a part of a race he was unaware of. The suitcases threatened to topple any second until a welcoming hand steadied them.

"Erm excuse me," Barrington voiced loudly with frustration.

Slightly louder than he had meant to. The man turned and shot a cold stare at Barrington that immediately made him regret his outburst, but urgency prevailed as the man continued without incident. The boy smiled, thankful to see Barrington again, his mother watched on with appreciation and also without.

"We're heading in the same direction," Barrington offered as an apology, and not wanting to undermine the boy's role.

"To be honest," he said, "I think I damaged my knee a few days back. Would you mind if I pushed the trolley? It would give me something to lean on."

The boy looked to his mother, who silently offered permission. As good an excuse as it was, Barrington wasn't lying about his knee. With all the excitement in the last forty eight hours, the first he'd noticed of it was while on the plane. Now it was a constant niggle.

"How did you manage to injure your knee?" the mother enquired.

"Running."

"Oh, so you are a runner?"

"A doctor."

"And now a patient," she jested.

"Yes," Barrington scoffed, amused. "I guess so. Although, not that type of doctor."

"I go to school," the younger of the two boys said.

"That's wonderful. And what are you learning?"

"I can count to fifty. 1…2…3…4…5…," the boy continued until his point was proven.

Thankfully customs was still quite a distance.

"That's very impressive," Barrington said when he finally reached his goal.

"Two and two is four."

"That's right. And do you know what four and four is?"

The boy looked at Barrington strangely, as though what he'd said had upset him. His mother noticed.

"Simi? The man asked you a question," she prompted.

"You should have buried that thing in the desert where it belongs," the boy said with sinister intent.

Barrington was horrified. His mother angry, not understanding what had gotten into her son.

"Simi?" she barked.

The boy suddenly snapped back to himself seemingly unaware of having said anything.

"Eight," he said. "Four and four is eight."

"Simi?" she said again. "I'm sorry, I don't know what's gotten into him."

Barrington smiled unconvincingly as the automatic doors slid open distracting the family to the attention of the waiting hordes, eyes wide with eagerness as they anticipated friends, family or loved ones.

Barrington's pace slowed behind the family, reluctant to cross the threshold. Only now in the eleventh hour did he appreciate what a lack of judgement it was in coming. How in a moment of desperation he'd thrown caution to the wind and was just waking up to that fact. Now he feared whatever waited for him beyond those doors, as though there was an evil he may never escape.

He saw his name held aloft on a handwritten sign though ignored it for now, still distracted over what the boy had said. It affected him to the point of wanting to leave that very second, to run away. But as smart as he was, he knew he wasn't that kind of smart, and in truth, where would he go? He didn't know if he was running away from people or towards them. Seeing this through was the only way of really knowing.

"Daddy!" the younger boy yelled as he rushed off into his father's waiting arms.

Barrington followed behind with the trolley as the husband greeted his wife and children. He was enthralled to see them all but the silent question in his eyes of who this man was required satisfaction.

"Thank you doctor," the mother said. "I hope your knee gets better."

"You are a doctor?" the husband said enthusiastically, as though there would be a follow-up question.

"He's not that sort of doctor, my love," the wife interjected

"Oh! Well, thank you for your help," he said not so reverently shaking Barrington's hand.

The elder of the two boys also shook his hand and the family said their goodbyes.

Did that really just happen? Barrington thought watching them walk away, suddenly he wasn't so sure. He tried replaying what the boy had just said, or what he might have said. Maybe he simply misheard. *Yeah,* he thought, *that had to be it*. He was more wired than tired and had hardly slept in the last forty eight hours. As there was no other possible explanation, or certainly not one he wanted to entertain in the middle of an airport, he looked for his driver.

He thought he was becoming quite adept at moving through crowds unnoticed. After leaving the plane an anxiety had taken hold of him, aware whoever was looking for him would be searching for a man travelling alone. The thought delivered a stiffness to his limbs, making his movement unnatural and cumbersome. He tried acting at being himself, but it was a poor copy and more likely to make him stand out than blend in. That was when he noticed the boy. The family were a good disguise to wear, just until he passed through customs.

As far as anyone was concerned Dr Ross was in town to deliver a talk at the Hilton, and as such would be expected to look the part, which he did. Despite the excitement and excursions of recent days, Barrington had brushed up well. He was wearing his favourite cream linen suit which always made him feel relaxed and confident, although he couldn't ever remember feeling quite so uncomfortable. Perhaps that was the thought of carrying an ancient dagger in his satchel with the power to unleash satan, and the real reason for his journey to place said dagger into the hands of a priest he'd never met.

With a welcoming smile the chauffeur seamlessly scooped up Barrington's wheelie bag under his arm.

"Good afternoon Dr Ross. I trust you had a good journey?"

"Yes, Thank you."

He wasn't much for small talk on the best of days, but any conversation was just a distraction from watching faces in the crowd, wondering if any were staring back.

"May I take your bag?"

The driver gestured toward the satchel.

"No," Barrington said sharply. "Erm, thank you"

Instinctively pulling it close to his body.

"I'm sorry, just err. I'm.. I'm very protective over my work, I like to keep it close, but thank you."

"Of course Dr Ross," the driver replied with a slight bow of his head.

The car was parked a distance from the terminal in a quiet section of the car park. Barrington hadn't noticed at first, but as the sounds of the daytime airport traffic began to fade into the background and the clip-clop of their shoes became the dominant echo over distant engines, his heart started to race.

The driver looked back at Dr Ross a couple of times with a slight smile, adding to his paranoia. His head swivelled nervously as they approached the car, expecting someone to appear from behind one of the hundreds of pillars; moistness speckled his brow. He needed to get into the car and quickly, like a child under a blanket that would somehow be safer. He snatched at the handle on the rear passenger door and pulled urgently with no success. His anxiety was starting to win over and adrenalin ate away at his energy as he pulled again and again.

"Sorry Dr Ross, one moment," the driver said.

Seeing the nervous panic growing in Ross, whose breathing was becoming noticeably more rapid, close to hyperventilating. The driver clicked the button on the remote a couple of times to reset the locks.

"You can try it now."

Ross pulled hard on the handle and the door finally opened with ease. He quickly got inside and tried to compose himself by taking deep breaths, realising it had been his impatience that left him locked out for longer than necessary. But now inside, he slowly started to regain control.

"Are you okay Dr Ross?" the driver asked with genuine concern as he entered the car.

"Yes, I erm." Knowing he'd made a scene he wanted to diffuse the moment. "I think I have low blood sugar," he said honestly. "You don't by chance have something sweet to eat do you?"

The driver opened the glove compartment and pulled out a chocolate bar. Ross quickly took the bar and ripped open the packet getting the bar into his mouth in the shortest amount of time.

"Thank you," he said mid chew. "I couldn't eat that stuff they tried to pass off for food on the flight."

He shuddered at the thought. Unscrewing the cap on the complimentary bottle of water he washed down the chocolate and followed it with another urgent bite.

"Would you like me to stop somewhere to get you something?" the driver asked.

"No, that's okay, I'll be able to get something from the hotel."

"If you change your mind, please just let me know, it really isn't a problem."

"Thank you," Dr Ross said.

The honest gesture helped him regain control and for the first time he saw the man as his driver and not a would-be assassin. Relaxing back into his seat, the chocolate had an immediate affect on his sugar levels which had been burning away with nervous energy.

Once the car was beyond the area of the airport and heading towards the city, Barrington began to feel slightly less anxious. However, he had to keep reminding himself that he was just an academic, allowing room to appropriately justify fear.

It was in these quiet moments he realised he was still coming to terms with Helena's death. Thoughts would often catch him unaware, raw and exposed. It was hard to know what emotions were for what situation, feeling so tired he could cry and so broken he was numb. All he knew for sure was that he'd never felt so lost in his own mind, the one thing he could always rely on without question.

He noticed the driver checking on him in the mirror from time to time, but given his behaviour at the airport that wasn't entirely surprising. In fact, it helped that he appeared to be showing genuine concern.

The journey into town had taken just over an hour. Now on the final stretch passing through the city, the sights and hustle became a welcome distraction. The car pulled up outside the Park Lane Hilton Hotel and the driver exited to open the door, keeping in tow with Dr Ross as he entered the reception carrying his wheelie bag.

"Will there be anything else Dr Ross?" the driver said standing to attention.

He spoke clearly enough for anyone in the close vicinity to hear. A subtle and warm smile graced Dr Ross, realising the driver had just graciously presented him to the hotel. *A classy move,* he thought.

"Thank you… for everything." Barrington said, discreetly passing a fifty pound note into his hand as he shook it. And with a nod the driver turned and left.

The receptionist smiled as she waited patiently for Dr Ross to turn his attention to her, watching him as he marvelled at the elegant surroundings and the people who had the good fortune to enjoy it. Not noticing that some had taken an interest at the announcement of his name.

CHAPTER 33

PROFESSOR LEHMAN

When Professor Lehman learned of the young student that lost his life, she'd agreed without hesitation to meet Father Michael in London. Had she stopped to consider the request, she may have ultimately declined. Her reluctance, while not strong enough to change her mind, was born of simple pragmatism. Regardless of gravity, she understood more than most what was at stake, she just wasn't sure what a 54-year-old Professor of Archeology could offer.

Father Michael was sheltering with a friend loyal to the Brethren, Archbishop Hammond, whom happened to reside at Westminster Cathedral. Lehman was a tad surprised at his choosing of such a prominent location, although had to admit she couldn't actually picture the church herself. He assured her as the Archbishop had assured him,

"While Westminster Cathedral may not be the most inconspicuous of locations, London has become an unkept garden, with the cathedral concealed within its growth."

Leaving the train station heading east along Victoria Street, the constant state of flux of the London skyline made the once home from home city feel unfamiliar, along with the entire area under a massive underground reconstruction project. Buildings now not only competed for height but shape as well, somehow managing to maintain an odd uniformity; collectively dull and uninspiring.

Only a few minutes into her walk, looking past the constructions and into the distance for signs or landmarks, a plaza appeared on her right, almost out of nowhere. And there, offset from the main road, shielded either side by an overgrown modern London, was the mother church of Catholics in the United Kingdom; Westminster Cathedral.

The building demanded a moment's pause, consuming the professor's attention while struggling to comprehend how she'd managed to erase such magnificence from her mind. Now it could only fuel imagination, how the Byzantine-Christian architecture would have risen to prominence in the early 1900s. A bell tower of striped red brick and white Portland stone rising 284 feet into the air, signalling to London with an explosion of colour, a new era of construction and design. It only added to her loathing of the concrete and steel curtains of modern design overshadowing its superior.

Crossing the square she climbed the steps to the entrance when a young lady with long blonde hair approached, her expression urgent.

"Professor Lehman," she said.

Surprised by the interruption, the professor could only look upon the woman with suspicion before quickly turning to familiarity.

"It's Dr Carden isn't it?"

This time it was Sarah's turn to be surprised.

"Father Weiss was a dear friend," Lehman continued with a rare smile. "He always carried your picture with him."

Sarah's expression and tone softened warmly.

"It's nice to meet you," she said. "Father Michael apologises he's not here to meet you himself, he got held up with the archbishop, bringing him up to speed. I thought we might grab a coffee and do the same."

"That would be delightful," Professor Lehman said.

The two ladies descended the steps and scanned the plaza in expectation. London teemed with coffee shops on every corner and then some. However, the only establishment in their current view offering refreshment was McDonald's. Sarah's pursed lips and raised eyebrows posed the question 'Shall We?'

"Absolutely not," Professor Lehman objected, walking away directionless for anything else.

Once back on the main road of cold concrete and steel, it was only a few minutes before their search was rewarded.

Cautious of her surroundings Sarah chose an isolated table in the corner of the shop, and over beverages and in as much detail as she could emotionally manage, shared the terrifying experience of Arizona. The professor listened with great concern as a broader picture began to emerge, but was still none the wiser as to the role she was expected to play.

"Barrington," Sarah said.

"Dr Ross?"

"He's here in London."

"I'm not sure I understand?" Lehman said, genuinely confused. "Why would Barrington be in London?"

Sarah had assumed the professor was privy to information pre-Arizona, quickly realising the conversation was about to take a turn.

"The archeologist that made the find... was found dead."

Professor Lehman slumped into her seat as if helped by a force, her stare disconnected as memories of her former student began to flood her mind.

"Helena," Lehman said with the distance of her stare.

Her eyes glazed a teary layer for just a moment, but the forthright professor was just too British to allow a public display to go any further. Sarah respectfully and silently waited while Lehman absorbed the information. It was almost a minute before she could bring herself round, but did so with a stoic and very British stiff upper lip.

"She was brilliant," Lehman remembered. "Truly. A terrible distraction for a promising young student by the name of Barrington," she smiled. "But very special. I was hard on her, I remember that."

"You have regrets?" Sarah asked softly.

"Oh no dear. Those crushed by pressure are never truly brilliant. But at least now I know why Father Michael asked me here."

"He thought after everything Dr Ross has been through, he just might need to see a face he knows, one he can trust."

"Indeed," she said reflecting on her former student. "He always did underestimate his value. I dare say he believes the knife is the only thing of importance."

"What do you mean?"

"The dagger on its own is useless without the knowledge to use it. It's said to wield power over the underworld, but to release that power requires ritual information that maybe three people on the planet have. And one of them is in possession of the knife."

Sarah became quiet, her expression grave.

"Are you okay my dear?" Professor Lehman asked, noticing her despondence.

"Yes," she said almost immediately perking up.

It was an unconvincing response leaving Lehman quietly concerned with her state of mind. She didn't know Dr Carden, but had heard on many occasions of her infectious bubbly energy, none of which was on display. It was perfectly understandable with everything she'd been through, but she got the sense there was something she wasn't telling her, something she wanted to say but couldn't bring herself to do so.

Sarah went on to explain Father Michael's plans and the role each of them had to play. For Professor Lehman it was simply to leave the hotel with Barrington. He'd been told not to trust anyone, so sending someone he didn't know and trying to convince him to leave with them seemed impractical. Not one for clandestine excitement, the professor acquiesced to their proposal.

"How is he?" she said. "Father Michael?"

There was a subtle change of energy when enquiring on the priest, a tone of affection, concern and warmth hidden beneath the persona, something the two women shared. Sarah thought about saying 'he's well' as a polite anecdotal response, but realising the professor's relationship with him far superseded her own, she hesitated, thinking perhaps her response should be as genuine as the enquiry. But the hesitation told Lehman all she needed to know.

"Beyond my reach." Sarah eventually surrendered, and strangely un-guarded. "Do you mind if I ask you something?"

"Of course," she said, wondering if this would be the source of her despondence.

"Are you a person of faith? I mean true faith?"

Lehman pondered the question with a sense of familiarity.

"With all that's going on, an apt a question as one might consider," she said. "Even after this conversation. I used to have a way of delivering my beliefs in a manner that wouldn't depreciate my profession. At least that's what I'd tell myself."

Sarah listened intently.

"I would say my faith was a little like my diet, low in calories."

The response was an amused smile.

"Yes," she acknowledged. "Unfortunately that's exactly the reaction it's designed to invoke; polite and amused. Because it doesn't really of-fend anybody does it? It's what so many of us do," she said shamefully. "Hide our beliefs so others may feel better about their own. The prob-lem is, the more you hide your faith the more disconnected you become, the more barren your existence, more hopeless. There's preservation in what we hide, consequences in denial, but strength in truth."

Professor Lehman drifted into raw and recent memories.

"But I supposed you're really asking me about my faith are you?"

"No, I suppose not," Sarah conceded.

"Even after all you've seen?"

"What is it I've seen?" she challenged.

Although not so much directed at the professor as much as a thought she'd been wrestling with prior to the conversation.

"Sorry I didn't mean to…"

"That's quite alright dear, perfectly understandable. You've been through a traumatic experience and I dare say without time to process. Faith does not always have to be as blind as you may believe. Often it's based upon an experience or understanding of an individual that can't be quantified. We both work in fields that theorise and hypothesise before embarking on a journey to find evidence that supports our conclusion, all journeys of faith. But in science when you run into a problem, you may consider that you're looking at something the wrong way, or perhaps asking the wrong questions."

"Yes of course, all the time."

"Then perhaps what you have or haven't seen is not the problem. I suppose the question I'm skating around is this, what could you see that would make you believe?"

It didn't take long to consider the question, so simple, poignant, but revealing.

"I don't know," Sarah conceded.

She realised the question was of course rhetorical, the professor already knew the answer Sarah was now discovering; nothing. It wouldn't have really mattered what she'd seen, the miraculous may have unfolded before her eyes and yet she would have tried to explain it through science, when that failed it would be because science had not yet discovered the necessary understanding. What it could never be was miraculous, because she'd closed herself off to the possibility.

Lehman's expression of understanding and empathy suddenly become concerned.

"Do you know what Dr Ross is in possession of?" she asked.

Sarah needed clarification.

"Barrington," Lehman confirmed.

"Oh, yes of course, some sort of ceremonial knife?"

"Yes, I suppose that's an accurate enough description. What he has you won't find in history books, because academics deemed it fantasy, and here we are. When I saw that… thing, it sent a cold chill into my bones. In part because I'd believed the academics, but when faced with the reality, then one has to consider the stories of its origin and purpose.

"So you believe this thing can actually invoke the spirit of Satan?" she said unconvinced.

The professor took a moment before answering.

"I don't know what I believe Dr Carden. What I know is an ancient parchment describes this day as prophetic. A dear friend of mine, your uncle, believed it enough to die in its protection. The problem I have is this, if the knife exists, then we should also assume the alignment does in fact point to the birth of a child. Beyond that, I guess I'm still trying to catch my breath."

Her thoughts drifted back to Father Michael.

"I dare say Father Michael is attempting to carry the burden for us all."

"Yes, unfortunately," she acknowledged. "Actually I should probably call him. See if he has finished with Archbishop Hammond."

Sarah stood up, a nervous tension had come over her.

"Maybe now might be a good time to call the doctor," she said with a hint of unease.

But the behaviour went unnoticed by Professor Lehman who was in her own mind, she took a breath. *This was all actually happening,* Lehman thought. Sarah went outside to make her call leaving the professor with some relative privacy.

CHAPTER 34

FATHER MICHAEL

At Westminster Cathedral, Father Michael was being hosted by Archbishop Hammond in his study, learning that he'd been kept abreast of unfolding situations through Brother Bonsu. However he was very keen to hear Father Michael's experience and perspective as he was the one at the centre of the whirlwind.

Father Michael did his best to honour the unseen truths, his thoughts and feelings, but faced a shortfall of emotion when it came to the archbishop. Not so much that he lacked emotion, only that his senior role within the Brethren wouldn't allow him to be distracted from the bigger picture, one he was now trying to paint for the priest who hadn't yet been able to see beyond this day.

"So you've finally reached the limits of your influence," the archbishop said.

"My influence?" he questioned.

"You've done all you can do?"

"Oh, I see," he said.

Worryingly reflecting on the question, but unable to focus, Father Michael became flustered.

"I think so," he said. "I hope so. Why? Do you think I've missed something?"

Archbishop Hammond smiled softly studying his senior ally with an empathetic understanding. The anxiety and worry he carried was palpable.

"You must allow your faith to take over," he said in a calming tone. "The prophesy does not live and die on your actions alone, it would be arrogant and foolhardy to think otherwise."

He was right, Father Michael thought, humbled by the archbishop's statement. The quiet admission also helped quell an overriding tension.

"I tried reaching Brother Bonsu," he said hoping not to reignite his worry, but after the experience in Arizona it would be reckless not to at least carry caution.

"I'm yet to hear anything back," he added.

There was a momentary pause before the archbishop spoke, as if selecting an appropriate answer.

"I'm sure he'll make contact when he can," he said. "Tensions are high and caution must be taken."

After a short pause of further study, he continued.

"You have gumption Father Michael, I like that. Brother Bonsu often voiced of the difficult circumstances that surrounded you in the Vatican, but said you conduct yourself with the grace becoming a saint."

Father Michael laughed.

"Not exactly, I'm ashamed to say."

"Oh of course that's right," the Archbishop was amused to remember. "I did hear of one rather famous incident. Of course these matters are often blown out of all proportion, however on this occasion I was rather hoping it hadn't been."

Father Michael remained serious and silent until knowing exactly what it was the archbishop had heard.

"Is it true you struck the Holy Father with a book?"

And there it was, he thought.

"I'm afraid it is," he admitted.

"Without giving light to speculation, do you mind if I ask why?" The archbishop's enquiry held genuine intrigue.

Father Michael had become quite accustomed to members of the clergy probing about the incident between himself and the Holy Father. While everyone approached it with the same excited and almost giddy enthusiasm, for Father Michael it bore an inescapable darkness.

"Information about several priests had come to light," he said. "Irrefutable evidence."

It was clear Father Michael was finding it extremely difficult to formulate the words. The archbishop leaned forward in his chair so that Father Michael would not have to raise his voice beyond a whisper.

"With every ounce of our being," he continued. "children are to be protected, not robbed of their innocence. But it seems protection is only given to monsters."

"I see," the archbishop voiced gravely before reflecting on Father Michael's words.

"Your actions created a powerful and dangerous enemy. One that will seek to satisfy his lust for revenge. Your dedication to the Brethren has not gone without notice, but I do wonder. You've been right at the centre of this whirlwind, I imagine you haven't had time to consider the prophesy?"

Father Michael was surprised with the response. Most people that made the enquiry were seeking either sensationalism or to appease their own curiosity, but it appeared the Archbishop's enquiry was not for himself.

"I'm sorry archbishop, I'm not sure I know what you mean?"

"Tomorrow? What happens if all goes according to plan?"

Father Michael felt embarrassed. Such a painfully simple question and one that he hadn't given consideration.

"He's sending a destroyer Father Michael, not someone to make peace. Those hiding behind walls of power will be crushed in the rubble."

Father Michael wasn't sure how he felt about that statement, not having had the chance to consider the implications of the prophesy. But it made sense. The symbols of their faith could no longer be represented by the buildings of their demise.

"When trust is broken, belief has nowhere to live," the archbishop said rising to his feet.

"Come. I have someone I'd like you to meet."

Archbishop Hammond led Father Michael back to the main cathedral where a young priest had just concluded service. He was standing by the doors thanking parishioners as they left, shaking hands and speaking as though each one were a close personal friend.

Father Michael smiled, the image reminded him of the way Franz would conclude service. Some parishioners used to wait up to an hour just to be able to say goodbye.

"A man went out to sow grain," the archbishop said beginning to recite a parable. "Some seeds fell on the path and the birds ate them. Some seeds fell on rocky ground where there was little soil. The seeds soon sprouted, but when the sun came up it burnt the young plants. Some seeds fell among thorn bushes which grew up and choked the plants."

From afar the two men watched their colleague with inspired admiration.

"Some seeds fell on good soil," Father Michael finished. "And the plants produced corn."

The Archbishop smiled.

"The people are the church," he said. "And it is built upon the word. The young man is Father Tobias Fischer."

Father Michael's expression creased. He knew that name, but couldn't place where from.

"He concluded his ordination under Father Weiss. He was there that night, the last person to see him alive."

The blood drained from Father Michael's face.

"You may be interested to hear what he has to say.

CHAPTER 35

COHEN

6:55am, for the last time Nathan unlocked the door to The Way of the Flower. He stood at the door for a moment, looking into the almost barren space with a conflicted moment of hesitation before eventually willing himself to cross the threshold.

Every step echoed with emptiness and yet everywhere he looked was filled with some of the most valuable memories he owned, forcing a smile of remembrance.

It wasn't just the shop that had become a part of him, but the area, the people, the clockwork familiarity of routine, and he was just as guilty of becoming a familiar cog in the routines of others as they were in his. While tomorrow may not have held the false sense of security that regiment offered, adventure lay within not knowing. A new country, new horizons and all the accompanying clichés. But for the sake of his friend, he wished with all his heart that today had never arrived and tomorrow was already here.

Since arriving back from Europe, Cohen's eagerness to return to the shop could have easily been mistaken as a need for distraction, an unwillingness to face his past or himself. But only someone who truly knew him could understand what the relationship offered, and that was balance. It was like a tea ceremony to a samurai.

But it also felt a little like old times, before the alcohol. Cohen hadn't changed so much, but something inside him had, like an ever present darkness had been lifted. Whatever it was, Nathan was fairly certain he wouldn't find out until sometime after the new shop in Spain had opened its doors, and even then wasn't entirely sure how important it was. He was back and that's all that really mattered.

Cohen was still upstairs, sitting in his favourite armchair staring endlessly at the sky, the same position he been in for the last several hours. Watching as the night shed its cloak and a chorus of machinery replaced the morning birdsong. He'd heard Nathan's arrival but wasn't stirred from his thoughts, continuing to reflect as he had done all night.

For obvious reasons Traeger had been weighing heavily on his mind, so after closing the shop the previous night, made himself an inspired green tea and readied himself to make the call.

Angela, Traeger's wife answered. He never made it home. All she could tell him was that his plane apparently ran into an electrical problem causing him to ditch somewhere over the English Channel. It was his last flight.

Death had surrounded Cohen his entire life like a torturous blanket and shock was nothing more than a numbed emotion, or so he thought. He was unable to manifest any words of consolation for Angela, or indeed himself. In fact it was Angela that filled the silence with gratitude, painful though it was to hear.

She would have rather seen Traeger pass doing what he loved than slowly deteriorate until the man in front of her became nothing more than a living memory. The electrical fault was perhaps just a softer blow. She assured Cohen that despite the tragedy, nothing had been left unsaid.

However, the same could not be said for Cohen, who would remain forever unsatisfied, believing there was still time to revisit the conversation they'd had in the hanger. Now he was ashamed that in those final hours, honesty hadn't prevailed.

Despite his vehement opposition, no longer could he voice with conviction that God didn't exist as he had suggested. But that his relationship with him was a contentious one at best. There was no solace in its revelation, only that what he hadn't shared now never would be.

He wanted to let him know that while peace may be a limited experience for him, it was through his flowers he would somehow find it. Ironically a conclusion that befell him staring into a sea of canola fields on his way to meet his old friend.

Death, the torturous blanket, God or whatever the kernel of torment was that used Cohen to manifest itself, he was now casting aside. He understood there was penance to pay for the life he'd lived and would accept that when the day arrived. But until then he would no longer walk the same path. The only danger Cohen wanted in his future was splinters and thorns.

The smell of warm baked pastries climbed the stairs and poked at Cohen's attention, almost as if to remind him the future was waiting with a friendship not squandered. Finally, with stoic resilience he rose to meet the day.

Making his final descent into the shop, he found Nathan as expected sitting at the work bench enjoying a morning coffee, chocolate filled croissant and the broadsheets. A predictable picture that was strangely comforting. Cohen took the seat next to him where a coffee and Danish awaited his arrival.

From a bag on the floor, Nathan pulled out a hooded sweat top and dropped it on the bench in front of Cohen.

"That Leeny dropped it in a couple of days ago," he said. "Don't worry, I had it dry cleaned."

Cohen sniggered. Nathan smiled and continued to read the paper.

The comfortable quiet lasted for several minutes as Cohen looked around the store. There was a lot more space with everything in storage, apart from the displays being used to cover their retreat and make them appear functioning.

It felt like winding back the clock and with it the natural inclination to reminisce. *It had all been just a cover,* he thought, a mask concealing his true identity, but moving forward it would be who he was to become, no longer a mask but a face, and he was okay with that.

While Nathan buried himself in articles of the highly politicised period, Cohen opted for keeping up appearances and made a start to the day. He struggled at first, putting together vase holder frames outside of the shop, forgetting there was a knack to it, but eventually found satisfaction in the smallest of tasks. Returning inside he collected the chrysanthemums left over from seasonal displays, and with delicate attention held the vase at face height, admiring its rich petals, breathing in its scent. He moved with great care towards the door never taking his eyes from the flowers.

It was important not to disturb the water or let the contents be thrown around with careless handling. The idea was that they represented an inner state of mind, to protect them from any turbulence or trauma was to protect oneself, sharing in the state of still waters.

"Interesting article?" Cohen said moving through the shop.

"What?" Nathan replied coyly.

"You haven't turned the page in several minutes. If you're just going to sit there and watch me, do you mind getting the door?"

Nathan chuckled as he put down the paper and shuffled passed him, wedging a stopper to keep the door open before returning to the bench.

"So you're just gonna continue pretending to read then?"

"If you're going to continue to pretend to open," Nathan said with a winning smile sipping his coffee with glee.

Cohen paused to respond with a clever remark, but nothing came to mind. Swallowing his amusement he returned for the next vase, and with the same slow steady pace continued the routine. For anyone else it would have been an arduous affair wanting the chore to be over in the shortest amount of time, but every motion was carried out with deftness as though meditation were hidden in the movements. It was both beautiful and painful to watch at the same time.

When he'd finally finished, Nathan was privately agasp at just how good Cohen had made everything look with so little, but playing along grabbed a broom and started to sweep the place through. Cohen then took Nathan's place at the bench.

As Nathan slowly worked his way to the front of the shop, he peered out of the window with the sense nostalgia, suddenly realising he hadn't seen the strange priest hanging around for a few days and they'd be gone the next time he showed up. He never did find out why he took such an interest in the shop, but disregarded the thought as just one of those things in life that would forever remain a mystery.

Cohen sipped his now tepid coffee and pulled the newspaper in front of him, realising how little he knew of current events or the world around him. It was a slightly daunting thought imagining himself as a regular citizen, although he could never see himself sharing the same concerns as the average Joe.

As he turned the page the smell of incense suddenly came upon him. Instinctively he stared up from the paper at his surroundings, tense and alert. Nathan was still sweeping undisturbed, although in quiet reflection. He knew his friend would miss the shop and though unspoken had left him with an unshakable guilt as it was his action that caused them to uproot, but otherwise everything was quiet.

He returned his attention to the paper and there in front of him was a picture of Archibald Montgomery, under the title 'Hope', the billionaire business man set to become the UK's next Prime Minister. Cohen's brow furrowed staring at the picture, but was soon interrupted by two men entering the shop. His eyes never left the page, though his attention was now firmly in the present.

"I'm afraid we don't open until eight o'clock," Nathan said.

He looked calm, although Cohen could hear the trepidation in his voice.

"You the florist?" one of them said ungraciously.

"I'm *a* florist," Nathan replied.

He was more concerned with his partner who intimidatingly circled behind him in the small space, eyeing the empty vases. Their attention was suddenly snatched away as the sound of rustling paper put them on alert. Cohen dramatically turned the page on the broadsheets, seemingly unperturbed by their company.

"You," the man called out. "Florist."

Cohen's attention remained firmly on the paper despite all eyes now being on him.

"As my colleague just told you, we don't open till eight," he said.

He turned the page once more, playfully exaggerating the movement. The two men shared a look of disbelief as if somehow this man didn't quite understand the dangerous element being imposed.

"He said you had a sense of humour," the man behind Nathan said, "we don't."

His attempt at intimidation was frustratingly muted with a void of response. He gritted his teeth and took a breath.

"But he also said that we're to treat you with respect," he continued frustrated.

"Didn't say nothing about the shop though, did he?" the other one butted in.

"No, he didn't," he said, picking up a large decorative vase from the shelf.

This got Cohen's attention. A darkness glinted his eye and then softened. He stared at the man holding the vase noticing a tattoo between his thumb and index finger. Three circles inside a soft triangle.

Not that he wasn't already aware, but it confirmed exactly who they were working for. However, the fact that they were in his shop was an indiscretion that angered him for reasons they couldn't begin to imagine. Folding the paper, he stood up.

"I'm sorry, what was it you two gentlemen were looking for?"

It was clear from their reaction they were not expecting such an imposing figure, but still they held their nerve, shaken though it was.

"Trenton wants to see you," one said.

Confirming what he already knew. Cohen looked at his watch.

"I can probably be with him in the next hour."

Unsatisfied with the response the man looked at his colleague who dropped the vase, smiling as it smashed scattering shards across the floor. Nathan watched anxiously, anticipating Cohen's response, quietly hoping for all concerned they didn't touch the flowers.

"I can probably be with him in the next hour," Cohen reiterated calmly.

The man picked up another vase.

"Please," Cohen asked politely. "Don't."

There was a gentle warning in his tone which was ignored. Now smiling directly in Cohen's face, he dropped the vase. Darkness quickly returned to Cohen's eyes, only this time it remained.

"Within the hour then," the man said turning to leave. "Don't make me have to come back."

And the two men left as abruptly as they'd arrived. Nathan exhaled almost as if he'd been holding his breath the entire time, agitated, he started to sweep the broken pieces of pottery while expectantly waiting to hear some kind of response.

"Relax your grip," Cohen said.

Nathan shot a look of frustration at his friend, but his eyes were already back on the newspaper, almost as if the incident had never taken place. Turning his attention to his grip on the broom only to see the whites of his knuckles revealing his tension. He relaxed his hold allowing the blood to circulate.

"You're not going?" Nathan said continuing to sweep.

But he knew the answer before he'd even finished asking the question. Cohen looked as though he was about to say something but was interrupted by his own thoughts. Nathan waited for the excruciating long pause to subside, eventually rising from the bench.

"Close the shop," he said.

CHAPTER 36

THE ORDER

Over the last several days in select countries across the globe, small plain white envelopes were being placed in the hands of world leaders and influential members of industry. Each one delivered by someone close to the invitee and all marked with the same tattoo as seen on the men inside Cohen's shop. Inside was a brilliant white card embossed with a golden serpent eating its tail. It was an invitation.

Its response saw a parade of official aircraft in an unofficial capacity landing at a military base somewhere in the South West of England, all under the cover of darkness. Each of the planes displayed a small flag of origin along its fuselage, which included most of the prominent countries from the European Union, the Commonwealth and the unmistakable stars and stripes of Air Force One. There were also a host of privately owned aircrafts and one that didn't display a flag of origin, but the coat of arms of the Holy See.

All invitees were transferred to military helicopters where they proceeded to a further undisclosed location.

Under the guise of preventing the civil unrest that plagued the city night after night and threatened to continue until the day of the election, entire units of police officers were being coached in from surrounding regional forces to bolster London's already heavy governing presence. Over one square mile of the legal and financial districts were cordoned off from the general public, with temporary fencing being patrolled by additional private security. Other than a few random comments on social sites, a complete media blackout meant no questions were being asked.

On the beautiful secluded lawn outside the mansion with the glass dome, seven private helicopters awaited their passengers. One by one members of The Order were led by heavily armed security to their individual aircrafts, each taking flight exactly five minutes apart and over the course of several hours would continue to land unseen in the very heart of London.

The last to leave was Sonja Gotha, wearing a silver gown worthy of a monarch and a hooded cloak draped from her shoulders that caressed the ground as she walked, and like the others was fiercely protected by a private and heavily armed security team. One of the men offered a gentle hand to help her inside the vehicle, in doing so he revealed a tattoo on his inner wrist; three circles in a soft triangle.

It was the last of the helicopters to leave the mansion, following the others on course towards London. Sonja relaxed quickly and comfortably into her seat staring towards the convergence in the heavens.

CHAPTER 37

ARCHIE & COHEN

It was like a moving piece of modern art watching the thick pale smoke of the cigar rise against the dark claret walls of the study. Archie was appreciating the contemplative quiet, gaining respect for an understanding of officers of war who'd savoured moments such as these, before the battle.

Sitting in his favourite armchair he kept the company of an aged single barrel whisky, the book: Menelik's Dagger by Dr Barrington Ross, which lay with its pages spread, face down on his lap, and Simon's picture sitting face up on the arm rest.

Taking another strong pull on the cigar he released the smoke, hypnotised by its form, valuing its intricacy and design as it twisted and spiralled in a seductive dance, as though having the ability to see its blueprint.

As it continued to rise, folding in on itself with wisps crossing realms between sight, he could see the complexity of his own plan unfolding in its layers, no less impressive in its design and at least on equal footing in its execution. *God was right to fear him,* he thought.

In the coming hours he would have overseen the downfall of a power that had resided since the dawning of mankind, one even the almighty had failed to eradicate. And, in the coming weeks, he would take a seat as the head of one of the most powerful nations on earth, and he was just getting started.

A polite knock at the door preceded Johnny's entry, slightly taken aback upon seeing Archie lost in the smoke.

"The florist is on his way," he eventually interrupted.

Not wanting to disturb the quiet for any longer than necessary he quickly turned to leave, when Archie said,

"How's our doctor doing?"

"She arrived with the priest this morning," Johnny replied.

"Good."

Never having fully emerged from his thoughts, Archie slipped back to his meditative state with ease as Johnny respectfully and gently closed the door. With immense satisfaction Archie took another strong pull on the cigar and exhaled the thick smoke once more, releasing him from his thoughts. He sat back into his chair and taking the book from his lap, continued to read.

As promised Cohen arrived at 26 Grosvenor Square within the hour. He was greeted by Johnny with the grace of a butler, one arm constantly presiding behind a stiff back gesturing for the florist to enter, both men eyeing one another as though seeing beyond the portrayal.

He was shown to a large elegant reception room which continued the regency theme of the building, from the wooden flooring and book cabinets, to tables and upholstery, the scent of buffered wax lingered. The only thing standing at odds with the room was Cohen.

He was offered a seat but rather strolled as he waited, feeling the eyes of the manager following his every step. He stopped at the bookshelf reading some of the titles. It was an impressive array of classic literature, everything from Hemingway, Twain and Homer, to Austin, Dickens and Dumas. All appeared to be rare editions. *More of a trophy cabinet than a book cabinet,* he thought.

The steady sound of footsteps reverberating from the wooden floors grew closer, foreshadowing Trenton's imminent arrival. Johnny exited the room facing Cohen as he closed the doors behind him, maintaining his watchful eye until the very last moment.

"Cohen," Archie said enthusiastically while entering from an adjoining room.

When the two men locked eyes there was a strange pause. They had both been expecting to feel a certain amount of trepidation, but this was something else. For now the answer would lay beyond their reach.

"Thank you for coming," he said, overriding the feeling. "Can I get you anything? A refreshment perhaps?"

But Cohen could only stare at him, remembering. Panama was a lifetime ago, but memories had the power to transport you across space and time, connecting you with history in an instant.

Having escaped to the jungle barely surviving the Columbian embassy onslaught, the unit had swapped one hell for another. Viktor was one of two men carrying wounds that impacted the speed of travel, and that was without worrying about the diplomat and his travel companion. Ammunition was on reserve, which didn't help in the running battles with militia when you can't see what you're shooting at. Best guess was to try and work out the trajectory of the bullet before returning fire without getting your head blown off, but every shot had to count.

As always, when they finally got the time to rest and recuperate, Cohen said he'd take the first hour watch. The men knew how much they needed each other to get through this, but without Cohen that percentage dropped dramatically. Knowing this, Trenton insisted he would take the watch so Cohen could rest.

When the diplomat refused to travel without the kid, in the heat of battle they had to do what was needed to be done to get out, though it went against everything Cohen believed. But he had no intention of ever leaving them alone. Once they were clear, he would take the boy and find him a worthy family, it wouldn't have been the first time and there wasn't an order in the world that would be able to stop him.

Frustrated with the constant whining of the pitiful, ungrateful diplomat and still wired from the battle, Trenton gave him the boy to shut him up. Cohen woke up to whimpering sounds of the child. In a flash he got to his feet, his movement disturbing the whole unit to wake. He turned to see Trenton standing there, watching as the diplomat violated innocence, statuesque and numb to its impact as if humanity had abandoned him.

When Cohen finished with the diplomat; to hell with the mission, Trenton was next. The men in the unit had been through enough, but Viktor said he wouldn't allow one brother to stand against another, so that night Cohen disappeared into the jungle.

"I guess it's been a while," Archie said.

"Not nearly long enough."

"I'm not the man you knew Cohen, no longer a man in hiding."

"Is that right?" he said.

Continuing to observe Archie's uncomfortable behaviour.

"The men you sent to my shop called you Trenton."

"Ahh, yes. I'm sorry about that," Archie voiced regrettably.

Knowing it was a transgression to enter forbidden ground.

"I had hoped by using that name it might impose the gravity of my request."

"Request?" Cohen sniped.

"Cohen, I didn't bring you here to open wounds. Please, can we just sit down so I can at least explain?"

Archie offered a seat on a couch, taking his own on the opposite twin, a coffee table separating the two.

"I'll stand," Cohen said.

Archie looked disappointed at the response. Cohen sighed, submitting to take a seat.

"Don't worry, everyone still believes you're a florist. Well, apart from Johnny of course."

"I am a florist."

After a slight pause of study, Archie said,

"Of course." Seemingly concerned with the conviction of response.

Cohen equally and undecidedly studied his one-time ally, and despite the remorseful appearance considered him an intellect to be feared, to underestimate him was a mistake.

"It's hard for me to know where to start," Archie said. "To have everything I do and yet be so indebted to someone that you could never truly repay them. You saved my son…"

Archie searched his mind for the end of that sentence, but no words encompassed his emotion. Impatient to wait for whatever fawning stifled him. Cohen said,

"Next time just send a text."

He then stood to leave.

"Wait," Archie pleaded.

There was something about the genuine vulnerability of Archie in that moment that caused Cohen to pause. It was a side he'd never witnessed before. Sinking back onto the couch and with a furrowed expression, he waited.

"What I'm about to ask of you, I don't have the right," Archie said. "But knowing your decrees, I fear the wrath it may inflict if I didn't."

"I'm not that man anymore."

"I beg to differ," he said. "My son's still alive."

Unable to justify further argument, Cohen listened.

"I know that you were aware I sent Leeny to you, regardless of whatever story she was going to give. And despite our past I was hoping that… well, that you were still you. And despite…"

Archie gestured to Cohen's slightly inflated appearance.

"You're still better than anyone else."

Cohen was unmoved by flattery.

"I had no right, but I had no one else to turn to," Archie continued, reflecting solemnly. "I know I got that boy killed in Panama and I've spent my life trying to make up for it."

Cohen flushed with anger, but his voice remained an example of calm.

"Is that what you tell yourself? You got him killed?"

Archie struggled to hold Cohen's stare.

"You stood by and watched while he was raped. I should have killed you that night."

"You were going to try, if I remember."

"If I tried we wouldn't be having this conversation."

Archie took a moment to consider his words.

"Fair enough," he said. "But still you chose to save my son. Like I said, I fear the wrath my silence could inflict."

Cohen was wary at his forthrightness.

"When you found Joshua, his blood had been drained."

Cohen nodded his acknowledgement, instantly angered by the memory of young Josh strapped down to the table.

"There was other blood," he said with enquiry.

Archie was reluctant to expand.

"Who's was it?" Cohen pressed.

After a short pause, Archie said,

"Other children." He Lowered his gaze, "All offerings."

"What do you mean offerings?" Cohen asked, his calm being tested.

"Blood offerings, sacrifices, the undesirables, homeless, the poor. Their blood is a commodity. Although as I understand, your decrees put quite a dent in production," he said trying to put a positive spin. "A death warrant for anyone else."

Cohen wasn't in the mood. But unfortunately with all he'd seen, not just through the bleak existence of his life, but more specifically present times, the claims Archie was making were not as outlandish as he would have liked.

"So why Josh?"

"A royal bloodline."

This time Cohen's expression didn't hide his disdain.

"Believe what you will," he continued. "But their belief causes them to act and these things have already taken place."

It was a fair statement, Cohen thought, but didn't necessarily make it any easier to hear.

"They were preparing him for sacrifice," Archie continued. "Tonight there's an alignment, one that was prophesied over a thousand years ago. They believe it signals the birth of a child, a destroyer. By sacrificing Josh they think it will invoke a spirit that would have the ability to kill the destroyer."

Cohen could see where he was heading, just not the destination.

"And without Josh?" he asked.

"The sacrifice is many."

Cohen's already furrowed brow lowered further.

"By saving Josh," Archie continued. "You've actually put many other lives in danger. But with your help I can stop them."

Cohen could now only feel the fire of hate as he looked at Archie, and was going to hate himself for what he was about to say.

"How?"

"They still require a ceremonial knife," he said. "A few weeks ago an ancient dagger was found in Ethiopia, a thing of legend. That knife just arrived in London. If we can stop them getting it…"

"Where is it now?"

A glint of a smile flashed in Archie's eyes.

CHAPTER 38

BARRINGTON

Barrington was oblivious to the subtle attention of faces that turned in his direction upon arrival, otherwise at awe with the venue, distracted by the opulence and preoccupied by a sign that caught his attention. Although not so much the sign that was simply advertising upcoming hotel events, but rather his name being displayed at the top in bold brass lettering.

He was being aggrandised as the guest speaker above the subtitle 'Sacred Traditions and Theology.' He allowed an internally proud smile to fill him with excitement that very quickly morphed into a stomach churning dread.

The only reason he'd accepted the event was for the convenient lie of bringing him to London, more importantly the dagger. Not once had he thought about delivering a lecture in what was probably the most prestigious location he'd ever been asked to attend. He was completely unprepared. The dragging feeling he'd tried so hard to resolve had now returned, this time it wasn't for fear of his life, but the death of his career. Now even the expansive elegance felt claustrophobic.

With his career flashing before his eyes Barrington collected the room key card, studying it, he tapped it six times and took the elevator to the 6th floor. First impressions were how basic and small the room was for a hotel with such a facade, but then he was just a single guest staying for one night and could only imagine the opulence contained on higher levels, an elevator ride, but still a world away.

The view however, did give him a moment of pause. A magnificent scene overlooking Hyde Park in the centre of London, giving the appearance of rolling green clouds carpeting the canopy of the park, as if looking down from a plane. Park Lane was directly below and one of the busiest roads in London, but triple paned windows held the city's ambiance at bay.

The moment of admiration brought a picture of Helena to mind. He could imagine her enjoying the four-star amenities in Ethiopia, sharing a bath overflowing with bubbles, champagne in hand and a smile on her face that lit up his world. The seed of what could have been had been planted and then yanked from the ground before its roots could take hold. For the rest of his life he would be plagued with similar un-tarnished images and scenarios, but tonight the thought moved him to take action.

Locking the door, he closed the curtains and switched on the small desk lamp. Taking the dagger from his satchel, he then gently unrolled the moleskin wrapping until the dagger revealed itself, staring at it while his conscience tortured him.

He had been so in awe of the find and distracted with sexual desire that he was too quick to impress with tales of the dagger's origins, not saying that which could have offered caution. Stories of people that had given their lives, willing and unwilling, just to protect its secrecy. The destruction of entire societies who unknowingly harboured the object and those ready to lay down their lives to realise its purpose.

There were many dark stories spanning centuries, but until now, that's all they were; stories. He had thought himself a man of strong faith, imparting rare tales that subtly ingratiated himself to the listener. *But it wasn't faith*, he thought. Just a naive self-righteous stand point seeking the recognition for the appearance of faith. Barrington stared at the dagger knowing that if he truly believed, the second he saw it he would have told Helena to bury it in the desert where it belongs. A theologian who had only just begun to grasp the essence of faith and belief. Humility was an emotionally painful lesson.

Soon enough he would be done with this hideous thing and could return to some semblance of a normal life, although what that looked like after all of this he wasn't sure. For now he just needed to do what the priest, Father Michael told him and stick to the plan.

Unpacking his blazer, shirt and trousers he set them neatly on the bed, dress shoes at the base and ordered dinner from room service. Steamed salmon, new potatoes, green beans, and a slice of banoffee pie for dessert. *Why not!* he thought. Finally, a gift box from a shop in the foyer, one large enough to house the dagger. He took a hot shower and had a fresh shave while waiting for his meal to arrive, ironing his shirt until it finally came.

The dagger sat on the desk beside him as he ate, the only time not staring at it was stopping to cut his food. It was about to leave his possession and once it was gone he never wanted to think about it again, though the chances of that were slim. But while it was there sat in front of him, it was hard not to consider. The forging of its metal, the design, construction and its journey through history, all remarkable feats in their own right and yet paled in comparison to the reason for its existence in the first place.

Leaving the food tray outside of the room for collection, he finally dressed for the evening's event. Separating his notes onto the bed, a single page laid side by side until it covered more than two thirds of the spread, he spent about five minutes perusing them all at once, walking back and forth along the bed eyes scanning the documents, pulling from them the odd word he knew could trigger an entire conversation.

A noise outside of the room paused him to listen. Unable to hear anything further, he approached the door still listening before carefully opening it to peer into the hallway. The tray had been collected and its carrier was making their way along the corridor.

Returning to the bed Barrington collected the pages and put them back inside the satchel, he was ready but for one last thing.

Sealing the gift box he finished it with ribbon and set a bow perfectly on top. *This was it*, he thought, catching his reflection in the mirror. He stopped and stared at himself as if he were looking into an abyss. Remembering Helena, he hooked the satchel over his shoulder and placed the box inside before turning to look once more. Determination was now staring back.

Watching the numbers scroll as the elevator descended towards the lobby, Barrington wiped the clammy residue from his hands onto his trousers. It came to a smooth, stomach-churning halt and the doors opened on an uncertain world. He took one last deep breath and stepped out of the elevator, moving with the illusion of confidence towards the concierge's desk. There were no families to disguise him this time.

An impeccably presented woman in her late twenties, black hair scooped tightly into a perfect bun, greeted Dr Ross with a well rehearsed smile.

"Good evening sir, I'm Abigail, the concierge for the Park Lane Hilton, how may I be of assistance?"

"Hello to you. I'm Dr Barrington Ross a guest at the hotel," he said stiffly and not at all like himself.

"Of course Dr Ross," she smiled with a hint of laughter, thinking he was trying to be amusing. "It's a pleasure having you as the guest speaker at the seminar this evening." "Oh," he said, surprised.

Quickly realising there must be something on the computer screen telling her whom she was speaking to.

"That's very kind, thank you. I was hoping I might leave an item in your care, it's my niece's birthday you see."

He delivered the line with the heartfelt sorrow of a man that would have rather spent time with his sister's daughter than have to work on such a special occasion, but such was life. And for an only child, he thought he did a pretty good job.

"Of course Dr Ross, that won't be a problem," Abigail said.

He tried subtly scanning his environment to see if anyone was watching, before carefully removing the gift box from his satchel.

"It's a delicate item," he said laying it onto the desk.

"I'll put it directly in the safe," she said. "Will you be returning for it after the seminar?"

"A family member will be sending someone, usually they just ask for me by name."

"Of course Dr Ross."

Abigail carefully picked up the box, surprised at its weight and placed it into the safe behind the reception. Ross watched her until the door closed and then it was gone.

"Will there be anything else?" she asked.

"No, thank you."

But his stare lingered on the space where the box had just been. It was hard to comprehend such an anticlimactic finale and an inescapable feeling he had dishonoured Helena's all too recent memory. A part of him just wanted to ask for it back, stick to his original idea and expose its existence, thwarting plans for all concerned. *To hell with them,* he thought, but it was too late. Anyway, who was he kidding? He'd seen what these people were capable of and his survival to this point was either pure luck or divine intervention. Instead he welcomed the relief of its burden, one that would later overwhelm him to tears, but until then he just needed to get through the next part of the evening. As alien as everything had been over the past week, this was the one thing he actually knew how to do.

The seminar's attendance was a resounding success, having to offer an excess of standing only tickets that brought the room to capacity, and were still turning people away.

Dr Ross sat on the left side of the stage drifting in and out of attention as he stared out at the sea of faces. Next to him was a friend from the circuit, Professor Evelyn Larson, who'd given an interesting and amusing theological insight into births, deaths and marriages. Having seen her talk on many occasions, he always admired the way she committed with such energy and humour from first minute to the last.

You could normally tell the seasoned pros who'd found a rhythm in their delivery. Karim Affas, who was just bringing his thirty minute lecture talk to a close at around forty five minutes, was not yet one of them. He was relatively new to the circuit and it started to show around ten minutes in. He was engaging and thoroughly likeable, but Barrington thought he'd skated over some of the more interesting points on the subject of 'Summa Theologica', however it's delivery was now sending him and the audience into a coma.

No longer worried with dark forces of the world, Barrington now faced the daunting and delicate task of resuscitating an entire audience.

CHAPTER 39

COHEN

The day began with a warning. From the very moment Nathan opened his eyes he could feel the weight of it pressing against his chest, making it hard to breathe. He thought perhaps it was because it was the last day at the shop and added to by the anxiety of the move. But by the time he'd arrived at The Way of the Flower, it had grown in strength.

When Cohen emerged from the flat, his mood was oddly light. In one sense Nathan was quietly elated, not sure he would ever see this day again, but now that it had arrived only served to fuel the ominous.

It was with melancholy he watched his friend that morning, slowly moving through the shop as he held the flowers, hiding the dark clouds that followed him to preserve a moment that could only be fleeting. Which wasn't always the easiest thing to do from the person who knew you best, and that went threefold for Cohen. He didn't know how or why his feelings had such certainty, only that this day wasn't going to end well. The arrival of Trenton's men was affirmation.

Unwilling to sit idly by and wait for Cohen's return before he could find out what was going on, he closed the shop and returned to familiar ground; the dark web.

It always concerned him how easily he slipped into old shoes when he'd hoped never to walk in them again, but for Cohen he would wear them every day for the rest of his life if needed.

With a feverish determination, he began to search the darkest recesses he could think of, trying to uncover why this day had been screaming at him from the moment he opened his eyes. It didn't take long before a picture began to emerge, but only telling him a part of the story.

The shutters rattled causing him to jump. Cohen was back. He entered the shop preoccupied with thoughts, but his friend saw that darkness had found him once again. Eventually the two friends locked eyes. They both knew what came next.

"What did you find out?" Cohen started, knowing Nathan would have been doing what he does best.

He closed the laptop with a snap.

"You first," he demanded with authority.

Taken aback by the unexpectedly sharp reaction, Cohen's brow furrowed but quickly softened realising he was right.

Nathan deserved so much more than Cohen had given him. After emerging from a self-induced alcoholic coma, he up and left the one person who'd cared for him, kept him alive all this time, just so he could run away at the first opportunity in the hope there was someone good enough out there to take his life; lying to himself it was in search of redemption. He'd made exactly one decision in the last eighteen months and that had managed to drag his friend directly into the firing line, uprooting his entire life. And yet what he was asking was so much bigger than he could have possibly conceived, Cohen wasn't sure where to start. His hesitation only sought to fuel frustration.

"I can't," he said.

Overwhelming disappointment washed over Nathan, crushed, believing their friendship had meant something that superseded some stupid code of discipline.

"I owe you more than an explanation," Cohen admitted. "And I swear, I will tell you absolutely everything. But right now, Nathan… there's no time."

In the instant it took for a heart to beat, loyalty swept disappointment aside.

"Three, maybe four contractors flew in, in the last 24 hours," Nathan said.

Cohen breathed a sigh of relief that his friend was on board.

"And?"

"That's just it, the contracts are on standby, as if they're waiting for confirmation of the target. Apart from one."

He'd written the name down.

"Dr Barrington Ross," he said. "But it's not a kill order."

"Capture?"

"Listen Cohen, there are different brokers attached to this, more than one player at the table. Honestly, I've never seen anything like it before. Whatever it is, whatever Trenton's asked you to do, you don't want any part of it."

Nathan looked at Cohen's blank unwavering expression.

"You're already a part of it," he said, as if scolding himself for mis-speaking.

Despite his frustration Nathan still craved a morsel of information to subdue his curiosity.

"What is this?" he asked.

The questioned deserved at least a moment in the light and in un-guarded thought Cohen said,

"God's and monsters."

Coldness stiffened Nathan's bones. He'd heard that phrase used on occasion, usually applied for dramatic affect to situations undeserving. Cohen however wasn't a man of drama, and as the words fell from his lips the coldness that entered him felt like it had been sitting there since waking that morning, and only now revealed itself as a truth beyond understanding.

Quietly, solemnly, Cohen returned upstairs to the flat studied by Nathan's worried gaze. Watching as his legs lifted over each step with great effort as if carrying an invisible weight.

When Cohen finally reached the top of the stairs his thoughts had consumed him to stillness. He'd meant what he said to Nathan that he would tell him everything, but now realised that would probably never happen, and for his own safety, the less he knew the better.

Entering the bedroom he opened the doors to a built-in wardrobe and removed two loose floorboards. From inside the hollow he took out a small old-fashioned suitcase with a thin rustic leather exterior, it was a little larger than a briefcase though with slightly more depth. Placing it on the bed he clicked the latches and opened the case to reveal a neatly folded, weathered, black leather jacket. Unable to bring himself to im-mediately touch it, he stared. Its sight had unexpectedly provided the answer to a question he'd been too afraid to voice... Why me?

But as he stood looking down at the past he witnessed his arrogance, that by wearing the jacket he'd allowed himself to embody a representa-tion of a servant of God; the angel of death. His journey was almost at its end, that was why he'd come home, but recalled his last moments with Traeger; the strong silent goodbye.

"When the dust settles, I'll come back," Cohen said.

But Traeger and Cohen hugged each other with the omission of two men that knew they would never see each other alive again. Traeger's bright blue eyes smiled with gratitude for being able to share just a small part of that with his friend, but Cohen's stare could only respond by falling to the floor. He was so ashamed of who he'd become and while Traeger's eyes held no judgement, he saw the truth they held.

Sobriety was beginning to crush him under the awakening weight of self-awareness, hiding behind the fear of others, behind a persona of death, when all he could see in its reflection was a coward.

Before even touching down at Le Touquet Airport he could feel himself beginning to unravel. It was no more than 10 minutes after Traeger and Josh had taken back to the air that Cohen found himself in Le Centenarie, a small brasserie situated along the beach.

They didn't have any of his favourite Johnny Walker Blue Label or even Black, instead and much to his disappointment, he would champion his demise with a bottle of spiced rum.

With Prague and Viktor behind him, thoughts were only just beginning to catch up. He stared out towards the horizon and to the couples who stopped on the beach, sharing in the splendour where the sea touched the sky, smiling to themselves and each other as though it held meaning, hope or possibility. But to Cohen it was just as bleak as his existence, a bland nothingness, a reflection of his life where death and destruction were his only contribution. *Redemption*, he felt stupid for even thinking the word.

Somewhere on the road to Hanau, in the midst of trying to save little Josh, Cohen had come to the decision not to return to his life, Nathan, or the shop. No good could come of it. For so long he'd been inviting death and now it was finally upon him. He could feel it, as real as the glass in his hand, all he had to do was go home, God had taken care of the details.

For that reason alone it was the first time he could ever remember fearing death, it was so much easier when he believed there was nothing beyond, when you didn't know it was waiting for you.

He may not have ever knowingly seen God or spoken with him, but his stomach turned upon the sudden revelation that God had always been speaking with him. But regardless of the silent admission and even in opposition to its truth, in shame he raised the glass that would appease his suffering and mark the final footnote in his demise, defying him one last time.

"I saved the kid," he said quietly to the heavens. "Now leave me alone."

As the glass touched his lips the scent of spiced rum made him pause. It was an unusual reminder of the incense he'd smelt on occasion, triggering a powerful stream of thoughts all accumulated from recent events.

What he had once hoped was madness delivered through a haunting of dreams, now bled into reality. He may not have acknowledged the shadows that surrounded him but he felt their presence, a supernatural will tempting him to embrace the darkness. What he'd initially assumed was a smell triggered by trauma, the incense, had in fact been a warning holding him to the light. He knew now had there not been someone watching over him he would have surely been dead already. Like that night in Prague, when he stood holding Joshua in the middle of the street, knowing he was in the crosshair of a kill shot. There was no rational explanation as to why he was still alive. And while he remembered it all, he knew his purpose had not yet been met, because he *was* still alive. But all of the memories paled in comparison to the one he'd been truly running from, where it all started, that night in Cologne Cathedral. Remembering the priest in his arms and the forgiveness he offered, the debt not yet paid.

A sudden loneliness began to inflict a pain on his heart that became an unbearable torture of his soul. Finding it hard to breathe he placed his hand on his chest when he realised, the pain wasn't his. What he was being allowed to experience was but a shard of an atom of the loneliness of God, and yet his outpouring of love remained unwavering. For so long he had spoken to so many and the response so few; could there be a greater loneliness? It was our own shame that saw us turn from God, hiding behind our fig leaves, behind our spiced rum.

Cohen placed the glass on the table and looked out once more upon the horizon. Suddenly and unexpectedly met with an unparalleled beauty revealed in its vastness, as though a veil had been lifted from his sight. He was surprised at his reaction when a watery layer glazed his eyes. *Only now at the end do I see.*

In the days that followed Cohen used his time and resources to make sure Nathan would have everything he needed in his absence. Securing the new site for the shop in the beautiful northern port city of La Coruña, Spain, along with an apartment only a few minutes walk that gifted a mesmerising view of the coastline. He was sad that he wouldn't get to witness Nathan's reaction, but imagination would suffice. Nathan had become more than just a friend or the lighthouse that refused to let him crash against the rocks. He was family.

Cohen finally lifted the leather jacket from the case allowing its length to fall free, forgetting just how heavy it was due to the titanium weave fitted between the lining, but it had served him faithfully over the years. As he slipped his arms into the sleeves and raised it over his shoulders it was the first time he felt righteous in its wearing, fear fleeing from him placed in his armoury to be used as a weapon. Tonight he was a soldier of God.

CHAPTER 40

THE HILTON

As Cohen made his way across the city towards Park Lane's Hilton Hotel, it was hard not to notice the unusually heavy police presence, particularly a helicopter that hovered ominously at a distance overhead and the host of blacked out SUVs inconspicuously parked in approaching side roads, cautiously aware he was now inside a net that was being cast over the city.

Once inside the hotel lobby, he took a moment to assess his surrounding while doing his best to ignore the lavish lifestyles he detested. He wasn't against the accumulation of wealth, only the expectant arseholes it turned people into. The building itself was not that vast but still an unfortunate maze that he wouldn't have time to absorb. Seeing the brass lettered signage directing him towards the lecture on Sacred Traditions and Theology, he followed.

It was standing room only, which was convenient for slipping inside without attracting too much attention. Dr Barrington Ross was easily recognisable from the picture Nathan sent to his mobile device, and as expected he was sitting onstage in full view of everyone. He seemed to be trying to give the appearance of an engaged enthusiast, but anyone taking the time to observe would see the distraction, his eyes periodically scanning faces of the audience while the speaker on his feet droned on.

Cohen subtly repositioned himself, slowly navigating pillars to better scrutinise profiles of the guests, already seeing a few faces that weren't there for an education.

On the left hand side of the third row was a man he knew as Ardent. Like himself, a westerner trained in the east, although formerly attached to the Japanese organisation the Yakuza, and not known for making subtle statements. Fifth row centre, Nash, an Irish hitman whom despite a surprising IQ matched only by his strength, liked to use his bare hands to make his kills. There were two posing as a couple, stylish, fresh-faced and seemingly invested in the talk, he may not have paid much attention had he not seen them enter together, now standing at opposite sides of the room and like Cohen, more interested in who was in the audience.

Sensing movement in his periphery, the fresh-faced assassin turned his head to discreetly survey the area. He caught sight of a shoulder passing behind a pillar before exiting the room. He wouldn't have thought much of it, but the section of clothing he saw was a leather jacket that didn't seem in keeping with the clientele.

"Someone just left the lecture," he said into a communication device hidden in his sleeve. "Check them out."

With Dr Ross otherwise engaged, Cohen began making his way back towards the lobby. He had no interest in the contract on the doctor, and by the look of some of his audience he'd be lucky to escape the blood bath they were going to leave in their wake. All he wanted was the knife Archibald said would be in his possession. He called Nathan, speaking from a bluetooth bud in his ear.

"I need you to access the hotel records," he said.

"Already ahead of you."

Nathan was focused on the screen in front of him, he had the information Cohen was going to ask for even before he'd arrived at the hotel. Now he was trawling through the hotel's CCTV footage, watching Barrington arrive, noticing one or two take interest, leaving the lobby and taking the lift to the sixth floor. Skipping through the feed found him returning to the lobby and leaving an item with the concierge.

"I figured you'd wanna check out his room while he was at the lecture, but viewing the CCTV footage, it looks like he left an item with the concierge. It's in a safe behind the front desk. I can see you now, just entering the lobby," he said. "Seems you have an admirer, cream blazer, white shirt."

"I'll get back to you," Cohen said, disconnecting the call.

Leading his tail away from the lobby on a wild goose chase of corridors until he found a service elevator, pressing the button quickly he entered. As expected, there was no camera. The man in the cream jacket saw the open elevator doors and quickly followed. The very second he crossed the threshold he was hit with a forceful impact to his throat by Cohen's extended knuckle, snapping his wind pipe. As he fell to the floor suffocating, Cohen pushed the button to the basement and exited, leaving the doors to close behind him before calmly making his way back to the lobby.

It was brightly lit and open planned, causing a cross section of chaos that maintained a relentless pace of coming and going. Pillars encircled a grand chandelier and below sat a large marble table with *a rather obvious floral display*, he thought, and a few chairs adjacent to the main desk. Taking a seat he continued to observe and scrutinise the faces milling through the lobby, particularly those loitering.

Amongst the persistent hustle an Indian gentleman entered the lobby with his wife, both dressed in an elegance he'd almost forgotten existed. He was distracted at seeing the joy on the woman's face as she looked at the splendour, almost as if it were being presented to her as a gift. The husband could be overheard telling the concierge they were there to celebrate their 20th wedding anniversary. The smile as he looked at his wife was more beautiful than anything the hotel had to offer, and the way she looked back was as if the world around them simply disappeared.

They passed by Cohen as they made their way to the restaurant and he continued studying the husband's face, as if looking for the truth, but it wasn't hiding. Cohen's ever present scowl lightened momentarily, wondering what that must be like. There were many experiences unique to him, but that wasn't one of them.

As they cleared his view his attention became focused again when catching sight of the exterior doors and a tactical armed unit positioning themselves outside the building.

He breathed deeply to control the rush of adrenalin his body just released, a response to the imminent unfolding situation. He realised a fuse was about to be lit and its explosion would take no prisoners. *There were so many people,* he thought, powerless to warn them. He'd already seen at least three tier one assassins and that was without the extra entourage. They wanted mayhem, devastation, collateral damage so truth could be buried in the confusion.

Suddenly the unnamed target on the contract dawned on him. His phone vibrated a text message from Nathan.

Nathan: IT'S YOU!… GET OUT OF THERE!!!

It seemed they'd both reached the same conclusion at the same time. This would normally be the point to abandon the mission and get the hell out of there. It wasn't just recognising reality that kept him alive, it was reacting to it, but still he sat there.

Cohen knew it went against his every instinct and that made him all the more uncomfortable, his mind started to panic, *Get the fuck out of here,* it was saying. *What are you doing?* It had always saved his life before, why was he refusing to listen now?

He dug his fingers into the rest of his arm to keep himself anchored, as if somehow his mind had the power to pull him free. The window of opportunity to get out was fast closing, when he saw a woman nervously enter the lobby.

Seeing the armed unit outside of the hotel, Professor Lehman was understandably anxious and now stood uncertain of herself inside the lobby, assessing the unfamiliar surroundings. Noticing the concierge desk she started towards it, not realising her presence triggered movements from either side of the lobby on a trajectory to intercept her. Cohen watched on.

At the same time the exterior armed police unit started to enter the building, their appearance immediately bringing fear and unrest to the hotel guests and inadvertently stuttering the momentum of the professor's interceptors.

Cohen could immediately see the police were missing small identifying marks that would authenticate the unit, something a layperson would be too distracted to notice. Not that they weren't legitimate, but whatever they were doing here wasn't.

Coordinating to swiftly create a barricade at the door, informing security that a terrorist threat had been made and they would need to start clearing the building floor by floor, filtering the guests outside to a waiting unit who would identify and release them.

It was a smart move, Cohen thought. If he had the man power that would have been the way he would have done it, to just throw a net over the whole thing.

The world was quickly closing in around him and still he sat there, only now the window of opportunity to leave had passed and he was quickly regretting the decision.

I don't understand? he thought, certain this was where he was supposed to be, convincing himself that the last few weeks weren't just some residual hangover of trauma or alcohol, but punishment of a higher calling. A dawning of shame fell upon him, wanting to laugh, belittling himself for how unbelievably stupid he'd been, preying upon his own fears to manipulate an unfathomable truth. Now after all was said and done, he would die for nothing.

Then it came; incense.

CHAPTER 41

BARRINGTON

Inside the seminar, Barrington's smile spoke to the conclusion of a journey as appreciative chuckles rippled across an audience poised for elation. Karim Affas watched on from the side with Professor Larson, excitedly humbled at witnessing Dr Ross's impeccable delivery, his connection with the audience and material. *This was how it was done,* he thought. Already having decided to invite him to drinks afterwards to pick his brains further.

It was all going better than Barrington could have ever imagined. As he looked upon the faces of the audience who were quietly reciprocating the gratitude, he could feel a pull towards ego. To let go of attachment and ravenously feed on its energy. Nights like this were springboards, propelling career trajectories into the stratosphere, and its temptation was irrefutably seductive.

He was sure no one would blame him for pursuing the fully deserved and earned success and even certain that Helena would have been elated for him. But although she was no longer here, he wanted to proceed as if she was, to be the man he felt when he was with her.

However, ego soon lost its grip on him and no longer could he feel its pull, instead he saw the strings of a puppet master. Something more insidious enticing him to return to who he was, as if a darkness was beginning to overshadow the world. Suddenly he realised with unequivocal certainty his part in all of this was not yet at its end.

As the crowd hung in suspension for what was to come, Barrington's attention was drawn to his right, to a man in the third row. He didn't know why, but his stare didn't share the anticipation of the audience, it was something more sinister.

Gunshots abruptly rang out close enough to send the room into an instant panic, people screaming as they ran for the doors. More shots were fired and alarms began to wail. Barrington froze. It was just long enough to see Ardent, the man from the third row, he wasn't moving with everyone else, but towards him.

The fresh-faced man who'd entered with the woman grabbed Ardent from behind, about to eliminate the competition, but by the time Ardent span around to face him he'd already shot him point blank from beneath his jacket, wasting no time to turn his attention back to Dr Ross, but only to see him moving with the surge of panic out of the room.

Ardent signalled to Nash that he was getting away, but he was in the middle of crushing the neck of the woman who had arrived with the now dead gentleman. She fought valiantly, but when her feet dangling from the floor finally stopped kicking, he dropped her like a rag doll and followed Ardent out of the room.

In the lobby, one of the two men on a path to intercept Professor Lehman suddenly lost his nerve and rushed towards the target. The action pulled deadly attention towards himself and a police unit member shouted. People hit the floor in response as the lobby quickly filled with the sound of gunfire. Several shots were followed by the panicked screams of guests and hotel staff caught in the crossfire. The man's opposite reacted unwisely, returning fire.

In the flurry of bullets and disorientating alarms that followed, Cohen rose, moving swiftly across the lobby floor shrouded by the sudden pandemonium. People began surging from every part of the hotel, all trying to exit the building at once.

The intended chaos was madness. A power cut triggered the hotel's emergency systems as guests trampled violently over one another, stampeding towards strobing lights that marked their escape.

Cohen fought against the rush, grabbing the arm of the professor and throwing her to the floor behind the concierge desk. She landed heavily, coming face to face with Abigail. The concierge was crying in shock, unable to comprehend what was happening or how she'd managed to get shot, now sitting with blood pooling all around her.

"Where's the knife?" Cohen screamed at her.

But Abigail could only look at her blood-soaked hands unattached to the reality of her situation while Lehman shielded from bullets and debris. The safe door was ajar and Cohen pulled it to, but the gift box was missing. He looked over the counter to see one of the armed agents exiting the hotel with the box under his arm. A hail of bullets ripped into the counter causing him to hit the floor. *They were covering their retreat,* he thought. He waited a moment before trying again, but they were already outside.

A well executed shock and awe. Other than himself and this woman, no one would have known what just happened.

The armed agent holding the box entered a vehicle and it sped away as another team moved in and began opening fire on the fleeing guests, creating a bottleneck of dead bodies piling up at the entrance. Further units secured the perimeter and once set, they began moving in to ensure there were no witnesses.

Terror was rising with guests and staff not knowing which way to run.

"You're coming with me!" Cohen shouted at the professor.

Dragging her to her feet, he made his way across the lobby showing no quarter as he shoved panicking bystanders from his path, making his way back towards the function room.

As he fought against the oncoming tide with Lehman in tow, she could see Barrington making his way towards them. Despite her fear she wasn't about to draw attention to him and hoped he hadn't seen her, but he had. She tried subtly shaking her head to signal him not to acknowledge her, but subtleties amidst the chaos were lost.

"Professor Lehman?" he shouted.

Barrington continued riding the surge, too busy looking behind him to notice Cohen until it was too late. Letting go of her arm he shoulder slammed Dr Ross into the wall with such a force it knocked the wind from him, and despite his distress he was still concerned about the men approaching from the rear. He wanted to say there was someone coming, but couldn't get his words out and wasn't sure if this man was with them. But Cohen followed Ross's fearful gaze along the corridor to see Ardent's head bobbing in and out of sight.

"Shit," Cohen vexed.

Seeing a corridor branching off, he pulled Barrington from the wall and pushed him in that direction just as a small explosion came from the lobby, then consecutively from other parts of the building, each one accompanied by screams before smoke started to fill the halls sending panic into overdrive. Lehman followed the man holding Barrington, feeling her chances of survival would probably be better with an assassin.

Managing to navigate off the main route, Cohen pushed Barrington through a set of frosted glass doors towards the hotel spa. It was a maze to the unacquainted.

Ardent had seen them turn and followed along the length of the corridor, losing sight he continued passed the frosted doors with Nash trailing not far behind.

Uncertain of his direction, Cohen slowed to check the various doors that surrounded them. All were private massage rooms. His frustration started to get the better of him.

"I don't have time for this," he said gritting his teeth, grabbing Barrington and pinning him to a wall. "You need to tell me where they're taking that knife?"

"How would I know that?" Barrington argued.

Though his confusion offered Cohen a slither of clarity. The armed unit had taken the knife and were now laying waste to whatever was left behind, it was clear that party wanted him dead.

"Who wants you alive?" he asked instead.

But the question only served to put the doctor into a state of shock, unable to reconcile that by implication someone wanted him dead. He remembered Helena's naked, lifeless body twisted in the middle of the street, her eyes staring at him. Cohen pulled Barrington off the wall only to shove him back with a greater force, the impact painfully jolting him back to reality.

"I don't know, I don't know, I DON'T KNOW!" Barrington screamed.

The angry tears in his eyes revealed a fracture with the potential to break, he was at the edge of his sanity.

"Listen to me," Cohen said.

Attempting to look him in the eye, but Barrington's tearful defeated gaze wandered with pity.

"Hey!" he continued with a sharp slap to the face. "Listen."

Barrington snapped from his wallowing.

"Wherever they're taking it, they planning to sacrifice children with that thing, so you'd better work out what it is you know fast or you're useless to me."

From the holster beneath his left arm he pulled out his gun and placed it against Barrington's forehead. It was without doubt the most terrifying moment of his life and yet his attention was distracted with bad information.

"That's not what the knife is for," he voiced bravely with a curious calm.

Cohen's grip eased as he lowered his weapon, but didn't let go.

"What do you mean?"

Barrington looked with worry at the professor, and she at him, both aware of the unique information he held.

"My book," he said.

"What about it?"

"In it I describe a part of a ceremony, which is the sole purpose for the knife's existence, extremely rare esoteric information and I'm telling you that's not what the knife is for."

Cohen was missing something

"So why the kids?"

But Barrington was also missing something. As he searched the extensive knowledge in his head for what the man could possibly mean, no quick answer was forthcoming. Seeing Cohen's patience waning, his worry intensified.

"He doesn't know about the prophesy," Professor Lehman said.

Cohen's scowl turned to face her, which was more than enough to instil her with fear. But Barrington's surprise was also poised with undecided anger, waiting to hear what she had to say, though instinctively betrayal was the overriding emotion before a word was even spoken.

Still searching for Dr Ross, Ardent reached the end of the corridor and scanned the merging crowds, unable to see the target he decided to double back. He met up with Nash and directed him back down an adjacent corridor while he pushed forward in another direction. Before setting off a faint shout pulled his attention towards the spa, he tried calling Nash back but couldn't be heard over the chaos. Alone he approached the frosted doors.

Cohen advanced on the professor with an expression of ill intent. Realising immediately that her age and gender afforded her no leniency, she faced him with an elongated neck and raised chin, a defiant posture of elegance in the face of fear.

"What do you know of the knife?" she said.

Cohen couldn't quite believe the audacity of this woman, interrogating him with a question.

"I'm not sure you get how this works," he said.

"Actually I'm not sure you're getting how this works," she snapped back.

But her words stunned him to listen, though she wasn't sure for how long.

"I'm willing to die for my beliefs," she reinforced with a light smile. "Are you? A soldier in someone else's war?"

He thought for a moment that she was referring to Archie, though realised it was an arbitrary and obvious statement. *But was this someone else's war?* He wasn't so sure anymore, only that he couldn't be the reason innocent blood was being shed.

"Okay," he said.

He grabbed Barrington and threw him to his hands and knees at the professor's feet. Taking a tuft of hair and yanking his head back so she could clearly see the fear in his eyes, he shoved the gun with force against the back of his skull. Barrington's life flashed before his eyes.

"Either you tell me what I need to know or you can watch as he dies for your beliefs. Then you can follow him."

But to his surprise Professor Lehman's expression didn't flinch.

"They don't need the knife to kill a child of prophesy," Professor Lehman said. "He's being sent to destroy what that knife will bring upon the world."

"And what's that?"

"Hell."

CHAPTER 42

COHEN

It was but a moment's pause and a thousand visions in an instant. From Nathan, Leeny and Josh to Viktor, Traeger and Archie, the light of birth and the fire of death, the forging of a great sword folded over eons under the weight of a hammer, a clock that began ticking the very instant a dying priest anointed his slayer with blood.

Incense came like a tap on the shoulder as Cohen let go of Barrington, spinning 180 degrees with his gun raised as Ardent entered the spa, his weapon trained on Cohen.

"That was just getting good," Ardent said with amusement. "I almost didn't want to interrupt. Will he find out? Won't he find out? It was like some shitty reality TV show."

He laughed manically.

"Now as far as the contestants are concerned, that bitch you can shoot in the face, but the doctor, he's coming with me… Oh," he continued as an afterthought. "And you have to die."

Ardent fired, but anticipating him Cohen turned, instinctively covering the professor, his weight on top of her as he dropped to the floor using obstacles for protection.

Everything happened so fast it was as though time slowed down.

As Lehman was falling backwards to the floor fearing of the man protecting her, she looked at his face, but it was his tortured existence she could feel. By the time she slammed painfully into the floor, the fear for her life was still present, just not from him and she didn't know why.

Ardent saw at least two of the shots hit Cohen but fall to the floor seemingly absorbed by his jacket, although it did little to stop the pain. Ardent stopped firing and Cohen stood turning to face him.

"Now that was fucking cool," Ardent impressed.

Holding his gun aloft, he said with nonchalance,

"By the code then?"

Cohen gritted his teeth until the pain dispersed and then imitated Ardent's action raising his weapon. Casting the guns aside both men pulled a blade.

"I'm definitely having that," he said intimating Cohen's jacket. "Titanium weave right?"

"Sorry. It doesn't come in a child's medium," Cohen quipped at his small stature.

Barrington scrambled out of the way as Cohen and Ardent circled each other in the narrow space. Cohen's size overshadowed his opponent by a degree that appeared unfair, but Ardent's size *was* his weapon and that quickly showed as he moved with a speed and low centre of gravity that was difficult to avoid. Cohen managed to block and attempt to counter but over extended and received a slash to the chest and stomach. Backing up to check the wounds, he found they were fairly superficial. However, he knew that two and two made four, and four and four made dead. He could see what he wanted to do, he was just no longer finely tuned enough to be able to achieve it.

Cohen made his approach but the engagement lasted only slightly longer before meeting the same conclusion. Ardent smiled, he could see Cohen was no longer the killer he once was and his next move would be his last.

Cohen thrust his blade forward but it was easily countered and Ardent's knife punctured his lower left side. It was the sacrifice that had to be made to get his opponent close enough. Cohen then brought the weapon down with an almighty force that penetrated through the top of Ardent's skull, leaving him lifeless before he hit the floor.

Cohen breathed through the pain as he carefully removed Ardent's blade from his side. Collecting his gun he turned to the Professor.

"How do I find the kid?" he demanded.

Barrington and Lehman were finding it hard to catch up with the reality they found themselves in, or comprehend the stoicism of this stranger.

"You can't," Professor Lehman said, starting to come around.

"Then how will they find him?"

"They won't, not specifically. They have no way of identifying him."

Identify who? Barrington thought trying to keep up. Cohen's pain was starting to push his frustration to a level beyond his containment, but Professor Lehman could only look upon him with sadness. *He doesn't understand*, she thought, now realising what he was trying to achieve.

"There's no way to save them all," she said gravely.

"What do you mean save them all?"

"It's as Herod in the time of Christ," she said. "Only this time they won't just kill the male born, any child born on this day is not safe."

Cohen's face skewed as though what he heard was more painful than his wounds, but with no time to assimilate his attention was taken by the sound of a radio coming from beyond a door several feet away. He gestured for them both to remain quiet as he approached.

The door slowly opened and the barrel of an assault rifle peered through, inches from Cohen's face. Yanking the barrel forward its operator was pulled through the door. The moment his head was visible Cohen put a bullet in it at point-blank range.

Gunfire followed from the hallway, exploding into the doorway, splintering the frame. Pulling a flash canister from the harness of the dead agent, Cohen tossed it into the hallway. A second later its burst filled the passage with an excruciating light rendering the agents immobile with sensory overload, giving him long enough to enter and execute the three remaining agents in quick succession. Tap tap, tap tap, tap tap.

The hallway was clear, but long and straight before they could reach the exit, which made him uneasy.

"Go!" he said, urgently directing them down the hallway towards an exit as he followed behind constantly checking over his shoulder.

Meanwhile, Nash found the frosted doors and entered. It wasn't long before he discovered Ardent's body amongst the massage tables and a trail of blood leading away, which he quickly followed.

By the time Cohen arrived at the end of the corridor, breaching the exit, Nash turned into the hallway, the two caught sight of one another just as the exterior door closed, cutting them off. Nash stepped over the bodies of the agents and calmly continued his pursuit.

Cohen led Barrington and Professor Lehman to a mews at the rear of the hotel and directed them on a route that would safely put a distance between them, their assailants and the hotel. Professor Lehman poised to say something, though not sure what, instead she could only watch with a surreal filter as this strange man disappeared into the night, suddenly gone from their lives as quickly as he entered. Although she suspected not for good.

"We need to go," Barrington said sharply with a tremble in his voice.

He walked at a pace with Professor Lehman needing to double step to keep up, and did so without complaint. However Barrington's sharp tone was something she was less accustomed to, but witnessing just a small part of what he'd been subject to, it was more than understandable. He had questions, that much a blind person could see. But Dr Ross wasn't the same man she knew only a few weeks ago. Suddenly his submissive, scared expression disappeared like an actor emerging from character.

"Did he get it?" Barrington continued.

"What?" Professor Lehman replied, confused at the sudden change.

"The knife?" Barrington pressed urgently "Did Father Michael get the knife?"

Lehman was slightly dumbfounded. While he hadn't said anything she wasn't aware of, with everything happening so quickly upon arrival, she'd forgotten about the plan, about Dr Carden. Fear for her new acquaintance took hold, overriding every other emotion.

"I don't know," she conceded.

CHAPTER 43

THE ORDER

In preparation for the ceremony, the evening saw a motorcade of incognito international leaders arriving at the Temple, a small district in the heart of London that was home to a large contingent of barristers, judges and legal chambers. It was in plain sight, yet concealed between the boundaries of Fleet Street and the gates of its southern boarder at Victoria embankment.

The many buildings preserved a vast and rich history that was romanticised in its direct connection to the 12th century Knights Templars. Particularly that of the Temple Church, a recreation of Emperor Constantine's memorial of The Holy Church of the Sepulchre, the burial site of Christ; Yahshua of Nazareth.

The slick cobbled stones of Middle Temple Lane were offered only faint illumination from the still functioning Victorian lamps, helping anyone that crossed its threshold to feel as if they'd been instantly transported to a time before the modern world, but for the carcade of executive vehicles now lining its periphery and armed personnel lurking in the shadows.

As an eerie still descended upon the evening's proceedings, a tall, masked hooded figure carrying a flaming torch appeared from a small narrow passage off the lane. The ominous sight triggered guests to emerge one by one from their vehicles, each concealed by identical black hooded cloaks and a plain black half mask with small horns protruding the forehead.

The procession of unidentifiable world powers followed the torch bearer, a single file of submissive obedience as rats to a piper, through the narrow passage, across the cloisters and under the archways, arriving at Temple Church.

As they passed inside the unusual rotund of the nave, each of the procession were given a chalice of blood before continuing to the north stairwell where they ascended to the circular triforium in preparation for the auspicious occasion.

Slowly and ceremonially with mumbles of incantations falling from their lips, holding in front of them a chalice of blood, they began to encircle its periphery, eventually and in unison coming to a sudden halt, turning inward to face the central viewing platform.

From beneath the arches of the cloisters, the seven hooded figures of Quod Order De Septem appeared behind seven torch bearers, their full faced masks of twisted demonic representations carried horns of pure gold. Witnessed by the attendees above, one by one they entered the lower church.

At the centre of the circular nave, Jonathan Montgomery IV placed a skull of the Magi, the religious artefact stolen from Cologne Cathedral eighteen months prior. Isabella, Melcher, Jessop, Wilhelm and Francis, each placed vessels containing the contaminated blood of young Joshua.

As the ceremony began to unfold, the armed unit carrying Dr Ross's gift box from the Hilton hotel was arriving at the West Gate of the Temple, quickly ushered beyond the police cordons and private security, coming to a stop at the Inner Temple. Alighting the transport a single agent carried the dagger towards the church, finally and unnervingly relieving its possession to a tall, faceless hooded figure. As he was returning to the vehicle a break in the clouds stole his attention, as it did the hooded figure.

CHAPTER 44

COHEN

Regardless of his wound, Cohen needed to quickly put some distance between himself and the hotel. If Nash was on his trail it might only be a matter of time before they ran into each other again. Circling back around the block far enough away from the Hilton, he headed south towards Piccadilly, the odd explosion could still be heard echoing into the night.

It gave him a stomach churning confirmation of how far they were willing to go to cover all of this up, and the resources at their disposal to achieve it. *If they could do this in the middle of London, then they could do anything anywhere.* The thought instantly turned his attention to Nathan.

Taking out his phone he dialled, Nathan answered before the first ring finished, just as a police car raced by with sirens wailing, Cohen ducked into the shadows.

"Are you still at the shop?" he said.

"Yeah," Nathan responded with semi focused attention. "Sounds like you made it outside. I'm trying to find out who's behind the contracts."

"I know who's behind it. You need to get out of there," Cohen demanded. "Now! Go dark, false papers."

Cohen's head was on a nervous swivel. He eyed the railing to Green Park across the street.

"Just like I showed you."

He disconnected the call, dropped the phone and smashed it under foot. Seeing an opportunity to cross the street he moved swiftly, but never ran. Climbing the railing was an easy job made hard with the injury, but once inside he stopped to catch his breath and assess the wound.

It wasn't the worst he'd ever seen, but not something he wanted to leave unattended for too long. He was relieved to hear Nathan's voice having momentarily convinced himself of the worst, but knowing he was okay meant he could focus on getting himself out of the city. Police cars continued scouring the area, most heading in the direction of the hotel, others he assumed were helping to widen the net.

Heavy rain began to fall which reduced visibility and helped cover his tracks. He pushed off the tree and began moving south, deeper into the park.

Nathan was sat at the workbench when the call disconnected. The sudden silence only enhanced the crying sirens that hung over the city keeping his heart in a state of perpetual torment. Heeding Cohen's warning, he closed the laptop to make a move when the shutters rattled causing him to jump for the second time today, but there was no one to be seen.

Understandably mistrustful, Nathan wouldn't dismiss the noise until investigating. Picking up an old set of sheers he slowly moved through the dark space, approaching the front window. He looked back and forth along the street, it was quiet. He was about to return to the bench to pack up his things when he smelt it. *Incense?* he thought. But suddenly realising what it was, he turned and ran.

A few moments later a massive explosion ripped through the shop, its burst fired a fury thirty feet beyond the windows. Silence followed, but for the song of another alarm rising into the night.

CHAPTER 45

FATHER MICHAEL

Amongst the stone eagles of the Campanile at Westminster Cathedral, Father Michael looked out over a remarkable view of London, though unmoved by its offering. Instead his gaze lingered towards the night sky and clouds that concealed a promise. He didn't doubt that beyond his perception an alignment foreseen a millennia ago was in conjunction, although his need for reassurance was beyond fathoming.

Only a few hours earlier after meeting Father Tobias Fischer, along with Archbishop Hammond, the three retired to his study. Despite Fischer's relative youth, his spirit seemed to hold a wisdom beyond its years and engaged with the earnest reflection of his mentor; Father Weiss.

Archbishop Hammond sat back to disengage, intrigued to simply witness, although occasionally distracted by a small muted television set displaying the news.

"It's good to see you Father Michael," he said.

"An unexpected gift," Michael returned. "I didn't see you at the memorial."

"No," Fischer said without offering further explanation.

But it set the tone for what was to follow, pausing momentarily to order his thoughts.

"Father Weiss always spoke of you with such reverence," he said. "And with sadness."

The latter part of the statement confounded Father Michael.

"He always felt as if he'd abandoned you," Fischer said.

"We had our callings."

"And yet clarity does not uncomplicated the heart."

Father Michael gave a stifled smile, a truer statement could not be heard.

"Father Weiss once said to me that silence could be the loneliest place when waiting to hear the voice of God. He said he'd heard his calling with such force, and then for over thirty years waited with no word. Doubt became a demon of torture, testing his faith, but while the tree shakes its roots hold firm."

His choice of words warmed Father Michael affectionately, as if hearing them from Weiss himself.

"His faith was eventually rewarded. But it's revelation will not be easy to hear," he said with warning.

It was a day he wouldn't soon forget, the 11th February 2013. Father Weiss had woken with an unplaceable agitation, stressing to his mentee the importance of placing the prophesy beyond reach of the Luciferians. But before sending, he removed a small section and with the flame of a candle destroyed it. He imparted the contents to Father Fischer alone that he should deliver the message to Father Michael at the appropriate time.

Being one of the younger men of the clergy, that day saw him draw the short straw to act as a tour guide for a group of visiting patrons. A task no one particularly wanted, but as it turned out was unexpectedly enjoyable. At one point the conversation turned to the Serie A, the Italian football league. Father Fischer had been frustrated at how his team, AC Milan were performing. They'd won the division two seasons ago, lost the following year and were becoming increasingly worse. That was when the news took the entire world by storm.

For the first time in over 600 years, the Pope had resigned. Within hours of the announcement, a bolt of lightning struck St Paul's Basilica and was broadcast on the internet and televisions across the globe.

Desperate to communicate the news and knowing it was important enough to interrupt Father Weiss' daily liturgy, Fischer led the group through Cologne Cathedral. Silence suddenly fell upon them all at once.

In the distance, alongside the Shrine of the Magi, the large figure of a man stood with his arm cradling Father Weiss, his other hand gripping the handle of a knife whose blade had already done its bidding.

Father Michael listened with pain as if having experienced the ordeal for himself and was now reliving it.

"There was much distress," Fischer said.

Which he thought an arbitrary statement, but for what followed.

REVELATIONS

"But not for Franz."

It was the first time using his Christian name and for good reason. In loyalty he wanted to honour Franz as the symbol he stood for, but now amongst friends he wanted to honour the man. He continued,

"There was a pain and anguish that befell his attacker that words paled to describe. And yet while Franz's life was slipping away he appeared cloaked in peace." Father Fischer seemed confused. "It didn't make sense," he said.

Father Michael was finding it difficult to hear the sympathy his colleague was finding for his friend's killer, but listened while he continued to recount. The archbishop continued to study Father Michael's reactions.

Holding the weight of his victim, the killer took extraordinary care in lowering the body to the floor as though a beloved family member were being laid to rest. The group along with their guide were stunned to silence, though just as Father Fischer was about to cry out he was further silenced by a vision, although one not shared by anyone else.

As clear as night from day, he saw an ethereal light appear over Father Weiss that extended to the dizzying heights of the cathedral. He would have fallen to his knees had he the function to do so. But rather realising his eyes were being held to witness not thrown to the floor in submission.

Despite having told the story before, Fischer still struggled to describe that moment, stumbling over his words with the frustration of inadequacy.

"I was struck with fear in its presence," he said. "Not certain of what I was supposed to be paying witness to."

The remorseful killer knelt over Franz's passing, tears forming like a baron well sprung to life. With barely the energy, Father Weiss raised his hand in one last embrace and caressed the cheek of his deliverer.

It was in that moment a light surrounded him, almost as if Father Weiss had transferred it to him, yet he was not aware. The killer got up and turned to leave but was quickly struck still by a force so powerful it left him paralysed to move, arms stretched out from his body as though crucified without a cross. The cry that followed he believed no human was capable of, but rather something was crying through him.

When the force finally released him, fear carried him away at speed. Father Fischer hurried to the side of his mentor, falling to his knees overwhelmed with grief as he took his hand. Franz' stare passed through

Father Fischer as though he were witnessing beauty that laid beyond our existence. He smiled.

"It has begun," he said.

Father Michael understood the story hadn't been told to make him feel better, but he really didn't know what to feel and sat silently. His colleagues waited respectfully. After much deliberation, Father Michael said,

"This man. The one with the light."

From the concerned look passed between Archbishop Hammond and Father Fischer, he knew he had concerned the right area of enquiry.

"What is it?" he pressed regarding the silent exchange.

"He showed up on our radar several weeks ago," the archbishop offered reluctantly.

"How?"

Father Michael's tone was now much more insistent. Hammond's hesitation was knowing how Father Michael felt about certain operations within The Natsarim.

"An asset in Prague," he said.

A suppressed sigh subdued Father Michael's distaste. He abhorred the idea that the church would have assassins on their payroll.

"I understand how you feel," the archbishop continued. "But we are at war Father Michael, a fact that should not be so easily forgotten. Even the apostles carried swords."

It was a contentious point that Father Michael didn't have time to get in to, and so nodded for the archbishop to continue.

"We discovered descent within The Order's ranks. They were holding one of their own. The target was a child of the royal bloodline."

"A child!" Father Michael exclaimed.

"He was rescued by the man from the cathedral. The asset was about to shoot him and the boy, when they witnessed the same light Father Fischer just described."

The information perplexed Father Michael.

"I don't understand," he said. "Who is he?"

"We don't know. But he's here in London. Father Fischer has been watching him, he owns a small shop across the river."

Father Michael was suddenly drained with confusion, memories of Franz weighing heavily upon him, when suddenly he remembered something.

"You said Franz tore off part of the prophesy?" he said addressing Father Fischer. "What did it say?"

REVELATIONS

"He would't allow me to see what the main part of the prophesy read," he said. "Only this… You will know the servant by the staff of a shepherd, and the sword of a soldier. Father Weiss believed that part of the prophesy was only ever meant for one person… You."

Archbishop Hammond was distracted once more by the television.

"It has indeed begun," he said.

His words were in response to what he was watching on the television, an interview with the Pope showering his praise upon the man of the hour, Archibald. T. Montgomery.

"The mouth of the serpent vomits its spawn," he continued.

The words caught Father Michael's attention, remembering Brother Bonsu uttering a similar phrase.

"What did you say?"

"The brotherhood have long known that the announcement of the false prophet would be delivered from the throne of the Antichrist," he said.

Father Michael turned to Fisher who shared the look of knowing, before looking back at the television and to the Pope being interviewed in the audience hall of the Vatican.

"It's hard to call something conspiracy or even coincidence when an entire building is constructed to be the shape of the head of a serpent," Hammond said. "And the audacity to place his throne right in its mouth, between two fangs. The Antichrist has paved the way for the rise of the false prophet, two of the unholy trinity are upon us. They will lay the foundation for the one to be revealed."

Before having a chance to absorb revelations that infuriated him for not already knowing, the meeting was interrupted by news of the asset's arrival. Father Michael chose to remove himself from their company. While he was interested to hear what was to be said, information he was certain would eventually reach him, he couldn't agree with The Natsarim's use of violence, and to be present was to be party. However he was surprised at the asset's appearance, expecting a burly gentleman whose light had long left his eyes, but rather faced with a young attractive woman, regardless of the bandaging to her ear and fresh scaring to her cheek, whose light was still present. Though his surprise was not enough to tempt his intrigue, he left them to reflect on any new information.

As Father Michael continued staring from the tower, towards the stubborn thick clouds huddling together as far as the eye could see, hiding what sight craved, he listened for the voice of God, but it was a lonely silence he heard.

The unexpected meeting with Father Fischer should have provided more than just clarity in his mission, but hope, reassurance in his faith, as opposed to instilling the doubt he now felt. His faith remained intact, but ego muddied the waters.

He was finding it hard to look past the journey he had taken with such blind faith, and yet at the end of every path someone else had been rewarded its information. It was as though everybody else was supposed to be there and he was trying to force himself into a story that wasn't his to tell.

He would never test God to ask him for a sign, but he could feel the question in his heart; and God knows your heart.

"Why would you stay silent in this hour?" he said.

But the longer he listened, the lonelier he felt.

What if silence was the answer? he thought. With panic his mind turned to Professor Lehman and Dr Carden. It was as Archbishop Hammond said, he'd been so focused on an objective, he hadn't thought about to-morrow, which meant he hadn't considered the consequences for those in his recruitment and the dangers they were being exposed to. He needed to stop this foolishness, abandon whatever crusade he thought he was on. If God needed this tired old priest, he would ask.

Just as he was about to leave the watchtower he noticed a faint illumination on one of the stone eagles perched around the platform. Turning to see its source he was faced by a break in the clouds in the only place that would allow him to witness the conjunction, shining with a brightness that was beyond this world. A tear graced Father Michael's cheek as he lowered himself to his knees.

CHAPTER 46

COHEN

Once Cohen eventually reached the southern outskirts of St James's Park, he gratefully noticed the sirens fading into the distance, though one or two still raced by not too far away. Putting his back to a tree, he rested for a minute while getting his bearings and trying to figure out a plan of direction.

He tried imagining a scenario where he would somehow be able to impact their plans, hopefully save a few in the process. Blood seeped as he checked his wound. Perhaps he could cut off the head of the snake, he thought. Maybe that would bring an end to this madness, but which snake?

Cohen's assured nature was held by knowledge acquired from a life devoted to study. An accumulation of disciplines that moulded his very essence into the weapon he'd become, and though its edges may not be as sharp as they once were, its forging was undeniable. Despite that, his knowledge remained blind to a solution.

His attention was pulled to an illumination further ahead, not the artificial street lights, but something else. With the energy of determination he pushed off the tree and continued towards it, thankfully there were no fences to climb on the southern side of the park.

The entire area around Victoria Station extending towards Westminster was under massive redevelopment of the underground system, almost like one continuous construction site. He assumed the illumination was coming from the floodlights of the work site. Unfortunately he soon found that the project had temporarily shut roads that blocked his path, and to redirect himself at this point would take him back to where he couldn't be.

Looking along the fence trying to see if there was another way around, he suddenly stopped to listen. The sirens, they had gone. But it wasn't just the sirens.

Coming through the park it wouldn't have been so obvious, however, now on the opposite side trawling the main roads, *where was the traffic?* He turned to look back in the direction of travel and there in the distance a stocky figure was emerging from the dark. It was Nash.

Taking on Ardent was an entirely different proposition, despite Cohen's lack of conditioning, Ardent's undoing was born of overconfidence, an infliction Nash didn't suffer with. Even at full health this would still be a problem.

Another figure began to emerge a short distance away, then another and another, and another. Cohen's head turned sharply back and forth scanning the roads, all of them empty, not a flashing light to be seen or siren to be heard.

Perhaps he'd been wrong about Nash, he thought. Maybe there was an overconfidence after all, a calmness in his pursuit, only it wasn't inspired from the self, but the power it would take to lay an assault on a high profile venue in the middle of London, and then be able to shut down an entire section of the city where he now stood. Nash was confident of the power at his employer's disposal. *And why wouldn't he be?* Cohen thought, feeling the perimeter constricting around him.

Along with the rain, fire reflected in Cohen's eyes as if sensing his nightmare; his dream. He could feel the end, it was close.

"Fuck it!" he said.

Submission just wasn't in his nature. As he turned to the fence, he curled his fingers into the wire opening and with a powerful grip, yanked it from its holdings, collapsing an entire section in the process. He felt the pain tear in his side, but stepped over the fence defiantly and into the construction sight.

Despite the floodlights, the illumination dimmed slightly, raising Cohen's attention skywards allowing the rain to grace his skin. A break in the clouds was closing over, taking away what he considered to be the light of the moon. He was about to continue when he paused spotting more men entering from the Victoria side. Looking behind him, it was too late to go back. He was trapped.

As the perimeter continued to close in around him, Cohen checked his wound and scoffed.

"One last stand," he groaned.

He was out of time and could see nothing inside the encircled construction site apart from deep shafts and the half-demolished remains of an old three-story Italian restaurant pressed up against the rear of the Victoria Palace Theatre. The smell of incense pulled his attention back towards the restaurant just as Nash stepped over the collapsed fence.

Cohen looked at the broken structure of the restaurant, part of the demolished exterior walls revealed an extensive and loving history that had all been erased in the name of progress, not unlike every war zone he'd ever been in. Only this time fear found him.

A part of him would have rather stood and fought, there was no way to win, but he would have found satisfaction taking some of them with him. Pulling out his gun instilled a sudden pause to the encroaching perimeter, all of them quick to raise their weapons on him. As he did with Ardent, he held his weapon in the air, only this time with one hand he released the clip from the gun allowing it to fall to the floor. Pulling back the chamber he released the loaded round, leaving the gun fully empty. Disregarding it, he pulled out his blade and like the gun, raised it aloft for all to see, before calmly following the scent inside the broken structure.

If they want me, they'll have to come and get me.

Nash's smile was like a toothless grin with teeth on the head of a man with no neck. With his prey finally trapped, it was with deep satisfaction that he looked upon this once symbol of fear now scurrying around like a rat in the sewers.

Standing where Cohen was just moments before, he viewed drops of blood leading into the ruin, happy that Ardent got a piece of him, silently he gestured for two of the men to follow the target inside. With obedient acknowledgment they raised their weapons and entered assertively.

In the waiting silence there was anticipation that became uneasy the longer they stood, a few subtle silent exchanges began eroding confidence.

A scream from inside was followed by a burst of gunfire that saw everyone clinch a tighter grip on their weapon. Then there was silence. Nash waited for a moment as his nose twitched with aggressive agitation before ordering two more men forward. This time the pair were not so confident.

Unlike before no scream could be heard, no gunfire, but a faint scuffle which resulted in the same outcome; silence. Nash snatched an automatic weapon from one of the armed units and opened fire on the already ruinous heap, following his lead the men all emptied rounds into the building. There was a short silence as Nash entered a new clip into the weapon and with fury let every one of the bullets fly. The men watched with concern as Nash's display of calm disappeared. He ordered one of the men to check the aftermath, but he stood defiant, unwilling to meet the same end as his colleagues. Nash then turned his gun on the man, but as he did the rest of the unit turned their guns on Nash. Frustrated with the outcome, he approached the unwilling man, pulling an incendiary grenade from his harness before tossing it into the already demolished building. Igniting at over 4000 degrees, the structure quickly began to burn regardless of the rain.

Cohen retreated to the back of the building as the fire began to rise, still distantly hoping to pull off one last escape he didn't stop searching for a route. His footing was made uneasy as old flooring crumbled beneath sending him crashing to the ground, providing a painful reminder of his wound. Suddenly distracting him from his own demise was a sound coming from the floor above. He tried to listen beyond the noise of rising flames and falling rain when he heard it again. It was the scream of a young child. He couldn't imagine what someone would have been doing there, homeless or runaway, it didn't matter. Scrambling to his feet he got to the stairs.

Outside Nash caught a glimpse of movement and again bullets ripped through the structure.

The flames moved faster than Cohen, as he reached the top of the stairs the wood gave way and the staircase suddenly fell. He managed to grab the ledge, the stretch tearing at his wound, and was able to drag himself up onto the first floor landing.

"Hello!" he screamed.

From outside the shout sounded like a cry, all assuming its expulsion was pain and they revelled in it with whoops and cheers. Nash's toothless smile returned.

"Help me!" the voice of a child cried out.

Desperately searching through the flames, Cohen called out,

"Where are you?"

Hoping the scream would carry over the flames. He wrapped his arm in front of his face to protect him from the smoke, but the heat was becoming so intense he could feel the oxygen in his lungs start to burn. He heard the voice again, barely managing to gage the direction other than it was coming from the floor above.

The inferno was now so intense Cohen wasn't sure he would be able to make it out alive, but he couldn't stop searching. Stopping at the next staircase as flames lashed through the slats, not sure it would be stable enough to take his weight, he ran as quickly as he could with flames whipping at his legs. Reaching the top he could hear the wood beneath him cracking as he jumped across a gap in the floor just before the staircase gave way, crashing to the ground taking out the floors beneath.

"Please help me!" the voice said.

Cohen froze upon seeing the face of an angelic little boy, his tears had washed lines into his face that had blackened from the smoke. He couldn't have been more than six or seven.

It was maybe ten to twelve feet to the end of the corridor and the floor between Cohen and the boy had collapsed. No matter what he did, he knew there was no way to reach him, but still, he wouldn't leave him.

The flames continued to rise beating both Cohen and the boy back from the edge pushing an ever-increasing distance between them.

"Look at me!" Cohen shouted trying to keep the boys attention on him, "I'm not going anywhere. You hear me. I'm gonna stay right here."

The sound of wood cracking pulled Cohen's attention upwards, when the boy said,

"I forgive you."

Cohen's attention snapped to the boy with the dread of disbelief as he remembered the words of the dying priest. In an instant he was stood in Cologne Cathedral holding a man who reached out to touch his cheek.

A thunderous crack overhead brought the roof to collapse and a heavy beam crashed into him, knocking him through the floor and falling through the flames, landing on the level beneath. Twice more it gave way until Cohen found himself staring up from the basement into a hole of flaming destruction with rain hitting him in the face. It was just enough time to see wooden beams and twisted metal engulfed in flames follow his descent, like an abyss descending upon him.

The structure crashed through the upper levels and landed with an iron spike piercing Cohen's shoulder, pinning him to the floor. The remainder of its structure lay only inches above him as a flaming cage that threatened to slowly melt the skin from his face.

Turning his head to the side to give a marginal difference to the heat, he tried to push against the metal but instantly scolded his hands to retreat. Using the sleeves of his jacket he pressed his forearms against two twisted iron poles and began to push, the leather buying only a few valuable seconds before it started to melt away.

With every bit of strength he could muster, Cohen pushed up with his forearms. The glowing iron rods made short work of the leather, burning through and fusing it to his arms as it continued to melt into his skin.

Cohen screamed in agony but still continued to push, slowly raising his prison as it excruciatingly retracted from his shoulder. Now clear but with not enough room to even turn on his stomach, he laid there as rain tapped his face with a continuing annoyance.

He tried taking a deep breath but struggled to expand his lungs, realising one had been pierced by the rod.

The sigh Cohen released was his final submission. He didn't think much of his coffin, but then it was all the same to him, he thought. Closing his eyes he tried to enjoy the coolness of the rain against his skin.

CHAPTER 47

DR SARAH CARDEN

There was more to Dr Sarah Carden than a bubbly Texan with a disarming smile, one that hid the truth of the pain she carried. Death could be hard enough on any family, but either you somehow find peace in its circumstance or torment becomes a lifelong companion. *Where was the peace in murder?* Sarah thought.

Unable to face her grief, Dr Carden distanced herself from the past by simply trying to ignore it, numbing herself to its affect, although there were days when she could feel it trying to catch up as though she were a hare in a race with a persistent tortoise. Work had been the excuse for not attending her uncle's memorial, but really it was the inability to hide her contempt for those calling themselves men of God, the ones who could offer no peace, no solace to a family in mourning. Working at the Vatican Observatory was one of the last attachments she had to that pain, but had taken steps to amputate her connection by relocating, possibly changing fields if the opportunity presented itself.

She had just been in the final processes of being considered for an alternative position by one of the observatory's main contributors, the Montgomery Institute, when she received the news that Father Michael would be attending this year's summer camp; the tortoise had finally caught up.

Unlike Weiss' other peers she adored Father Michael, partly because of the way Uncle Frankie held him in such regard. Perhaps it was just simply the common bond they shared, but despite herself she'd avoided contact or communication with anyone he associated with, particularly those from the church. It was times such as these Uncle Frankie might have said,

"Be careful what you fill in the void of loss. Happy memories are recommended, but anger often stakes a claim."

And it had. Admittedly, loss had taken more than just an uncle, a brother, a mentor, a man of the cloth, it had taken her faith. She couldn't conceive of a God that would allow one of his servants to be struck down in a house of his own worship, sacrificed in vain.

Upon hearing Father Michael's name she was reminded of the item taken into possession shortly after her uncle's passing, however, along with swathes of overwhelming memories of that time, it was just another thing she'd managed to erase. Sarah wasn't sure what she was running from, but upon the arrival of the priest, Trentini, she knew it had found her, and with it came death.

As a scientist she'd never seen anything to convince her of the supernatural, but had experienced first hand the destruction religious extremism left in its wake, enacted with savage conviction.

Heinrich was the next victim on that list, then young Philippé, for which she would forever have his blood on her hands. How many more had to die before their actions revealed themselves for what they truly were; insanity.

Philippé's death returned the pain of her own loss with heart-wrenching fury and a bitterness to her palate that made the world taste rotten. As much as she loved Father Michael and wanted nothing more than to honour her uncle, she now realised as a scientist the best way to do that was to bring truth into the light, let it have its day, let people finally see that gods and monsters are nothing more than tales of morality. Because in the real world you can't invoke spirits into human vessels, and the longer they held on to such fantastical beliefs, more people would die.

Alone she was powerless to affect change, and although she didn't yet know it, that night would also provide her with the most unlikely of allies in Archibald. T. Montgomery.

She thought it beyond belief that someone as important as the founder of The Montgomery Institute would take the time to call *her*, to make sure *she* was okay. Father Michael was busy with his own call and for the briefest of moments she thought she might say something, tell him the truth, but then she could probably kiss goodbye to any plans she'd made to relocate. As it was, the drama of that night had not yet reached its conclusion and the brief encounter passed by barely forming a memory, that was until she arrived in London.

Having only touched down within the hour, the timing of the second call should have acted as a warning, but finding herself in an unfamiliar city in the middle of an unparalleled situation and admittedly girlishly in awe to have this larger than life, philanthropic man of the hour calling her cell phone, didn't see any red flags. Had there been time to assimilate the information she would have undoubtedly acted with more caution, but riding on the crest of chaos Mr. Montgomery stressed a dire urgency to meet.

Sarah had only ever seen him on TV and the extensive fawning of him in newspapers and magazines, things she didn't pay much attention to. This would be the first time seeing him in the flesh. She thought his entry into the political sphere was a breath of fresh air, one that could be used the world over, but any interest in him to this point had been purely academic.

An executive chauffeur driven car pulled up to the curb and Mr. Montgomery alighted to hold the door open for Dr Carden. It was almost as if the sunlight bent to his will, the way it reflected off surfaces and windows of passing cars to highlight his arrival, and yet his smile paled to that of even the sun. It was hard not to be struck with just how beautiful he really was.

Feeling like pinching herself, Sarah found herself sitting in the back of a vehicle with the Archibald. T. Montgomery being chauffeured on a small circuit of central London. It was a position she was sure millions of women and men could only dream of. She assumed his interest and enquiry would revolve around the occult nature of the incident at the observatory, things people left out of the papers. She could never have envisaged what she was about to hear.

"They took my son," Archie said, shaking as he spoke.

The staggering revelation stole every syllable from Sarah's vocabulary, stunned to a statuesque figure unable to utter a word for fear of missing a single in return. She listened with overwhelming empathy as he divulged details of an elaborate government operation to recover his son, Joshua, the sacrificial element of his abduction and the warring factions of The Order and The Natsarim that brought devastation to so many lives, including her own.

She couldn't conceive of why this brilliant man, someone who was fast becoming the face of a generation would be reaching out to her, but now she understood. They weren't just connected by events that had uprooted and shaken both of their lives, or the desire to see its end, but the object that made it all possible; an ancient dagger.

"I know you arrived today with his good friend," Archie said. "A man whose standing reaches beyond the boundaries of the church."

"You know Father Michael?"

"Only by reputation," he said warmly. "But I can see how easy it would be to follow someone whose righteous condemnation challenges even that of the Holy See."

"I hold no attraction for conflict," Sarah said.

"But you do for truth. Conflict is just the battlefield you must cross to reach it. Why else would you have come all this way? While Father Michael's pursuit is a noble one, it's his grief that drives him, and though not aware, he uses your grief to rally you to his cause. But you already know this," Archie said.

His stare instilled Sarah with vulnerability as it penetrated her projected facade.

"You're a scientist, you search for truth. And where else would you start but with his closest friend."

He wasn't altogether wrong, she thought, but it didn't make it any easier to hear someone else bare your soul.

"The conflict you face is inside you," he continued. "Between your loyalty to those who believe, and the reality of those whose lives it touches and destroys. Mine, yours, and that's just the tip of the iceberg. How many more have to suffer before they realise?"

He wasn't saying anything she hadn't already thought about but her sanity appreciated hearing it from someone else, someone of vast intellectual superiority to momentarily relieve her of the burden she carried. While she'd agreed with everything Archie had to say, deceit and dishonesty still wrestled with her heart.

"I know what it is I'm asking of you," Archie said, placing a warm reassuring hand on top of her own.

Sarah's thoughts rested with Father Michael, a beautiful, humble and earnest man whose nature wasn't born of egotistical pursuits, who believed the path they walked offered more than just meaning to loss, but to avert a greater one to come. But the object of their grief was shared, so why should she consider her own to be any less valuable? Especially now she had learned the extent of just how far they were willing to go, kidnapping children, blood sacrifices. She wondered how much Father

Michael actually knew, and how much he wasn't telling her, after all The Natsarim were no choir boys.

She concluded her logic and reasoning were sound, but if what she was going to do was so righteous, why didn't it come with the appropriate feelings?

Following her brief, albeit surreal encounter, for the first time Sarah met with Professor Lehman. She hoped a woman of such impeccable standing and someone that held the admiration of her peers would be able to offer an alternative insight, one she may not have considered. But as the conversation unfolded it only reminded her of that which she'd forgotten, the death of archaeologists Helena Braithwaite-Duncan. If anything the encounter only worked to solidify her resolve, though did little to help her escape the underlying feeling of betrayal.

For the greater good, Sarah knew what she had to do, although unrealistically she hoped time would allow a short respite that perhaps offered a clearer solution. But as she sat in the lobby of Park Lane's Hilton Hotel, that hope was taken upon hearing the announcement of the name, Dr Ross.

Father Michael's plan was quite simple, despite having chosen civilians for its execution rather than operatives. Sarah checked into a room on the sixth floor based upon how many times the doctor had tapped his keycard. He was aware he was being watched, but not by whom. From there all she had to do was wait. Dr Ross would order room service and once finished with his meal, place the dagger under the napkin on the tray and leave it for collection outside the door.

Sarah was lucky enough to book a room a few away from Dr Ross on the opposite side of the hallway, listening at the door and reacting to every sound she heard, constantly opening it to check. Discretion was not her best trait. Eventually she saw the meal arrive and around fifteen minutes later Dr Ross placed the tray for collection outside the door.

This was it. As she left the room her heart was beating so fast she thought she might throw up, but she collected the tray with the confidence of an employee and made her way back to the lobby. Concealing the dagger in her bag, she left the tray inside the lift and crossed the foyer to exit the building where Archie's driver Dave would be waiting for her.

Dr Carden thought that once the hard part was over, she would feel better about what she was doing, still convinced it was the right thing. But as she sat in the back of the car staring hypnotically from the tinted window, she caught her reflection staring back. In that instance she knew if she went through with handing over the dagger, the hollow of betrayal inside her would never leave, never able to look at her reflection again without seeing deceit staring back.

"Stop the car," Sarah said.

She met Dave's eyes in the mirror, but he returned them to the road without response.

"Hello, did you hear me? I said can you stop the car?"

Panic rose as her breathing shallowed and heart quickened, accompanied by a sickening fear. Suddenly she was very conscious of her reality. Quickly turning her attention to the door with the mind of jumping from a moving vehicle, Dave engaged the locks, but in her hysteria she pulled at the handle regardless.

"Open the fucking door!" she screamed. "Open the fucking door!"

Leaning back on the seat she began to kick the door and window with all her strength. It just wasn't enough.

Dave waited for the right opportunity to calmly pull the car to the side of the road. Sarah's panic started to dissipate, relieved the situation wasn't what she'd thought. Until Dave leaned over his seat and pointed a gun at her face. She noticed he was sporting a fresh tattoo on the inside of his wrist, in such a situation it wouldn't have been the first thing to absorb, but she'd recognised the symbol as the logo for the Montgomery institute, the soft triangle with three circles. It was said to represent three basic pillars of science but in the height of the situation she realised exactly what she was looking at, three sixes interconnected; 666.

The car door opened and two ominous looking men were waiting for her.

"I'm sorry this seems over cautious," Dave said. "But it's for your own protection."

Of course she didn't believe him, but what choice did she have? As she was about to leave the car, he handed her a delicate jewellery box.

"Take it. Archie said it's important."

Fearful but with an overriding rush of anger, she snatched the item from his hand and opened it. Nestled inside was a beautiful silver bracelet with thirty charms circling the chain. Offering Dave a vicious expression of disgust and with no choice, she exited the car to her waiting chaperones.

CHAPTER 48

ARCHIBALD

Inside the Temple Church beneath the triforium and the ravenous eyes of half faced demons peering on, the moleskin cloth was removed from the box, handled with the veneration of religious royalty and placed at the centre of the nave beside the two thousand-year-old skull of the Magi. The anticipation was palpable

Sonja, the central member of The Order stepped forward and knelt before the skull. Jonathan followed, stepping forward taking his position opposite, opening his cloak to reveal his bare chest in preparation to become the elected vessel. Pouring the first of the containers of blood into the skull, Sonja presented it to Jonathan. Upon taking the skull in hand, the world powers watching from above raised their chalices of blood and drank. As they continued their murmuring unholy scripture, slowly and carefully Sonja began unwrapping the cloth.

Despite age, her heart pounded with childlike excitement as she reached the final layer. Hundreds of eyes watching on, waiting to see the dagger historians relegated to myth and legend, a knife that tore the fabric between worlds. Pulling back the last layer of cloth, she revealed a cluster of cutlery embossed with the logo for the Hilton Hotel.

On the roof terrace of 26 Grosvenor Square, the very same heavenly event witnessed across London, now fully consumed Archie's attention.

"They're ready for you," Johnny said entering the terrace.

He bowed his head with extreme reverence, one held for this night and all that would follow, but not before noticing a sky that quietly instilled him with dread. As Archie turned to face him, Johnny descended to one knee, raising his hands he presented The Dagger of Menelik.

In the Temple Church, Sonja's eyes seethed through her mask at the sight of cutlery. Without hesitation she rose to her feet, knocking the skull from Jonathan's hands and spilling the blood across the floor.

"Destroy it," she ordered. "Without the skull, he cannot perform the ceremony."

Turning on her heel she immediately started towards the exit, deceit needed no second invitation. Jonathan stood, kicking over the other vessels leaving a river of blood flowing down the aisle and with great force, stamped upon the ancient skull, smashing it to smithereens. Following Sonja and the other members of The Order, he proceeded to abandon the church.

With the mumbling incantations continuing to fall from overhead, The Order's journey was abruptly halted upon reaching the doors, sealed from the outside.

The seven members turned to each other, eyes peering through golden horned masks as they became reacquainted with a primal emotion position had long insulated; fear.

The relentless monotonous murmuring which only moments ago filled them with empowerment, now felt like shards of glass slowly burrowing the canals of their ears.

"Oh shut up!" Melcher screamed up at the platform of half faced demons, unable to bear the sound a second longer.

But the ceremony had already begun and what he saw staring back was no longer half faced, but a manifestation, a presence of evil. Shadows no longer moved with subtlety, but purpose, which was to be expected, only this time the seven were not in control.

On the terrace, Archie paused upon seeing the dagger. Knowledge of its existence was in no way preparation for the reality of coming face to face with an object imbued with power from the source, a gift from God.

The very second he took the knife in hand, light descended from the break in the clouds. Closing his eyes, he inhaled deeply and with every fibre of his being could feel the collision of worlds. As he turned to victoriously face his divine oppressor, a low groan of thunder surged across the heavens, lightning streaking above the clouds charging them with brilliant flashes of electric blue. He smiled with sadistic amusement.

Leeny and Dave joined them on the terrace and following Johnny's example, in servitude fell to one knee. Their fealty filled Archie with righteousness. In rising he allowed Leeny to further her adoration with a kiss on the lips, though the action was only received, not given. Archie was otherwise engaged, consumed with the overwhelming experience of transcendence.

Upon receiving the seal his mind had begun to absorb an expansion, insight that laid beyond the boundaries of human existence. For a man of already superior intelligence, it was ecstasy. Though before it could be fully realised, there was still one thing left to do.

He gazed upon the object resting in his hands as a heavy rain began to fall with the sound of a thousand racing chariots. The seal God gifted to Solomon to enslave his kin was now the keys of his release, the architect defeated by his own creation. He held the dagger aloft in defiance of divine presence.

"Eloi, Eloi, lema sabachthani?" Archie screamed at the heavens, tears in his eyes. "Why have you forsaken me?"

Leeny quickly ushered the men from the terrace allowing Archie a private audience. After a short period of reflection, trying to fathom the magnitude of the object held in his hands, he continued with a calm as though his audience of one now stood next to him.

"I didn't want this," he said. "There was a time I tried running. Not from a diminishing bloodline desperately clinging to power from dark rooms, but from you."

He scoffed at his admission.

"Where was I supposed to go? An existence predetermined by your scriptures, not exactly a level playing field. I was only four when Simon told me this day would come. Four, when I was told I was all that stood between you and them." He referred to humans with disgust. "Why was I not your testament to the world? Your glory? Perhaps I should just be slain by my father that he may inherit the burden you've placed upon me? A father too willing to sacrifice his son, I wonder where he gets such fantastic ideas?"

He smiled at the thought, one that brought liberation from servitude.

"If I allow that, then your enemies will have defeated themselves and there will have been no reason for you to send your destroyer. No, you're coming for a fight."

There was excitement in his voice at the suggestion.

"But this is not the Holy of Holies," he scolded raising his voice. "This is the place of *our* banishment, of *our* exile. You should have never sent the Adamite's here. But then your sadistic cruelty knows no bounds, you lie to them too. Telling them they are free to choose when you know full well true freedom is chaos. To act upon the impulse of desire without moral consequence, without conscience. If choices are ladened with burdens how can one ever truly be free? Look at you," he said with contempt. "All the power in the universe and shackled by your own laws of morality, you're not free. I do not stand here in challenge to your throne, it is you that has come to challenge mine. And when the dust on this world finally settles, your existence will be that of a barren desert. The end has not yet been written."

Turning his back on the heavens, Archie joined his waiting subjects. Johnny was holding the skull from the safe, the skull of the Magi.

"They're ready for you," he said.

CHAPTER 49

COHEN

As Cohen lay trapped in the concrete foundations of a redevelopment site, rain continued to accumulate around him slowly filling the makeshift coffin. He raised his head looking towards his feet, realising if he stayed there he'd drown before dying of his wounds. Passing a look up through the hole towards the sky, he hoped God was paying attention to how pissed off he was. Slowly he tried working his position like a snake on its back until he could see the water running off towards his feet. With much effort and pain he continued inching towards the run off as water started to cover his face. With his legs starting to dangle into an opening and being unaware of what was beneath, he had no choice but to continue on. His face was now fully submerged, but once far enough forward the water helped to release him sending him falling once more. This time it was only several feet but the pain on impact was no less. With no obvious exits from the concrete cavern, Cohen was forced to shimmy on his belly, following the rivers of water along a horizontal shaft not much bigger than his frame, all part of the redevelopment.

He crawled with no urgency and at the only pace his body would allow, laboured and fading. It was hard to estimate how long it was, perhaps fifty or sixty metres, but once clear he found himself exiting an adjoining site under the dark arched walkways of Victoria Street. It reminded him of Cologne Cathedral and Father Weiss' liturgy, walking in and out of sight beneath the transept, where it all began.

This is it, Cohen thought, *only a matter of time before my body's discovered.* He was losing blood fast and had seen enough of these types of injuries to know the outcome was just minutes away. An almost alien feeling of weakness began to take hold of him as his legs started to shake and lose strength, barely able to carry his broad 6ft frame another step, stumbling into the road.

It was around 2:00am and the rain was now falling from the heavens like a monsoon. His long leather mac weighed heavily on his shoulders absorbing more water by the minute, his scruffy shoulder length hair matted across his hard-worn unshaven face as he shuffled forwards aimlessly.

A lone silhouetted figure stumbling through the night like the image of a monster from Stoker's fables. No longer with the strength to lift his feet, dragging them scraping along the floor, head bowed from its own weight forcing him to watch as the water cascaded over his worn and trusty leather boots. Weakness finally overcame as his legs buckled sending him crashing to his knees. Extending his right arm at the very last second to stop himself face-planting into the concrete, his left hand still instinctively covering the gaping hole in his side a couple of inches below the rib cage, with blood seeping through his fingers.

He gritted his teeth, sucking the air into his mouth with sharp shallow breaths as he tried dispersing the pain that coursed through his body. It took everything he had, but Cohen struggled back to his feet.

He stood for a moment to get his balance before moving on, but only made it a few feet before once again crashing to his knees. He could do nothing but watch as his blood diluted and washed away in the rain. Death was breathing down his cold wet neck. His eyes were tightly closed revealing lines of history that flowered from the sides, connecting with other lines like the intersection of a road map.

Defying death he crawled through a steady stream that flowed in the opposite direction, his knees scraping the concrete. Suddenly the cooling summer rain was no longer a comfort as Cohen felt a chill run down his spine, quickly engulfing his entire body.

He never smiled, but on this occasion couldn't help but let the edges of his mouth curl. *Finally*, he thought. His arm gave way collapsing heavily onto his stomach trapping his left arm between himself and the floor, his skull almost bouncing back off from the concrete before finally coming to rest, face half submerged in a puddle.

His breath created small ripples in the water, the only sign that he was still alive. He listened to the steady drum of his heart pounding in his ears like a slowing rhythm that would send him to a sleep he would never wake from. With his eyelids somewhere between being closed and open, the horizon was now vertical as he looked on. Cohen's peripheral vision began to darken and narrow, about to close his eyes for the very last time.

In an instant the rain stopped falling and a warm breeze blew gently against his face causing the water to ripple towards him. A light flickered as it reflected off of the water catching his eye. At this point it really didn't make a difference what the light was, but for some reason Cohen needed to know. Fighting to keep death at bay for just a few moments longer he strained to lift his cheek clear of the puddle. He didn't know if he would be able to hold his head up long enough for the surface of the water to calm, but as it stilled he saw it.

An electric blue neon light outlining a religious cross, but Cohen's vision was quickly obstructed by the legs of someone stepping between him and the reflection. Having held on to life for longer than he would have ever wanted, his vision finally faded to black.

CHAPTER 50

FATHER MICHAEL

After light from the heavens had disappeared and clouds once more concealed the convergence, Father Michael remained on his knees staring at what had been, wiping the tears from his cheeks. Eventually and with much effort he rose to his feet, feeling heavier than when he'd taken to his knees. A subtle light adorned his face, one that emanated from within.

In its presence the truth of reality had become apparent; innate. Love was the emotion overriding all others, though in its absence reality was beyond the veil of our experience; where faith is born.

Father Michael knew true faith was not acknowledged by outward displays of the miraculous, but by an inner voice that lays beyond the treacherous journey of silence, beyond the incessant screaming of temptation to dismantle, discourage and dissuade you from ever finding that path. As a witness his faith had been reinvigorated, but disappointment became a heavy stone knowing his heart had craved a sign.

With his thoughts returning to the wellbeing of his colleagues, his brothers and sisters in arms, he was just about to leave the tower when something from the street below caught his eye, something in the shadows.

On the opposite side of the road under the pillared walkways of Victoria, a figure stumbled in the dark. Father Michael looked on curiously, concerned for the individual as the figure moved in a manner that appeared injured as opposed to inebriated. Eventually losing his footing the man fell into the road. Now in the light of the street he watched as the figure struggled back to his feet, as though his purpose to do so was greater than his life. But his will was overcome once more as he plummeted heavily to the concrete and his body lay still.

In the company of Father Fischer, Archbishop Hammond was being debriefed by the asset know as Gina, when Father Michael passed the office with an air of urgency.

"Father Michael," he called out jovially.

But his lack of response instilled a concern that required the satisfaction of investigation. Disregarding the debriefing and without word Archbishop Hammond left the room and followed. As though concern was contagious, Father Fischer and Gina also followed. The group's pursuit persisted into the main area of the cathedral, continuing to call out, but the only response was that of Father Michael's rushing steps ominously reverberating and dominating the empty expanse, coming to a halt once he'd reached the exit door.

"Father Michael?" the archbishop reiterated. "Is everything okay?"

Still without response Father Michael pulled at the door bolts and locks, but with limited success. There was a knack to the order of locks, for which Father Fischer was happy to help. No sooner had he opened the doors when Father Michael urgently and unapologetically pushed past, quickly descending the steps outside where he finally stopped and stared into the pouring rain. The group instantly joined Father Michael, the rain stopped falling and there in the middle of the road they witnessed the source of his distress.

Father Michael made his approach, but stopped a few feet short of the body. He knew exactly whom he was looking at and upon seeing Father Weiss' killer laid out before him, his heart hardened. The asset known as Gina rushed past the priest and knelt by the dying man.

"You're just going to stand there?" she snapped.

But Father Michael could do nothing but stare. The victim's long wet hair was matted across his face, somewhat concealing his identity. Gina carefully stroked it to one side with an affection she hadn't known since Angel, her mini lop.

"It's the man from the flower shop," Father Fischer exclaimed.

But like Father Michael, Gina knew exactly who she was looking at.

She had never told anyone why she named her rabbit Angel, and being a little girl no one considered to ask. But the name was chosen after her saviour, the angel of death, the one she would honour with her life by walking in his footsteps. The only time she'd ever failed in the execution of those duties was in Prague. Her devotion to God was resolute and born of an imperfect soul, the same life she was being asked to take and would have; only thankful for God's intervention.

The man she knew from her childhood was compassionate, loving, paternal and smelled of flowers with a hint of gunpowder. As far as she knew he was a real-life angel. It was with distinct clarity she could remember the entirety of her small hand concealed within his as they walked through the favelas, a place she'd been taught to fear since birth, where danger didn't hide around every corner, it lived in the open and consumed the weak. But the snarl on every tattooed face and dead eyes that peered ominously from shacks nodded with respect. Something she had never seen before or since.

She hadn't understood at the time, but as the body of the small-time assassin Luiz Alves hung cooking in the sun, the angel of death was revealing his identity to the favelas as a warning, a protection of the little girl at his side, Isabella.

"You're not to help him," Father Michael said coldly.

"What?" Gina exploded with a fierce look in the priest's direction.

"If this is the man the prophesy speaks of," he continued without emotion. "Then he must be born again. For that to happen he must first die."

"And if he's not?" she said.

Father Michael didn't respond, but Gina knew the look of a man that wanted the end of someone's existence even if they couldn't bring themselves to say the words. But unfortunately she knew he was right.

With Cohen's face half submerged in a puddle, the only signs of life were light ripples caused by the faintest of breaths. Eventually they stopped, the three men of the cloth and Gina the assassin waited. She hadn't cried since she was six years old and wasn't about to start now, but she wanted to.

After an excruciating time, which soon became too long to resuscitate, watching the still of the water it became clear this was nothing more than a wretched soul, a pawn in unfolding events.

"Leave him," Father Michael said. "His body will be discovered in the light of day."

The words stunned his colleagues, but none dared speak. Turning his thoughts to Dr Carden, Professor Lehman and Dr Ross, he said,

"Right now we have other people to worry about."

Gina was somewhat disappointed the men of the cloth had not exhibited more alarm over events, a sign of lost innocence. As she rose to her feet to join them returning to the cathedral, she noticed a light ripple across the puddle. Not sure if it was caused from her movement, she stilled herself and watched, waiting. Suddenly there was a second and then a third.

"He's alive," she said rushing back to his side.

Quickly raising his head from the puddle, she turned him onto his back aided by Father Fisher. Archbishop Hammond made the sign of the cross over the man and began a quiet prayer. Noticing the charred sleeves of his jacket and the movement having released a waft of burning flesh, Gina carefully inspected the wounds to his forearms. Parts of the jacket had fused itself to his skin but she managed to peel away small strips to reveal the fresh wounds. Both forearms bore a branding.

"Look," she said.

Showing the group what they could already see. The burning rods that impaled Cohen, pinning him to the floor had branded a symbol into each of his forearms. One appeared as the staff of a shepherd, the other a sword of a soldier.

Printed in Great Britain
by Amazon

41326802R00189